To Love a
*Sunburnt
Country*

To Love a *Sunburnt Country*

Jackie French

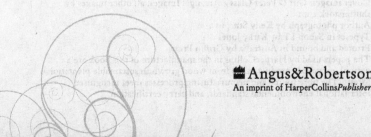

Angus&Robertson
An imprint of HarperCollins*Publishers*

The title of this book and the text on the cover 'All you who have not loved her, You will not understand ...' come from the poem 'My Country' by Dorothea Mackellar. Reproduced by arrangement with the Licensor, The Dorothea Mackellar Estate, c/- Curtis Brown (Aust) Pty Ltd.

Angus&Robertson
An imprint of HarperCollins*Publishers*, Australia

First published in Australia in 2014
This edition published in 2015
by HarperCollins*Publishers* Australia Pty Limited
ABN 36 009 913 517
harpercollins.com.au

Copyright © Jackie French and E French 2014

The right of Jackie French to be identified as the author of this work has been asserted by her under the *Copyright Amendment (Moral Rights) Act 2000*.

HarperCollins*Publishers*
Level 13, 201 Elizabeth Street, Sydney NSW 2000, Australia
Unit D1, 63 Apollo Drive, Rosedale, Auckland 0632, New Zealand
A 53, Sector 57, Noida, UP, India
1 London Bridge Street, London SE1 9GF, United Kingdom
2 Bloor Street East, 20th floor, Toronto, Ontario M4W 1A8, Canada
195 Broadway, New York NY 10007, USA

National Library of Australia Cataloguing-in-Publication data:

French, Jackie, author.
  To love a sunburnt country / Jackie French.
  2nd edition.
  ISBN: 978 1 4607 5042 1 (paperback)
  French, Jackie. Matilda saga ; 4
  For ages 14+
  World War, 1939–1945—Juvenile fiction.
  World War, 1939–1945—Evacuation of civilians—Malaya—Juvenile fiction.
  World War, 1939–1945—Prisoners and prisons, Japanese—Juvenile fiction.
  World War, 1939–1945—Australia—Juvenile fiction.
  Families—Australia—Juvenile fiction.
  Australia—Social conditions—Juvenile fiction.
A823.3

Cover design by HarperCollins Design Studio and Astred Hicks
Cover images: Girl © Peter Glass / Arcangel Images; all other images by shutterstock.com
Author photograph by Kelly Sturgiss
Typeset in Sabon LT by Kirby Jones
Printed and bound in Australia by Griffin Press
The papers used by HarperCollins in the manufacture of this book are a natural, recyclable product made from wood grown in sustainable plantation forests. The fibre source and manufacturing processes meet recognised international environmental standards, and carry certification.

There are many ways to love your country:
to Virginia, Beth, Barry, Peg, Noel, Geoff, Fabia,
Angela, Lisa, Nina, Trish, Kerry, Penny, Tony, Robyn,
my brother Peter, my mother Val, my father Barrie,
whose military service, memories and analysis I have
given to Michael in this book, and most of all to
Bryan and Edward, always.

Chapter 1

Gibber's Creek Gazette, 1 December 1941

HMAS *Sydney* Sunk, 645 Crew Lost

The Prime Minister John Curtin today announced the sinking of the HMAS *Sydney* off the Western Australian coast by the German commerce raider *Kormoran*, disguised as a Dutch merchant vessel. In half an hour of fighting both ships were crippled ...

Michael Thompson
St Elric's School
Sydney
5 December 1941

Nancy Clancy
Craigiethorn Plantation
via Kota Bharu, Malaya

... it's grand news about the 9th Division ending the siege of Tobruk, isn't it? I'm pretty sure Jim's one of the 'rats'. Of course he can't tell us where he is, but in his last letter home he talked about using half his cup of tea to shave with, and said he'd had enough sand to last him the rest of his life, and would everyone please not even say 'sandwiches' when he gets back.

Mum worries, but when I told her that Jim can look after himself as well as any bloke I know, she just smiled and said it was a mother's job to worry, and that she worries about me getting my teeth knocked out at rugger or my train getting derailed on the way back from Sydney, and that ninety-five per cent of being a mum is worry anyway. But you know Mum.

Well, that's all, I think. I'd tell you about school and all that, but sub-Junior Year is enough to bore anyone to concrete. At least I'm off home on 'holidays' in a few days, which means dagging a thousand sheep when it's ninety-six degrees in the shade. Actually, I can't wait.

Wish you were going to be at the Christmas party this year. Maybe you even will be. I'll look up from the punch bowl and there you'll be, in the spotted voile dress you told me about. What is a spotted voile anyway? It sounds like a small English animal, the burrowing kind. If someone made you a dress out of them, I hope you've trained them not to bite.

I'm glad Moira and Gavin are doing so well now. We are all longing to see you home at last. Dad says that war with Japan is inevitable, even if the government won't admit it publicly. Can't you stuff Moira and Gavin into a wheelbarrow and push them onto a ship, even if Moira refuses to go? Or just come home yourself? But be careful sneaking past all those German U-boats and ships disguised as innocent Dutch traders.

If you're not at the party, I'll sit by the river and think of you. Wishing you were here, or if not, that I was there, with you.

Yours, always,
Michael

CRAIGIETHORN PLANTATION VIA KOTA BHARU, MALAYA, 9 DECEMBER 1941

NANCY

Her name was Nancy of the Overflow, and she could do anything, except stop the entire Japanese Army, even at sixteen. She could not even stop the six Japanese soldiers in their dull green uniforms slipping silently across the plantation compound outside, without endangering those she loved.

If those soldiers saw her lying there on the study floor, peering through the window, they'd kill her. They'd kill Moira, her sister-in-law, and her baby nephew. Then they would invade her country, if Gentleman Once, and Michael, and Michael's father, were correct.

Had war really come? There'd been no bombing, no thud of guns, none of the tragic clamour of war she'd heard in newsreels. There'd been a far-off booming noise at dinner, but she'd taken it for thunder.

Back in her own world she knew the voice of thunder, could tell if it was circling around or heading away, whether it would spark a bushfire or bring a deluge to put one out. But this was not her land. Not her trees: too green, too heavy. Nor was it her air, thick with moisture that erupted into rain.

Had those growls in the sky been gunfire?

What were Japanese soldiers doing here, if war had not erupted like a small silent volcano in the night? The Japanese Army was supposed to be far to the north, in Thailand. Australia couldn't be at war with Japan with no warning. Both countries had signed a treaty saying that they would formally declare war before any attack was made.

There'd been nothing about war with Japan on the wireless last night, just the war with Germany in Europe and Africa, how the Russian winter was slowing the German advance towards Stalingrad. No worries, Ben had told her and Moira last week. The Japs aren't going to risk war with the British Empire. And if they do try to land in Malaya, we'll stop them easily.

Moira was reassured. Nancy wasn't. She knew her brother well enough to sense the worry behind his easy smiles.

Ben and 'Pig Iron Bob' Menzies said that war between Australia and Japan wasn't inevitable. But Mr Menzies wasn't even Prime Minister any more, and if the Japanese weren't preparing to invade, why was Ben up north with the local Volunteers?

Australians would stop the Japanese, of course. She knew that as surely as she knew the colour of the paddocks after rain. But, here and now, the safety of her nephew and sister-in-law was up to her.

She stayed lying on her stomach on the wooden floor of the bungalow, still as a lizard on a rock, watching the small secret men in their grey-green uniforms move out the gate towards the jungle, bayonets held ready.

Ben had also said the Japanese Army didn't travel at night. They were as blind as bats without their glasses. Yet there they were, disappearing silent in the darkness ...

She peered into the dark of the compound as the soldiers vanished, becoming one with trees and shadows. She could almost make herself believe they'd never been there.

They had.

If she was invading Malaya, she'd send scouts ahead, just like a rider went ahead when you were droving, seeking out grass and water for the cattle. If those men were scouts, then she and Moira and Gavin might be safe. For now. Whatever the soldiers had been looking for tonight, it probably wasn't women and children in a bungalow, nor their servants.

She forced herself to wait, counting her heartbeats, to make sure the compound stayed empty before she moved. She wanted to move. Wanted to run after those soldiers, grab their bayonets, stab them, as they'd stabbed women and children in China, stab the whole Japanese Army, stab the whole mess of politicians and diplomats who failed to keep those she loved safe, stab any invader who might try to take her country.

And she couldn't. For the first time in her life here was something no amount of determination could change.

She took a deep breath, smelling the lavender furniture polish Moira had sent out from England, and her own sweat. She *could* get her sister-in-law and baby nephew to safety. Now, before more soldiers arrived, and planes and bombs. South, to Singapore, so strongly defended by British, Australian, Indian and Malay forces that no Japanese invaders could take it, and from Singapore onto a ship to Australia, to Overflow, sun-drenched paddocks and men and women who'd use the rifles that potted rabbits, the shotguns kept for snakes, even bayonets made with carving knives if they had to, before they would accept an invader on their land. Moira should have left for Overflow a year ago — that was the reason Nancy had come here in the first place, to help Moira pack up the bungalow and leave.

How could she get them to Singapore? Yesterday she would have driven to Kota Bharu, where Ben was stationed, to get a ship from there.

Kota Bharu was to the north. If the Japanese were already in Malaya, then Kota Bharu would be their first target. Maybe even now it had been taken ...

Impossible. The Japanese Army could not defeat her brother, or men like him.

And yet Japanese soldiers had been here ...

Were there many more out there, marching down the road in the darkness, slipping between the jungle tangles? Was it even safe to take the car? A car was obvious, a large target to fire upon.

No choice. It would be hard enough to persuade Moira into the car tonight, impossible to persuade her to walk along the road, much less scurry through plantations. Nancy could become a shadow between the rows of rubber trees that even the Japanese Army would never see. Not Moira, with her thin white ankles and high heels, her English cheeks that had only felt the sun when protected by a hat and veils, still weak after a difficult pregnancy. Nor was Nancy entirely sure that even she could evade an army carrying a five-month-old baby. You couldn't tell a five-month-old to hush.

But you can lug a baby wherever you want it to go, thought Nancy. She couldn't lug Moira.

They must drive to the railway station. The stationmaster might have news that the wireless lacked, telegraphed directly from Kota Bharu or wherever the Japanese had landed. Take the train to Singapore, then a ship home. No more excuses: that Moira's troubled pregnancy and Gavin's premature birth meant they were

5

still too delicate to travel, and that impregnable Singapore meant Malaya was safe from attack even if the Japanese did declare war. If Moira was well enough to go to a dinner party with the District Commissioner and his wife last week, she was well enough to take herself and her child south to safety. Moira must now admit she and Gavin would be safer in Australia, even on a voyage through seas patrolled by increasing numbers of German ships.

Nancy believed her sister-in-law was as delicate as a goanna, and just as stubborn, like the old one behind the chook shed at home who'd dug up a whole paddock of potatoes, thinking they were eggs, goannas being fond of eggs: he had bitten every spud, unwilling to accept that none of them were eggs.

Moira had spent the last three months refusing to admit there was any danger to her, her baby, her husband, to this southern part of the Empire. Or perhaps Moira simply didn't want to go to Australia at all. Or at least not to Overflow. Nancy suspected there were aspects of her new family that Moira was not prepared to accept.

For Gran was Aboriginal. Unmistakeable: dark skin, dark eyes. And proud of it, wearing a white dress, her white hat with cherries, to church, even to the Bluebell Tea Shop in town where the sign said, *No Aboriginals Allowed*, daring anyone to ban her from their building, to even think of hauling her or her children to a reservation. Granddad had been white, whatever that meant, for his skin was saddle leather, from years on horseback. Only his hair had been truly white, leached by old age. She'd been named for him, Nancy for his Clancy, Clancy of the Overflow. Nancy Clancy sounded stupid, but she was stuck with it. Mum was white. Nancy and Ben could pass for white-with-tan, with Mum's schoolteacher accent and the affluence of Overflow behind them.

Moira must have known Ben was a quadroon. Ben would never have kept something as important as that from the woman he loved. But a well-off plantation manager with slightly too-dark skin could pass here in Malaya, where many men had a dark tan. In Australia Moira would have to abandon her servants and picnic parties for life on an Australian station with a 'native' grandmother-in-law. 'Native' was such a Moira word: 'Nancy, darling, don't wear that. It's what the natives wear ...'

All was still outside. Time to move. Nancy inched along the floor to the hallway, still on her stomach, in case more soldiers peered through the windows, keeping her head down — Gran always said your head was the most recognisably human part of you. You kept your head tucked into your body and your eyes down when you were hunting. She was prey now. She supposed the same camouflage rules applied. They were all prey, every civilian in this land, running from the beast with a million tentacles called war.

Moira has no choice now, thought Nancy, finally, gladly, standing upright in the shelter of the hall. If it would take the entire Japanese Army to get Moira south to Overflow ... The Japanese had come.

Chapter 2

Bruce Clancy
Overflow
via Gibber's Creek
8 December 1941

Ben Clancy
Craigiethorn Plantation
via Kota Bharu, Malaya

Dear Ben,

Just a short note to tell you that your mother and I are increasingly worried about the situation in Malaya and the growing possibility of war with Japan. I know that sea travel at this time is far from ideal, but we feel strongly that the danger from German ships is only going to get worse. If Moira still refuses to leave Malaya, then Nancy must come home, now.

I know that Nancy believes that she must stay to look after Moira and Gavin, that she must do her duty as you are doing yours. But she is still only sixteen, no matter how capable and independent she seems. Son, you must, somehow, convince her to come home, now, with Moira and Gavin if possible, but without them, if necessary. I would urge you to come home too, but know your loyalty to your unit and your friends.

No matter what the papers and politicians say, Malaya is no longer safe. Your mother is writing to Nancy today too, but I hope I can rely on you to get your sister on a ship back to Australia, as soon as possible.

Your loving father,
Dad

Populate or perish, says Australian Minister for Information, Arthur Calwell. Unless Australia expands and develops its population and economy, there can be no guarantee that any victory over the Japanese is permanent. Women must have more babies, said Mr Calwell.

This reporter asked Mrs Joseph McAlpine, wife of Gibber's Creek Dr McAlpine, now serving with the AIF, what she thought of Mr Calwell's proposal.

'An excellent idea,' she said. 'Send my husband back on leave and we'll get started immediately.'

CRAIGIETHORN PLANTATION,
9 DECEMBER 1941

NANCY

'Darling, don't be ridiculous. Soldiers, here?' Moira blinked up from her white froth of pillows. She reached for the matches to light the lamp by the bed.

'No! No lights!'

'What? Nancy, you've had a nightmare.'

'I wasn't asleep.'

'What were you doing out of bed anyway?'

'Shh. Couldn't sleep. I went to get a book from the study. That's when I saw them.'

'It was probably one of the servants.'

'They were soldiers. I saw six of them, in uniform. They had bayonets.'

'Bayonets ...' Moira looked uncertain. She whispered, 'You're sure?'

'Yes.'

To Nancy's surprise, Moira stopped arguing. She swung her legs out of bed, stylish in a pink silk nightdress. 'You'd better go and get changed, then start packing.' She reached for the bell pull to call the servants.

'No.' Nancy grabbed her hand. 'We can't risk waking anyone.'

Guilt raked her. Servants. Darling Choi and Rah and all the others. But the Japanese in Thailand had called themselves liberators, ousting the European colonisers. The servants would be safer without her and Moira. Safer if they stayed here and could be 'liberated', could say truthfully that their employers had simply left.

How safe that would be she didn't know. She suspected that there was no safety for anyone in war. Bombs fell, hit whoever was below. Bullets were almost as imprecise. But this was the servants' home, even if they did not legally have title to the land. Moira may have lived here for the three years since she had married Ben, but this land was not her home.

'No noise. No lights. One bag, something you can carry. A change of clothes.' What else? 'Jewellery. Any money ...'

'Nancy, I can't fit all Gavin's things in one bag. You simply don't understand —'

'If there has been an invasion, we have to hurry. Now. If we get to the station and find it's a false alarm, we can come back and pack up properly.'

Moira stared at her, then nodded. 'Very well. But I warn you, if this is a wild goose chase I am coming back, and not to pack. You understand?'

'Yes.' Nancy hesitated. 'I'll load the car, then come back for you and Gavin.' That way she could check the compound for strangers, silently, unseen.

Moira nodded again.

Jodhpurs, not a dress ... no, jodhpurs were too pale, too easily seen if they had to retreat into the jungle. It would have to be a dress, the green one with blue flowers. Sandshoes would be sensible, or plimsolls as Moira called them, but Moira would have a fit if she wore sandshoes on a train, even if the entire

Japanese Army was attacking. Low-heeled shoes then, and stockings, which meant a suspender belt and more time, but the train conductor probably wouldn't let a 'mem' on the wretched train in this country if she wasn't wearing stockings, or at least not in a first-class carriage.

She thrust a change of clothes into her haversack, hesitated, then shoved in more, including the blue spotted voile dress she had described to Michael. She had recently discovered the joy of clothes, even if sometimes they were a nuisance. If only one didn't have to wear stockings with dresses, and horrors, gloves.

She threw a pair of stockings into the bag too. If they had to run, she could ditch her clothes, and just carry Gavin's things: a mosquito net, nighties, booties, blankets, nappies. The local women didn't bother with nappies for their babies, just held them out at the right time. Less washing, of course, but it did mean you had to be careful where you stepped ...

Ben had insisted they keep more cash in the house the last few months, in case the local bank closed and businesses stopped taking cheques or money orders.

She reached to stuff the banknotes in her pockets, realised dresses didn't have pockets and swore; remembered she was no longer droving and trying not to swear; thrust the notes down into the brassiere that Moira insisted she wear, which would make the bl— *wretched* thing even hotter and gave her a bust like Bette Davis. The notes would probably get wet with sweat. No, horses sweated: men perspired; ladies glowed. Ladies be b— *blowed.*

What else? Water. A Thermos and one of the water bags Ben used to take out into the plantation, slowly seeping moisture to keep it cool, like a Coolgardie safe. Food ...

The kitchen was in the hut across the compound, next to the garage, so that the cooking wouldn't heat up the bungalow, nor fill it with cooking smells of onion, garlic and cabbage, as well as the local spices Ben and Moira seemed to love and she still found peculiar, not at all like Mum's curried eggs, and sometimes too spicy to eat. She slipped to the door, listened ... the chirp of some strange frog or insect. She'd had no chance to learn the night sounds here, with Ben away so much, and no one else seemed to know what they were. No sound of humans except the click of Moira's heels on the wooden floor.

She should have told Moira to take her shoes off, though if no one had heard them moving and talking by now, hopefully no one would.

She crept across the compound, haversack in one hand, water bag in the other. The air smelt of chickens and yesterday afternoon's rain, and the ever-present rotting scent of the jungle, so that she longed for the clean dry air of home. Another hour until dawn.

She tiptoed into the kitchen, swore, mentally, which didn't count and also made no noise. Of course Moira had the larder keys. The larder held wine and rum and whisky, powdered milk, canned turtle soup, tinned peas: expensive staples of colonial life, things that might be worthwhile to steal.

She opened the food safe instead, took out bread and most of a fruitcake to nestle on top of her clothes in the haversack. Back home, she thought wistfully, there was always the remnants of a roast leg or shoulder of mutton, or stuffed rolled ribs. But people rarely ate cold meat here, except chicken at picnics. Meat rotted fast. She looked around, added half a dozen mangoes from a basket, a pineapple and, as an afterthought, a fruit knife.

Time to run.

Gear in the car. Back to the house for Moira's suitcases — three of them, despite Nancy's insistence on only one. Moira stood, neatly dressed, gloved and hatted, Gavin in her arms, wearing a long white nightgown with a white lace cap that Nancy privately thought made him look sissy.

He blinked up at her, still too small for his age but no longer fragile, with Gran's dark eyes, and hers and Ben's, and grinned, a pure joy grin, entirely his own. 'Gooruk?' he crowed, as if delighted to be out of his cot, heading out into the night. He waved one tiny fist.

She grinned back, unable to help it, then whispered, 'Out to the car. Be quiet.'

'I know.' Moira sounded irritated, but at least she didn't object. If they were not at war, Moira was going to be very annoyed indeed. She settled into the passenger's seat, Gavin in her arms.

Nancy cranked the engine, wishing Ben had bought a newer car, had insisted his wife go to Australia two years ago, had married anyone but Moira. She stopped herself from thinking that, heard the engine catch, flung herself into the driver's seat and wished, at the very least, that Ben had bought a car with a roof, not an open tourer. Did a car roof stop bullets?

All her life, except the year she had spent droving to Charters Towers and back, she had known the land and people around her so well that tomorrow was almost as clear as yesterday.

Now she knew nothing, nothing that mattered, like how much power Japanese bullets had. Shotgun pellets passed through the shed wall at home, when she and Granddad had used it for target practice. When he had thrown up an old tin can and she had shot it down with his .22, the bullet had pierced it. She thrust away the image of a bullet like that spearing into Gavin. A baby was the most precious thing in all the world, Gran said. And Gavin, darling Gavin, with his gummy smile and tiny toes, the most precious of them all.

Must keep him safe.

The car lurched forwards.

'You've forgotten to turn the lights on.'

'Shh! I don't need lights. People can see lights.'

'They can hear the engine,' said Moira, reasonably, and in a whisper.

'You can see lights further than you can hear an engine.' Out on the plains you could see a fire fifty miles away, a tiny star through the dark sky of the trees. But trees move. The night sky didn't, except for the slow turn of stars that guided you back home …

Home, where they should all be now. She couldn't think of Overflow. Not yet. The car backfired, making her wince, then slid out of the compound, down the avenue of palm trees, out onto the thin white line of road.

'Ben would have let us know if the Japanese had invaded.' Moira's voice was once more too loud. Gavin stirred in her arms. He pulled off his hat and began to chew it.

'How?'

'Sent a telegram. Or a messenger, if he couldn't come himself.' Nancy gritted her teeth. 'He might be ... busy ... now.'

The car lurched over a bump. She wrestled with the wheel. She could drive. Just. Three lessons from that nice lieutenant, laughing ones, after picnics up on the hill. Why *hadn't* Ben let them know? Sent a telegram, a message. Or was he ...?

Dead? No. If the Japanese had invaded tonight, there might have been no way to get a message through.

B— *blast* Moira. Moira should have left Malaya two years ago, when the war with Germany began. For the hundredth time Nancy wished she'd never even come to Malaya. Homesickness was so strong she could taste it: the glow of hot earth after rain, dogs that smelt of sheep, the pong a wombat left, lingering over the soil for days, air that seeped sweet and dry into your lungs. She had almost written to Dad asking for him to book her a passage home time after time. But she couldn't leave Moira, threatened with miscarriage. Could never leave Gavin with war with Japan brewing and his mother unwilling to accept the danger. Darling Gavin so incredibly tiny at first, his red face shocked and disapproving of the world he'd been thrust into. There were things you sometimes had to do for love, like swallow your longing for grey-green trees and water with a tang of rock, not earth and leaves, for Michael and her family.

She glanced at Gavin, dribble soaking his hat. She'd never guessed you could feel so much love for something so small, a whole new person suddenly appearing in the world.

'I still don't think —' Moira's voice rose again.

'Shh! If there's nothing wrong when we get to the station, we'll go back again. Be home in time for breakfast.'

'What are we going to eat while we wait for the train? If you think I'm going to buy food from the native hawkers —'

'I brought food from the kitchen.' Nancy suddenly realised that Moira would turn up her nose at food from a haversack; might even refuse to accompany her if she carried it. Well, a haversack was practical, easier to carry than a suitcase. If …

She shut her mind to the 'if'. It was possible to think of herself carrying Gavin, slipping away from the Japanese through the jungle. Add Moira to the image and it became ridiculous.

She remembered how Moira had turned up her nose nearly a year earlier when she, Nancy, Moira's sister-in-law, arrived carrying the haversack, instead of a lady's leather suitcase, suitably embossed with her initials. Moira's slightly-too-dark-for-polite-society sister-in-law.

Men were tanned. Women protected their skin from the sun. Her brown skin was not just from heritage, but sun-kissed from a year in the saddle, after she'd bunked off from school to go to Queensland droving. Add brown eyes to her brown skin … Twice she had heard whispers from the oh-so-proper English ladies. 'She's not Eurasian, is she? Anglo-Indian?' And then the reassuring, 'Australian. A large property I hear. Too much sun, I expect: so unfortunate.' Money, and the prestige of a large property, meant a tan might be forgiven. But she saw the query linger in the eyes of her hostesses nonetheless.

Being Eurasian here was as great an impediment as being Aboriginal in her own country. Mine, she thought. My land. Her hands trembled on the steering wheel. For a second she wanted to leap from the car, track the Japanese soldiers she'd seen like she'd track a snake back home, plunge their own bayonets into them.

She didn't. She couldn't. Couldn't track in this damn jungle where the ground was littered with old leaves and unfamiliar smells. Couldn't take on six men by herself. Two, maybe three, if they were smaller than her and she took them by surprise. She'd managed to get rid of those two shearers up past Nyngan, smashing a rock into the nose of one and a foot in the kidneys of another, just like Granddad had shown her, enough to leave them doubled over and gasping and her running.

But the shearers hadn't had bayonets. Her duty now was to get Moira and Gavin to safety; and to warn others, if warning was needed, that war was on these shores. To get home to Overflow, then do whatever was needed there ...

She wondered if she'd broken the shearer's nose. She hoped so.

Moira dozed on the leather seat beside her, Gavin asleep again in her arms. The car shivered through the darkness. Three lessons weren't quite enough for even Nancy of the Overflow to learn to drive. But they had stayed on the track, had missed a pig — or possibly the pig had missed them.

The sky gathered its greyness up from the horizon. The moon had gone, that bright full moon that had lit the way along the track. Nancy thought of moonlit rides through the timber shadows back home. Had the Japanese used the full moon too, to show them where to go? Not just the soldiers like the ones she had seen, but the pilots of the planes too?

A far-off drone whispered across the too-still air. For a moment she thought it was a plane. But it was the cicadas, waking with the sun, the first hard golden rays bringing forth a buzzing that became a roar as the sunlight flooded across the jungle top.

Daylight smudged the world. The black wall of the jungle turned into trees. The car lurched on a larger bump than usual.

Nancy grasped the wheel more firmly. Perhaps the nightmare of the past few hours would vanish with the light. Perhaps when they got to the station they'd find that the Japanese had already been captured, had only been a handful of paratroopers drifting down beneath their domed parachutes, just as she'd seen in the Movietone News at the picture theatre down in Kuala Lumpur, about the invasion of Denmark.

But Denmark was at the other end of the world, where the war with Germany was. It was so hard to truly believe in war here. War was for *real* countries, like England and those in Europe. Malaya, Thailand, Australia floated in the southern seas, forever untouched by war. She frowned.

Or had they been? She had never learnt the history of this part of the world at school. Schools taught English history, with just enough European to make sense of English wars, like with Napoleon and the Battle of Waterloo and the Kaiser in the Great War.

She had not even learnt the history of her own land, except for the First Fleet, the early governors and the crossing of the Blue Mountains. Only Gran had given her that, on their Sunday afternoon walks, her small hand in Gran's big-knuckled black one — stories that she only later realised were history too, far-off stories, some older than humanity, of rock and ancestor animals and water.

And tales of only a few generations before too, of Gran's grandparents, aunts, uncles, cousins, of battles with the white men who were her relatives on Granddad's side, and Mum's. Her ancestors fighting her ancestors.

Had there been wars in Malaya, ones she had never heard about? The sultans had troops. If they needed troops, perhaps there had been wars. Maybe many wars ...

War could be here too. It was.

Daylight glowed up from the horizon. The sky turned hot, clear blue. Monkeys chattered above them, and once she saw a flash through the trees that might have been a tiger but that she told herself was more probably jungle flowers that the movement of the car made flicker.

Gavin gave a small sharp cry. Moira opened her eyes. 'There, there, precious.' She looked about and opened her dress discreetly, draped a scarf over her shoulder and bosom, and began to feed him. 'Are we there yet?'

'About a mile from the main road.'

Moira peered at a hut through the trees. 'See? Nothing's happening.'

'We'll see.'

'Bup erp,' said Gavin conversationally. He'd been babbling baby sounds for the last few weeks.

The car passed another hut. A child waved from the garden, picking bananas for breakfast. A woman in bright native cloth swept a compound with a twig broom. Normal. Quiet.

For the first time since leaving the plantation, Nancy wondered if she really had dreamt the soldiers. Sometimes under the ceiling of stars her dreams had been so vivid she'd expected to be still in them when she opened her eyes. Dreams of her grandfather holding her close as they rode across the ridges; her mother's voice laughing as she read a story by her bed. Mum read them a story every night, right up until the day Nancy had left home. She had almost hoped Mum would start again when she got back. She hadn't.

Moira reached for her handbag with her free hand. 'This is insane. I must look a mess! What if the Commissioner's wife sees me like this? I don't even have any lipstick on ...'

'If the Japs have invaded, it won't matter.'

Moira hunted through her handbag. She tried to hold a mirror steady, as well as Gavin and her lipstick. 'Things like lipstick always matter. It's called keeping up appearances. If we English don't maintain our standards, how can we expect the natives to respect us?'

With force, thought Nancy, thinking of the pistol at the Commissioner's belt, the rifle Ben took even for a day's work on the plantation, the shotguns lined up in their rack in the study.

She should have taken the guns. Now the Japanese would get them. Or the servants, the men of the plantation. Please, she thought, take the guns before the Japanese find them. Hide them, if you can't use them now. If the Japanese do take your land, you can break free ...

Could they? Would they? She tried to think of any land that had been conquered and had won its freedom back. The English ruled Malaya. The English had taken her grandmother's land. Her grandfather's ancestors had killed her grandmother's ancestors. Yet they had loved each other, and deeply …

Japan needed rubber. Malaya had rubber. Japan needed iron. Australia had iron. You need iron to fight a war. Gentleman Once had told her that, the old boozer up near Charters Towers. She'd sipped warm lemonade while the men drank their beer and Gentleman Once had sounded off, calling Prime Minister Menzies 'Pig Iron Bob' because he'd sold Australian iron to Japan. If they don't have iron, they can't make planes and ships, he'd said. Sell it to them and they'll build them.

'So we shouldn't sell it to them then, eh, Gentleman?' asked one of the drovers.

The old man had looked owlishly over his whisky. 'If we don't sell our iron to the Japanese, they'll take it. The next war will be in the Pacific. Not Europe. You mark my words. We took this country because there were more of us than them. Well, there are more Japanese than Aussies …'

They'd laughed, 'One Aussie is a match for twenty Japanese,' and started talking about the odds on the favourite for the next week's Cup. By dusk the old man was slumped against the bar. Bluey and Ringer had carried him home.

But his words had lingered, like the echoes of the kookaburras' morning call — if you listened closely, you could still hear the laughter through even the midday sunlight. And over the last year as the Japanese moved closer, and closer still, from China down through Thailand, the words had become a constant whisper.

Gentleman Once had been wrong and right. The next war — this war — had begun in both Europe and in Asia, as Germany invaded country after country, as Japan invaded China and surged south. Had war between the British Empire and Japan really come now?

There were only six soldiers, Nancy thought. Maybe they weren't invaders at all, just Japanese, like the barber in the village, who had decided to wear uniforms for some reason. Or Chinese like Ah Mee. Could she really tell Japanese from Chinese in the dark? They might have put on uniforms for a joke, or a festival to frighten devils.

And the bayonets?

The car turned the last corner. The road lay before them, but they could not see it.

For what had been a road was now a torrent of crawling, jogging humanity — juggling luggage, babies, bundles, pigs, hens in bamboo cages. Wide-eyed children, men with bloodied faces: a river of terror heading south.

Moira said nothing. What was there to say? She clutched Gavin closer.

'Bobble um?' he said.

Nancy clutched the wheel and began to manoeuvre the car into the river of people.

Chapter 3

Sylvia Clancy
Overflow
via Gibber's Creek
8 December 1941

Nancy Clancy
Craigiethorn Plantation
via Kota Bharu, Malaya

Dearest Nancy,
Your father is writing to Ben today. You know it is serious
when your father manages to put pen to paper! He is urging
Ben to send you home now, even if Moira still refuses to come
with you.

It is not just that we miss you. War with Japan is too terrible to
contemplate, and your father and I remember too well what it was
like in the last war for those caught up near the fighting.

I will write again next week with more news of home, but I
hope by then there will be no need to write and you'll be on a ship
for Australia. Wire us as soon as you can and your father will book
your passage.

Gran sends you her love, and hopes if you can't be with us for
Christmas, you can for the New Year. I imagine Michael hopes
the same thing. His mother sent you her best regards, by the way,
when I met her at the CWA 'Comforts for Soldiers' fete. She
had even donated a pair of socks she knitted herself. I wish you
could have seen them to prove you are not the worst knitter in the

world. Matilda Thompson is admirable in every way, but she is
not a knitter!

Delilah sends you a woof, and Timber a whinny.

Love always, my darling daughter,
Mum xxxxxxxx

Gibber's Creek Gazette, 9 December 1941

War with Japan Begins Yesterday!

Today the Prime Minister, Mr John Curtin, and the Governor-General, Lord Gowrie, formally signed a statement at the meeting with the War Cabinet. Mr Curtin said the war began from five pm yesterday.

At the Gibber's Creek Council meeting, Councillor Bullant said that all of Gibber's Creek stands behind Mr Curtin and the war effort.

MALAYA, 9 DECEMBER 1941

NANCY

The railway went through the middle of the village (or perhaps the village had grown about the station), built to carry barrels of crude rubber from the plantations, woven baskets of rice from the paddies, bananas and pineapples. A scraggle of bamboo huts, squawking chickens, more women sweeping up the fallen leaves and flowers of the night, vegetable gardens in roughly fenced-off allotments, and then the huts closer together. This was not where white people lived, the colonials from Britain and Australia, but Malays, Chinese, Tamils ...

The dull jungle greens gave way to colour: yellow flowers in the vegetable plots; red flowers, purple bougainvillea; the bright blue top and pants of the rickshaw pullers; the Tamils' clothes of lolly pink; and the red, green and purple Malay sarongs. Nancy could smell frying onions, hot peanuts, cardamom, coconut.

Her stomach growled as she swerved to avoid a black-and-pink patched pig, majestically stepping across the road, and then a water 'boy', at least ninety years old, stooped under his pole with its buckets of water at each end.

The station car park was full. Nancy found a spot further down the road, left Moira in the car changing Gavin's nappy and dressing him in a cream linen travelling suit, and lugged their baggage to the cloakroom, taking a ticket from the attendant. She went back for Moira, Gavin and the haversack, reluctantly leaving the water bag. It would be stolen, of course, by the time they got back. But they were not coming back. The car would be stolen too. Should she find someone to look after it for Ben?

She knew no one to ask, just Moira's friends on plantations out of town, and Ben's comrades in the army, and none of them could take a car now. Nor could she manage to drive it as far as Singapore, or even Kuala Lumpur, even if they could buy enough petrol, which she doubted. They had just abandoned the whole bungalow, its furniture, bedding, clothes. What did it matter if someone took the car as well?

For the first time she felt the magnitude of Moira's loss. Her house, almost everything she owned, her way of life, swapped for this undignified flight to an unknown farm in New South Wales where she must know, from Nancy's reaction to being waited on by servants, that the only help in the house was Mrs Perkins twice a week to 'do the rough'. Moira would have to make her own bed, mend her own clothes. No amah to look after Gavin …

Gavin would love it at Overflow. She'd take him down to the billabong, let him dabble his tiny feet in the slow, muddy water, show him how the golden lizards soaked up the sun …

The waiting room was full too. She left Moira standing on the platform, Gavin over her shoulder, patting his back with her gloved hands to bring up the burps, cloth ready to catch the white curdy baby vomit. There had always been an amah waiting to do this before. Nancy was relieved that Moira seemed to be able to manage it by herself.

Now to join the queue for tickets, and ask the attendant if he had any news.

Half an hour later she pushed her way back through the crush of people on the railway platform. The train sat, steaming gently, making the hot air even damper. Moira still patted a fretful Gavin over her shoulder.

Nancy reached over and took Gavin from her, breathing in the sweet baby smell of his hair under his hat. She patted his back automatically and smiled at his burp. Gavin always burped for Auntie Nancy.

'What's happening?' demanded Moira.

'It really is war. The Japanese attacked Kota Bharu the night before last. Not just bombing. The Japanese have seized the airport, at least.'

'Ben is up there!' Moira's gloved fingers clenched.

Nancy tried to make her voice reassuring. 'Ben can take care of himself.'

'Yes, of course.' Moira's voice was forcefully calm. 'How close is the fighting?'

'Still up around Kota Bharu, the stationmaster thinks. That's all he's heard on the radio.'

'But you saw Japanese soldiers at our place!'

'I saw six men.' Nancy tried to find the word, as Gavin tugged a lock of her hair and began to chew it. 'I think they must have been what Ben calls reconnaissance, sent ahead to spy out the land. If the Japanese Army were close, they'd be bombing us already ...'

Moira stiffened.

I shouldn't have said that, thought Nancy tiredly.

'Do you really think Ben ...?'

'I think Ben is fine.'

She didn't. She had no idea how her brother was. Gran said she knew if her children and grandchildren were safe or unhappy, and even when they were coming home. If that was true, Nancy hadn't inherited the gift.

'If he'd been involved in fighting, he should have let us know if he is all right.'

'Moira, no one is delivering telegrams out of town right now. He wouldn't have had time to send a telegram anyway.'

'He'd want us to be safe!'

Which is why he sent for me to help you go to Overflow, thought Nancy. And a fat lot of good that did. A year of having dresses fitted and learning how to talk about the weather to the Commissioner's wife — not even real talk, like 'Will the rains be late this year?' but 'Isn't the heat dreadful?' — while Moira felt well enough to go on picnics but not to travel. They'd have been closer to a hospital at Overflow than at the plantation. But no point thinking about that now ... 'The good news is the trains are still running.'

'What's the bad news?' Moira's eyes were shadowed, her face even paler than usual.

'No tickets.'

'But there have to be!'

'Bobble bobble erk,' said Gavin indignantly on Nancy's shoulder, almost as if he agreed with his mother.

'Not till next week at the earliest,' said Nancy, patting his back wearily. 'Not even in second class.'

'Second class!' Moira looked at her as though she was mad. 'You'll have to drive us.'

'Can't risk it. The petrol tank's nearly empty.'

'What about the jerry can?'

'The petrol in the jerry can wouldn't even get us halfway to Kuala Lumpur. We can't risk being stranded alone on some road in the jungle.'

To her relief, Moira didn't argue. 'Then we have to get train tickets somehow.'

Nancy took a deep breath. She gave Gavin her finger to chew, forced herself to make her voice quiet and persuasive. 'There's a third-class local train later today. If we sit right next to the train line, we can make sure we get on it ...'

'What? Crammed up with all the natives! Pigs and chickens and men chewing betel?'

'It's our only chance! We don't even have anywhere to stay here. It's not safe to go back and we don't have enough petrol to get anywhere else.'

'It's not safe for Gavin to travel with natives! Heaven knows what he might catch.'

Why should Malays or Chinese have any more diseases than Europeans? thought Nancy. Her best friends at school had been the Lee twins. But she had given up trying to change Moira's view of the world months ago. She hunted for the right ammunition. 'Moira, Ben would say you have to keep Gavin safe. That means getting any train we can south.'

'I am not travelling with a bunch of natives! If you had any idea at all of the proper way to do things ...'

'Mrs Clancy?' The well-bred voice came from the window of one of the first-class carriages.

Moira checked herself, slipping effortlessly into her garden-party persona. She stepped over to the train, her high heels clicking on the platform. 'Mrs Armitage! We met at the Smithertons' dinner party, didn't we? How do you do?'

Mrs Armitage was in her fifties: severely curled grey hair under a purple hat, with mauve gloves and impeccable black shoes. And perfect lipstick, thought Nancy. 'As well as can be expected, my dear. Such dreadful news.'

'Do you know what is happening?'

'My husband had a telegram from Head Office this morning. Mr Armitage is with the Federated Malay States Railway, you know. There has been an attack on Kota Bharu. Have you heard?'

Moira nodded.

'Mr Armitage insisted that I go south at once. I'm just glad that we decided that the German U-boats made it too dangerous for the children to come to us from England these school holidays.'

'You're travelling down to Singapore?'

'My dear, it won't come to that! Our boys will stop them soon enough! No, to Gemas. I'll stay at the club house there.' The older woman hesitated, as though unsure of the words to use. 'My dear, I'm afraid there are no seats left. But if you wouldn't mind sitting on your luggage, I am sure no one would mind if you shared our carriage.' She looked at the other occupants — two elderly women, an elderly man, moustached and as thin as a greyhound, a mother with two teenage girls.

'Quite all right,' said the motherly one. 'In times like these ...'

Mrs Armitage glanced at Nancy. 'I'm sure your amah could squeeze in somewhere in second class. I can have a word with the stationmaster ...'

She takes me for a Eurasian, thought Nancy grimly, shifting Gavin to her other shoulder. Then, more charitably, realised that her crumpled clothes, her bird's-nest hair and lack of make-up, not just her skin colour, might have caused the misapprehension.

'This is my sister-in-law,' said Moira expressionlessly. 'Mrs Armitage, this is Nancy Clancy, my husband's sister. She has been visiting us from the family property, Overflow, in Australia.'

Mrs Armitage's expression cleared. 'Ah, the Australian outback.' The additional 'so your skin colour is from the sun' went unsaid. The flash of calculation on the woman's face also possibly meant 'Australian property name: therefore money'. Particularly with a brother managing a plantation. One thing Nancy had learnt in Malaya was the incessant evaluation and re-evaluation of one's acquaintanceship, each person in their place, but that place shifting according to rank and wealth, connections and antecedents. And always, always, colour of the skin.

'I apologise for my appearance,' said Nancy carefully. She couldn't remember the last time she had apologised for anything. But getting Gavin and Moira to safety was more important than worrying what a mem thought of her. 'I saw Japanese soldiers in our compound early this morning. I only thought of getting Moira and Gavin to safety. I threw on the first things that came to hand.'

'Ah, I see. Well, you can tidy yourself up in the train. One can't let the side down, especially in times like these ... You had better hurry,' she added, as the stationmaster blew his whistle.

Nancy handed Gavin back to Moira, then ran for the luggage as Mrs Armitage waved discreetly to the stationmaster to keep the train at the station. Nancy shoved the suitcases into the carriage, then hauled her haversack over her shoulder.

'But our tickets,' protested Moira.

'You can pay the conductor,' said Mrs Armitage. 'And if he objects,' she gave a small cough, 'I am sure if we mention Mr Armitage's name there will be no problem at all.'

Chapter 4

Gibber's Creek Gazette, 9 December 1941

Important Meeting Town Hall Tonight

A large attendance is expected at the Gibber's Creek
Town Hall tonight when Councillors Bullant and Ellis will
announce the measures that will be made for safeguarding
the community in the event of a national emergency.

Six pm Town Hall. Ladies, please bring a plate.

MALAYA, 9 DECEMBER 1941

NANCY

There wasn't.

Nancy sat crammed in the middle of the seat, with Moira facing
her on the other side. Predictably moustache-man had given his
seat to Moira, and the two girls gave theirs up too. They now
sprawled on the floor, legs out, passing Gavin from white-frocked
lap to lap while he delightedly pulled their hair and examined their
noses. The elderly moustache-man (in rubber, he said, which made
Nancy think of a small rubber moustache-man on the mantelpiece)
perched on the suitcase that couldn't fit on the luggage rack. Nancy
doubted the conductor could have even found room to come into
their carriage, much less to eject three unwanted passengers.
And why should he, when they could pay their fare and had the
agreement of the first-class passengers they were travelling with?

29

'Tea?' asked Mrs Armitage. Moustache-man politely reached up to bring down her picnic basket, and then his own and the one belonging to the motherly woman. The atmosphere was almost festive, as with each mile chugged south through the jungle and rubber plantations the war was left further behind.

'I would love a cup,' said Moira.

'I always carry a spare. You wouldn't mind drinking from the lid?' This last was addressed to Nancy.

Nancy shook her head. She thought of their own fruitcake, probably reduced to crumbs in the haversack, and rejected it. She took a slice of Mrs Armitage's instead and nibbled. 'It's delicious,' she said, then tried to remember if it was correct etiquette to comment on the food. Actually the cake tasted like someone had mucked up the recipe, adding native spices and chunks of pineapple. But she couldn't leave it uneaten now.

'A Ceylonese recipe. Mr Armitage was stationed there, before the war. Ah, happy times.' Mrs Armitage offered Moira an egg and lettuce sandwich. Moira took it gratefully.

The motherly woman proffered fish-paste sandwiches from her tiffin basket, or cheese and tomato; rock cakes, which had turned indeed to rock in the heat, and had to be nibbled slowly; and buns, suitable for satisfying the appetites of teenage daughters. Moustache-man passed around his Bath biscuits, then slices of mango cheeks that he removed with a Swiss army knife. 'Never eat a fruit you haven't seen peeled,' he instructed Nancy.

She didn't say that she had been told that by almost every European since she arrived in Malaya. She was too grateful for the hospitality, the seats in the train, the food, the comfort of company — even just to have others making decisions. Mrs Armitage had already decided that she and Moira and Gavin would stay with her at the railway accommodations overnight, and promised that Mr Armitage, in absentia, would arrange for tickets to take them to Kuala Lumpur once she had spoken with him on the telephone. 'So much easier for your husband to reach you there, rather than going all the way down to Singapore,' said Mrs Armitage.

'Excellent golf course at Kuala Lumpur,' said the motherly woman, diluting her tea with a judicious measure of hot water from yet another Thermos. 'You must join the golf club. Do you play?'

'Of course,' said Moira.

'No,' said Nancy.

'Oh, my dear, you really must learn. Spiffing game.'

'I think my brother would prefer us to go straight to Singapore,' said Nancy carefully. 'We can get a ship there to Australia.'

'Stuff and nonsense,' said moustache-man. 'Sail to Australia with German ships about? You heard they sunk the *Sydney*? It is quite impossible that the Japs will actually invade Malaya. Not with British and Indian and Australian forces here. There are only two possible routes down the peninsula. Any invasion force would be wiped out in days. The Japanese only travel on bicycles, you know.'

Then they've bicycled a long way from Japan, thought Nancy sceptically. She suspected a bicycle could go almost as fast on the rutted roads as a car. And what about the Japanese planes, ships and parachutes? The men she had seen early this morning couldn't have bicycled from Kota Bharu if the attack had only been yesterday. Which meant parachutes, floating down below giant puffs of silk, like the German paratroopers she had seen on the newsreels.

But there was no point spoiling the conviviality of the carriage.

The heat grew, despite the open windows. Smuts fluttered and clustered on the girls' white dresses, on Moira's neat suit and moustache-man's tie. Moira dozed, as did the motherly woman. Moustache-man slept with curious half-snores, as if his moustache was too thick to let him make a proper one. The girls played with Gavin, who smelt just slightly of milky burp and dirty nappy.

Mrs Armitage turned curious eyes on Nancy. 'Have you been in Malaya long?'

'Nearly a year. I came to help Moira pack to return to Australia,' she added. 'But she felt too ... unwell ... with Gavin ... to travel that far.'

'Ah, I see,' said Mrs Armitage.

Nancy wondered exactly what she did see. Did Mrs Armitage think Nancy's family had sent her to Malaya to find a husband, as so many female visitors did in India and other colonies, where white women were in such short supply that even a girl or woman who had failed to find a suitable husband back home might have a chance?

'And is there a young man waiting for you back in Australia?' asked Mrs Armitage archly, settling the question. 'Or perhaps there's an officer who's caught your eye?'

'I'm only sixteen,' said Nancy, hoping that was answer enough without having to add, 'Too young for husband hunting.'

'So no young man then?' Mrs Armitage persisted. Perhaps Mrs Armitage had a son of suitable age in England, thought Nancy, and wanted an Australian heiress for him. Which she supposed she was, if you counted the value of Overflow in the pounds, shillings and pence for which it never would be sold. Mum and Dad had never discussed what would happen after they died, but she supposed that, as with her Sampson cousins' property, Overflow would be divided between Ben and herself — one reason perhaps why Dad bought up any of the surrounding land that came on the market. Overflow was half as big again as in his father's day.

Mrs Armitage still waited for her answer.

'I have a ...' Nancy stopped. How would she describe Michael? Friend was too little, fiancé too much. It had been a year since she had seen him. People changed in a year. She had changed in the year droving to Queensland, and changed in her year here. Michael was still at school. Even if school was endlessly the same, Michael must have changed too.

Except at heart he would still be Michael of Drinkwater, as she was Nancy of the Overflow. They were ...

She didn't know the words, and there was no way the older woman would understand even if she could have found them.

Mrs Armitage noticed the blush on her cheeks. 'Ah, there *is* a young man. Do your parents approve?'

Did they? She had never given the matter much thought. 'Yes, of course,' she said.

'And his parents?'

Was Mrs Armitage thinking Michael's parents might object to a ... tanned ... young woman?

Did Michael's parents approve of her as a possible daughter-in-law? She imagined Michael's mother, still called Miss Matilda by half the district, daughter of the famous swaggie who had died at the billabong in Australia's most loved song. Drinkwater was Miss Matilda's kingdom, and half of Gibber's Creek too. Thought of Michael's father, Tommy Thompson, called 'legendary industrialist' in the Sydney papers, a small man with baggy-kneed trousers, and eyes that were both shrewd and kind.

She suspected that Michael's parents, like hers, would let their children discover the hearts of their own lives.

Did they like her? She smiled, remembering that last Christmas party. She'd yarned to Miss Matilda for hours before it began, telling her about her trip to Charters Towers while they'd inspected the improvements to the shearing plant. How could a woman like Mrs Armitage understand Miss Matilda, gumboots over silk stockings so she didn't get her green leather shoes (from Paris before the war) stained with lanolin in the shed?

'I've known his parents all my life,' she said instead. 'They're family friends. We spend Christmas at a cousin's property next to theirs every year. It's only a couple of hours upriver from ours, almost next door. There's a party at Drinkwater on Christmas Eve, then a picnic down at the river on Boxing Day and, well, all sorts of things.'

Mrs Armitage smiled approvingly. Nancy realised it sounded terribly respectable — parties of women in white dresses and big hats, like the picnics in Malaya, and servants in white gloves, instead of food laid out on trestles in the shearers' quarters.

At the Boxing Day picnic, women dressed in anything from jodhpurs to bathing suits to the latest Sydney fashions, and waved the flies from the doorstops of bread, and lettuce or beetroot salads. A tribe of kids splashed and yelled or fed carrots to Sheba, the elephant left by the circus that had ended its days in the Drinkwater paddocks, kids brown from the sun or from Aboriginal heritage, kids with Chinese parents or grandparents, like the Lee twins, or Mah McAlpine's children. The men barbecued mutton chops over glowing coals, yarning about the price of wool or the next contender for the Melbourne Cup who might just be running now in their back paddock. The cricket game afterwards where everybody played, women as well as men, the toddlers with their grandfathers showing them how to hold the bat, just like Granddad had shown her ...

It was so vivid she was back there, the buzz of flies, the scent of river water, the plock of the cricket ball on the bat. Gran and Ben cheering and Granddad holding her in his arms to make her first run ...

'And what is his name?' persisted Mrs Armitage.

'Michael,' said Nancy. 'Michael Thompson.'

34

Chapter 5

Gibber's Creek Gazette, 9 December 1941

Subscribe to the *Gazette* today!

As the war in the Pacific is likely to disrupt the supply of newsprint, it will be necessary for the *Gazette* to limit its print run. Readers who order their paper for regular delivery will be guaranteed a copy, but casual buyers may miss out.

Subscriptions can be made at Lee's Newsagency or the *Gazette* offices, in Albert Street.

DRINKWATER STATION, NEW SOUTH WALES, AUSTRALIA, 9 DECEMBER 1941

MICHAEL

Michael Thompson sat on the sand and watched the water. The river pondered between its banks as if there was no war to ruffle its world. Yesterday Australia had been part of Europe's war, its armies fighting for England. Today Australia was not just formally at war with Japan, but already fighting on battlefields in Malaya, the enemy heading south. The world had changed overnight, but not the river. Men might fight and women weep. The river obeyed the rain and sun, not humans.

A year ago he'd sat here and watched the water with a girl.

It had been Christmas Eve. His parents' annual party. Everyone came to it: the workers from his father's local factory and their families; the whole McAlpine clan and the women who worked at Blue and Mah McAlpine's biscuit factory too; his mother's maternal relatives, the Sampsons; and every neighbour within driving or riding distance and a few from beyond that.

Christmas Eve 1940 had been the same as every other year, till you looked closely: saw the absence of nearly every man between twenty-one and forty; saw the wives, sisters, mothers, smiling too brightly, lipstick defiant, seams drawn on the back of the legs to replace the silk stockings already in short supply, with shipping and factories devoted to the war effort, not luxuries.

He'd spent the day mopping the shearers' quarters, the afternoon loading the buffet tables while guests arrived, a few in cars but mostly on horseback as they might have come decades earlier, because of the war's petrol shortages, the women vanishing upstairs to change out of their riding clothes into party finery, the men heading down to the stockyard to inspect the new rams.

Flinty Mack and her husband had ridden down from Rock Farm in the mountains for their annual visit to her brother Andy McAlpine, Drinkwater's manager, and his wife, Mah. Flinty's three kids kept riding, expert on their ponies, down to Moura to stay with Blue McAlpine. Blue was married to Flinty's other brother, Joseph McAlpine, now a doctor in the Medical Corps in Malaya, and she and Mah ran the Empire Biscuit Factory. The Mack family had camped out the night before on their way down from their valley in the mountains, a four-hour car journey turned into a two-day adventure.

Laughter and the stamp of horses, and behind it all the thump of the generator. His mother had decreed that for this night only, despite petrol shortages, the generator would be going; too much danger of fire in the summer's heat if they had candles or slush lamps.

Which meant Mrs Mutton and Mah McAlpine had taken advantage of the electricity to make ice to freeze ice cream, and he was put to churning, churning, churning custard while Blue

McAlpine tied satin bows on all the dogs, even three-legged Brute, and no one mentioned Joseph, or his brother Jim doing basic training with the AIF, or the Sampson boys in North Africa, or Kirsty McAlpine working up on a property near Darwin for the duration.

Tablecloths on the trestles from the shearers' quarters; the big silver punch bowl filled with Mrs Mutton's special recipe of lemonade, ginger ale, fresh lemon juice from the trees out the back, sugar, ice cubes, crushed mint leaves and canned pineapple juice carefully hoarded in the larder — this might be the last year for a long time they added pineapple juice to the punch. Lamingtons too were becoming a rare species — one needed desiccated coconut for a decent lamington and although most larders had begun the war with a good supply, it was also becoming scarce. Nor would there be hams tonight — all pigs, ham and bacon must be sent to Britain, so home-corned legs of mutton took their place.

But most of the party's staples had always been local anyway: cold chicken, dispatched and plucked by farm manager Andy McAlpine in an orgy of clucking, with pin feathers still flying around the courtyard; roast turkey, bred at the Lees' market garden; potato salad, with salad cream dressing; pickled beetroot; sliced tomato, cucumber and lettuce salad dressed with cream and vinegar; vast bowls of fruit salad and whipped Jersey-cow cream; almost as many kinds of pie as there'd be women here tonight, each one bringing her speciality — late cherries, early apple, early plum and apricots, mock ginger made with spiced choko that tasted and looked like pears, blackberry, raspberry; jam tarts, the pastry traditionally made with suet, from boiled mutton fat, which made a lighter and moister pudding than butter; sponge cakes light with duck eggs, filled with more Jersey cream and strawberries and the passionfruit that clambered across most backyard dunnies; pikelets already topped with jam; plain scones or pumpkin scones with lemon butter or strawberry jam; and giant plum puddings that Michael knew had been eked out with grated carrot because he had wandered into the kitchen while Mah McAlpine and Mrs Mutton were grating them. They'd demanded he stay to give the pudding bowl a stir for luck. Sandwiches, because after all there was nothing like a sandwich at a party — you could hold them and not need a plate or fork: cheese and tomato; cheese and grated carrot; cheese and salad, the beetroot staining the top bread slice red; curried egg; mutton and chutney.

Tonight there would be ice cream too. And music. Dancing. Laughter.

There was also a girl.

He saw her as his parents led the first dance, with Andy and Mah McAlpine and Flinty and Sandy Mack following, an old-fashioned polka fast and bright to push away the dark of war, the bombs' savage descent on London and Berlin, the triumph and tragedy of an army lost and saved at Dunkirk, the worry about where Jim was headed after training.

Black hair. Brown eyes. A dress that looked thrown on, three sizes too big, not fitted to her shape like those the other young women wore. Darkish skin that might be tan but he reckoned more likely made her one of the Sampson clan, which meant she was a second cousin five times removed, or fifth cousin two times removed, something like that. She saw him too. Their gazes cut through the crowd under the oak trees.

'Ah, Michael, good to see you. How's school?' One of his Sampson cousins.

'Good, thank you,' he answered automatically. 'Excuse me a moment …'

He made his way towards her. The same age as him, he thought, or maybe a year younger. Skin clear as river water, eyes deep as a billabong. You could see the stars reflected in her hair.

'Michael, how you've grown! How's school?'

'Good, thank you, Mrs McAlpine. Will you excuse me? There's someone I need to see.'

The girl stood and waited till he reached her, then grinned as he stood there, suddenly unable to think what to say. 'Are you going to ask me to dance, or stand there and let the mozzies fly into your mouth?'

'We've met?'

'Of course we've met, you drongo. I'm Nancy. Nancy Clancy. And if you say, "You're a poet and you don't know it," you'll get a plate of ice cream in your hair.'

'Don't you even think of wasting that ice cream. I spent half the afternoon churning it.'

She was Pete Sampson's great-niece then, old Mr Clancy's granddaughter. Nancy of the Overflow, two hours' drive down the river, or three hours' ride if you took the shortcut. The Clancys came for Christmas every year, spending a week at the Sampsons'. But he couldn't place Nancy. 'I'm sorry,' he said frankly. 'I can't remember meeting you.'

'You have,' she said dryly. 'Just this year I'm wearing a skirt.'

Now he *did* remember her. Not from the year before — he was sure he hadn't seen her then — and not the year before that either. That was the Christmas he'd stayed with Taylor's family in Sydney, because Sydney had sounded so much more exciting than coming home, then regretted it, missing the hilarity of the Christmas week.

Yes, she had been different three years back. She'd been what? Twelve? Eleven? Tattered moleskins, hair cut as short as a boy's. She'd been one of the mob he'd splashed in the river with, Christmas after Christmas; they climbed trees, rode branches like they were horses, collected cicadas, hiding them in the darkness of their cupped hands then opening them to hear them sing.

He remembered his mother's gossip, eighteen months earlier: Nancy Clancy had abandoned school at fourteen, a year before her Qualifying Certificate, left her parents a note to say she'd gone to Queensland droving. Remembered Dad laughing and saying if the Clancys had wanted a daughter all lace and proper, they shouldn't have called her Nancy. 'I doubt she'd suit the office, Nancy of the Overflow.'

'Did you really run away from home and leave your parents a note?'

'I rode away from home. I didn't run. And we were only fifty miles away by the time Dad caught up with me.' She looked at him, laughter in her eyes. 'I had to do something to make them realise I didn't want to be a schoolteacher like Mum.'

'Did it work?'

'Oh, yes.' The grin was wicked now. 'Dad arrived with a new swag all packed — fruitcake and books to read and all — and instructions that I was to wire home from every town we passed, and if I wanted to come back he'd send me the train fare.'

'Just like that?'

'Yep.' She shrugged. 'I thought I might get a walloping, but he didn't even seem that surprised. Old Ringer Bailey was boss anyway. He and Dad go way back. Been droving with Granddad too. Mum and Dad knew Ringer would keep an eye on me. Mum might even have thought that I'd decide to come home after a week without a bed.'

'But you didn't?'

'No.' Her eyes shifted, looking back towards the river, the dark plains. 'It was ... wonderful. Just that. A year of wonders.'

He thought of the poem written about her grandfather. *And the bush has friends to meet him, and their kindly voices greet him, in the* — how did it go? *The whisper of the river and the murmur of the stars?* He didn't think he had the words right, but they were the ones he felt.

He wanted to say that he had heard them too, the stars singing out of the depth of night, a clarity you never got at boarding school in Sydney, the river muttering so you could almost make out what it was trying to say.

Instead he said, 'You're back home then? For more than Christmas?' Her shoes looked too big for her, he noticed. Worn shoes, polished but showing cracks.

She said lightly, 'Pretty soon I will be. Just one more adventure before I settle down. Ben's up in Malaya, managing a rubber plantation. He's just joined the local Volunteer Defence Corps. I'm going up there to help his wife pack up and come here.'

'Seriously? Half the country is trying to leave Malaya and you're going up there?' The previous night at dinner with the McAlpines Dad had said that war with Japan was inevitable; that the Japanese must strike further south to keep supplying their country and their forces. But Andy McAlpine argued that Japan would never be stupid enough to attack the British Empire. Prime Minister Mr Menzies had worked hard to keep relations good with the Japanese. There was even a Japanese ambassador in Canberra now, and an Australian one in Tokyo. Andy had fought in the Great War, of course, but Dad knew about things like trade and resources. And perhaps Andy too hadn't wanted to worry Blue, with Joseph with the army in Malaya.

But whoever had been right, this wasn't a time to go travelling unless you had to, with the Empire in retreat and so much of Europe falling as Hitler's armies advanced, so much damage wreaked on England's major cities, children evacuated, much of its army lost at Dunkirk. Though surely Malaya was safe, protected by the impregnable might of Singapore in its south. Other towns might fall, but Singapore — and the lands it protected — could never fall.

'Ben was pretty insistent. I've never met Moira, but it sounds like she can't even pack up the house without help.' She grinned. 'Just for a few weeks, then I really will be home for good. It'll be fascinating to see Malaya. Your dad wangled me a passage on one of the cargo ships. American — neutral, so there's no worry about attack by German U-boats. Your family has useful connections.'

'Yes.' Dad's factory here and the ones in Sydney were now devoted to war work, manufacturing a new wireless of some kind, invented by his father. Michael had neither asked for nor been given details. As the paper said, loose lips sink ships. He also knew vaguely that much of his father's money had been made with a similar invention in the Great War. Government contracts and export licences did mean contacts in all sorts of places, and he supposed with shipping companies too. 'Who'll run the plantation?'

'Half the blokes in the local Defence Corps are like Ben, with a property or business to manage. He's got a good foreman and he can get back there every week or so. But it sounds like Moira — Ben's wife — is going all to pieces with him being away so much. Moira's English,' she added, as though that explained going to pieces, though with what England and the English had borne the past year, Michael thought that 'even though she's English' might have been a better way to put it. But Moira was her sister-in-law, not his.

Yet, said a whisper in his mind.

His brain hiccupped so he missed what she was saying next, about packing and passports and the passage booked to bring them home.

Was he seriously thinking of marrying a girl he had just met — well, just noticed anyway — thinking of marrying *anyone*, when he was only fifteen, with another two years of school ahead of him? Marriage was something another fifteen years away, another life …

A jigsaw assembled itself in his mind. The pieces had been there waiting, just needed the final piece to make a whole.

The music, the laughter of friends and neighbours, the complaints of sheep in the river paddock, the whicker of horses greeting each other closer to the house, the feeling when a mob of sheep flows over the hill, like a brown flood of wool and baas. So many pieces, waiting for him now.

Not another life, in fifteen years' time. *This* life. Yes, more of his life — much more — before marriage would happen. But for the first time he knew that the soil of his life was here, under his feet. Not as a doctor or lawyer or banker, like some of the distant cousins, or with inventions and factories, like Dad. His parents had never discussed who would inherit what. He suspected that with two substantial but quite different inheritances, the farm and factories, and two sons, they were waiting to see who fitted what. He knew too without it ever being spoken, that both farm and factories were too deep in the hearts of his parents for them ever to pass them to someone half-hearted. Whole heart, or not at all. If neither of their sons loved them, or wanted another career, farm or factories would go to a trust, with managers, like Blue McAlpine's family's firm, leaving the boys free to find their own niche in the world.

And this was his. Even if he never inherited Drinkwater, he would be a drover, earn enough for his own property ... '*And the bush has friends to meet him ...*'

He had said the words aloud.

Nancy's eyes narrowed. 'You making a joke?'

'No.' He wondered how many people had taunted her with the words of the Banjo Paterson poem about her grandfather and almost namesake.

She heard the truth in his voice. The grin reappeared. 'All right then.'

Someone clapped him on the shoulder. A woman, powder, scent and lipstick, kissed him on the cheek.

'Michael, merry Christmas. How is school? What year are you in now?'

'Going into sub-Junior,' he said. He waited till the couple had passed, then his eyes met Nancy's again. 'Look, we can't talk here. Come down to the river with me?'

She looked at him assessingly. He flushed, suddenly realising what the invitation must seem to suggest.

At last she said, 'All right. Do you need a lantern?' The last was almost a challenge.

'Moonlight's enough.' Besides, he thought, a lantern would show everyone that two young people were slipping off into the dark.

He stepped out of the pools of light around the shearing shed. She followed him, walking through the tall English garden trees, planted by his great-grandfather, then the smaller, more sparsely branched fruit trees, carefully pruned, then into the

43

sheep paddock. Three hundred sheep turned towards them as one, assessed them, then turned back to grazing, chewing cud, dozing. Humans did not bring hay or do in fact anything of interest after dark. Further down river Mah McAlpine's elephant helped herself to hay.

Nancy walked as he did, eyes down at the ground, adapting to the dark away from the relative light of the sky. Only when he'd led her to his favourite spot, a bald knoll above the river, did they look up. The moonlight turned the river into a shimmer of silver flowing between sandy banks growing shaggy with tussocks and thorn bush now, after the last big flood three years back.

Doubt flooded in as soon as they sat down. He had no idea what to say. Or do.

Would she expect him to kiss her? He had kissed Morrison's sister last Easter break, but someone's sister didn't count and, anyway, it had really been she who'd kissed him.

He'd been crazy, back by the shed, to think he had anything in common with the Clancy girl. Loving Drinkwater, yes, that was a small solid walnut in his mind. But this girl had left school at fourteen, not even doing her certificate so she could go to high school. Nor had she gone to boarding school, like all his friends' sisters: just the one-roomed school her mother had taught in before she'd married and taught in again now that so many male teachers had gone to war, even though married women were not supposed to teach.

Had Nancy ever read a book in her life, except school textbooks? What would Morrison say, or Taylor? Had they even spoken to someone with dark skin? There was a name for men who went with Aboriginal women, and it wasn't a polite one. Her dress looked like one of her mother's. And those shoes …

He was being a snob, his mother's worst insult for anyone. But was it snobbery to feel that someone's world was too different from yours to ever meld, despite what he had felt back among the light and chatter? Was it prejudiced to acknowledge that skin colour did make a difference, simply because it *did* matter to so many, despite what Dad said about everyone being the same under the skin? How could he have thought about marriage to someone from another world ...?

The thought stopped as if it had been cut off with a knife. His world — the part of it that he realised mattered — and hers were only a few bends of the river apart. And even if he had carefully never mentioned it at school, one of his own maternal great-grandmothers had also been Aboriginal, the beloved Auntie Love who had helped bring his mother up, and many — including those at school — knew it.

Overflow was a good property. Prosperous. Wealthy, even. Nancy's brother was a plantation manager, for all that his skin colour — and hers — was probably too deep a shade of brown for them to have ever got into a decent boarding school. But Ben had gone to agricultural college, hadn't he? And Nancy had mentioned her father had put books in her swag to take to Charters Towers. You didn't do that unless the swag carrier loved books.

He was glad thoughts couldn't be heard. His head circled, leaving him exactly where he had been a few minutes before. He liked this girl. More than liked her. Knew her deeply, even though in one way they had only just met.

A breeze ruffled the river, sending silver feathers shivering along its surface. The lights from the shearing shed and house reached here, he realised. He could even see the freckles on her nose.

'I didn't know Aboriginal girls had freckles.'

She looked carefully at the river, not him. 'Dad's half-caste. Mum and Granddad were white. Reckon I take after the three whites, not Gran.'

He wanted to say his great-grandmother had been Aboriginal. Wanted to say that it didn't matter. But of course it did. His mother's acknowledgement of her black relatives meant that invitations from other squattocracy families to the Thompsons had been conspicuously lacking. His mother's crime was not having Aboriginal ancestors, but openly acknowledging them.

At school he'd been called 'abo legs' — Hawker said you could always tell an Aborigine by his skinny legs — till he got picked for the under-sixteen rugby team. Footballers stuck together, and every one of them was bigger than Hawker and his mates. There had been no more insults after that.

Nancy would know about his great-grandmother anyway. The whole district knew every bit of gossip about the Thompsons of Drinkwater. She seemed far away in the moonlight and the pale yellow edges of the electric lights.

What could they talk about? Most of his life had been spent at school, home too far away for any but the long vacations. He didn't resent it, even if he didn't like it. That was just what one did. His life was made up of blokes at school; the only girls he met of his own age were the sisters of friends, town girls, with hair carefully curled. Soft hands. Soft lives.

He tried desperately to find words. To ask what it had been like, spending a year droving up to Charters Towers and back. But everything he thought of sounded too much like that poem. She'd think he was making fun of her. Or that he thought an Aboriginal girl, even a quarter-caste, was fair game for the son of Drinkwater.

Something moved in the shallows. All at once she seemed no longer made of wood. She leant forwards, breathed, 'Look.'

A swan glided from the reeds. Silent, not even seeming to paddle, she rode the water. Behind her came three smaller swans, almost half grown.

'It's the light. She must think it's day again. Funny, I haven't seen swans here before. River's too fast for them, mostly.' Michael glanced at Nancy as he spoke. Her face glowed as if the starlight shone on her alone. She looked ... he wasn't sure how she looked. Like she thought life was on one page but had found it on another. As if the swans were wondrous. Meaningful ...

Like Mum with his pelicans. It had been the first Parents' Day at school. Mum'd been there, with Dad, in her go-to-Sydney silk, and what he suspected was the most elegant fresh-from-Paris hat among the crowd of parents. They had gone for ice cream at a café by the river, sitting on the veranda. A pelican had landed on the railing, right by their table, its beak full. And Mum had said, as casually as she'd said she'd like strawberry ice cream, 'They'll always protect you, you know.'

'I don't understand.'

Mum kept her gaze on the big bird gulping down its fish. 'The day you were born. Before they even put you in my arms. I looked out the window and there were the pelicans, flying above the house. And I thought, they're here to look after him. I knew you'd be safe, after that.'

He'd glanced at Dad. Dad just looked tolerant, vaguely amused, like he often did with Mum. Mum was normally one of the most sensible women around, but sometimes …

A shadow passed across them. He looked up as a pelican came in to land on the water, its legs forwards, pushing at the water like a seaplane braking.

Suddenly it was hard to breathe.

Nancy said, 'Look! The light's drawn him too. Maybe he was flying and thought, hey, it's still day by the river.'

His voice seemed to speak without him willing it to. 'Mum told me once that she saw pelicans flying around when I was born. She said they'd watch out for me.' It was the first time he had told anyone that story. The first time he had ever admitted to himself that at some level he did indeed believe it. But the stars didn't crack from the sky. Nancy looked at him, assessing, approving, then back to the birds on the river. He let himself continue. 'I was hating school — all the people, all the noise after life here. And Mum said, "If you see a pelican, you'll know it'll be all right."'

A pelican gave me something to say to a girl, at least, he thought. Something that might make her laugh at the quirks of parents. He waited for the giggle.

None came. Nancy said, 'The swans are mine. Gran told me. She was there when I was born. So were the swans. This year,

47

coming home, when the floods nearly got us, a line of swans flew right up high above us. Travelling west, like us.'

'Warning you about the floods?' He tried to keep the incredulity from his voice.

'Telling me I'd be all right. To do what was needed and I'd get home safe.'

'Have they ... told you ... other things?'

'It's not really telling, is it? You see them, and you know.'

She made it sound as if he knew what she meant. As if he didn't think the idea crazy, old women's superstition.

And she was right. He did know and he didn't judge it crazy.

'I row at school,' he said. 'It gets me down on the river. Sometimes the pelicans almost seem to be telling me something too.' Like before that exam, he thought, when he was in a blue funk, and he saw one paddling by, eyeing him as if to say, 'All you have to do is glide along,' and the panic had gone. He'd steadied, had written well.

'Pelicans and swans together on the river.' Nancy grinned at him. The light gleamed on one chipped side tooth. 'I know what Gran would say to that.'

She looked back at the river, not completing the thought. She won't put it into words either, he realised. We are too young. But what we aren't saying is still there. Will always be there. Drinkwater. Overflow. Us.

Words came at last. 'What did it feel like, the day you left for Queensland?'

'Good. Cleared my head out, after sitting at that desk in school. Mountains instead of four walls. The sky instead of a window. I could breathe again. Find out who I was away from Mum and Dad. Nine years of school was bad enough. Plus Mum eagle-eyed over homework every single night.'

'And the team let you go with them?'

'Like I said, Ringer had known Granddad. Everyone knew Granddad, all the way to Charters Towers.'

'Were you the only girl?'

'No. I don't think they'd have taken me if I was. Mrs Bailey was there too. Said it was because she wouldn't trust Ringer not to stop at every pub they came to. But she loves being in the saddle, just like him. It helped that I looked like a boy though.'

She said it as though it was no big thing at all for a girl to join a man's world, as if it had never occurred to her that a girl should spend her life only in kitchens, or with her children on her knee. Just as it never seemed to have occurred to Mum, he thought, or Blue and Mah McAlpine with their biscuit factory.

'So Nancy of the Overflow was allowed to go to Queensland droving?'

'Yep. But they knew where I was. All the time. Used up most of my wages sending them all those telegrams.'

'Would you go again?'

'No. I'm only leaving now because Ben needs me.'

He looked at her as she watched the dark water. Nancy's voice almost seemed the whisper of the river. 'I realised on the way back home that it was, well, home. Nancy of the Overflow. It's who I am. But I had to go to Queensland to find out. What about you? Who are you?'

'Me?' He watched the pelican, gliding across the light. The mother swan ducked her head under the water, looking for food. One of the cygnets copied her. 'I go back to school at the end of the hols.'

He was embarrassed, a schoolboy compared to a girl who had done so much. 'Four more years, if I want to go to university. Don't know after that. Maybe Hawkesbury Agricultural College, or even Christchurch in New Zealand. Army or air force if we haven't won the war by the time I'm twenty-one.' He met her eyes. Dark eyes, like the sky. 'Then back here. No matter what.'

She nodded. He realised with a shock that he didn't have to say any more. Never, perhaps, would need to say more about the heart of his life to this girl, or the woman she'd become.

They watched the swans, ducking in the shallows. The pelican hunched by the reeds. It seemed to be asleep. Music swam around them, a waltz now, played on the piano in the shearers' quarters, not the gramophone. Someone who played well.

'That's Mum,' said Nancy. 'She tried to teach me.'

'Not interested?'

'A singsong is all right for a wet afternoon.' She laughed. 'Poor Mum. She tries so hard with me. Like this dress.'

'It's pretty awful,' he said frankly.

'I know. But none of my old ones fit and there was nothing ready-made in Gibber's Creek that would do, not with all the shortages. Mum went on like it was her fault — she should have stocked up on dresses for her growing daughter before the shops emptied. So she tried to fix up one of hers for me.'

'And her shoes too?'

The grin was wicked. 'How did you guess? But my moleskins are pretty tatty after a year away. Even my boots are falling to pieces.'

'How will you manage in Malaya?' From all he'd heard society there was more formal even than in Sydney.

'Doesn't matter how I look on the ship — it's a cargo boat anyway, not a passenger liner, so there's no dressing for dinner. Moira has a dressmaker who'll run some things up for me. I'll come back looking like Princess Elizabeth, except for the gravy stains.' Another glance at him. 'Mess likes me.'

'So do I.' He'd said it before he knew what he was going to say. She just nodded again.

'Will you write to me?'

'Of course. I'll be back by the end of March. When are your next holidays?'

He realised with relief that she seemed to be taking it for granted they would meet again as soon as possible.

'Easter.' That seemed an eternity away. 'Would your parents mind if I rode over to Overflow before you go?'

'They'd be ecstatic. 'Specially Mum. A boy coming to call would be the first properly daughterly thing I've ever done in my life.' She flicked him a cheeky glance. 'And you're sober.

Wear decent boots. And won't boast to Mum that you can dock a hundred sheep an hour like poor Bluey Smith did when they brought me home.'

He wanted to kiss her. Not, like Morrison's sister, because she was a girl, but because she was Nancy. He wanted to breathe her in. He leant towards her, waiting to see if she drew back.

Instead she leant to meet him.

She tasted of lemonade and ginger sponge, of sunlight and water and the bush. A lifetime later he pulled back. If they kissed again, they would keep going.

Not here. Not yet.

'We'd better get back.'

She let him help her to her feet. A girl who had ridden to Charters Towers and back didn't need his hand. But it was what a man did for a woman and, besides, it meant his hand was in hers. He kept it there, as she looked at him, serious, in the soft gleam of distant light.

'Can I tell you something? Something I've never told anyone. Will you keep it secret?'

She liked him. She had to like him or she would never have asked him that. She might let a boy kiss her ... and he'd punch anyone else who tried ... but to tell him a secret ... The wonder of it prickled through his skin. He wanted to stomp a dance of triumph all around her, sing till the birds woke up again. Instead he said, 'Yes. Of course.'

'I want to tell you about the letter,' she said.

For a moment he didn't know what she meant, then realised. *The* letter. The one in the poem by Banjo Paterson. *I had written him a letter ...*

'The one your grandfather never got because he'd gone to Queensland droving?'

'*And we don't know where he are.* But Granddad *did* get it. They kept it at Overflow for him.' She took a breath of river air, glanced for the swans: they had vanished, realising at last that it wasn't day.

'The letter said, *Don't do it, my friend.*' Her voice was obviously a quote, from something read a hundred times. '*Don't throw your life away on a native girl. Come and stay with me in Sydney and I'll guarantee you'll meet girls you can take home to your family with pride.*'

'But he didn't,' said Michael.

'No. He'd married Gran before the letter arrived, and they went droving and Dad was born in a camp up by the Condamine. Then years later my great-grandfather died and he'd left Overflow to Granddad anyway, even though they'd never even spoken again. Maybe he forgave him for marrying Gran. Maybe he never got round to changing his will. Granddad never knew. Dad had bought his own place next to the Sampsons' by then, but after Great-Granddad died we all moved to the main homestead. Mum told me last year that Granddad had told her he never regretted it,' she added softly. 'Said riding with Gran was like being an eagle, flying across the plains. Said Gran was the land, the sky and the rain to him, all the years that they were married.'

Michael thought of the dark-skinned elderly woman he'd last seen helping Mrs Mutton mix the punch. Nancy's grandmother must have been decades younger than her husband. Had she regretted marrying a man so much older, leaving her so long a widow? He didn't think so. He suspected that Nancy's mother had no regrets about marrying a half-caste either, that in telling her daughter of her father-in-law's happiness she was talking about her own fulfilment too, even if so much was closed to her children because of the colour of their skin.

He reached out, and touched Nancy's cheek. No, he thought. He was wrong. Nothing — not even the touch of the tarbrush — would stop Nancy of the Overflow from doing what she wanted, what she felt was good.

Nothing at all.

The daylight was seeping from the world. Michael scrambled to his feet, stiff. The river still flowed. But Nancy was gone.

They'd had the New Year picnic, too crowded with kids and gossips and friends and relatives to slip away together; two half-days together after that, at Overflow. Dinner with her family, her mother playing Bach on the piano afterwards, and then a family game of Scrabble. Nancy's gran's eyes on him, watchful, almost amused; her father judging him and, he hoped, approving.

And then that hour at dawn the next day, the only time they'd had alone, sitting together in green shadows as the water spilled across the rock, before her parents woke. Had she meant what she said then?

Her words had moved him so much he hadn't known what to say. He'd thought of a hundred things since then, but you couldn't put something like that in letters. They had walked back to breakfast, the bustle of loading her haversack into the car — no neat leather suitcase for Nancy of the Overflow. He'd said goodbye to her on the station with the rest of her family, had kissed her cheek, in front of her aunt and her grandmother and half the district, and felt her skin on his lips for days after. It had faded at last, but not the memory.

She had written, as she had promised. He'd written back. Letters that anyone could read, if they'd wanted to, with little that was personal in them, except *I miss you* and *I hope you will be home soon.*

Had Nancy really meant what she'd said that last morning? Was it as important as he thought? More even than saying 'I love you' which neither had yet, even in the letters.

She had not been home by Easter, nor had the situation in Malaya been quite what she had expected. Moira was worried for her husband, but not in pieces, or at least those pieces had come together to competently arrange new clothes for her sister-in-law and suitable amusements — picnics, dances, tennis parties, even driving lessons with the young officer she'd met at one of the picnics.

Moira was also pregnant, which was possibly an unexpressed reason Ben had wanted his sister to come to Malaya to help her pack and travel, with the nearest white neighbour an hour's drive away. But the pregnancy had not been easy. The travel plans had been delayed, and then delayed again. The baby had been born three weeks early, with Moira bedridden at times, and for all of the last weeks of her pregnancy.

Nancy had written of longing for home; that she missed him, and the river, and the horses, though she had never quite said she missed them in that order, of her disappointment as month after month dragged by and Moira's condition remained too uncertain to travel. But she had seemed to enjoy herself too, with the parties and picnics when Moira had felt up to it, or even by herself, chaperoned by the Commissioner's wife.

Why did no one ever tell me clothes could be fun?! she'd written in one of the early letters. *This tiny little Chinese lady in the village makes them. I have an evening gown of beaded silk, pale blue. Wait till you see it! I have even learnt to walk in high heels. Moira lent me her lipstick for the party last night. Mum would have a fit if she knew I was wearing lipstick.*

He had wanted desperately to see her in anything; had been reassured too, at some deep level, that the harum-scarum girl was learning to dress well, to hold her own in polite society. He had counted out the months of pregnancy, added one more, and tried to wait till then.

But even after the baby's birth he still hadn't seen the evening dress, nor the blue spotted voile, whatever that might be. *Blue because Moira says my skin is too tanned to wear white. She makes me wear a hat with a veil whenever we go out, and my arms covered. My tan is fading, fast. You can't even see any freckles!*

The premature baby was even more fragile than his mother. A boy, Gavin. *With the tiniest hands you ever saw,* said Nancy in her letter. *We were so worried at first, but he is feeding well now. We should be able to travel in another month or two, I hope.*

But in another two months the danger from German U-boats and destroyers was greater. Moira had declared that it was safer to keep her baby son in well-defended Malaya than risk German torpedoes. And Nancy, it seemed, had felt that she needed to stay with them, despite the longing in each letter to him, and he suspected to home too.

It had been a strange year. A waiting year. Waiting for newspapers, the lists of dead or wounded, the campaign maps; waiting for the news on the wireless after prep, the boys crowded into the housemaster's living room. Waiting, waiting, waiting, while the war was lived by others, beyond his school grounds.

More Australian troops were sent to Malaya in February, to bolster defences there. Michael didn't know whether to be relieved about that or worried that it was necessary, with Nancy not yet home.

That was the month Banjo Paterson died, the 'poet of the bush' who had made her grandfather a legend, had played a part, perhaps, in sending Clancy droving up north with his wife, away from disapproving tongues and faces — and letters.

Michael felt strangely bereft by the old man's death. The poet had been there for so much of his family's history, creating the poem and song 'Waltzing Matilda', inspired by the death of his grandfather in the billabong, watched by a twelve-year-old girl who was now his mother. The man who had heard the story of the Man from Snowy River's exploits, had written the words that had inspired Flinty Mack on the ride where she had helped capture Snow King, sire of the winner of the Caulfield Cup; who had perhaps inspired Flinty to write the books for which she was now almost as famous as the poet. The man who had made Nancy's grandfather famous.

And he was gone, an article in the newspaper, read after prep, with other boys around him, far from the bush and its folk that Paterson had celebrated. An era seemed to have vanished with him.

Australians, including perhaps his brother, had taken Tobruk in North Africa and twenty-seven thousand Italian prisoners of war too, but German Field Marshal Rommel was on the attack again.

The year had worn on. Telephone operators were instructed to say 'V for Victory' as they connected calls, but the order was withdrawn after too much stumbling and mumbling. Blue and Mah McAlpine's factory started baking biscuits for army rations, instead of their famous 'squished fly' Empire Rich Teas. Andy McAlpine was elected Captain of the Gibber's Creek Volunteer Defence Corps, as well as of the bushfire brigade, the same men being in each.

Prime Minister Menzies had lost the support of his party and resigned from the leadership after his return from a four-month overseas trip during which he had presented the case to the British War Office for greater forces to defend Australia, not just the Motherland. Arthur Fadden was elected Prime Minister, but he also resigned after only a month. Labor leader John Curtin took over. Michael's parents seemed pleased about this political outcome. 'A hard worker' was Dad's verdict, one of his highest compliments to any man.

Letters. Letters, letters and waiting. He wrote his letters after prep at school, the weekly letter to his parents and the twice-weekly letter to Nancy, sitting at the table in the library, where anyone could look over his shoulder and read what he was writing. Trying to hide away to write was impossible, would draw attention even more to anything he wanted to keep private.

He imagined Nancy writing to him on a dark wooden desk in Ben's study, on thick cream notepaper, her writing curiously bland and neat, he supposed a product of her mother's drilling, the teacher who'd have insisted on copybook after copybook until each letter was an exact duplicate of what an educated hand should be. Each one began *Dear Michael*, and he tried to tell himself the 'dear' meant exactly that. Each was signed *Yours always* which was how he signed his too, both carefully avoiding the word 'love'.

She missed him, she told him. But as Gavin grew older and stronger and Moira recovered, she also described a dinner party and a friendly lieutenant who'd taken Moira and herself on a picnic and given her driving lessons. She seemed unaware that Michael might be jealous. Perhaps because he had no reason to be.

But she was far away, beautiful, in her new clothes in a social life far removed from his schoolroom, separated from him by an ocean and German ships, guns and torpedoes. Had he misunderstood what she had told him, on that morning at Overflow? Had she changed her mind now that she had seen sophisticates like the lieutenant?

He had so little to tell her in exchange. What would Nancy of the Overflow want to know about his life at school, afternoon prep and evening chapel, rowing or rugby practice and swotting for exams, where afternoon cadet practice and weekend cadet camps were as close as he got to real life and the war?

He told her instead of his weekends and holidays at home, that there were more pelicans on the river, but he hadn't seen the black swans again. Told her about the last round-up, getting the scrub bull that had been breaking down the fences, how he and Andy McAlpine had potted over two hundred rabbits in a night. Told her the gossip from his mother's letters to which Dad contributed a weekly PS — how two of the stockmen had joined the air force, how the air force had refused to accept Kirsty McAlpine as a pilot for the second time, despite all her prizes and experience.

The British government might allow women pilots to ferry aircraft from the factory to the airbases, but the Australian authorities wouldn't even let women do that, not even one who had flown her own plane across Southeast Asia from Europe and had paddock-bashed her way around Australia more times than she could count.

He told her how Kirsty had put her plane in a shed for the duration, a lightweight racing aircraft, like its owner deemed unsuitable for war.

With every letter from the world outside, he felt more and more a schoolboy, while the men she mixed with prepared for war. But he didn't tell her this. Didn't tell her either how the day Jim had left, his embarkation leave over, his unknown destination probably the Middle East, his mother had saddled up Lady Grey and ridden down the road. Michael had been given special permission from school to be there for his brother's final leave; also, he now realised, simply to be there for his parents when the house was empty of Jim's voice.

He had mounted Billy Buttons as his mother rode down the drive, followed her horse's tracks in the dirt, keeping well behind. She had gone to a bend in the river beyond the Drinkwater boundaries. He'd left Billy tethered, had walked towards her, then stopped when he heard the howling.

For a moment he thought it was a dingo, then realised it was Matilda. Mum never cried — never — not even when his father had had his stroke. Especially then, perhaps.

He thought maybe she wasn't crying now. The noise was grief, pure and artless, the lament of ewes when their lambs were taken to the slaughter, as if they knew the abattoir they'd never seen would turn their babies to chops.

He couldn't go to her. She had ridden this far to be private and alone. He must allow her that.

And slowly the sounds stopped. There was silence, and then the slow clop of Lady Grey coming back.

He met her on the road. He saw in her face that she knew he had followed her, knew he had heard. She reached out a hand. He urged Billy Buttons over, held her hand for a long minute. They didn't speak till they were almost at the homestead, when she said, 'Don't tell your father. Or Jim.'

And he'd said, 'No.'

He didn't tell his father. But he would tell Nancy when he saw her again.

But when was when? It had been simple when she'd left. But every month that passed now made the passage from Malaya to Australia more dangerous. Malaya was defended by its army and air-force units, by the strength of Singapore. The seas were not. Until war with Japan was a reality — if it ever was — he'd reassured himself that perhaps it really was safer for Nancy and her brother's little family to stay in Malaya, as her sister-in-law wished, and not venture home.

A week ago the government had finally released the news that the HMAS *Sydney* had been sunk by a German raider disguised as a Dutch merchant ship off the coast of Western Australia, with the loss of all six hundred and forty-five of her crew. The HSK *Kormoran* had been crippled in the battle, but almost all her crew survived to reach the Australian coast.

And then the news on the radio this morning. Malaya was not safe now. Had anyone in Australia dreamt of news like this morning's? Not just the Japanese attack on Malaya, not just the final declaration of war, but worse, much worse, the grim announcer's words of devastation by the Japanese far across the world. All around the earth today people would be trying to cope with what the last twenty-four hours might mean.

And like him, perhaps, each would be wondering what the affairs of the world would mean to those they loved.

Was Nancy all right? He bit his lip. Tucked away on the plantation, with most of the white men gone, did she even know of the disasters that had struck across the world last night?

He was afraid for her, so afraid he could not even speak of it to his parents at breakfast; nor would he be able to speak of his fear to hers when they came to the Christmas party his mother had insisted still go on however disastrous the news.

Or would her parents not come to Drinkwater this year? Because if ... something ... happened to Ben or to Nancy ... If ... something ... had happened last night, might happen tomorrow or today ...

He could not allow himself to even think the words. She had to be all right. And now, at least, one thing was clear.

Nancy must come home. Now.

Chapter 6

Gibber's Creek Gazette, 9 December 1941

Our First War Aim is to Win the War

Councillor Bullant's entry has won the 'new slogan' competition for the *Gibber's Creek Gazette*. From now until the end of the war Councillor Bullant's words will be below our masthead: Our First War Aim is to Win the War.

Other contributions included 'All In to Win the War' by Councillor Horace Ellis, and 'Save Australia!' by Alice McAlpine, aged five and a half, daughter of Mr Andrew McAlpine, manager of Drinkwater Station, and Mrs McAlpine, co-proprietor of the Empire Biscuit Factory.

MALAYA, 9 DECEMBER 1941

NANCY

The heat grew as the day progressed. So did the smuts. Gavin subsided into sleep, his eyes smudged with tiredness and overexcitement, stretched across the laps of the girls, Arleen and Irene. Nancy was not sure which was which, and they seemed to answer to either.

Mrs Armitage nodded into sleep too, her curiosity sated. Nancy wondered if it would have been 'good form' to have given Michael's pedigree, hinted at his family's wealth and connections. No, probably not; nor did she want to. Michael was private, not discussed with Moira or even Ben, though they knew about the letters between them, and Mum would have written to Ben, telling him that the Drinkwater heir had ridden over to their place, stayed the night before his sister left and come to the station to wave her off.

Nor was she even sure if Michael was 'hers'; if he ever had been. One kiss, she thought, if you didn't count the kiss on the cheek goodbye, in front of everyone on the platform, Mum already in the train to accompany her to Sydney.

His visit to Overflow had been crammed with packing, and a brush fire in the house paddock had taken away even the chance of a quiet walk together in the dusk. By the time it was out they all were grubby, tired and hungry and had to scrub off the grime before the roast chicken farewell dinner Gran had made, the evening of piano playing and Scrabble. She had stayed awake too long regretting their lost walk and was still asleep when a handful of pebbles thrown at her window woke her.

She had peered through the window, glad that she hadn't taken her nightdresses droving, that for the first time she was wearing something that wasn't either far too big or tatty, even if it did have the rosebuds and lace Mum considered suitable for her daughter. 'Michael?'

He laughed quietly. 'Anyone else likely to be throwing pebbles at your window at five am?'

'Is that the time?' She grinned at him. 'Give me three minutes.'

'Two.'

She was ready in one, the nightdress thrown off, an old dress thrown on. She realised she should have put on shoes as soon as she climbed through the window. Young ladies wore shoes. But none of the other kids at school did and, despite Mum's best efforts, she got rid of hers as soon as she was out of sight of the house, except of course when she was riding.

The grass was dew wet and chilly against her soles. She held a foot up. 'Do any of your girls in Sydney wear bare feet?'

'I don't have any girls in Sydney. No girl at all, except you.'

She flushed, suddenly extraordinarily happy. 'Why do we say "wear" bare feet?'

'Never thought about it. Don't you get bindiis in them?'

'My feet are tough.'

'Snakes?'

She shrugged. 'Mostly I know when a snake is about. The birds give alarm calls if it's a brown or a tiger. And I see the snake tracks. There's a scent to black snakes too.' She looked at him curiously. 'Your mum didn't tell you any of this?'

'No.' He frowned. 'No, wait a sec. Before I went to school. We used to take a walk and she'd talk to me. I even remember something about listening for snake warnings. School put it out of my head till now. How did you know Mum told me?'

'Gran said your mum was brought up by Auntie Love. She was related to Gran somehow. Niece or great-niece, I think. Gran thought a lot of her.'

'And she was my great-grandmother. Funny to think of history being not so very long ago.'

'We'll be history one day. If we do anything interesting enough.'

'I think,' he said, 'that being history is uncomfortable. I'd rather breed Corriedales. But there won't be a choice, if the war keeps going. Where are we heading?'

'You'll see when we get there.'

Over a small hill, sheep watching curiously from the dew-damp grass. A mob of roos, the old buck thoughtfully scratching his stomach, wondering if they were a threat. His females bent to eat, unconcerned.

They could see the river from here, a pattern of small channels and then the main branch, silver in the early light. But Nancy crossed the hill, instead of heading down to it.

She pushed through thorn bushes, growing on such rocky ground that it had never been worthwhile clearing them. And there it was. A small gorge between two hills. Rock broke to the surface here, patched pink and grey almost like goanna skin. The water flowed steeply a few feet deep over a polished lip of rock in a tiny waterfall, before twisting snake-like in cascades down into a round deep pool below a native fig tree, carpeted with maidenhair and a low red-tinged fern. It was strangely like the pool at Moura, the property his mother had lived on as a girl with Auntie Love, and now rented to Blue and Joseph McAlpine, but the water here flowed more forcefully and deeply, though the pool was as rounded and serene.

The world was hushed around them, even the bleat of sheep muted by the hills on either side. Nancy sat on the rock beside the water, cross-legged. The waterfall spray made a slight haze in the early light, its drops winking silver and gold.

Nancy looked at the water, not at him. 'Gran showed me this place when I was small. I've never brought anyone else here before.'

'Why did you bring me?'

She'd looked at him then, at his serious face, his hair like bleached grass, so much nicer without the pomade he'd worn at the party and yesterday, before she answered.

Now, a year later, she bit her lip at the memory of what she'd told him. It wasn't what girls said to boys in romance novels. She wondered if anyone had ever said it to a boy before.

She shouldn't have said it. Or should she? He hadn't answered; had so obviously not known what to say. But he had seemed moved, as if he understood.

Had he?

Boys were companions to chase goannas with, to lead droving among the trees. She'd had no experience of being with a young man like this. Nor did she want the sort of courtship you read about in books, dressing up to go to the picture theatre or to dances. Flirting and making your young man jealous. She'd had no time for that, not when she'd had to leave later that day. Suspected she never would have time; would always be open with those she loved ...

There, she'd said it to herself, at least. But surely what she had said to him instead meant a hundred times more than simply love. What they had together meant more than kissing, or what

63

came after kissing when you were married, which she knew the mechanics of, had even seen with ewes and rams, but suspected was somewhat different for a human couple.

Had he understood? He hadn't replied, but he hadn't laughed either. She'd thought perhaps he was too moved to speak.

He had never mentioned her words in his letters. Nor had she. You didn't write about such things — or, if you did, she didn't know how. He had written faithfully twice a week. But good though the letters were, you couldn't see the whole person on a page. She liked Michael the letter writer. But it was the look on his face as he watched the swans and pelican at the river, the sudden joy when she had shown him the cascades, the wonder as he gazed up at an eagle balanced on the morning air — that was what she'd fallen in love with. She needed to see him again to know that she hadn't imagined the bond between them.

She bit her lip. What if he met another girl in Sydney? One who didn't 'wear' bare feet, whose hair was done by a hairdresser, not hacked off when it grew too shaggy? At least hers looked decent now too, or would when she had a chance to comb it.

He was at a boys' school, so there were no girls to meet there. But he had mentioned staying at a friend's house in Sydney in one letter, and there were girls enough in Gibber's Creek too. Perhaps he wrote to her just from friendship ...

She thrust the thought away. Damn — no! *Bother* Mrs Armitage, making her think like that. Michael was Michael as surely as she was Nancy of the Overflow. And when they met again, she'd ask him if he remembered her words at the cascades, if he felt like that about her too.

She leant back on the leather seat, the sweat trickling under her dress, listening to the clack of wheels, the beat of the engine. A clearing appeared, paddy fields, a cluster of small children and a woman in bright native clothes who waved. It was all so normal, so peaceful, she wondered if she had indeed panicked this morning; if the refugees on the road had been panicking too; whether even those fleeing in this carriage had no need. The

Japanese may have attacked; had obviously sent scouting parties ahead. But surely they had already been pushed back.

At least she was getting Moira to move south, even if it was only to Kuala Lumpur. Once there she had to be able to persuade her to go all the way to Singapore, then onto a ship home. Their plantation was clearly too close to the Thai border to be safe, even if the Japanese Army was repulsed this time. Moira must know it now.

Soon, she thought — Michael, Gran, the river, riding up into the hills. She had been away too long, almost as long as it had taken to drove to Charters Towers and back again, and she had needed home then. She wanted it even more now. This land was too green; the flowers were too bright. Or rather it wasn't the land's fault, nor the people's either, not even condescending busybodies like Mrs Armitage, who after all was kind as well.

The fault of this land was that she didn't know it, hadn't absorbed its scent and songs since the day she was born, had never been introduced to it by those who understood it, only by those who trod temporarily on its surface, like Moira and Ben. For Ben, Malaya was an adventure, work experience — a chance to prove himself his own man before, inevitably, he too came home to Overflow.

She wondered if Moira knew that he'd be drawn back there? Or did she hope that one day they might retire to England, in a cottage by the sea?

Chug a chug a chug a chug a ... Jungle gave way to rice paddies, rice paddies to swamp, swamp to plantations, plantations to slopes. The song of the engine changed as it pulled its carriages uphill. *CHUG a chug chug CHUG a chug chug.* Nancy felt her eyes closing, the night's lack of sleep taking over from the energy she'd needed earlier. This train was evidently an express, not stopping at the smaller stations. *CHUG a chug chug CHUG a chug chug* became a lullaby. *CHUG a chug chug* ...

The train jerked to a halt. She woke with a start, the air clammy and her dress damp with sweat, and peered out at jungle.

'What's happened?'

Japanese, she thought in alarm. They've captured the train. There could be no other reason the train should stop here in the jungle.

'Loading firewood, I expect,' said Mrs Armitage blearily. Arleen/Irene were still asleep, Gavin sprawled in what had been a clean suit, giving tiny baby snores, still across their laps. 'The engines have been converted to firewood since the war. Shortage of coal, don't you know.'

'Shortage of a lot of things. Damn Japs and Huns. Pardon my language, ladies,' added moustache-man. He too looked as if he had just woken from sleep.

'Excuse me.' Nancy rose, and peered out the window, still half expecting to hear shouts in Japanese, though she was not sure how they would sound different from the many languages already spoken in Malaya.

There *was* a station, a small one, long enough only for the engine, loader and first carriage. A stationmaster in the traditional blue English uniform yelled an order to two men loading firewood, just as Mrs Armitage had suggested, then leant into the first carriage. Voices rose in excitement.

'What's happening?' demanded moustache-man.

'I don't know. The stationmaster seems to be telling the people in the next carriage something ...' She broke off as the man limped towards her, his gait explaining why he wasn't in a different uniform, like almost every other man from twenty-one to thirty-five. 'Excuse me, ladies, sir, but have you heard the news?'

'The Japs have attacked Kota Bharu? We'll soon see them off,' said moustache-man, mopping sweat and smuts from his forehead with a once-white handkerchief.

'Not just Kota Bharu. We're holding them off there all right. They've bombed Singapore too. But that's the least of it.' He paused to give them the full effect of his words. 'Have you heard about Pearl Harbor?'

'Where's that?' asked Mrs Armitage.

'Hawaii. Those islands where the American fleet is based. Was based I should say.' The stationmaster almost seemed to be enjoying the melodrama. 'The Japanese have bombed the lot of it. The entire American fleet sunk. All their aircraft too.'

Moustache-man sat straighter. 'Impossible, man!'

The stationmaster shook his head. 'No, sir. The BBC's had news bulletins out all day. Happened just like I'm telling you. The whole American fleet just sitting there, like ducks on a pond, for the Japs to hit. All their munitions stores. The lot. Just gone.'

'What a rotten thing to do,' said Arleen/Irene. 'America isn't even in the war.'

Rotten? Nancy looked at her incredulously. America the massive, the force that had finally decisively ended the previous world war, neutral so far in this one, taken so totally by surprise. And now America's entire fleet gone! Didn't the girl know what this would mean?

'Can't do something like that,' said moustache-man. 'You have to declare war before you strike.' He too seemed to think the unsporting nature of the attack the most important aspect of it.

'Well, they've gone and done it anyway.' The stationmaster moved on to give the next carriage the news.

'This means Japan is at war with America as well as the British Empire,' said Moira slowly. 'England will have to declare war on Japan now they have attacked Malaya. So will America. And Australia will have to declare war on Japan too,' she added as an afterthought.

And England is only just managing to hold her own against Germany, thought Nancy. They don't have planes or men or ships to help us down here. Most of our men are in the Middle East, defending Britain. And the might of America, the ships and planes that could have carried America to war in the Pacific, had been demolished in one shock attack.

She gazed out at the jungle, just as the wet air melted into rain. We are on our own, she thought.

Chapter 7

Gibber's Creek Gazette, 12 December 1941

New Call-Up

Single men aged eighteen to forty-five and married men aged
eighteen to thirty-five, except those in reserved occupations,
are to be called for service in the armed forces under new
regulations announced yesterday. Councillor Bullant stated
today: 'It is every man's duty to save our country now.'

KUALA LUMPUR, MALAYA, 18 DECEMBER 1941

NANCY

The Anzac Club kitchen was hot, hot not just from the day,
closing in like a fist in the unmoving, humid air of Kuala Lumpur,
but from the heat of five stoves. Nine white women volunteers
and nine native cook boys were on duty to feed the thousands
of men — troops and government workers — who had no other
place to eat now the hotel and clubs that were still open were no
longer serving meals. Six months back there had been more than
enough mem volunteers to work buffet at the Anzac Club. Now,
with most of the white women gone, those who were left worked
all the hours they could.

But there were not enough hands. Never enough hands,
thought Nancy, balancing two plates of sausages and eggs in one
hand and a bowl of fruit salad and ice cream in the other.

It was good to be doing something again, after almost a year of leisure. Boredom was harder work than droving. Work also helped keep away worry about Ben. Was he safe? Had he even got the message that they were here?

They'd sent a wire to his regiment as soon as they arrived at Gemas, as well as to Overflow, and to Moira's parents in England, to tell them that they were safe, and heading to Kuala Lumpur. The initial attack at Kota Bharu had indeed been repulsed, but all of the British colony agreed — even Moira, to Nancy's relief — that it was out of the question to go back north.

Gemas was too crowded with evacuated railway families to stay more than one night, but Mr Armitage's name had carried them efficiently on to Kuala Lumpur next morning. By the time they had arrived there the Japanese forces had struck Kota Bharu again.

And this time they prevailed.

Day by day the Japanese Army surged further south, though the Allies were expected to take a stand any day now. General Heath, the commander of the British Indian III Corps of the Malaya Command, could hold his position for months, according to the wireless. There was no danger ...

Yet everyone knew there was.

Evacuees streamed through the city on the way to Singapore, from Kedah, then Perak. Women and children mostly, piled into cars, bundled with cots, pillows, blankets, suitcases, the women bleary from driving all night, the children wide-eyed, too quiet and understanding too much. Most had been ordered from their homes with an hour's notice and told to take no more than two suitcases, their husbands already vanished to the volunteer Selangor Defence Force.

Like Moira, few knew where those husbands were now, whether they were fighting, wounded, alive or dead. Women stopped to plead at headquarters, asking for information, or at least a way to get a message to men who might not know that their family had left for England, India or Australia for weeks or months or even longer. Others stopped for petrol or a few brief hours' sleep, then drove on.

Planes buzzed overhead each day: Japanese, no Allied planes now, circling and studying, then dropping a cluster of bombs, almost as an afterthought, while the ack-ack guns fired fruitlessly from below. Every cricket pitch and golf course was hilled and sandbagged to stop enemy planes landing there. Every major building had its air-raid shelter prepared, even if it was made of concrete pipes and sandbags.

But Moira still refused to go on to Singapore. 'Ben will expect to find me here,' she said, as the train pulled into the crowded station at Kuala Lumpur and Nancy tried once more to persuade her to take a ticket south.

'He'll expect you to go to Singapore. Or go home! His home,' she added, to make her meaning clear. 'That's what he's wanted all year.'

Moira didn't meet her eyes. 'I'm not going anywhere till I know Ben is safe. Till I've spoken to him. There's far more chance of him getting leave to see us here than down in Singapore.'

'But what about Gavin? You're putting him in danger too.'

'His father is in far more danger. Once we go south it may be a year or more before Ben sees his son again. Besides, everyone at Gemas said that the Japanese will be stopped any day now. We're in no more danger here than we'd be in Singapore, with the bombing there, or in a ship.'

She's probably right about that, thought Nancy, frustrated. Nowhere in Malaya was safe now; nor was Singapore, bombed nightly if the gossip at the Club was right. Ships were in more danger than ever. But at least if they went they'd be going towards safety. She quelled the thought that perhaps her own longing for Overflow, for Mum and Dad and Gran, to talk to Michael again, instead of the frustrating almost-talk of letters, made her wish to get to Singapore more urgent.

And it was true that their present house was probably safer from bombing than Singapore. They had journeyed from the railway station to the Anzac Club in two rickshaws. Nancy had hoped that, like Gemas, Kuala Lumpur would be too crowded to tempt Moira to stay, but it had been surprisingly easy to find a house, fully furnished, even with bed linen and staff. Many of the colonialists' houses were deserted, their owners fled to Singapore, and from there to England, India, Batavia or Australia. The secretary of the Club even had a list of homes where the owners would be glad of respectable tenants, to prevent their belongings being looted.

An hour later Nancy was driving a borrowed Austin Minor, also deserted by its owner, to a bungalow edged on one side by a rubber plantation and behind by jungle. She was met on the trellised veranda by a forty-year-old boy, Ah Jong, who accepted the arrival of two strange mems as calmly as he produced the endless paw paws, pineapples, local vegetables and eggs that were the only household staples available in the markets now.

The house was eerie, another family's photos of relatives on the side tables, music abandoned on the piano, even underwear and nightdresses in the drawers. The family who had left had gone in a hurry, carrying only what their car could hold. Just as Moira left her home and possessions on my say-so, thought Nancy.

Kuala Lumpur was eerie too. Streets of empty houses, and not just the colonial bungalows. Many Chinese, Indian, even Malay residents had left the city too, fleeing to the country or at least a smaller village, anywhere hopefully safe from the bombing. Blocks of flats shone empty eyes onto the street; others stood seemingly intact, but when you looked behind only the façade was left, the rest rubble. Lines of cars stood looking perfect, but were in fact perfectly useless: their tyres all flat from flying shrapnel, their windscreens shattered from the concussion of exploding bombs, even if the paintwork was hardly scratched. The Japanese bombs were small and spread low. And each plane seemed to hold a lot of them.

Nancy glanced out through the tape on the Club windows. Please, no raid tonight until the dinner rush is over, she thought tiredly. One more hour here and the worst would be done.

'Feet hurting?' Miss Reid smiled at her, her arms full of greasy plates.

'Not too bad.'

Miss Reid looked down at Nancy's flat Chinese slippers. Nancy flushed. The slippers were comfortable: you couldn't wear boots with a dress and it was impossible to wear jodhpurs to the Club. There was no way she was going to totter all day and part of the night between the kitchen and dining room in high heels, even the sensible heels that Miss Reid and the other women wore.

But Miss Reid just looked approving. 'I must see if my boy can get a pair of those for me at the market. I had to soak my feet for an hour before I could get to sleep last night.'

Miss Reid was Australian, not English. She had come to Malaya to work for a rubber exporting firm, though she now worked at military headquarters. Perhaps as a working woman, thought Nancy, she was more tolerant of quirks such as wearing comfortable shoes than the mems whose only work had been ordering servants around and the parties, golf and picnics of colonial social life.

'There are some back at the house that would fit you. I'll bring them in tomorrow.'

A few days ago it had been hard to use others' possessions, from the pale yellow dress with lace collar she now wore under her apron to the green silk dressing gown embroidered with red dragons she'd found in the bedroom and guiltily adored. Now like everyone else in Kuala Lumpur, Nancy tacitly acknowledged that those who had fled would not return. Even if the Japanese were pushed back — *when* they were pushed back, Nancy told herself — this would remain a land at war for months, or years, with the Japanese bases in Thailand and Burma so close. Dresses, shoes, slippers and sheets left behind would rot, or be captured by the Japanese troops, or be blown to debris in the almost daily bombing raids. And Miss Reid had been so kind, practically single-handedly trying to locate the men from the volunteer Civil

Defence Forces, to put them in contact with their evacuated families, neither having any idea where the other might be.

'Thanks.' Miss Reid hesitated. 'I haven't been able to get any news about Captain Clancy. But I did get a call through to Tanjung Malim. A few of the local Defence Corps men I know there are liaisons with the regular army. They've promised to get the word out that Captain Clancy's family is here.'

'You'll let me know if you hear that ...' That Ben was dead, wounded or taken prisoner — all-too-possible reasons why he had not yet contacted his family.

'If there is any news at all, I'll let you know at once.' And she would, thought Nancy, as Miss Reid moved on, setting down the plates with one hand while picking up another round of sausages and mash with the other. Miss Reid was one of the most capable women she'd ever met.

Nancy placed the bowl of fruit salad and ice cream in front of a sweating major, then clattered the plates of sausages in front of a middle-aged civilian and a young lieutenant at the far table. 'Dinner is served, tuans.'

The young officer stared at his plate, his eyes shadowed.

The civilian grinned at the mockery in her voice.

'Thank you, miss,' he said, tucking in his napkin. 'First meal I've had since lunch yesterday. My boy ran off in the raid last night, leaving dinner half cooked. Had to give the chicken to the dogs.'

'You should have brought it here. We'll cook anything for you. Be glad of the supplies.'

'Roger, will do.' He forked in a hunk of sausage with a generous splodge of mash. 'Come on, lad. Eat,' he said to his companion.

The young officer lifted his fork as if he wasn't sure what to do with it.

The dining-room gong tolled behind them.

'Air raid,' said Miss Reid calmly. 'Gentlemen, if you would step this way ...'

Nancy followed her, then glanced back. The young lieutenant still sat at the table. She stepped back, and gently touched his arm. 'Come on. The spotters usually only give us fifteen minutes' notice.'

He nodded numbly. She took his hand to urge him up, then kept hold of it as they crossed what had been the lawn, now piled with hillocks and raw wood poles. The air seemed to shiver with unspilled rain, the sky above a sheet of grey, as if it had agreed to give camouflage to the bombers. 'In here.'

The shelters were big concrete pipes set in among the newly made hillocks, thick with humidity and fear. Young Malay troops were already inside, their rifles and bayonets on their laps as they crouched against the curved walls. Nancy privately felt that they might be in more danger from the unseasoned and nervous troops than the bombers.

The first shelter was already full, and the second. She shoved the lieutenant into the third, then reached over to pull the door shut behind them.

The darkness closed around them, the heat, the damp, the smell of sweat. She tried to listen for the first sound of aircraft, or the answering fire of ack-ack guns. Kuala Lumpur had no air defences, no planes that might attack the enemy. The few lumbering old Brewster Buffalos — chronically short of spare parts and with many years' back-log of repairs despite the pleas of their Australian pilots — had been shot down in the first days of attack in what gossip said were impossible raids, ordered against the advice of the men who had to fly them, and die in the attempt. Now the town's only defence was the ack-ack guns that might — or might not — hit a plane or two while the others unloaded their bombs. Twenty-seven planes, always in formation, following the lead plane …

She felt the lieutenant tremble beside her. 'We haven't been introduced,' she said brightly. 'I'm Nancy Clancy.'

She hoped he'd make the usual joke about the rhyme. Instead he said, 'Bruce Ruddley.'

74

'Pleased to meet you, Lieutenant Ruddley. What brings you to this part of the world?'

She could hear the effort it took him to keep his voice steady. 'Assistant manager at the tin mines.'

'Ah.' The Japanese will want the tin, she thought, just as they need Malaya's rubber.

'What about you, Miss Clancy?' His voice sounded as if he had had to heave the polite words from some far-off place.

'I came to stay with my brother and his wife. He runs ... ran a rubber plantation up north.' Would he and Moira ever be able to go back there? Ever *want* to go back? At least Moira and Gavin should be safe from the air raids tonight in their house by the jungle, too far from the central buildings for the enemy to bother bombing.

She could hear the first drone of the enemy planes now, the chatter of the ack-acks. The shock wave of the first bombs hit. The man beside her gave a small cry. She reached for his hand again. 'We're quite safe here.'

Actually, she didn't know if they were safe or not — the hastily constructed air-raid shelters had never had a direct hit. But they *were* safe from flying debris and shrapnel, more likely killers than taking a direct hit from a bomb itself.

'Not safe,' he whispered. 'They're coming for us. Coming for us all.'

It was too true to argue with. 'Then we'll fall back to Singapore. There's no way the Japanese can take Singapore.'

She felt rather than saw him turn towards her. 'You don't understand. They don't move like a normal army. You march up the road and there they are, these little men on bicycles. And you think, this will be easy. No one can move through the jungle. The only way north or south is on the road, or up the river. But before you even take aim they're behind you too. Paratroopers with machine guns, dropped in the night before. They come through the jungle too. No one can come through the jungle! But they do, carrying those damn bicycles ...'

His voice was a thin croak in the darkness. She leant closer to listen, despite the noise of the aircraft, the guns, the shattering of who knew what around them. 'They opened fire. Six of us left alive, the others lying all around. We put our arms up, held our rifles in the air, called out that we surrendered. The Japs made us kneel.' His words leapt out now, as if he couldn't stop them. 'Six of us, kneeling by the river. They shot us, one by one.' The words stopped as if the tap had been turned off.

'But … you're still alive.'

'I was number six,' he said flatly. 'I shut my eyes. I tried to pray, but all I could think of was Grandma's Christmas pudding. She'd promised to send me one. I thought what a thing to think about at the end of your life, a Christmas pudding. And then I heard a scream …

'I stayed there with my eyes shut, waiting for the shot. And then I opened them. And there were these big men surging from the river, naked as the day they were born, waving great curved swords like they were chopsticks. That's what they did with them — chop, chop, chop — and every single one of those Japs was dead. And I was still alive.'

She tried not to let her mind see what he had described, but the image came nonetheless. 'Who were the men who saved you?'

'Gurkhas. They'd heard we'd been ambushed. Stripped off, swam underwater with their swords strapped to their waists with cords.' She heard him take a breath. 'They gathered up the heads they'd chopped off and hung them about their waists, then they plunged back into the river.'

'They left you there?'

'I can't swim much. Besides, there was … no one … no one at all … I was safe. Safe!' She could hear that he was sobbing now. 'I walked through bodies, their bodies and ours. I walked and walked. Walked past the bodies, walked along the jungle track and there was no one. No one. Then I came to a crossroads and a dispatch rider rode up and he gave me a lift on the back of his bike. He said he needed dinner. Dinner.' He gave a small shudder. 'So we came here. He saw some friends in the bar and I ... I just sat where you found me.'

Did anyone even know this man had survived? she wondered. Or that his comrades had been killed? 'Have you reported in?' she asked gently.

'I ... I don't know who to report to here.'

Miss Reid will know, she thought, if they could catch her before she vanished to work at the Defence Headquarters after serving breakfast (sausage with bread instead of mash). She wondered if the young woman ever slept.

The ground had stopped shaking. The ack-ack guns were quiet. She could hear the drone of the planes getting fainter. She reached over the lieutenant and opened the door.

The world was white. For a moment she thought it was dust and debris, the club house bombed to shards, then realised it was paper. She clambered out and picked up a leaflet.

It was Japanese propaganda, very like ones she'd seen before, dropped after the bombs. Some were printed in Chinese, others in Malay and Indian dialects. She could read none of them, but had been told by Miss Reid that they promised freedom and prosperity to all Asians once the British colonial oppressors were defeated.

This one had no words, just two images — one that showed an English officer with a giant moustache and bucked teeth, sitting with a luscious blonde on his knee, a tankard of beer in his hand. Below was another scene: Indian troops dead and dying, their shattered bodies among barbed wire, the blood — the only colour on the page — dripping down the paper.

Liberators, she thought. No English person she had met had considered that anyone might think the Japanese were truly liberating the country. They wanted the Malays' rubber, tin, rice, and the local labour force to get them. But she had heard her grandmother's stories, of land taken, of uncles, cousins killed. She could hear Gran's quiet voice now. 'I was born at the end of a war. We lost.'

It was easier for her to think of the British as an invading force than it would be for most of the other people in Malaya, colonists or locals, not the spearhead of civilisation that they thought themselves to be. But the Japanese as liberators? No. Instinctively she knew that once you came as a conqueror, you stayed one. There was no freedom for anyone in Malaya coming from the north.

The young lieutenant stumbled out into the open air beside her, blinking at the daylight. She took his arm, and led him over to Miss Reid, who was clambering out of the first bunker. 'Miss Reid, would you mind finding out who Lieutenant Ruddley should report to —?'

'Nancy!' The voice came from over at the club house.

She turned. It was Ben.

Chapter 8

Gibber's Creek Gazette, 18 December 1941

Cabinet Approves Employment of Women in Factories

Prime Minister Curtin has announced that as a war measure Cabinet has decided to approve the extensive employment of women in industries where men are not available. The Prime Minister assures us that such employment will only be for the duration of the war, and that the women will be replaced by men as soon as male labour is available. A sub-committee will be formed to prevent the encroachment on men's jobs by cheap female labour.

KUALA LUMPUR, 18 DECEMBER 1941

NANCY

He looked like he always looked, rumpled, even if these clothes were army uniform. He even had a beer in his hand. Trust Ben, Nancy thought, to find himself a drink in the middle of an air raid.

He drained the glass, placed it on the ground, then enveloped her in a hug. He even smelt the same, the sweat that was essentially Ben sweat, still, she thought, with a tang of gum leaves.

He pulled back. 'You're looking good. I like that dress.' He grinned at her. 'Even wearing lipstick.'

She flushed. With Miss Reid managing to wear lipstick, it had seemed — to use Moira's phrase — to be letting the side down if she couldn't keep her lips rouged too. 'Where have you been?'

The grin grew wider. 'Fighting a bloody war.'

'Don't you swear at me, Ben Clancy.'

'Who was it who called Mrs McNaughton a silly old —'

She punched him, hard, on the shoulder. He stepped back, laughing, the exchange the same as it had been since she was four and he was thirteen, and she discovered that if she punched him he wouldn't hit back. Some things, at least, were easier as a female, and punching your brother — or that shearer up past Nyngan with the (she hoped) broken nose — was one of them.

'Moira all right? And Gavin?' His voice lost its laughter.

'They're fine. Gavin can sit up all by himself! We're staying in a bungalow up towards the tin mine — no danger from the bombs there, the Japs won't want to damage the mine.' She was about to offer to drive him home, then realised that he might want — need — time alone with his wife and son, without worrying what a sister might hear. 'Ben, you have to get Moira to leave. Down to Singapore, and a ship to home.'

'I will.'

'She says she's been waiting to see you.'

She thought he'd be as exasperated as she was at Moira endangering Gavin by staying in Malaya. Instead he gave a half-smile. 'I married a good 'un, didn't I?'

She stared at him. Moira a good 'un? Spoilt, snobbish. Thinking if she went to Overflow, she'd be expected to sit in the kitchen and drink her tea with a black woman, and call her Gran. And she'd be right. But Nancy had never tried to talk to her brother about his choice of wife. This was not the time to begin.

'I'm glad she's here. I know, I know,' he held up his hand as she began to protest, 'I tried to get her to go south months ago, as soon as she was strong enough. But the way things are going, well, I may not get a chance to see them for a long time. But I'll tell her she needs to go now. For Gavin's sake. For mine, so I know they're safe. And you. But Moira makes her own mind up about things.' His smile was different now, the one he always had when he spoke of Moira, or saw her when he came in from the plantation or manoeuvres. 'Gavin's tooth come through yet?'

'Not yet. But he's drooling enough to fill a bathtub. Here.' Nancy handed him the car keys and its piston rings — all vehicles had to be immobilised now so no Japanese paratroopers who might come down after the air raids could use them. 'Take the street to your right, then drive towards the tin mine. It's in the last street, the house with the bougainvillea in front and a million nappies hanging up under the veranda. Can't miss it.'

'Thanks, sis. How will you get back though?'

'Have to stay on duty here till late,' she lied. 'Then be up to start breakfast. We're shorthanded.' Which was no lie. Nor was, 'There are plenty of spare bedrooms now.'

'With locks on them? Wouldn't trust some of these chaps as far as I could chuck them.'

'With locks on them, big brother. How long can you stay?'

'Got to be back on duty by six am.'

'You want some food?'

'Is there food at the house?'

'Plenty,' she assured him. 'Well, eggs, fruit, rice.'

'That'll do me.'

They looked at each other. There was so much she wanted to say — that she loved him, that she would look after Moira and Gavin, would give her life for them if necessary (except that would mean no one to look after them, so she'd make sure it didn't come to that). But one thing must be said.

'Ben, when this is over, come home. Please. Not to the plantation. Your real home. Overflow. Dad needs you. We all need you.'

'All right.'

She had expected him to argue, to tell her of the career he was building for himself, that he didn't want to just take over a family property. To say that Dad could hire a manager, if he needed to take things more easily.

'You really will?'

'I really will.' He met her eyes. 'I've seen the world outside now, sis. Enjoyed it too. But when we've got the Japs beat I'll be home. And Moira and Gavin will be there with me. For good.'

'Oh. Well then.' She hesitated, hugged him, hard. Whispered, 'Stay safe.' Kissed his stubbled cheek, as brown as hers, then forced herself to walk away, back to the dining room, so that he wouldn't waste precious minutes he might spend with his wife and son with his sister.

He had left when she got back after serving breakfast the next day, the yellow linen dress rumpled, crumpled, the silk slippers caked in grease. Moira lay on the chaise longue on the veranda, idly pulling the punkah to fan herself and Gavin, who was lying on a blanket at her feet, drooling and gumming a slice of lime Ah Jong had given him to distract him from his emerging teeth. He waved his arms and legs at her. 'Mnmmert!'

She picked him up, kissed his soft cheek and breathed in his baby smell. 'Hello to you too, froglet. Did Ben get here all right?'

For once Moira made no comment about Nancy's appearance. 'Yes. He left before dawn. He wouldn't say where he was going.'

'Might not know.'

'That's true. Thanks for giving us time alone,' she added.

'No worries.' She saw Moira frown at the Australian colloquialism. 'We were busy at the Club so I was useful anyway. Did Ben convince you to go to Singapore and get a ship home?'

Moira's face closed off. 'He tried. I don't want to go quite yet. Another week or two can't make any difference. Ben might get leave, or even be posted here. And anyway, Mr Sanderson at the Club says that the army can hold back the Japs for months.'

'Did Ben tell you that?'

Moira hesitated. 'No.'

'Well then.'

'We didn't talk about the war.' Moira got to her feet. 'Gavin's nappy needs changing.'

And you have no amah to do it for you, thought Nancy. No maid to button your dress and slip on your stockings. No boy even to pull the punkah to keep you cool. 'Moira, please. Think of Gavin. Even if you don't want to go to Australia, at least let's go to Singapore.'

Moira looked at her expressionlessly; Nancy knew it was not her face she was seeing, but Ben's. 'Soon,' she said. 'Ben might even get stationed here. Just a week or two, and we'll see.'

Chapter 9

Gibber's Creek Gazette, 3 January 1942

Motorcycles for the Army

Gibber's Creek was visited yesterday by a party of military officers concerned with the impressment of motorcycles for the use of the military forces. Owners of suitable vehicles have been notified of the place set for the examination of their machines. The machines will be taken at a valuation set by the authorities.

KUALA LUMPUR, DECEMBER 1941–JANUARY 1942

NANCY

Christmas was just another day, though one without an air raid. Neither Nancy nor Moira had made any effort to find presents for each other, or even for Gavin, who at least was too young to know what the day should mean. Most of the shops had been abandoned by their owners so there were luxuries for the taking, even if necessities like bread or car tyres were hard to find. But anything they gave each other would have to be carted off when they evacuated again, or left behind. Nor was there any chance of mail or packages from Australia, or even sending a wire to say merry Christmas.

Instead Nancy rose at dawn, as usual; drove in to the Anzac Club, glad of the petrol ration Miss Reid had wangled that kept her on the road; served all day with one other woman and the two remaining cook boys, till Miss Reid left work at four pm to join them.

There was little they could offer the men. Just a month earlier there had been a flourishing canteen, soft drinks, a library, billiard room, ping-pong, darts and a piano and the room where dances were held each Friday night, bands from each of the hotels taking turns in entertaining there.

Now they had bread, eggs, bacon and milk, not even sausages any more. Bacon sandwiches for Christmas dinner. But one of the men played the piano. They sang carols as she carried out the plates of sandwiches. They had sliced the meat thinly to make it last and fried the bread in the fat to make up for the butter they lacked.

She crept home at almost midnight. A single lamplight shone in the house through the crack in the curtains. Nancy hoped it was not enough for a Japanese plane to see. She used her shaded torch to find her way up the stairs, across the veranda and down the hall.

Moira sat in the armless chair in her bedroom, Gavin in her arms. He was asleep, sprawled on her lap, all legs and arms. For a moment the love on Moira's face made Nancy gasp. She had never seen the Englishwoman's emotions so open before.

She knocked on the doorway. 'Just wanted to let you know I'm back.'

She expected self-possession to close Moira's face again. But the softness remained as she asked, 'How was today?'

'Not too bad.' She tried not to think of the Christmas party they'd have had at Drinkwater the night before. Who had Michael danced with? Had he sat by the river and remembered her?

'No news?'

'No,' she lied. There had been nothing about the fighting up north, nor about Ben, it was true. But this afternoon the BBC World Service had announced that Hong Kong had fallen to the Japanese. Nurses in the hospital who had stayed to care for the patients had been bayoneted. Miss Reid had whispered, 'Probably after much worse.' American General MacArthur's forces were falling back under attack from the Japanese in the Philippines.

Mr Churchill was in Washington, urging the Americans to give more help for Britain. Help was needed on the Russian front as well. But after Pearl Harbor, how much did America have to give?

The only other radio station was the local one at Penang, now taken by the Japanese. The canteen had listened to five minutes of what the Japanese Army would do, flattening towns like Kuala Lumpur, dropping Japanese money that anyone of Asian descent could use as soon as 'liberation' was complete. Five minutes had been enough.

But she would not tell Moira that. Not on Christmas Day. Not when, for a moment, mother and child had reminded her of a scene in a stable, almost two thousand years earlier. Instead she said, 'We sang carols.'

'Even you?'

'My voice isn't that bad.' Except it was. 'I hummed along. How is Gavin?'

'Chewed my finger for an hour. Ah Jong put lime juice on his gums again. It seemed to help. Nancy ... he'll be all right, won't he?'

She didn't mean Ah Jong, or even Gavin.

'If anyone can make it through, it will be Ben.' It was the truth, though perhaps not tactfully phrased. But it seemed to comfort Moira.

'At least there wasn't an air raid.'

'Perhaps we're finally pushing them back.'

She didn't tell Moira that there'd been a raid that day on Singapore, that the enemy planes must have been focused there instead. 'Good night,' she said.

'Good night, Nancy.' Moira gazed down at Gavin's peaceful face again.

The bombs fell on Kuala Lumpur the next day, on Boxing Day. Hour after hour of them, all through the morning, Nancy crouched in a shelter next to Miss Reid on one side, a Malay policeman on the other.

At last she crawled from the shelter, her legs so stiff they hurt. Beside her Miss Reid stretched too. 'At least the Club is still standing.'

Nancy nodded. She was feeling relieved on several counts. The sound of bombs had come from the side of town as far as possible away from the bungalow where Moira and Gavin were.

'Miss Reid, look.' She pointed to a small puddle of clothes on the ground. There was another over by the next shelter. It looked as though the person who had been inside the clothes had simply vanished. But how could an air raid do that?

'Malay police uniforms,' said Miss Reid, as if that explained it all.

'I don't understand.'

'It's only to be expected. The police are taking off their uniforms, heading back to their villages. It'll be safer for them not to be associated with the British when the Japanese arrive. Most of the office workers have left already.'

When the Japanese arrive, not if, thought Nancy.

The day's rain hit as they made cocoa in the canteen with the last can of powdered milk while the ARP volunteers collected sodden bodies and carried the wounded to makeshift hospital wards. Miss Reid smiled tiredly. 'You'd best head home while there's still light. It might take you a while to find a route through the rubble.'

Nancy nodded.

The rain had stopped as abruptly as it had begun. Her car, miraculously, still had three of its four tyres intact. She hunted along the street of abandoned vehicles till she found another, laboriously jacked up the car, kneeling in the puddles, then surrendered the job in relief to a passing sergeant. He finished the job, then gave her a half-salute. 'Best take yourself home, girly,' he said.

'You think the bombers will be back tonight?'

He shook his head. 'Why bother flying at night when there's nothing we can do to them during the day? But there's bad men around. Looting downtown, and no one left to keep it in check. Best to stay clear.'

'Is there much damage?'

He stared at her. 'Damage? Most of the town is gone. The government buildings, the Post Office, the Selangor Club. Street after street just rubble. And now I'd better get to work.' He gave her a tired grin. 'I'm the only one left in the entire Pay Corps. All the native clerks have left. If this war is going to get its bills paid on time, I'd better try to make sense of the paperwork.'

A truck rumbled down the street as he spoke. He waved to it. It stopped. He clambered in, waved to her. She waited till it vanished down the street, hoped that if there was any rubble blocking the way they'd clear it before she reached it, then got into the car and followed them.

The canteen shut on 3 January: with little food, and few staff, there was no point trying to keep it open. Even Moira had to acknowledge now that Kuala Lumpur must soon fall to the invaders. Ben would not be stationed here. The question was not if they should evacuate to Singapore, but how.

The train station seemed to have a small army all of its own, loading tin, rubber, anything which might be of use to the Japanese. The banks had already sent all their securities down to Singapore. Bridges in the city and along the route south had been mined, the explosives waiting till evacuees were clear and the order came to set them off.

In the centre of town, hundreds of mine workers stormed the remaining shops, carrying off rice, blankets, whatever was to hand, while the remaining police and the local Defence Corps tried vainly to stop them. Hot, almost smokeless flames came from the grounds of the Club and the main hotels: all alcohol and any other supplies that could not be taken were being burnt to stop them falling into enemy hands.

Nancy and Ah Jong packed the car with bedding and clothes.

On the 8th the order came, brought by a tired sergeant. An hour before dawn, they were to rendezvous with other cars at a plantation out of town to make a convoy to travel down to

Singapore. 'Take what food you can. Don't suppose you have a rucksack?'

'Yes,' said Nancy.

'Good. Make sure you've got water in it, a change of clothes. If the road's blocked, you may need to walk.'

Or run, thought Nancy, dodging bullets or bombs.

It was impossible to sleep, even with the alarm clock set. At last, Nancy got up, slipped to the kitchen to get the last of the supplies. Ah Jong was already there, packing a hamper. 'Bread,' he said. 'I baked the last of the flour last night. Bananas, good for the baby. Oranges ...'

'You could come with us,' said Nancy.

He shook his head.

He's right, she thought. He is safer away from us. It had been good of him to stay as long as he had. She suspected the notes they had paid him with would be worthless as soon as the town was under Japanese control.

She took one of the baskets while he carried the other. To her surprise, Moira was already on the veranda, tying a piece of paper to the post.

'A note to Ben,' she said briefly.

'Moira, the army is going to blow up the bridges behind us. The railway bridges too. Ben won't even be able to get here.' Or if he did, she thought, the area would be full of Japanese soldiers, and he'd be fighting them. 'He'll know we've gone to Singapore,' she added. She had said it a hundred times. Knew that Moira knew it too.

'Just in case,' said Moira, tightening the string.

They drove in darkness down the silent street, out of the town and along the empty road. Two cars waited at the plantation compound and a harried corporal with a list in his hand. He ticked off their names, nodded at buckets of mud beside his truck. 'Cover the car with clay,' he said shortly. 'Camouflage. There's a four-gallon drum of petrol for each car.'

'What if that's not enough?' asked Nancy.

'That's why you're travelling in a convoy.' He spoke as if to a toddler. 'If your car breaks down or you run out of petrol, get a lift in another.' He left as another car rumbled down the road.

'I'll do the clay,' said Nancy. 'No point us both getting dirty.'

Moira nodded. 'I'd best feed Gavin now, while it's private.'

She opened her blouse and arranged the silk scarf over herself. Nancy dipped her hands in the clay, slapped it on the car's roof, the sides, the doors. There was a washtub at the other end of the compound. She used it, careful not to splash any on her face — unboiled water carried disease.

They waited.

It was light by the time they left, other names on the corporal's list still unticked. He had evidently decided that there was no option but to leave whoever hadn't made it behind.

The convoy snaked and wove between the rubber trees out to the main road. We look like a lumpy caterpillar, thought Nancy, a patchwork of clay and blue and green and brown, bulging with hampers, baskets and what looked like a full-length mirror in the car ahead. At least when we stop we can check our stocking seams are straight, she thought, and suppressed a giggle.

Gavin woke, cried, was entertained by Moira playing Peepo, peering at him from behind her hands until he laughed. At last he settled on her shoulder, gazing at the jungle they passed as if the journey was made entirely for his pleasure.

Past Klang, and then Kajang and the AIF casualty clearing station, past troop camps, carriages, trucks and tents and men, and all the way the spires of black smoke rising from the rubber supplies, burning to deprive the Japanese of the resource.

And yet, despite the stench of smoke and the tiny convoy creeping along the jungle roads, life went on around them. Children picked greens in a wet ditch, giggling and whispering as the cars passed; Malay women with baskets walked along the side of the road, almost as if they were shopping in the main street of Gibber's Creek; women in black trousers and coolie hats bent, their hands in the water of a paddy field. They didn't even look up as the convoy passed.

Normal life: working and eating, laughing with friends, going to bed in your own house. The Europeans were leaving, yet the beat of life went on.

Did we matter at all? Nancy thought. Managers like Ben and mems like Moira? So many other races have come here and found their place. Did we just float across the surface of Malaya, and can now vanish, with little changed, after the scars of war have healed?

Other conquerors were coming. Yet, somehow, looking at another group of children playing by a stream, she suspected that they too would be as ephemeral.

The sky emptied its rain mid-afternoon, quenching the fires, washing the clay from their car, turning the road into a small river. The cars forged on. At least her driving skills were better now.

Gavin grizzled, then realising this car was his destiny for the foreseeable future, began to bounce, trying to clamber up the back of the seat, paddling Moira's lap with his small fat feet as she supported his back. Twice Moira changed his nappy on her lap, awkward and leaving her skirt (and once Nancy's dress) slightly damp.

It was dark when they reached that night's destination, a deserted rubber camp. The beds were all taken; nor was there any food. Nancy made a makeshift bed for the three of them, a pile of blankets under mosquito netting, with a sheet to cover them, and rolled-up clothes for pillows.

They shared supplies with the women next to them: Ah Jong's bread with canned sardines, canned bully beef, canned cheese.

To Nancy's surprise, they slept.

No bacon and eggs for breakfast. The bread was gone, but there were buttered biscuits, more sardines, boiled water to drink and to refill their Thermos. Then she applied more clay.

Drove on.

The convoy broke up the next morning. One large convoy was too easy a target, the corporal decided (or perhaps a passing officer pointed this out).

They travelled now in groups of six cars. For a while they tried to travel on back roads, but the going was so slow they headed back to the main road south.

Troops passed in trucks, in cars, each with a smile and wave. They saw no other women the entire day. Mile after mile, stopping only to fill the petrol tanks, to eat sardines and oranges for lunch. The heat increased. The road glared. The whole world was pounding trucks and once an arrow of Japanese bombers overhead.

They were in paddy country, with no place to shelter if bombs fell.

They drove on.

Rain started, lashed the cars, turned the road to a river and the windscreen to a creek, stopped. Houses thickened into a city. Three cars broke away from the group as they crossed the causeway into Singapore — those who had friends or relatives in the city heading there. For Nancy and Moira there was no choice but to follow the others to the Evacuation Bureau.

They stood in the meandering line outside the bureau till Gavin began to grizzle again. 'No need for us both to stand here,' said Nancy. 'You wait in the car.'

Moira nodded her thanks. Her face was pale, her eyes shadowed. She's not used to travelling in the day's heat, thought Nancy.

Nor was she. Not heat like this. Suddenly she wanted to cry, to have someone look after her, say, 'There, there, now here's a bed for you.' But there were only weary women, crying children, the straggle that had tried to stay until forced here by war.

It was late by the time she got to the head of the queue. She tried to smile at the clerk. 'No hotels, I suppose? We have enough money ...'

'No hotels at all. You'll have to be billeted.'

'There're two of us. Three, I mean. My sister-in-law too, and her baby.'

'Three of you.' The clerk made it sound as if three was the most unreasonable number of all. He sighed. 'You'll need to be registered properly tomorrow, then go to the Shipping Office and put your names down with P&O. Name?'

'Nancy Clancy. My sister-in-law is Mrs Benjamin Clancy.'

The clerk looked up from his papers. Nancy thought he saw her properly for the first time. 'Nancy Clancy?'

She waited for the joke. It didn't come.

'There's a cable for you.' He rummaged in the drawer of his desk, then handed her the yellow paper. 'Next!'

She moved aside, but not too far, ready to reclaim her place when she had read the cable.

HAVE BOOKED ROOM AT RAFFLES HOTEL
STOP MISS NANCY CLANCY MRS BENJAMIN
CLANCY MASTER GAVIN CLANCY STOP PASSAGE
BOOKED STOP CONTACT MR OREILLY P&O
OFFICE FOR DETAILS STOP STAY SAFE STOP
MICHAEL SENDS HIS LOVE STOP BEST WISHES
ALWAYS THOMAS THOMPSON

She moved over to the wall, the cable still in her hand. Tears came, and would not stop: tears for the kindness of neighbours, the goodness of friends; tears because somehow, miraculously, a hand of comfort had been extended across the sea; and tears because there would be beds tonight and food. Tears mostly because Michael had sent his love.

Love, in a time of war. Despite the stench of burning rubber clinging to her clothes, her hands shaking with weariness, she felt as revived as if she had already slept a week at the Raffles.

Michael had sent his love.

93

Chapter 10

Gibber's Creek Gazette, 4 January 1942

Australia Looks to America, Says Prime Minister Curtin

Prime Minister Curtin has announced that 'Australia looks
to America, free of any pangs as to our traditional links or
kinship with the United Kingdom'. The Prime Minister said
that the USA would be the cornerstone of Australia's defence
in the Pacific.

SINGAPORE, 11 JANUARY 1942

NANCY

The Raffles hummed even so late at night, though its exterior
was dark, blackout curtains drawn to stop any sliver of light that
might attract an enemy plane.

A uniformed footman opened their car door, ignoring the
coating of mud; another collected their luggage, not even blinking
at the mosquito nets and bedding. Nancy suspected that these
days even guests at the Raffles arrived carrying odd assortments,
or even possibly no luggage at all. Another man in livery helped
her out, then slid into the driver's seat to park the car.

A doorman opened the door with a subtle flourish. She
stopped, entranced.

Polished wooden floors and Persian carpets; white-painted
walls; green palms in bronze tubs; the scent of food, proper

food, as well as the tang of spices; ceiling fans whirring; and somewhere nearby an orchestra played and people laughed.

They were expected. 'Only one room, madam, I am so sorry. But with the city so crowded … And there are two beds, and a cot for the little one.'

Up in a grillwork, clanking lift; down a long corridor with dark panelling, the wood creaking under their feet. Their luggage preceded them to a bedroom with wide windows muffled in heavy curtains.

And beds. Two as promised, with starched white sheets …

'Tea, madam?'

'Please,' said Moira.

The tea came while Moira was in the bathroom down the hall, a wheeled trolley with silver service: teapot, hot-water pot and thin china cups, a silver tea strainer, a plate of thin bread and butter, crustless watercress sandwiches, a covered dish which revealed steaming curry puffs and a platter of jam tarts.

Nancy settled Gavin on her knee and began to eat, slipping him crumbs of bread and butter, of jam tart.

The door opened. Moira, wrapped in a dressing gown, stared at her and sighed. 'Heaven knows how I'll get him back to a proper routine. And no jam tarts! Not at this time of night. He'll take forever to settle.'

'No, he won't. He's as tired as us. How are the bathrooms?'

'Wonderful. So much hot water and, oh, the soap.' Moira stretched out on the bed. The shadows under her eyes had turned to purple bruises. Nancy handed her a cup of tea and a plate of sandwiches.

'I could sleep for a week,' said Moira.

'So could I.' Nancy settled Gavin in the white-painted cot. He stared up at her and gave a sudden gummy grin. She grinned back, wondering why his expression was familiar, then realised it was hers, seen in the mirror every day.

Strange to think of this small person with her smile. Not Ben's. Not Moira's. Hers and Gran's.

Both Moira and Gavin were asleep by the time she got back from the bathroom, clad in the silk dressing gown with dragons she hadn't been able to bring herself to leave behind, clean for the first time since they had left Kuala Lumpur. The bed was not as soft as the princess's in the fairytale. She slept deeply regardless, woke in darkness, then realised the blackout curtains were still drawn; one tiny sunbeam was escaping and wandering across the room.

Moira snored softly in the other bed. Nancy had vaguely heard her rise in the night to feed Gavin, who was now sprawled on his back, his arms and legs outflung. She smiled at his soft pale face, then tiptoed out, down to the bathroom for yet another bath, dressed in one of the garments gleaned from the house in Kuala Lumpur, this one blue polka-dotted linen, only slightly too long when she'd hauled the skirt up a little over the belt. She combed her hair, decided not to risk disturbing Moira and Gavin by going back to borrow Moira's lipstick, then went down the stairs — forsaking the lift and its alarming creaks and groans — towards the smell of food.

'Breakfast, madam?'

'Please.'

The waiter surveyed the room. 'I am sorry, madam, there is no table free. The hotel is full, you see. If madam would not mind sharing?'

'No, of course not.'

She expected to be placed with an elderly lady, perhaps, or even a family. But the other single diners were mostly men. The few tables with families were already full. Instead the waiter led her towards an elderly man peering down at papers on his table.

'Mr Harding, if you would be so kind, this young lady wishes breakfast and there is no table free ...'

'What? Of course, of course.' He stood politely. 'Cyril Harding, at your service.'

'Nancy Clancy,' she said, as the waiter held out her chair for her.

96

'Someone either had a warped sense of humour, Miss Clancy, or you were named for a relative.'

'My grandfather.'

He sat again and raised grey eyebrows. 'Your grandfather was called Nancy?'

'His surname was Clancy, and "Nancy" was as close as they could get to it.' She risked a grin, unsure how familiar one was supposed to be with a stranger at the breakfast table. 'Everyone just knew him as Clancy.' She decided to omit 'of the Overflow'.

'I know the feeling. Prefer Harding to Cyril any day. Only the wife ever called me Cyril.' His accent was educated Australian. In his fifties, perhaps, too old for the services unless he was in the regular army, but he wore no uniform. 'I recommend the porridge. They know how to make it here. Some places add milk and sugar. Turns it into a sort of pudding.'

'I eat it with milk and sugar,' she said apologetically.

'That's different. Adding it after is the right thing to do. How do you feel about fish curry?'

'Strongly against.'

'Ah. Devilled fowl?'

She shook her head.

'Recommend an omelette then. Not the choice there used to be.'

'That sounds good.'

'Excellent. The young lady will have porridge and an omelette. Fruit for both of us. Toast and my usual. Tea for you?'

'Please. You stay here often?' she asked, as the waiter left them, and another approached to fill their glasses with chilled water.

'Lived here for nearly ten years now, since my wife died.'

'I'm sorry.'

'That I am reduced to living at the Raffles? No, my dear, don't apologise. I'm joking. Ah, porridge,' as the waiter slipped a bowl in front of Nancy, and another in front of him. He winked at her. 'All the waiters ran away into the jungle. Had to fend for ourselves for a night. But the next day the place was staffed again. Good management. Nothing like it. Tuck in.'

She helped herself to sugar, a pool of milk. Mr Harding, she noticed, added only salt to his, despite his words of approval earlier.

'How are things up north?'

'How did you know we came from there?'

'I doubt you've come to Singapore for a holiday,' he said dryly. 'And if you had been here before now, you'd have a regular breakfast table. "We" you said. Mother, sister or sister-in-law?'

'Sister-in-law. And nephew. You'd make a good fifth columnist.'

He choked slightly on his porridge. 'You are a perceptive young lady. I suppose you came with the convoy last night?'

She decided not to answer that one. He smiled. 'You'll need to register today. All new arrivals do. And be inoculated against smallpox and typhoid. Unless your ship is leaving soon.'

Since she didn't know when it was leaving, or even its name, she limited her reply to, 'Thank you.'

'Happy to be of use. Good thing you landed here. Some of the billets can be a bit rough. Bombs might fall, shells whizz across the rooftops, the Cricket Club may be rubble, but the Raffles goes on. Though they did bomb the dhobi hut last week. The washing hut,' he added, seeing she didn't recognise the term. 'Lost two of my shirts. The Raffles is the only place in Singapore where you might see a maharajah dining at the next table. Doesn't matter what colour a chap's skin, he's welcome at the Raffles.'

She looked up, wondering if this was a veiled reference to *her* skin. But he continued to spoon his porridge mildly, then sat back and let the hovering waiter take his bowl. She suspected Mr Thompson, or his agent, had been careful to book them into a hotel where there might be no question of accepting her, especially in times like these.

'Do you know what's been happening? I haven't heard any news since we set out,' she said.

'And you've only been listening to the BBC World Service before that? Ah, thank you,' as the waiter slid an omelette accompanied by baked tomatoes and a small puddle of rice in front of Nancy, and a far larger serve of rice topped with something brown and green and fragrant in front of Mr Harding. 'Tuck in. The BBC will have us know that General Heath is holding back the Japanese at Johor Bahru. Only problem is that the Japs have already taken Johor Bahru. Which means they have also captured Singapore's main water supply. Not to worry — it's only been connected the last few years. The city has enough cisterns to go on with.'

If the BBC could not be trusted to tell them the truth about Malaya, considered Nancy, what might it be concealing about the rest of the world? The news they had heard back in Kuala Lumpur was desperate enough: landings on the islands of New Britain, New Ireland and in the Solomons; the surrender of the Australian forces in New Britain, the RAAF sending one last message home: *We who are about to die salute you.*

'What's really happening here?'

He studied her for a moment, then nodded, as if he had decided she was someone who preferred the truth. 'A mess. Mess after mess. Fools of British officers who can't accept that the Japanese aren't marching in neat lines towards them, but creeping around behind, wading through jungle swamps, climbing palm trees, coming down by parachute, landing on the beach. Unsporting of them, but it works. Know what we should do?'

She shook her head.

'We could wipe them out in a fortnight. Give me two thousand men and I'll lead them behind the Jap lines. Attack them from the rear, like they are doing to us. I know the country, which is more than these damn fool Pommies can say.'

'Are there a spare two thousand men?'

'Plenty that aren't being of use. But they don't even have to be army men. Put out a call for Chinese volunteers last week. Hoped for two thousand. Got six thousand volunteers in a day.

Make fine guerrilla soldiers, the Chinese. Look what they are doing back on the mainland.'

'Gorillas?' She had a sudden image of training large, hairy gorillas to fight Japanese soldiers.

He grinned, a surprisingly youthful grin despite his grey hair. 'Fellas who don't obey the rules of war. Hide out in the bush, attack when they're not expected. Blow up supply depots. Six thousand Chinese guerrillas could keep Malaya free. Know how many of those volunteers the British Army put in uniform? None. By the time they get round to it, it will be too late.'

'Too late' must mean Singapore taken, she thought. For there was little else left of the peninsula. She watched Mr Harding fork up his curry. Everyone had been telling her that Singapore was impregnable, that Japan would never attack Malaya, and when it did, that Japan could never take it. This man seemed to have come to terms with the impossible.

'Do you really think there is a chance to beat the Japanese? Even now?' She thought of the burning rubber, the bridges exploding behind their convoy.

'Of course. We outnumber them. Look at Malta, how it's held out against the Germans. We could do the same here.'

'So Singapore won't be taken,' she said thankfully.

'Of course it will.' He said it as though no one could possibly think otherwise.

'But you said we outnumber the Japanese.'

'Ah, but they have strategy, and we don't. Our guns point to the sea, and not the land where the enemy is coming from. They can't even be moved. Those in command won't listen to army intelligence. Intelligence! Don't know the meaning of the word.' He peered at her over his fish curry. 'Old Chinese chappie said it best. Clever people, the Chinese. Old Sun Tzu: "If you know the enemy and know yourself, you need not fear the results of a hundred battles." Eat your omelette before it gets cold,' he added.

She attacked her omelette. It was good: filled with a slightly spicy green filling, but delicious anyway.

'Know what the one great failure in war is? Seeing your enemy as less than you. Means you don't truly see them at all. All the talk about Japanese on bicycles. Brilliant bit of strategy that. Of course they have vehicles too. But bicycles can move faster on crowded narrow roads. You can carry a bicycle through the jungle.' He shook his head. 'Most of the desk wallahs talk about Japanese "sneaking through the jungle" as if it puts them on the same level as jungle animals. Just means they are superb soldiers who were trained for just this, as our blokes weren't. Those men are wading chest deep, covered in leeches, facing deadly snakes. Magnificent warfare. How is your omelette?'

'Good.'

'Excellent. And excuse an old man sounding off.' He smiled at her over his curry. 'You are forced to listen to me, or not get breakfast.'

'No, really. It's fascinating. No one else has ever talked to me seriously about the war before.'

'I'd like to think that's because you are a beautiful young lady and the men you meet want to talk about you, not the war. But I suspect they haven't thought about the war themselves, just swallowed decades of clichés. Anyone with half a brain could see what was going to happen here a mile off. The Japanese foreign minister signed a treaty with the Soviets nearly a year ago so the Japanese won't have to fight a second front in Manchuria or Korea while they're advancing south. Japanese agents have been collecting information about Malay defences for years. No one put a stop to it — the Japanese have been allowed free movement as part of the policy of appeasement.'

He snorted. 'You'd have thought that after Munich the British would have learnt that appeasement doesn't work. Ah, toast,' as the omelette and curry plates were removed and two silver toast racks were placed on either side of the table. A silver dish of marmalade and another of strawberry jam appeared, and two of butter, neatly curled.

'You don't seem angry,' she said tentatively.

He snorted. 'Used up my anger in the last war. Two armies of equal stupidity butting their heads together in the mud for four years, till the Americans arrived just as our side was finally discovering what the word "tactics" meant.' He gave her a sardonic glance as he offered her the toast. 'Look up the dictionary sometime. You'll see "intelligence" then underneath it "military intelligence". Dictionary is right. Two separate animals.'

He helped himself to butter, spreading the marmalade thickly. 'Can't beat grapefruit marmalade. Though it's not proper grapefuit here. This will be pomelo. What was I saying? Could have stopped the whole invasion in its tracks if it hadn't been for command back in England. American intelligence, and British too for that matter, knew about the Japanese convoys days before the attack. Local commanders asked permission to take them out. Half an hour and the whole invasion would have been stopped in its tracks if the Japanese had lost those two transports. Bally desk wallahs refused. All this,' he waved his hand, taking in the waiters in their uniforms, the trays piled high with fish, strange messes on heaps of bright white rice, the silver porringers but also, presumably, the smoke and rubble of Singapore outside, the burning spires of rubber dotted through the jungle, 'one decisive action could have stopped it all. Now we are on a two-hundred-square-mile island, penned up like a mob of sheep while the Japanese guns bark at us from the mainland.'

'What do you think will happen?'

He swallowed a mouthful of his toast, signalled to the waiter. 'Coffee, if you please. Ah, yes, that's the ticket,' as something more resembling thick black tar than coffee was poured into his cup. 'Hot and black, that's the way to drink it. I imagine old Percival is going to surrender, that's what's going to happen. Surrender to a force less than half the size of the Allies. The Japanese adapt to the terrain. The British haven't learnt how to.'

She put her toast down on her plate. 'So Japan will win the war?' Japanese masters of Australia, of Overflow, of Drinkwater.

I'd die before I let that happen, she thought, and so would Michael. And Dad and Mum and the Thompsons. We wouldn't run, as we've done here. We'd stand and fight.

Somehow she must get back —

'Oh, no.' Mr Harding took another bite of toast, swallowed. 'Japan will lose.'

'But you said —'

'Said the British haven't learnt how to adapt ... yet. But they will. Look at the Great War. No real tactics till the last two years, and then we whipped them. But it's not going to be Britain who saves Australia this time. We'll need to do it ourselves, with Yankee help.'

'But the American fleet, their planes have been destroyed ...'

'As most of ours have been lost in the Middle East too. Don't underestimate the Yanks. They have what Japan doesn't.'

She thought he meant courage. But he continued, 'Natural resources. Oil. Iron. Factories. They'll be making new planes and ships already, while every ship, every plane that Japan loses means one more lost to them for good. And we,' he meant Australia now, 'have food.'

'How does that help?'

'Takes food to fuel an army. Japan doesn't even send rations with its troops. They can hardly grow enough for themselves on those small islands — they're mostly mountains. The Japanese armies have to live off the land wherever they are, a land disrupted by war. They can manage that in China, in Thailand, even here. But they won't find it so easy in Papua or the islands, or north Australia for that matter. America has its cornfields, we have our wheat and meat. We'll win. But it won't be soon.'

She thought of the sheep at home, the eggs from the chooks, the paddock of pumpkins Dad put in each spring, the Lees' market garden. Could those really make a difference and win a war? Did this old man know what he was talking about, more than the generals in command?

Yes, she thought. Like Gentleman Once, who'd predicted all this.

'What are you going to do now?'

She meant, was he too waiting for a ship to take him back to Australia. But the grey eyes twinkled at her. 'Put on my uniform and go to work. Not supposed to be in civilian dress, but I always spill marmalade at breakfast. Can't do a good day's work without a decent breakfast.'

She looked. Yes, there was a spot of yellow marmalade on his tie. He wiped it off with a finger, licked it, grinned again at his own bad manners, then stood up.

He must be one of the very intelligence officers he had talked about, she realised. She wondered why he had told her so much. She met his eyes, and saw the steel. Not a kind old gentleman. Well, yes, he was, but not just that. Anger simmered deep inside him, despite his words, seeing a battle being lost that might have been won.

'You eat up, my girl. You're going to need it. And get yourself on a ship out of here.'

'We have passages booked for us. I don't know when we sail though, or even the name of the ship.'

'Captains keep information like that close to their chests. You just get yourself down to the Shipping Office every day and see what's happening. Make sure your name is on the list and make sure it stays on the list.'

'Please ...' He was about to go. 'If ... if the Japanese take Singapore before we can get out, what will happen to us?'

'You'll be interned as enemy aliens. Anyone in the military becomes a prisoner of war — unless they know the islands well enough to get to Batavia from here.' There was something in his face that said he knew those islands very well indeed. 'If you have the bad luck to be taken prisoner, you might be exchanged for Japanese prisoners after a while, but I doubt it — Japan hasn't signed the Geneva Convention.'

She hadn't heard of that; didn't want to waste his time asking what it was. His face was sombre now.

'I wish you had left here months ago. I spent a year of the last war as a prisoner of war in Germany. If worst comes to the worst, Miss Clancy, remember this. We'll win. Not by next Christmas: not for years. But we have the resources, and they don't. We'll win in the end. All you need to do is survive, and you'll get home again. Can you remember that?'

'Yes.'

'I think you will.' He looked across the dining room. 'And now, if I'm not mistaken, that is your sister-in-law, who is going to give you a stern telling-off for talking to strange men. Good morning, Miss Clancy. And good luck.'

'Good luck to you too.'

She stood as Moira approached, Gavin in her arms. Moira accepted Mr Harding's polite nod with a slight inclination of her own, then waited till he was out of earshot. 'Nancy! What on earth were you doing talking to a strange man?'

Just what Mr Harding said she'd say, thought Nancy. Was he correct about everything else too?

'The hotel is crowded. I couldn't have a table to myself. And it would have been extremely rude not to make conversation with the person who allowed me to share his.'

'Then you should have waited till I came down.'

There was no point arguing. Nancy reached over and lifted Gavin from Moira's arms. 'They have porridge! I'll give Gavin some while you have breakfast. You'll feel better when you've eaten.'

The waiter appeared at the table, proffered a menu. Moira took it. Her face brightened. 'Porridge — two servings, please, one for the baby. Oh, devilled kidneys.'

'I am afraid, madam, that we have no kidneys today.'

Nancy suppressed a smile at the thought of all of the Raffles's guests and staff suddenly minus their kidneys.

'The devilled fowl is particularly good this morning.'

'I will have that then. And a pot of tea now, if you please.' Her eyes raked Nancy, gave grudging approval to dress, stockings, shoes and hair, lingered on the lack of lipstick.

'I'll go down to the P&O Office straight after breakfast.' Nancy took a breath. 'You need to have the bags packed in case we have to sail straight away.'

She waited for argument. It didn't come. Moira nodded. 'I'll be ready. Ah, thank you,' to the waiter bringing their porridge; she bestowed a smile on another who brought fresh tea and handed Nancy a teaspoon to feed Gavin. 'I'm not stupid, my dear. If ... when ... Ben manages to get to Singapore, he'll be evacuated with the army, just like at Dunkirk. Civilians like us would just get in the way. Oh, you've got porridge on your dress already!' She reached over and wiped off the spot, then tied a damask napkin around Gavin as a bib.

Nancy fed Gavin another spoonful, smiled as he gulped it down. Despite their flight the day before, despite Mr Harding's words, a strange sense of peace enveloped her. In a few weeks' time she'd be at Overflow, maybe even before Michael had to go back to school. Mum and Dad and Gran. The river and the hills. And paddocks that stretched across the plain — wonderful wide paddocks where she'd be moving sheep, dagging them, carting hay, back in her working clothes.

And if Moira tried any nonsense, Mum and Gran would deal with her.

Chapter 11

Gibber's Creek Gazette, 19 January 1942

Subscribe to the Hundred-Million-Pound
AUSTERITY LOAN

Advance subscription may be made now.

Interest accrues from date of subscription.

OR BUY NATION WAR SAVINGS BONDS AND
SAVINGS CERTIFICATES.

DRINKWATER, 24 JANUARY 1942

MICHAEL

'Michael, just the person I need.'

Michael looked up from the kitchen table, where he'd been devouring a late lunch of cold mutton and last night's potatoes after mending the fences in the hill paddocks, and thinking of Nancy. A few weeks more and she'd be back in Australia, safe. Or as safe as the rest of the country ...

He stood up politely as Blue McAlpine strode into the kitchen. Red hair as bright as a bushfire, and a bushfire's energy harnessed into a slim-skirted suit of bronze linen with a matching blouse of bronze and green chrysanthemums. She looked like what she was: a successful businesswoman, though her biscuits were now reserved for the armed forces, and wife of the local doctor, now with the AIF. She did not look like a retired circus mermaid.

Blue inspected him, much as he suspected she inspected the conveyor belt at the biscuit factory she owned with her circus friend, Mah, now married to Drinkwater's manager. 'You're filthy.'

'Sorry. I planned to go out again after lunch.'

'Anything urgent?'

'Just inspecting the rest of the fences.'

'Good. I need a hand getting Sheba on the truck for the War Bonds parade.'

Sheba was an elephant, retired from the Magnifico Family Circus, which had sheltered Blue, then a runaway teenager, and Mah, a homeless orphan. Now the women were married to the McAlpine brothers. Michael looked sideways at Blue and grinned. Blue McAlpine as a mermaid seemed as impossible as the extremely proper Mah McAlpine as a magician's assistant, with her brother in a top hat sawing her in half nightly for audiences around the country.

Blue raised an eyebrow. 'What's that grin for?'

'Wishing I'd seen you as a mermaid,' he said frankly.

Blue laughed. 'You'll get your chance. I'm going to be in costume for the parade this afternoon. So's Mah.'

'That'd be worth seeing.'

She looked at him mock sternly. 'You weren't planning on watching our parade?'

He wondered how to say politely that mending fences was more important than watching parades, especially now when so many men had left for war. That he had more urgent things to think of than watching an elephant, even if it carried two young women in revealing costumes.

'I don't have any money to invest in War Bonds. It'd be wasted on me. I doubt there's anyone in Gibber's Creek who hasn't put anything they have to spare into War Bonds already either.'

'That's not the point,' said Blue.

'What is the point then?'

'Morale. Makes us feel we are all in this together, not each one with our own worries. Stops us brooding. Gives us things to do.'

Like knitting army socks, he thought, making camouflage netting twice a week at the Town Hall, Red Cross meetings and collecting ivory and saucepans and paper for the war effort, and the hundreds of other jobs women across Australia dedicated their few free hours to, after the demands of family and the factory work many had taken up to keep the country going with so many men away.

He looked at the woman in front of him, at the shadows under her eyes, the mouth that was a little too firmly smiling. 'Have you heard from Dr McAlpine?'

'A letter from him yesterday.' Her voice was carefully light. 'But you know what the post is like. All I know is that he was well when he wrote it.'

Nor would Dr McAlpine have been able to tell his wife where he was, or if he had, the censor would have blacked it out. But he had told her on his last leave that he was headed for Malaya. At least, he thought, Nancy is headed home. She might have boarded the ship already. Even his father didn't know when the ship that his agent had managed to book berths on for Nancy and her sister-in-law would sail.

'Any news of Nancy?' It was as if Blue had guessed his thoughts.

He blinked. He hadn't been aware that their ... attachment ... was so well known. But it was impossible to keep a secret in a place like Gibber's Creek.

'Dad got a cable to say Nancy and Moira had arrived safely in Singapore.' He flushed. The cable had ended, *THANK YOU EXCLAMATION MARK PLEASE GIVE MY LOVE TO MICHAEL STOP NANCY.* Which meant that everyone at the Post Office, from the postmistress to the delivery boy, knew that Nancy Clancy had sent her love to Michael Thompson. By now the whole district would be gossiping.

But Nancy had used the word 'love', just as he had done. That was worth a bit of gossip.

'Nancy'll be right,' said Blue seriously. 'The Japanese have more to worry about just now than torpedoing passenger ships.'

He nodded. That was what his mother had said the previous night. His father, however, had said nothing. His father's silence worried him.

'Come on,' said Blue McAlpine. 'Elephant.'

None of the fellows at school had quite believed his family had an elephant in their river paddock, even when someone (Michael suspected Jim) posted him a photograph of Sheba inscribed *To Michael. Love always, Sheba* and he'd opened it with everyone gawking and laughing. He wondered if he'd have time to get Dad's camera and take a photograph of the Mrs McAlpines riding her this afternoon.

Sheba stood at the edge of the river, hosing herself down in the midday heat. A rack of hay stood nearby — even the river paddock didn't have enough grass for an elephant. Her small and mildewed teddy bear — Blue and Mah presented her with a new one each Christmas — sat on the hay, regarding the sheep in the next paddock.

He still remembered the excitement of coming home from school to find an elephant by the river. She had lived in a paddock by the factory for a while, but had terrified delivery boys on their bicycles, peering inquisitively over the fence and helping herself to their packages. She had been at Moura next, the farmhouse that had been his grandfather's, but which for some reason his mother had wanted Blue and Dr McAlpine to live in. But the Moura paddock had proved too small, and the company of wombats and wallabies not enough to occupy an elephant used to admiring crowds.

So Sheba and her beloved teddy bear had come back to Drinkwater, to be admired — or at least respected — by the neighbouring sheep, where she could watch the comings and goings of the small village that was Drinkwater: the main house, the shearers' quarters, the workers' cottages, Andy McAlpine's more substantial house, the horseyards and the sheep pens and cattleyards.

He and Jim had tried to ride her, of course, even though their mother had forbidden it. Sheba had kindly but firmly pushed them away with her trunk each time they'd tried. Would she really let Blue and Mah on her back now?

The old elephant saw Blue and gave a welcoming trumpet. She plodded up the hill, pausing only to grab the teddy bear with her trunk. She held it out to Blue.

Blue took it, offering a handful of carrots in return. The elephant conveyed them to her mouth, crunching, eyeing them both as though to say, 'What's happening now?'

'Show time again, old girl,' said Blue softly. She held out an apple. The elephant munched it. 'But just me and Mah on your back today. Not Gertrude.'

'Who's Gertrude?'

Blue smiled reminiscently. 'She was the best trapeze artist and acrobat I've ever seen. Mah and I had acts that just looked impressive. But Gertrude was the real thing.'

'Where is she now?'

Blue grinned. 'Did you see To Love and To Serve?'

Michael nodded. The movie had been on at the Gibber's Creek picture theatre for a week.

'The girl who captures the German spy ring? That's Gertrude.'

Michael shook his head. 'That was Gillie O'Gold. She's American.'

'Gertrude used to be a harem dancer one minute and one of the Boldini Brothers the next,' said Blue dryly. 'She could turn herself into whoever she wanted to be. Just like Fred. But Gertrude wanted to be a star.' She looked at Michael assessingly. 'You're too big to fit into a Boldini Brother costume, but you're about the same size as Fred.'

'Fred?' he asked warily.

'Mah's brother. He was the circus magician.' Blue's smile changed, almost wistful now. 'And a harem dancer when he had to be. Fred was a magician in other ways too sometimes.'

'Did Fred go to Hollywood as well?'

'No.' Her tone made it clear no more would be said about Fred. 'You'll make a fine magician.'

'I don't know the first thing about being a magician.'

'Nothing to it,' she said airily. 'Just march in front of Sheba and keep pulling bunches of flowers out of your top hat. And smile. Don't forget to smile.'

'Look, Mrs McAlpine —'

'Call me Blue. And it's for a good cause.'

She's not talking about raising money for the war effort, thought Michael, or not entirely. This was a woman who must be as anguished about her husband as he was for Nancy. More — for she had the loss of years of closeness while his bond with Nancy had only just been glimpsed. But today they'd give themselves and their neighbours something fabulous and funny to think about instead. Doing their bit.

Blue lifted her hand, and stroked Sheba's leathery neck. 'Come on, old girl,' she said softly. 'Time for the Big Galah.'

Three hours later Michael found himself, somehow, dressed in a frayed dinner jacket and black silk-lined cloak, only slightly moth eaten, pulling fake flowers from a top hat and marching in front of an elephant, draped in gold and green, carrying a small grubby teddy bear in her trunk. On her back sat the doctor's wife and factory manager, now a mermaid in a sequined tail, blonde wig and what looked like nothing else but was, in fact, a tight flesh-coloured top down to her wrists. Mah McAlpine flashed surprisingly shapely legs under a ballerina's skirt, with spangled wings on her back. Her wig was blonde as well.

The two women were clearly enjoying themselves.

Behind them marched the Gibber's Creek town band, or what was left of it — elderly men with trumpets, kids with flutes from school, a boy his own age beating a drum. The fire brigade came next; the Women's Christian Temperance Union, reduced to three members now but still valiantly carrying their banner; the fishing club, with a ten-yard-long papier-mâché Murray cod; the Girl Guides and the Cubs; and, finally, in uniform, their heads proudly erect, the Gibber's Creek Central School Cadet Corps.

He had left his cadet uniform at school. Didn't regret it. They were not his corps and, anyway, just for the moment, he could forget the worry about Nancy, forget he was a schoolboy with the war and world passing him by. This was true magic, far greater than the flowers from his top hat.

He glanced behind him at Blue and Mah on the elephant's back. Who would have thought Mah McAlpine had legs as good as that?

Blue caught his eye and winked.

He flushed and turned back, pulling out another bunch of dusty paper flowers for the crowd's applause. Blue was right. It made no difference how much this procession raised. It was good to march: a small defiance. Hitler's bombs might fall, Japanese parachutists might flutter over Malaya and the islands, but just now he marched with an elephant, as the crowd — slightly smaller perhaps than the number of marchers, and perhaps more dogs than people — cheered on either side. He wondered if this was the real reason women gathered in their precious 'free' hours at night to roll bandages, wrap comfort packages, or organise fundraisers. There was comfort in being together.

He gave himself up to the pleasure of the day.

Chapter 12

Gibber's Creek Gazette, 24 January 1942

Japan Seizes Port of Rabaul

A force of five thousand Japanese troops has taken the strategic port of Rabaul on the island of New Britain, vastly outnumbering the Australian 2/22nd Battalion with more than one hundred aircraft-borne divisions. The Australian RAAF commander of the outnumbered and mostly obsolete Wirraways that were left to defend Rabaul against the sweeping tide of the enemy has sent a message in Latin to Australia which translated reads, 'We who are about to die salute you.'

SINGAPORE, 27 JANUARY 1942

NANCY

She travelled to the Shipping Office by rickshaw again, as she had ever since they had arrived in Singapore. Cars were not permitted, except military or ARP vehicles, though as there were no air-raid warnings in Singapore, nor any air-raid shelters beyond the wide concrete gutters, Nancy wondered how the Singapore Air Raid Patrol deserved its name. From England, she supposed, where enemy bombers were met with British planes and barrage balloons to protect the most important sites. They had been lucky their car hadn't been stopped the first night they arrived here, either by the military or by an air raid.

The rickshaw driver wended his way through the wreckage, the stinking ooze of broken sewage pipes and, once, bodies lined on stretchers, waiting for collection. Dust hung in the air, strange-coloured dust perhaps tinted with explosives. Singapore looked worse in daylight. That first night Nancy had been too exhausted to realise how bad things were.

The line at the Shipping Office was as long as usual, mostly women, and mostly with tired children clinging to them like baby koalas, as if frightened that their mothers too would vanish as the world around them crumbled. But today, at least, there was good news at last. She and Moira had passage booked on *The Lady Williams*. They were to bring only what they could carry, including bedding and five days' worth of food, and be at the docks at one am.

The Raffles's butlers cleaned and repacked the bedding from their car; the kitchens filled Nancy's haversack with food: fruitcake, packets of dried fruit, more canned sardines, which could be opened without a can opener, green bananas that would ripen by the next day or the one after, hard and unfamiliar avocado pears. 'Good for the baby,' said the soft-voiced butler. 'Will ripen like bananas and be soft.'

The hotel arranged the rickshaws, one for their luggage and one for them. Nancy stood with Moira, an amah in white holding Gavin, while the two porters loaded their motley array of goods onto one of the rickshaws. Even so close to midnight, the orchestra still played behind them. A gust of laughter floated out from the Palm Court, and the scent of fried chicken, spices and pastry.

Nancy gazed back at the Raffles. It was hard to leave this haven for a ship and the dangers of the sea. But even the Raffles must face the storm to come. And beyond the sea was Overflow ...

'Excuse me? Miss Clancy?'

It was Mr Harding, or whatever his rank was. 'Mr Harding, how ... nice ... to see you.' She hoped she sounded properly Malaya-society polite. 'Moira, this is Mr Harding, who kindly allowed me to sit at his breakfast table. Mr Harding, my sister-in-law, Mrs Benjamin Clancy.'

Mr Harding lifted his hat to Moira. 'A pleasure to meet you, Mrs Clancy. I hope you don't mind. I have brought you a going-away present.'

'I ... er ... thank you,' said Nancy, staring at the two life jackets in his hands.

'Delighted to meet you, Mr Harding.' Moira sounded anything but delighted. 'Thank you so much for thinking of us, but I'm sure the ship will have life jackets.'

'No, I'm afraid they won't, Mrs Clancy,' said Mr Harding bluntly. 'Or at least they won't have enough for the number of passengers that will be aboard. I'd wish you "bon voyage", but I'm afraid it will be anything but a "bon" one. May I wish you a swift and safe passage instead.' He handed the life jackets to the porters to put with the luggage. 'One more thing.'

He held something towards Nancy. For a moment she thought it was a scrap of drab paper.

It was a gum leaf, dry and crackling when she gripped it too tightly. She relaxed her hand, and held it to her nose.

It smelt of summer and cicadas. She could almost smell the mutton chops on the fire, the scent of the river in flood.

Mr Harding looked at her steadily. 'A lesson I learnt in the last war. Keep believing in home, Miss Clancy, and you will get there.'

He stepped back, up under the darkened Raffles portico. 'I'll wave you off,' he said. 'Everyone should have someone to wave them goodbye.'

Nancy sat in the rickshaw, took Gavin on her lap. She lifted his chubby hand. 'Wave to Mr Harding, darling. Say bye bye.'

'Shllobbims?' asked Gavin, drooling gently onto her knees.

The rickshaw glided off into the even greater darkness around the drive. Nancy glanced back. It was almost impossible to see Mr Harding, but she knew he was there. She lifted the hand that held the gum leaf and smelt it again. But there was no scent now. Had she imagined it before? How old was this leaf?

It didn't matter. Believing mattered. She would get home, with Moira, with Gavin. When Singapore fell — and it must fall — Ben would escape. Another Dunkirk. Ship after ship would bring their army home again ...

Gavin pulled at her hair and began to chew it, more drool dripping down his chin. She wiped it with one of the Raffles napkins, tied around his neck by the amah and forgotten as they left. She wondered why she was crying.

The rickshaw drivers cycled through the rubble. Behind them searchlights raked the northern sky. A low familiar rumble turned into planes. Nancy waited, her skin tingling, for them to come closer, for the dull thud of bombs, for the crash of walls and exploding cars. Should they ask their rickshaw drivers to stop, so they could shelter in the gutter?

But the planes stayed to the north, skimming in and out of the searchlights. The first bombs dropped, the explosions flaring into the sky, redder and brighter than the searchlights for a moment, then dimming back to a distant glow of firelight.

Please, she thought, don't let them bomb the docks tonight. Let us get away from this place.

The rickshaw with their belongings stopped. Theirs did too. Their driver pointed to a new mass of shattered rock on the road, a leaning tree festooned with broken telephone and electricity lines. He shrugged.

It was obvious the rickshaws could go no further.

'Will you help us carry our luggage?' asked Moira.

Their driver looked blank.

'Helpee carry luggage!' said Moira more loudly. She held out a note.

The man took the money, his face still blank. He helped the other rickshaw driver unload the luggage onto the side of the road, then, still expressionless, climbed onto his bicycle and pedalled away. His companion followed him.

'Stupid man. He can't have understood,' said Moira.

He understood, thought Nancy. She thought of Ah Jong back at their borrowed house in Kuala Lumpur, of the Malay police removing and leaving their uniforms behind to vanish back through the jungle to their villages. This was their home. Why risk their lives — or their rickshaws being stolen — for strangers?

The bedding had been rolled up into a kind of swag, held in place by the mosquito net. Nancy shrugged her arms into the haversack, wriggled the life jackets onto each shoulder, hoisted the bundle in one hand, and a suitcase in the other. She was about to say that Moira would have to carry the other suitcase when she saw that her sister-in-law already held it as she picked her way through the night, Gavin perched on her hip. Nancy staggered after her.

The only light came from the searchlights and the glow of fires. But the breeze came from the sea, smelling of salt and smoke and the tang of coal, and the road went in the right direction.

At last they reached the docks. Nancy produced her pass, with the name of their ship. A tall corporal pointed down to a far wharf, past boxes of ammunition, piled or dumped like children's blocks, a patchwork quilt of soldiers, some huddled on haversacks and swags, others marching in formation, coolies lugging boxes.

'Thank you,' said Nancy wearily.

The corporal looked at her again. 'Here, I'll take those.' He relieved her of the bedding, hoisted it under his arm, and took the suitcases that she and Moira were carrying in his hands. They followed the path he forged through the crowd.

'Here you are.' The corporal plonked the luggage down at the end of a straggling line.

Moira stared. 'This can't be right! We're booked on *The Lady Williams*.'

'That's her all right.'

'But there can't be cabins for all of us on that.'

The corporal looked at her with sympathy. 'Won't be cabins for any of youse. But it's your ticket out of here, missus. Just wish I was going with you.'

Nancy stared at the ship bobbing quietly at the end of their line. She had glimpsed ships that morning; knew from the chaos of the Shipping Office that not only would they not be travelling first class, in a cabin to themselves on a luxury passenger liner, but had accepted they would be six to a cabin on a far lesser vessel, perhaps, with more beds made up in the dining room ...

She had not expected this.

The Lady Williams was a cargo ship, despite her aristocratic name. She was not much bigger than a Sydney Harbour ferry, but shabbier, paint peeling from her funnel, barnacles on her sides. The decks already looked crammed with women. If there were cabins, they would be full.

But it didn't matter. Nothing mattered, except Overflow, somewhere ahead. She could face bombs, face even the Japanese Army, if only she had her family, which was not just people, but the land she knew.

She glanced at Moira, expecting protest. But Moira just held Gavin closer. Her face held nothing but exhaustion, and a glimpse of loss so great that Nancy had to look away.

'Ben will be all right,' she muttered.

'Yes. Of course,' said Moira. Her voice was hoarse. She wore her pearls, Nancy saw, rings on three of her fingers, her good emerald brooch on the lapel of her sensible travelling suit. Keeping up the side, thought Nancy, then realised that jewellery could also be sold; could be used if necessary to provide them with food and shelter and help, and that it was safer worn, not in luggage that might be lost or stolen.

She looked at the life jackets sitting on their bedroll. If the ship ... If they had to use the life jackets, money would be sodden, useless. She suddenly wished that she hadn't been so steadfast in refusing jewellery for birthdays or Christmases. She too might have had pearls, in case ... She thrust the thought away.

The soldier gave a tired grin. 'Hang on a sec.' He strode over to a pile of boxes, already opened, and rummaged inside one.

He held up a teddy bear and a box of chocolates. 'Christmas has come a bit late.' He held them out to Moira.

'We can't take —'

'Don't belong to nobody now, lady. Unless the Japs want them.'

Nancy tried to imagine the Japanese commandos she'd seen — was it not yet two months back? — clutching teddy bears as well as bayonets. The image wouldn't work.

'Thank you,' said Moira.

The man gave a sketchy salute. He vanished back into the dappled dimness of a thousand uniforms.

They stood in the ragged line, old women, young women, European and Eurasian, women with babies, children holding the hands of amahs or clutching their mothers' necks, like Gavin, now draped over Moira's shoulder blissfully asleep and unaware of both his new teddy bear and the danger behind, above and soon below.

They ate the chocolates rather than start on their other food. Chocolates would not keep, and these were already patchily white and floury on the surface from the heat. It seemed surreal to be deciding between orange cream or almond whirl from the menu on the lid. Nancy let the chocolate melt in her mouth instead of chewing it, making each one last longer. It filled in time. There was comfort in the taste of the familiar too.

Gavin woke. He blinked at the chaos around him, and gave a small whimper.

'I think he's hungry,' said Nancy.

'I'm not going to feed him in the middle of the docks,' said Moira. 'He'll have to wait till we're on board.'

'Can I give him a chocolate?'

'He's too young,' said Moira tiredly, and then, 'Oh, very well. Just the plain milk chocolate one, and break it into pieces first.'

Nancy bit off a small piece. She pressed it to Gavin's small warm mouth.

He wrinkled his nose as if she had fed him dog droppings, and spat it out onto the Raffles napkin, then seemed to change his mind and reached for it again.

'He likes chocolate.'

'Everyone likes chocolate,' said Moira, closing her eyes.

'Here, I'll take him for a while. I'm going to sit on the luggage.'

The eyes opened. 'You will not. Making a spectacle of yourself.'

We are about to try to sail between enemy ships and mines, she thought. German U-boats below us, Japanese planes above. And Moira is worried about me sitting on my swag. But nothing mattered except escape, and Overflow ahead of them.

She remained standing. She would not add to Moira's weariness and distress.

By two am they were on board, had climbed down the narrow hatch into the meat locker that would house more than five hundred women and children crammed below decks, the only ventilation coming from the jammed-open hatch.

They deposited their bedding. Nancy stood, skirts out, to give Moira a modicum of privacy while she fed Gavin. The chocolate might have satisfied his hunger, but he needed a drink, and any water in this land was suspect unless you had seen it boiled yourself.

At last they made their way back up to the deck. Despite the order to be there so early, the ship seemed in no hurry to cast off. More and more women shuffled aboard. We were lucky, thought Nancy, looking at a ship just beyond theirs, with women and children clambering out of a rocking ship's boat and climbing a dangling rope ladder, sailors leaning over to heave them on board. At least we didn't have to climb up the side.

Another roar of planes, closer now. An ack-ack gun fired from the wharf, the ship rocking in protest. The planes were coming closer now. Bombs thudded, near enough for her to hear the screams, the fall of bricks and concrete. They waited, huddled in the crowd, each one knowing there was no shelter. This was the only escape. If the docks were lost, then so were they.

But no bombs fell on the wharves or ships. At last the engine noise faded to a mutter, then disappeared. Daylight seeped through the smoke and dust. There was no shade. A sailor distributed packets of biscuits and already opened tins of bully beef to the women on deck, one packet and one tin between Moira and Nancy.

They sat and ate. Neither had any appetite nor was the food appetising, but they had experienced enough by now to know that they needed to eat when food was available.

'Not exactly the Raffles,' said an elderly woman next to them, dipping a biscuit into a can of meat. She wore emeralds at her throat, and a tiara — Nancy tried not to giggle — an emerald tiara in daylight, peeking out from under a respectable sun hat.

Nancy smiled agreement.

They finished the beef — there was no point saving some for later as it would soon go bad in the heat. Nancy kept half the biscuits, in case there was a wait till their next meal. They might need all the food in their pack before the voyage was over. Nancy stood in front of Moira again to give her some privacy while she fed Gavin.

The heat grew. Water, she thought. We have forgotten to bring water. Somehow she had assumed that with the ocean around them there'd be no need of water. Stupid, she thought, stupid … just as another sailor rolled a forty-four-gallon drum on board. He shoved in a bung, turned a tap and began to fill jugs of water. He followed another sailor holding a tray of tin mugs around the deck. 'Keep the mug, you'll need it later.'

'Do you know where we are headed?' The woman next to them looked Eurasian, her grey serge suit too hot and dark for the tropics, with gold earrings and gold rings.

Moira pretended not to hear.

'Darwin,' said Nancy.

'I heard it was Broome,' said another woman, fat as Mrs Flanagan from the Gibber's Creek Post Office.

'Batavia,' said the elderly woman with the tiara.

Nancy said nothing. She had assumed the ship was heading to Australia. Darwin had been her last Australian port. Perhaps the ship was heading to Batavia first, and would then sail on to Broome and then Darwin. Or perhaps there'd be another ship at Batavia, and, hopefully, their passages booked on it. Nothing she could do about it now.

How many nappies were they going to need to get to either port? Would there be any way to wash them? The air below was bad enough now. What would it be like with twenty-four dirty nappies in the tropical heat?

They ate more bully beef at mid-afternoon, the water jugs coming around every hour or so. The boat rocked. More planes, more bombs, but still neither docks nor ships were hit. The single lavatory already stank; there was invariably a long queue of women waiting to use it. Could they wash Gavin's nappies in seawater?

When, oh when, would the ship finally sail?

At dusk the order came to go below. They lay half sitting, crammed on their bedding — there was not enough room to lie down fully — with Gavin grizzling at Moira's breast. She had given up any attempt at modesty, except to hold her blouse across. Besides, there were only women here, who tactfully avoided noticing a mother feeding her child.

The ship rocked. The darkness grew. They dozed, on and off, except Gavin, who slept, stretched across their laps. Yet another explosion thundered in the distance. At last, some unknown amount of time later — it was too dark to even glimpse her watch — the rocking changed. The motor rumbled purposefully. A small surge knocked Nancy into the woman next to her as the ship got under way.

Nancy felt Moira's hand reach for hers. She grasped it. 'We're going home,' she said.

'Your home,' said Moira, her voice distant. 'My home is Ben.'

Chapter 13

Gibber's Creek Gazette, 28 January 1942

The War Relief Dance
By Elaine Sampson, aged nine and a half

Yesterday our school had a dance for Comforts for Soldiers. At lunchtime we took all our books off the shelves and the boys moved the desks in front of the blackboard so they would not be in the way.

We had good music. Mr Henderson played the mouth organ and Mrs Harrington the banjo. We paid a penny to dance. A good time was had by all.

We raised one shilling and eightpence halfpenny. The halfpenny was because Billy Snogs only had a halfpenny but we decided he could dance anyway because he is the tallest boy in class and can dance like Frank Sinatra does in the movies, except he wears shorts instead. We will buy pencils for the soldiers so they can write to their families. The girls wanted to buy soap too but the boys voted no.

SOMEWHERE SOUTH OF SINGAPORE, 29 JANUARY 1942

NANCY

The bomb hit with the first shreds of daylight. Nancy had been asleep, propped against Moira. She woke as the boat shuddered, twisted, then forged on. Gavin woke with a start and began to whimper. Around them women screamed, or hugged themselves, frozen with fear. Children wailed, in protest and terror.

'What's happened?' Nancy's voice was hoarse with thirst, her dress damp with sweat.

Something hit the water nearby, so close they could feel the swell the instant before the explosion knocked them sideways. Even the children were silent. Nancy held her breath too, waiting for the ship to sink.

It didn't. Nancy rummaged under the end of the bedding for their life jackets.

Another explosion. Another. The ship lurched upwards, sideways, twisted in the water, but the walls around them stayed intact. Nancy found Moira's hand. The older woman was silent, holding Gavin to her, his ears jammed between her body and her free hand to shield him from the noise. He gave small hiccupping cries, too caught up in the surrounding terror to properly cry.

Another sound, like cloth ripping. A splintered hole appeared in the deck above them. Nancy peered around, wondering if the bullets had penetrated below the deck, but there was no sign of blood on any of the women and children in the dimness of the hold.

They waited, now hearing only sobbing children and men's yells from overhead. I'm getting good at waiting, thought Nancy. More shouts from above, the sound of running feet, the chatter of gunfire. Explosions on either side of them ...

Was it minutes or hours? She thought the latter, but time had lost its meaning. Was it minutes or hours before her ringing ears registered that the bombs had stopped, the throaty roar was dropping as the planes receded?

The hatch was opened wider. 'Everyone all right down there?'

No one answered, then a woman called back, 'Seem to be. Was the ship hit?'

'Bit of damage aft. Nothing to stop us though. It's safe to come on deck if you want some air.'

Nancy grabbed Gavin and made her way towards the companionway before too many could crowd the way, climbed with one hand on the rail, the other holding Gavin. As she emerged through the hatch, she took a deep breath of fresh and smoky air and felt some of her sweat dry.

'Water over there, love.' A sailor nodded towards a drum amidships.

'Thank you.'

Moira appeared beside her as she helped herself to water, drank fast and deeply before the drum too was crowded. She'd had enough of bodies pressing against her.

'Do you think it's safe to give Gavin a drink of water?'

'Better not.' Moira took him from her. 'I'll feed him. Let's go forwards. It should be less crowded there.'

The deck was rough with bullet splinters below their feet. Smoke pillowed the rear of the ship. They passed a lifeboat. Moira gave a small laugh. 'Well, we won't be using that.'

'Why not? Oh, I see.' The wood was ripped so badly that there was no way the boat would float. Nancy thought of the life jackets under their bedding. She should have brought them with her. But they'd look ridiculous carrying them around. As if they expected defeat. Not keeping up the side, she thought vaguely. Poor show, what.

It was cooler in the small space forwards. There was even a little early-morning shade next to a wooden crate. Gavin fed, nuzzling for comfort long after the feed had finished. Moira let him, sitting back against the bulkhead, her eyes closed.

Nancy went over to the rail and peered out across the ocean. Singapore had vanished. Over on one side there was a thin blue line of land. An island, she thought, trying to remember the scatter of Malaya's outcrops on the map that had hung in Ben's study back at the plantation, might hang there still.

Who was living in the house now? A Japanese officer? Or would the house be abandoned, too far out of the way? No, she thought. The Japanese will want the plantation to keep producing the precious rubber. A new manager would live there, a local man, perhaps even the foreman who had been effectively doing the job during Ben's absences.

She gazed back the way they had come again, searching the sky for planes. Over on the horizon was a larger shape she took to be a destroyer, and three more ships, one larger and two slightly smaller than theirs. Was the destroyer protecting them? But no one had shot the enemy planes from the sky.

Something bobbed, perhaps fifty yards away. At first she thought it was another crate, then realised it was too round, with spikes, like a too-fat echidna.

A mine. She had seen them on newsreels. The ship had to touch the mine, didn't it, before the mine blew up? This looked to be too far away to be an immediate danger. But there might be — must be — more.

But at least there were no more planes ...

Something rose above the thin line of the island. A bird, she thought. Another and another ...

Bombers.

'We need to go below.'

'No.' Moira's voice was surprisingly calm among the new tide of screams from the deck behind them. 'Go and get the life jackets. Bring them back up here.'

'But we might be hit if we stay up here.'

Moira touched the crate behind them. 'We can shelter behind this and the bulkhead.' She looked at Nancy directly. 'If the ship is sunk, the companionway is going to be blocked with women. We'd have no chance of getting out of there alive.'

Nancy bit her lip, nodded. It should be me thinking that, she thought vaguely. But Moira had far more experience of ships than she had. Though not, she thought, of ones that might soon sink. She slipped between the other passengers, struggled down the companionway, women pushing on either side. They'll panic if we are hit again, she thought. Moira is right ...

She grabbed the life jackets, waited till the worst crush had come down the ladder and then pushed her way back up, along the boat.

'Back here.' Moira crouched above Gavin between the crate and the bulkhead. She straightened and slipped on the life jacket, fastening it in front, then resumed her crouch. Gavin gurgled and grabbed at her pearls. She pushed his hand away absently, gave him her finger to chew. 'Put your life jacket on. If we're badly hit, swim towards the island. Fast. If you're near the ship when it goes down, the suction will take you with it. Hopefully one of the other ships will pick us up, if they're not damaged too.'

'Moira ...'

'What?'

'I can't swim.'

'What?!' Moira stared at her. 'All Australians can swim. All those beaches.'

'We live hundreds of miles from the beach!'

'You can't swim at all?'

'A bit. Mucking round on the river.' She'd never swum more than a dozen strokes across a swimming hole. The river was too shallow to swim in, except when it was in flood and too dangerous. No one swam in the billabongs, not with tangles of waterlilies and the chance of bumping into black snakes cooling off.

'Bloody hell.' She had never heard Moira swear before. 'I can't manage you and Gavin both.'

'You can swim?'

'Four-hundred-yard school champion,' said Moira shortly.

Bully for you and your swimming pool, thought Nancy. She looked at the sea around them. The bombers were almost on them now.

'Dog paddle or overarm?'

'Dog paddle.'

Moira looked at the land on the horizon. 'Dog paddle might get you there. The life jacket will keep you afloat. Once you're in the water use your hands like paddles and kick like hell. And that,' she said grimly, 'is the best swimming lesson I can give you right now.'

'Perhaps they won't hit us.' Nancy tried to count the planes. Fifteen, twenty, twenty-five ...

The first bomb fell. The ship heaved as the water exploded around them. A plane zoomed lower. The screams from the other end of the boat took on a new note, agony now among the fear.

Time slowed. A dark ball slipped down the blue of sea and sky. Into the funnel of the ship. The ship shuddered. As if it knows, thought Nancy. Then it exploded.

The world shrieked into fragments. The shock rolled both her and Moira across the deck. Instinctively Nancy lunged back, grabbing Gavin, forcing him below her as bullets strafed the deck. She began to roll again, sheltering his body with hers.

The ship was sinking.

Flames danced across the deck behind her.

Another explosion. The ship vanished. What had been solid deck was noise so loud she couldn't even hear it, was splintering wood and flames. She felt the ship lurch wildly to one side, flinging her against the bulkhead. It lurched again, the prow rising higher and higher against the sky. She saw rather than heard Moira's yell, 'Jump!'

The prow was too high and steep now to reach. She stumbled to the side, held Gavin while Moira climbed onto the rail, then passed him up to her, a small wailing ball of baby. Moira jumped, holding the baby high, her bent legs neatly scissoring the water. For a few seconds she vanished, then appeared again, lying on one side, stroking solidly with one arm, Gavin gasping and screaming in the other.

Screaming. He was alive. Tiny, terrified, in the vastness of the sea.

Nancy shut her eyes and jumped.

—⁕◎

Water. Green water, which was strange, because it had looked blue. Green and bubbles, so many bubbles. She must be sinking down, onto the bottom of the sea.

No, the other way. She was floating up, a golden, wave-rippled ceiling above her. The life jacket.

She popped through the surface, gasping.

Cold. How could the water be cold here in the tropics? Then realised it was not cold, not really, it was that she had been so hot.

Where there had been a ship was nothing but flames. She wondered if they had more flammable cargo than women and children.

No one could live in that. Ten seconds before, or twenty, she had been there. Moira's order had saved her life.

The heat burnt her even from here. She turned her face away.

'Moira!' she yelled. A wave slapped her face. She realised she had automatically managed more movement in the water than she had ever attempted before.

'Moira!' she cried again.

No answer.

She managed to lie, her legs out, dog-paddling her hands. Someone screamed behind her. Not Moira. Another voice yelled, 'No, no, no, no!' Someone shrieked, 'Glenys!'

She couldn't help them. Couldn't help anyone but herself. And Moira — hopefully — was swimming like the school champion she had been, holding Gavin up above the waves, towards the distant island.

She bobbed up to make sure she was heading in the right direction, and kicked like mad.

Chapter 14

Gibber's Creek Gazette, 29 January 1942

Letters to the Editor

Dear Sir,

I would like to draw readers' attention to the words of poet Henry Lawson. Though written decades ago, they are even more relevant now. Britain may have failed us; America may befriend us; but in the final stand, Australia must fight alone.

Yours faithfully,

Mrs Thomas Thompson

'In the Storm that is to Come' by Henry Lawson

*By our place in the midst of the farthest seas we are fated to
    stand alone —*
*When the nations fly at each other's throats let Australia look
    to her own;*
*Let her spend her gold on the barren West for the land and its
    manhood's sake;*
*For the South must look to herself for strength in the storm
    that is yet to break.*
*The rain comes down on the Western land and the rivers run to
    waste,*
*While the townsfolk rush for the special tram in their childish,
    senseless haste,*
*And never a pile of a lock we drive — out a few mean tanks we
    scratch —*

For the fate of a nation is nought compared with the turn of a
*   cricket match!*
I have pictured long in the land I love what the land I love
*   might be,*
Where the Darling rises from Queensland rains and the floods
*   rush out to the sea.*
And is it our fate to wait too late to the truth that we have been
*   blind,*
With a foreign foe at our harbour gate and a blazing drought
*   behind?*

DRINKWATER, 29 JANUARY 1942

MICHAEL

Four shirts, with name tags. Four pairs of trousers, long, with name tags, freshly starched and ironed. Socks, with name tags.

There was something forlorn about socks in a suitcase, rolled up like baby echidnas, always pushed into the corners or even stuffed into shoes. Gym bag. Hair oil, wrapped in a towel in case it leaked. Two fruitcakes, from the miraculous Mrs Mutton, who hung bunches of home-grown grapes and long strings of halved figs and plums up in the hay shed to replace the dried fruit it was hard to buy now. Mah McAlpine provided the property's butter now, from the three patient Jersey cows in the paddock overlooking Sheba's.

Could you milk an elephant? he wondered. They were mammals after all and so, by definition, milk producers. But if you could milk elephants, then Malaya would have cheese ...

He sat on the bed and thought of Nancy. Unfair that now she was so near home at last, he would be at school. But she'd have to pass through Sydney, even if she landed at Brisbane or Melbourne and came by train. He could take the day off. Mum was a good sport and could wangle something persuasive with a note, and anyway, these days boys were always vanishing for a few days to see brothers on a final leave, or to welcome them back before they headed off again …

How would Nancy have changed? He hoped she hadn't cut her hair, or had it permed in fashionable curls. He supposed she wouldn't be wearing a drooping dress, as she had at the party and on the train when he waved her goodbye. Nor the moleskins, worn through at both knees and ragged at the cuffs, that she had worn at Overflow. Would she wear the blue spotted voile she had told him about?

Surely there'd be a chance to be alone with her, even in Sydney. The Botanic Gardens perhaps. Somewhere they could talk and hold hands. It wouldn't be the same as being here, but it wasn't long till half-term. He'd come back for that, even if it meant a night on the train each way, so he'd have two whole days with her …

Did she still feel what she had said that morning at the cascades, before she left? Please don't have changed too much, he thought. Wear a spotted voile, and even lipstick, but still be Nancy of the Overflow.

The phone shrilled down in the hall. Two long rings and three short ones, which meant it was for them. He heard Mrs Mutton's tones: 'Drinkwater, Mrs Mutton speaking.' And then, 'I think he's in the study.'

He went out into the corridor, curious. Phone calls about work mostly came to the factory, and not so early in the morning.

'Thomas Thompson speaking. Yes, operator, another three minutes. As many as it takes. Hello?'

Silence. And then, 'I see.' More silence. And then, 'I see. Thank you for calling me. There's no other news?'

Another pause.

'I see. Yes, I see. Yes, of course. Please call at any time if you have word. Many thanks indeed.'

The phone clicked back in its cradle.

'Dad? Is everything OK?'

'Don't speak like an American.'

Which meant that Dad was worried. He was always easy-going except when he was worried.

Michael ran down the stairs. 'Dad, I'm sixteen now. If there's a problem at the factory —'

'What? No, nothing like that. Nothing to worry about. Finished your packing?'

'You *are* worried.'

His father looked at him. Really looked at him, assessing. He nodded. 'Come into the study.'

Michael followed him, then sat in one of the shabby leather chairs by the desk. His father sat too, with the slightly awkward flop that was one of the last reminders of his stroke a decade earlier. 'Michael, can you keep this to yourself?'

'Yes.'

'Are you sure? Don't say it lightly.'

'Yes. Of course.'

'That was my Sydney agent. He's just had word from Singapore ...'

'Nancy!'

His father nodded. '*The Lady Williams* has been sunk by a Japanese bomb. One of the other ships nearby saw it.'

Nancy. He felt for loss, for agony. It wasn't there. He'd know if she was dead. He'd have to know it.

Wouldn't he?

'We have to let them know at Overflow.'

'No! Michael, it's not public knowledge yet. In wartime, well, it's not our decision who to tell and when. We might be worrying them unnecessarily too. The ships were travelling in a convoy. Still are. That's how they know *The Lady Williams* was sunk. If the wrong people find out where the convoy is, it will be easier to target them. My agent didn't know how many passengers were picked up by the other ships. Won't know till they reach port.'

'When will that be?'

'I don't know. I don't even know where they are heading.

Information like that is confidential these days too. You know that, Michael.'

Other ships nearby. Nancy had been picked up. She must have been picked up.

'They're not all like the *Titanic*,' his father added gently. 'There's a good chance they had enough time to get the boats launched. And with other ships in the area ... there's every chance that they would have been picked up, so. A very good chance.'

Somehow, hearing it repeated made that chance seem smaller, not greater. Michael asked dully, 'What do we do now?'

'Wait,' said his father.

'I can't go to school not knowing.'

'You can, you know. If you don't go to school, we'll need to give a reason.'

Yes, he could. If Nancy could survive a sinking ship, he could manage the afternoon train to school.

'Mrs Mutton is cooking roast chicken for lunch. And peach crumble. Your mother agreed to the generator being used for three hours to make ice cream.'

He tried a smile. 'You mean it is my duty to eat ice cream, to thank Mrs Mutton, and to not worry Mum?'

'Yes,' said his father.

'Well,' he said lightly, 'if that's all I can do for the war effort today, I'd better get on with it. It's ... it's hard, Dad. Being at school in times like these. I could at least be working at the factory. Or here.'

'You'll be more use when you've finished school.'

He didn't believe that. Perfecting Ancient Greek and Latin grammar was not going to make him a better farmer, or even factory assistant. But he knew his parents — neither of whom had even done their Fourth Form exams, much less their Leaving Certificates — put an inordinate value on both their sons' educations. He knew that they hoped he'd go to university, or at least to agricultural college. Leaving school might be an infinitesimal help to the war effort. It would be a mighty slap in the face of his parents.

'You'll let me know as soon as there's any news?'

'Of course. I'm sure the Clancys will let us know as soon as they get word too.'

Thomas Thompson looked at his son. Said nothing. Just looked. Michael knew without the words being said that if the news was bad, his parents would be at the school when he received it. That they'd make sure he had whatever time he needed before he faced his friends again.

You did not hurt parents like his without an overwhelming reason to cause them pain. He would stay at school, for them.

None of the fellows at school, he thought, would understand his bond with Nancy. None could understand what her loss would mean either. Could his parents? His mind automatically veered away from thinking about the depth or nature of their relationship.

Nancy was alive. Had to be alive.

'Thanks, Dad,' he said. He stood. 'See you at lunch.'

'I'll be there,' said Thomas Thompson. He reached up — when had Michael grown so tall that his father had to reach? — and hugged his son.

Chapter 15

Gibber's Creek Gazette, 29 January 1942

WASTE PAPER MAKES MUNITIONS!

You can help by saving ALL FORMS OF WASTE PAPER.

Newspapers, flat or crushed, letters, receipts, envelopes, old books, wrapping paper, flat or crushed, cigarette packets, cartons, cardboard boxes, magazines.

A USED ENVELOPE MAKES A .303 CARTRIDGE WAD.

All donations to be left at the rear of the CWA rooms, Tuesdays and Saturdays.

SOMEWHERE SOUTH OF SINGAPORE, 29 JANUARY 1942

NANCY

Time passed, and so did water. Waves kicked at her and slapped. The screams behind her grew more frantic, and with them the guilt that she was here, not there, helping no one but herself, increased. But for now that was all that she could do.

She had felt the ship sink behind her, a giant gulp, fingers of water dragging her down. She struggled, but in a minute it was gone, and new waves were punching her, trying to drown her.

Then they too were gone, leaving only flames that flickered above the water.

Something new pushed her now. It was like the current in the river. But the sea didn't have currents, did it? She tried to remember geography at school, vaguely remembered that it did. It must, for there could be nothing else to push her now. Which way was it taking her? She pushed herself upwards for a second, saw the land no further away. At least she was still heading in the right direction.

She called out, 'Moira!'

No answer, except the screams behind her.

'Gavin,' she whispered, and felt her heart bleed, for his tininess, his helplessness. For love.

She stroked and kicked.

Night was a blessing. Her body ached with heat. Then it became a curse, as she felt the current change around her. How could she know where land was now?

Stroke and kick. Kick and kick and stroke. Perhaps she was swimming away from land. Perhaps she should just rest …

She woke from a doze, her face in water. For a second she panicked, then realised the life jacket still held her up. God bless Mr Harding, she thought.

'Moira? Moira, can you hear me?'

A voice, not Moira's, but speaking English, came back out of the watery darkness: 'Who's that?'

'My name is Nancy Clancy.'

'There are five of us here. We're holding onto a crate. There's room for another if you can get to us.'

Others had survived then. Had they jumped, like she and Moira had done? 'Thank you, but I've got a life jacket.'

'Good luck then.'

'Have you seen a woman with a little boy? Moira Clancy?'

The voice, fainter now over the suck and clap of water, 'No. You're the only one we've heard. Hope she made it.'

'Do you know how far we've got to swim?'

No answer. Had they even heard her?

Nancy kicked, and kicked again, tried to hear if anyone else was swimming nearby, but could only hear the slap of waves and somewhere the drone of an engine. Plane or boat?

She should have swum towards the others. At least there would have been company, and she would not have been alone in this great sea. She called again, 'Hello?'

No answer.

'Hello? Where are you?'

Only the waves replied.

'Hello! Can anyone hear me?'

She kicked. Stroke and kick and kick and stroke. I am alive, she thought. If I am alive, then Gavin and Moira may be too. Stroke and kick and kick and stroke. After a while she dozed again.

She felt the dawn before she saw it, a lightening of the air. The current changed about her. She tried to see through the darkness; she failed to make out anything — or perhaps there was nothing but black water to see.

Her body ached, ache beyond pain. It was as though the salt had dragged all the water from her body. Her skin felt dry, even as the waves slapped it.

The water pulled at her now, wet arms that pushed and tugged. As the light grew brighter, she managed a vague heave up.

And saw the beach. Strange pink sand. No, not sand, pebbles. Palm trees. A curl of waves.

She sank back in the water, wondering if she had the strength to cry. Decided that she didn't, but that she could still kick. Her feet seemed feeble against the strength of the water. She let the current carry her instead. A wave, stronger than the rest, picked her up and rolled her over, her face down in froth and water. She struggled frantically up towards the light.

The beach was closer now. Grey things lay draped across it. She tried to block her mind to what they were, but brain and eyes computed nonetheless.

Bodies. Women's bodies, in dresses streaked with red. A man stood there, above the women. A small man, in grey and green, a helmet on his head, a rifle in his hand.

She had to help. She had to run. She could do neither.

She tried to duck back into the water, but another wave pushed her up. The man strode forwards, raised the gun. He pointed it at her …

The bullet bit. She screamed, grabbing her waist, saw the blood …

He raised the gun again.

Her body reacted before she could even think. She flopped back, as if she was as dead as the grey shapes on the beach, her face down, head tilted sideways a little to allow her to take brief gulps of air in the seconds when her mouth was free of water, letting the life jacket keep her up. She felt the waves drag her this way and that. Her arms flopped and folded as the water tossed and sucked at them.

She waited for the next shot, the last one, the one that would leave her dead.

It didn't come.

The waves lifted her and tossed her, back and forth. She felt sandy gravel under her dangling hands and feet; she didn't dare move towards the safety of the land, which was no safety. Nowhere was safe at all.

At last a wave retreated, leaving her on the prickles of the beach. She felt water tickle her waist, felt coldness seep from her side, another wave touch her toes. Now there was time for pain. For grief that swallowed up the world, but no strength to even remember why she grieved.

And that was all.

The world was dark. She wondered if she was dead or unconscious — then realised that if she was either, she would not be wondering, nor would her side scream like a tiger had bitten it.

Not a tiger. A bullet.

She moved her head cautiously. Her vision blurred, but she could see the sand, the white froth of waves. Something wet licked her foot, and then her knee.

A wave. The tide must be coming in. Panic shivered across her skin. She could be sucked back into the immensity of the ocean. What the sea had spat out it might grab back. She dug her fingers into the pebbles, found that she could move, a slow slide up the beach. At last the rocks were dry, beyond the high-water mark, she hoped.

She dared not try to stand nor even look around; nor did she think she could. Everything was pain, her side worst of all. She lay, puffing weakly against the stones. Darkness spread across her once again.

'Mem, mem, wake.'

She felt her head lifted, something held to her lips. She drank automatically, then thirstily, something sweet and cool and vaguely familiar. Coconut water, she realised, blinking at the waves of light that crashed across her from the sea and the sky.

'Mem must come now.' A woman, young, brown-faced, a shapeless patterned dress, bare feet and covered head.

'I don't think I can.' She had been shot. You couldn't move when you'd been shot. She tentatively pushed her hand down to her side, half expecting it would go into a welling hole and then she'd die.

Instead it simply hurt. She felt again, held back a cry. The bullet had hit the life jacket, then dug a small hole across the edge of her waist. But though her hand came up red, the bleeding had almost stopped. Certainly it hadn't welled onto the sand.

She let the thin arms help her to sit, and then to stand. She looked across the beach.

Bodies. All women, as she'd thought, though one might be an older child. All dead, their blood already black on the strange pinkness of the beach. A tangle of wood had been washed up to one side. She wondered if the dead women had used it like a raft. Had theirs been the voices in the night?

Her heart clenched. Moira? She peered again, body after body, looking for the olive green of Moira's suit, a small form that might be Gavin. But the only body that was Moira's size and hair colour wore a white dress. White, except for blood.

'The soldier?'

The woman didn't seem to understand the word. 'Come.'

Nancy staggered up the beach, leaning on her rescuer. Or was the woman leading her to the Japanese, to a firing squad?

The trees were replaced by grass, shoulder high, that cut her arm when she brushed it. Its dried ribbons cut her bare feet, too soft after a year in shoes. Hers must have come off in the sea. The world whirled.

'Come, mem.'

On, through the grass. Palm trees and red soil, and then darker green, one massive tree, its multiple trunks defying the sea wind.

The woman stopped, and slowly helped her sit on the ground, undid the life jacket and eased it over her shoulders.

'Mem, stay. Stay!'

Like a dog, thought Nancy. She nodded. There were things she had to do … she was not sure what but there were *things*. But she would think about those later.

She shut her eyes. This time it was true sleep, fuelled by the coconut water. The sun was high when she opened them again, and a hand was brushing a dark green paste against her side.

'That hurts!'

The woman stopped.

Nancy looked down, winced, then drew the woman's hand back. 'Thank you. Please, keep doing it. Thank you.'

The woman nodded. More of the paste, then leaves, held on with twisted grass, plaited in some way so it wasn't sharp. The woman reached down and brought up a coconut-shell bowl.

Water.

She drank, and felt her head clear slightly. The woman offered her another bowl. Nancy sniffed it, felt her stomach lunge, lifted it anyway and sipped. It seemed to be fish soup, milky in some way, heavily spiced, with many chopped greens. She wondered if it was medicinal, or simply all the woman had.

She put the bowl down. 'Thank you. What is this place called?' Perhaps she'd remember the name from Ben's map.

The woman looked nervous. Had she understood?

Nancy pointed to the soil. 'Here? Called?'

'Pulau Ayu.'

Was it the island's name? Or the word for 'earth'? Or even the woman's name? Nancy tried another tack. 'Have you seen any other mems? Mem and a little boy?' She sketched Gavin's height in the air.

The woman looked at her, her expression now half wary, half concerned.

'This mem was in the water. Like me. The sea.' Nancy pointed towards it. 'Not … not on the beach. That beach.' How much English did the woman understand? If only she had tried to learn Malay while she had been staying on the plantation.

The woman's voice was soft. 'Mem stay? Yes?'

'Yes. I will stay here.'

Her mind was clearer now. She watched the woman vanish into the shadows of the trees. She should find Moira. If she had made it to the island, Moira and Gavin could have too. Or had they been shot?

Five bodies on the beach, what might have been a crate. Five women kicking together might have got here before her. She had heard no shots. Had the soldier stabbed them with a bayonet, one by one, as they crawled from the waves in the darkness?

They should be buried before the vultures found them, or the crabs or whatever bird or animal scavenged around these parts. Or had the tide already carried them away? She tried to think where they had lain in the sand. All at low-water mark, she thought, yes, they would be gone now, drifting with the tides.

Her eyes pricked at the thought of their bodies, forever homeless, then she realised she was too dehydrated to cry.

Was this the island they'd seen from the ship? Or had she drifted somewhere else in the night? If it was the one Moira had pointed out, how big was it? It had looked long, from the ship, but perhaps it was long and narrow. Or even wider than it was long. Were there villages, plantations?

More importantly, how many Japanese were here? Had the soldier on the beach been a scout from a small group, like the ones she had seen the second night of the invasion, or from a larger force? Were the Japanese in control here yet?

The woman would know. She'd ask when she came back. If she came back. She'd ask if there were villages, other beaches where Moira and Gavin might have come ashore. Please, she thought, let them be safe. Not smashed on rocks or eaten by sharks. Not cold and floating in the water. You can't do that to Gavin! Please let Ben be safe too. She paused and added, please, let Gran know that I am alive. And Michael. Make Gran convince Mum and Dad I'm safe. Amen.

She wasn't sure why Gran might know, or Michael either. Just that Gran sometimes *did* know some things that it would seem that she couldn't really know about. Like the day she had arrived back from Charters Towers a week before she was due, and there was Gran with the roast dinner ready, and her favourite apple crumble.

Michael ... Had she imagined how much he understood, that linking without words?

Her brain faded in and out. Michael and gum leaves. She had lost the gum leaf with the rest of her possessions. Would she lose Michael too? Would he think she had drowned, get engaged to someone else ...? What was that poem Mum used to recite, about the sailor who comes home after being shipwrecked and on a desert island for ten years when everyone thought he was dead? The sailor looked through the window and saw his wife happy with another husband, and another's child. The sailor had slipped away, leaving her to her new life ... 'Enoch Arden', that was it.

Enoch Arden had left so his wife could be happy with someone else. But she didn't want Michael to be with anyone else.

She let her hand rest on the life jacket that was lying beside her on the sand. What had Mr Harding said? You must believe.

I believe, she thought. I believe that home is there, the cascades and the pool under the fig tree. I believe that Michael understood, that morning I took him there. I believe that we will be together, me and Michael and Overflow ...

She slept again, or at least the world vanished for a while. She woke to footsteps, too close to clamber to her feet and try to hide.

It was the woman, Gavin in her arms. Sunburnt Gavin, red-skinned, wide-eyed, chubby arms bare, in a strange-looking skirt of flowered cloth. And next to them was Moira.

Chapter 16

Gibber's Creek Gazette, 30 January 1942

Blackout for Gibber's Creek

Police yesterday received orders that all homes and businesses must be blacked out during night-time hours. By seven-thirty pm police had closed all businesses until blackout arrangements can be made.

PULAU AYU, AN ISLAND OFF MALAYA, 30 JANUARY 1942

NANCY

She lay in the not-quite shade of the multi-trunked tree, the sand breathing heat about them. The air was too bright, a reflection from the sea or her own weakness. Nancy still felt too dizzy to decide.

Moira sat beside her, sponging Gavin to cool his sunburn. 'I think we were in the water a couple of hours. I kept trying to keep Gavin out of the water and shelter him from the sun with my skirt. I didn't even know the canoe was there till someone bent down and grabbed my arm. A fisherman. He hauled us into his canoe. Well, it was bigger than a canoe — more like a proper boat. It even had a sail.'

Trust Moira, thought Nancy, to talk about 'proper' boats when the owner was saving her life.

The woman had gone again, leaving them with a wooden bucket of water, and another with more cold fish curry. Now they lay against the tree trunk, only moving as the shade moved. Gavin curled on the sand next to them — it was cooler than on their laps — while Moira tried to cool his flushed skin with a wet handkerchief. He was shadow-eyed and curiously limp.

'I looked and looked, but I couldn't see you. The oil from the ship had spread. There were tiny fires everywhere. I saw one of the ships from the convoy, but it was too far to hail. The fisherman wouldn't paddle over to it either. I don't know if he was scared of bombs or it was too far away.' She felt Gavin's forehead. 'I don't think he's as hot now. Anyway the fisherman paddled up to some rock and told me to stay there, out of sight. That was the first time he spoke any English. The woman came to fetch me today. I think she must be his wife. Or sister. What about you?'

'I washed up on a beach. The woman found me.' She didn't mention the bodies. 'The Japanese are here.'

'I know.'

'You've seen them?'

'No. But why else would they be hiding us, instead of taking us to the authorities? What happened to your side? Did you get hurt by the debris?'

'A soldier shot me when I reached the beach. I pretended he'd killed me.'

'Shot you! How bad is it?'

'Not all that bad. No big hole or bullet, just a chunk out of my side.' She stroked Gavin's cheek lightly, relieved when he grabbed her finger and began to chew it.

'You need a doctor.'

'I'm all right. The woman put some stuff on it.'

'Native muck,' said Moira. 'We should probably wash it off —'

'Don't you touch it.' Suddenly she was furious, fear and relief boiling up with anger. 'Gran makes "native muck". And it works. We use her poultices whenever we cut ourselves. If it hadn't been for you and your prejudices about natives, we wouldn't be here. If you'd been able to face living with a grandmother-in-law who was Aboriginal, we'd have been home safe months ago.'

'What!'

'Ben wanted you to go a year ago! That's why he sent for me!'

'I couldn't go then. You know I couldn't.'

'But you could have gone months ago. You put Gavin in danger ...' And me, she thought. You've kept me from home, from Michael.

'How was I to know the Japanese would invade like that? I thought we'd have weeks of warning. Days at least.'

'We could have kept going to Singapore instead of staying in Kuala Lumpur. We could be home by now!'

Moira said nothing, her eyes on Gavin.

'It's true! You could have killed us all. Gavin too. Just because of your stupid prejudice ...'

'How dare you say I'm prejudiced?'

'Because you are.'

'You stupid child. If I were prejudiced, I'd never have married your brother.'

Her wound felt cold. She wondered if it was bleeding again, under the leaves, decided there was nothing she could do about it. Putting more pressure on it might just dislodge any developing scab. If they were going to die here, she could ask one thing first.

'Moira?'

Moira still looked at Gavin. 'Yes?'

'What did you tell Ben when you found out his grandmother was Aboriginal?'

'That I still wanted to marry him.'

'What?' Nancy rolled towards her, winced. 'You knew about Gran before you married him?'

'Of course.'

She hadn't thought Ben would have married anyone without telling her about his family. But she hadn't been able to believe that Moira would marry a quarter-caste either, not unless she assumed that no one would find out, either in Malaya or back in England.

'He told me at the New Year's Eve dance at the golf club.' Moira's voice was suddenly far away. 'He looked so handsome in his dinner jacket. I wore my white brocade and silver shoes ...'

She blinked as Gavin began to cry. Moira forced herself into a sitting position and held the baby to her breast. 'I hope my milk doesn't dry up. Some of the native women feed their babies till they are two years old. My mother was scandalised when she heard I was feeding him myself, but with all the uncertainty of war ... well, thank goodness I did.'

She looked back at Nancy. 'Ben was so scared of what I'd say. I said, "Is she?" and then, "Are you going to ask me to marry you?" because I was afraid he wouldn't. And he laughed and said, "Only if you're going to say yes."'

'You ... you knew? Then why wouldn't you come to Australia? Why don't you like me?'

'I should have left for Gavin's sake. But it's easy to know that now. I ... I just couldn't leave Ben. What if he was wounded? If he needed me.'

'And me?'

Moira shrugged. 'I don't dislike you.'

'You don't like me either.'

Moira sighed. 'You haven't made it easy. That first afternoon when I tried to get you to put on lipstick before Mrs Anderson's mah jong afternoon ...'

'I said I'd rather paint war stripes on my face than wear lipstick.'

'And that rag of a dress you arrived in. Heaven knows what the District Commissioner's wife thought. But I'd promised Ben I'd do my best with you.'

'You promised Ben!'

'Ben asked me to try to ... to tidy you up a bit. Show you how to behave in society, how to dress.'

'Ben!'

149

'Your brother cares about you. My dear girl, has it ever occurred to you that if you marry that young man you keep writing to — or anyone else of good family — you need to know how to behave in public? Your mother's done her best, but oh dear, even after you had some respectable clothes you'd keep putting on those rags you arrived in to go around the plantation. There was no way to get through to you that some things are acceptable, and some are not. Your mother even wrote to thank me when Ben told her that at least you were wearing dresses and had had a proper haircut.'

'Mum!'

The hurt bit sharper than the bullet. Her mother — her brother — wanted her reshaped as a 'lady'. Had Michael also wanted her to look 'acceptable'? Was that why he had never sent the word 'love'?

No, she thought. Whatever is between me and Michael is honest. But he still might like her to ... to dress well sometimes. And she did know how to dress properly now ...

Vaguely she was aware Moira was still speaking. '... you never even understood the impact your behaviour might have on Ben. A sister who —'

'Won't play the game?'

'Exactly. It reflects on him. Do you have any idea how hard it has been for Ben to succeed, despite his background? The way you dress and behave doesn't just affect him. It reflects on your whole family.'

'Not on you?'

'On me too.' Moira's voice was even. 'People would think I didn't care enough to help you dress properly, do your hair properly, insist you sit like a lady instead of a cowboy ...'

'Drover. Or jackaroo.'

'Jackaroo, kangaroo, what difference does it make? If you had just once *tried* to do the proper thing ...'

Why should I? she thought. What does it matter? But of course it did matter. She had seen how much it mattered. And perhaps you didn't have to play the game all the time, just show that you knew the rules enough that you *could* play it when you wanted to, and ignore it when it didn't suit. Like Michael's mother with gumboots over her silk stockings.

And she did know the rules, and not just the ones Moira had nagged her with. The ones Mum had taught her. The ones she had taken pride in ignoring — make sure your shoes are darker than the hem of your dress; don't wear patent leather after five pm; wear gloves and hat to go to church or town, even if you only put them on after you slide off your horse — thinking that by ignoring them she was proclaiming herself her own person.

But there was no need to proclaim to anyone. She was Nancy of the Overflow, and she'd loved her spotted voile, her poor spotted voile blown to shreds in the sea. For a moment sadness for the dress blended with grief for all those women and children lost to the ocean, a sense of loss so profound that she knew she must shove it away and let it out some other time, when she could bear it.

Gavin burped, bringing up a froth of white. Moira wiped his face with her hand, then wiped that on her dress. 'Thank goodness he's drinking well. And my milk hasn't dried up. I was scared it would. I think his temperature is normal now too.'

The Nancy who returned home now — and she would return, she must return, and Gavin and Moira too — would not be the urchin who wagged school to go adventuring in tatty moleskins. I know how to dress and behave for the Melbourne Cup or a drover's camp, she thought. I am Nancy of the Overflow and I can do *anything* ...

Including survive.

'Moira, I'm sorry.'

'For what?'

'For everything. For ... for not being grateful enough about the dresses, all you tried to teach me. For not getting you to safety.'

'What?' Moira looked at her, shocked. 'I should be apologising to you for not looking after you better. I should have got us on a ship much earlier. To India if we couldn't get to Australia. But if there was any chance at all of seeing Ben, I ... I wanted to be there.'

'It was my job to look after you.'

'I am the older one,' said Moira dryly. 'And a married woman.'

And I am Nancy of the Overflow, thought Nancy. Not Nancy of Malaya. I have been a stranger ever since I arrived on the plantation.

'I'm so sorry,' she said again. 'I promise I will ... do my best from now on. Wear what you tell me to. Put on lipstick as soon as I hear visitors arrive.' She lay on the sand and stared at the blue sky between the treetops. A giggle seeped up.

'What are you laughing about?'

'Here we are on an unknown island without even any shoes between us and I am promising to wear lipstick.'

'I still have my lipstick,' said Moira. 'It's in my pocket.'

And suddenly they were both laughing, weakly, but laughing, as Gavin burped again.

Chapter 17

Dr Joseph McAlpine
AIF headquarters
Singapore
30 January 1942

Mrs Blue McAlpine
Moura
via Gibber's Creek

Blue, my darling,
Well, the 'holiday abroad' has certainly ended. Woke this morning
to find that some blighter had poured a bag of flour on the road to
make an arrow pointing to headquarters for the Jap bombers to follow.
A few of us got rid of it quick smart. Luckily I was at the hospital
when headquarters was hit. Got back to find my hut ashes. But there
are homes deserted all over the place so within an hour I had found
myself quite a palace. I even had a BATH. Luxury of luxuries.
Then put on clean clothes. Well, when I say 'clean' I mean they had
been washed recently. Ironing and starching have been forgotten in this
corner of the army for the last few weeks.

Today we began the battle of Singapore. The causeway to the
mainland has been blown up. All the places where I have spent
the past year are in the hands of the enemy, and I fear many of
the men I have patched up in that time have been taken by the
Japanese too. If only we could patch up the British Army.

I hope to get this letter onto a flight this afternoon. One
advantage of being an MD is that you get all sorts feeling grateful

*to you, including RAAF pilots. Have no idea when I'll be
able to write again, or get another letter to you, and doubt that
any you write to me will reach me. But do keep writing, darling.
Just to know you are writing is almost as good as getting the
letters, and miracles may happen yet, and a whole bundle will get
through. But I don't think there is a miracle big enough to save
Singapore. We can only hope that its evacuation is better planned
than its defence.*

*If you don't hear from me for a while, don't go and think the
worst. I WILL get home again. What do you say we try for twins by
Christmas? It will be hard work, old thing, but someone has to do it.*

*Give my love to Sheba, and to Mah, and Matilda and Tommy,
and tell them to look after you even if you don't think you need
looking after. I know you too well, my darling. I won't say, 'Don't
worry about me,' because you will. I admit I am a bit concerned
myself. But I also know deep within me that I will be home with
you, sitting on the veranda in the dusk, watching the wallabies
drinking at the creek — and don't forget those twins.*

Take care, darling. I love you always,
Joseph

PULAU AYU, 30 JANUARY 1942

NANCY

Light pulsed, throbbed, or was it her wound? Mosquito bites
itched. Her body felt baked in salt. It itched too. But Gavin's tiny
body seemed free of bites. Mosquitoes spread malaria and other
disease. Moira must have sheltered him somehow.

They waited.

The woman returned as the sun began to slip down from
the midday sky. This time a man was with her, wearing black
trousers and a white shirt. He looked impatient, even angry.

'Looks like he's wishing he'd left us to float somewhere else,'
said Moira wryly.

Nancy didn't want to know what the fisherman had seen that had changed his mind.

The woman carried two more buckets; more water in one and, in the other, a hand of bananas, small ones, finger length, and coconut shells filled with some sort of gooey paste. She knelt and held out a coconut shell to Moira.

'Cassava,' said Moira, spooning some up with her finger. She offered it to Nancy. 'You eat, then I'll share the rest with Gavin.' She peeled a banana and held it to Gavin's mouth. He shut his lips and turned his head away listlessly. Moira ate it herself, then took the cassava from Nancy.

The woman and man watched them eat, silent. Nancy sat, self-conscious, and drank some of the water. The man waited till she had finished. 'Nippon here. You must come.'

The woman said something sharply to him, in another language. The man answered angrily. The woman broke in again.

'I think she is prepared to look after us. But the man wants us to give ourselves up to the Japanese,' said Moira.

Nancy was silent. If this was Australia, she could hide in the bush; find food and water; make sure the Japanese never found them. Natives went from island to island in their fishing boats, didn't they? Perhaps fishing boat after fishing boat might even get her to Australia or some place where the Allies still had control.

Could she survive here, or on other islands? If she had been here alone, she'd have risked it. Moira too could probably manage, this new Moira who had taken charge to get them safe from a sinking ship. But Gavin was too small to survive days at sea in a small boat, to live without shelter from rain, mosquitoes.

She looked at the man and the woman, both silent now, watching them. The Germans shot collaborators. She was pretty sure the Japanese would too. These people might die if the invaders knew they had been helping them.

What was safest for Gavin and Moira? Had the killings on the beach been an isolated incident? Would the Japanese shoot them as soon as they surrendered? Or would they take them to a prison camp as Mr Harding had suggested? Was this island even big enough to have a camp on it? It was big enough for the Japanese to bother with, so she had to presume it was. Mr Harding had been right up till now. She had to trust he was right about prison camps too.

You could survive a prison camp, as Mr Harding had done. It occurred to her that the Japanese might be more merciful to meekly surrendering women than they would be to two found skulking around in the jungle.

Nor, if she was honest, was she convinced that she herself could survive on her own in this strange jungle. And if they refused to come, then this man — this kind man, who even if he was scared and angry now had saved Moira's life and Gavin's — might feel he had to tell the Japanese about their presence on the island, in case he put his own family in danger.

She glanced at Moira. Should she tell her about the bodies on the beach?

No. It would only worry her more.

'I think we should go with them. What do you think?'

Moira nodded faintly.

There was really no choice at all.

For some reason she had expected a long walk, dreaded it: her legs still felt as weak as ice cream. But the village was perhaps a mile from the beach, next to a slow seeping river with a wide jetty, and big sheds. No wonder the couple were nervous, she thought, as they walked up the narrow road, with the 'mems' so close to their homes and Japanese authority.

Children crouched by thatched stilt houses, looked at them curiously. Dogs panted in the shade.

The police station was the only concrete building in the village. Two bicycles were parked outside it.

The woman had melted away, somewhere among the houses. The man knocked, opened the door and bowed.

Two Japanese soldiers sat at the big wooden desk. One of them barked out an order.

The man rose from his bow, then pressed Nancy's and Moira's backs to make them bow too.

More words, sharp and angry. Both soldiers stood, seizing their rifles with bayonets fixed to them. The man said something. He backed out of the room without saying anything to Moira and Nancy. The younger of the soldiers followed him to the door, yelled at him, the words sharp, even if unintelligible. He shut the door and looked back at the women and the child.

Nancy rose from her bow. It had hurt her side. She hoped it hadn't made it bleed again. It wasn't going to do her any favours if the Japanese found one of their number had already tried to kill her. More words in Japanese. The tone was different now. The older of the soldiers — he looked no more than twenty, if that, while the other looked about sixteen — pointed to two chairs. They sat.

Two cups of water were placed on the desk. The older guard nodded to them to drink.

They drank.

To Nancy's surprise, the younger officer held a banana out to Gavin. The baby took it, shoved it against his mother's neck, then stuffed the remnants into his mouth.

The soldiers laughed.

It was such a ... human ... response that she felt like crying; she almost believed that maybe everything would be all right, that these men might even let them go, to try to make their way back home. She drank more of the water, watching them, put the cup down at the same time Moira drained hers.

The older one said something: obviously an order.

They stood, Moira holding Gavin. The soldiers picked up their rifles and nodded towards the door. They followed Nancy and Moira out into the hot sun.

Along the road again, out of the village, the soldiers with their rifles behind them. No one spoke to them, or even looked at them. The children had vanished. Only men looked from doorways now, bowing as the soldiers passed.

At least we don't make people bow, thought Nancy, then remembered Moira and Ben's major domo back at the plantation, politely bowing to guests as they arrived. Butlers bowed in moving pictures too. But they were paid to bow. Did that make a difference?

To one side of the road were patches of trees, too scrubby to be called jungle, and more of the long grass she'd seen by the beach, as well as a few coconut palms. The other side seemed to be a plantation, though the trees and vines were unfamiliar. Men who looked Chinese planted rows of seedlings in bare ground. Others chipped at weeds between rows of young trees. It was just as she had thought it might be — their overseers had changed but their lives had not, even though the new regime was only days old.

Once beyond the houses the guards' demeanour changed. They lowered their rifles, wiped sweat from their faces and pushed back their caps. The older one held out his hands for Gavin.

'I don't think you should,' began Nancy, but Moira had already handed him over.

'Snommle ump,' said Gavin, patting the guard's cap. Despite his sunburn, he sounded happier than she had heard him since they had left Singapore.

The soldier bore the child's weight easily. He made a face, laughed again when the baby smiled, said something to his companion. They walked on either side of Moira and Nancy now, talking between themselves. The younger soldier put his cap on Gavin's head, to shade him from the sun.

Another mile. Her salt-soaked feet throbbed and Moira limped, her face flushed. Nancy wondered if she had ever been outside so long without a hat.

Another bend in the road. A tin-roofed warehouse stood in a clearing and a charred patch where something — or many somethings — had been burnt.

The soldier took back his cap. The other handed Gavin to Moira again. They raised their rifles and indicated to the women to walk in front.

The warehouse door was open. They walked inside, the soldiers still behind them, and blinked in the dimness.

Two women sat on bags at the back of the warehouse; a single soldier, no older than the other two, stood guard. He motioned with his rifle for Moira and Nancy to join them.

Had the other women come from their ship? Nancy didn't think so. Both wore shoes and hats which they'd have lost at sea, unless one of the lifeboats had been usable and launched before the ship blew up. The first was young, in her twenties perhaps; the other was elderly, stout and red-faced, too many rings on her fat fingers that may have been a way to keep them with her like Moira's pearls and brooch, which was still fastened to her limp, grubby dress. A case each and a roll of blankets stood nearby.

No one said anything. Which meant, Nancy decided, that the women had been ordered not to speak, otherwise they'd have acknowledged them at least.

They sat down, on the furthest sack.

'Bibbole?' said Gavin in baby speak to the soldier who had carried him. The man ignored him. Gavin looked at the other women then, disappointed in the possibilities for any further entertainment, settled on his mother's lap and chewed her finger.

They waited, heat around them like a blanket. No air moved in the warehouse; neither did the guards.

An engine noise. The guards stood straighter as a car pulled up outside.

Two men in uniform, one older, obviously senior, his face with no expression at all. The other was forty perhaps, with glasses so like the Japanese in the newspaper cartoons that Nancy almost giggled.

If she had giggled, she would have cried. She bit her lip instead.

'You will stand,' said the man with glasses, in clear English, his accent educated and surprisingly like Moira's. 'You will bow to the Japanese officer.'

They stood. They bowed. Evidently the other women had bowed before, as none of them protested.

'Pick up the suitcases. You will march outside in single file, and stand against the wall. You will not speak or you will be shot. You understand?'

Nods.

'Argle,' said Gavin.

The soldiers — and the translator — ignored him. Moira put him over her shoulder, where he would be less inclined to make a noise. Or maybe, thought Nancy, to prevent him from seeing what happened next.

Prison camp? Or are we too much trouble, four women and a baby on what was probably a small island? Was that why the women had been killed on the beach, to save the Japanese the trouble of guarding them?

They walked out into the sunlight. Stood against the wall, the sunlight striking their faces, except the two with wide-brimmed hats.

The officer snapped an order. The three guards raised their rifles.

Nancy closed her eyes, then opened them. If these were her last few seconds, she would live them all.

Overflow, she thought. Michael, remember me when you see the swans on the river. I hope they have a hundred cygnets, and their cygnets have more babies too. Babies that I will never have ...

The officer snapped another order. Nancy watched him, seeing the river too, the young man sitting next to it, the swans and home.

Chapter 18

Gibber's Creek Gazette, 16 February 1942

Singapore Surrenders

The once-mighty Fortress Singapore has fallen to the Japanese. Of the thirty thousand AIF posted there, it is hoped that many, or most, have been evacuated, possibly to Batavia, but as yet there has been no word.

DRINKWATER, 16 FEBRUARY 1942

MICHAEL

He sat on the Drinkwater veranda, the Latin textbook forgotten in his lap.

Singapore had fallen. It seemed wrong to care so much about one person, when tens of thousands, perhaps hundreds of thousands, were killed or missing. It was hardest, perhaps, not to know what to feel: you could not, should not, feel grief until you knew someone was gone from you forever. But he did feel grief, because she was not here. Was it irrational to feel cheated, because the promise of her arrival, and her safety, had not been met?

She should be here, now, down river, at Overflow. For he was still at home, had been saved from school by food poisoning.

Had he been saved by ice cream? The custard must have gone off in the heat before it had been frozen, because his parents and

Mrs Mutton had food poisoning too. Food poisoning meant no train to school, and flat lemonade and grated apple and dry toast for all of them, prepared by Mah McAlpine before she headed off to the biscuit factory each morning.

He'd been up again after two days, but Mum and Dad and Mrs Mutton had been laid low for a fortnight. A fortnight of being able to look at familiar paddocks, gold and comforting, the hot air shimmering above the hills, instead of the claustrophobic walls of school.

Here, at home, it was possible to feel that Nancy might come riding along the river bend; that he might hear her laughter in the murmur of the river. School would not just be a wrench from home this term, but a cutting away of his links with her as well ...

He'd taken over the apple grating, squeezing the lemons and adding sugar and boiled water, persuading Mrs Mutton to stay in bed too. He could tend his parents and Mrs Daggins was fine doing the rough alone, the bathrooms scrubbed, the floors mopped, before she went off to her half-days at the factory.

But Mum and Dad were now back to their usual selves. Which meant that tomorrow or, at the most, in two days' time, they would drive him to the station and the train to school. Meanwhile, he sat on the veranda with his Latin grammar, trying to look studious, but instead looking at the hills, the road, hoping the telephone bell would ring or, better, a car come down the road and it would be Nancy, freshly landed in Sydney by the ship that had picked her up, she'd caught the morning train ...

Even as he thought it a dust cloud appeared. A slow one. Horse, not motorcar. Mrs Flanagan with the mail. Mah McAlpine waved to him as she flashed past the veranda on her bicycle, on her way into town. 'I'll get the mail,' she called. 'Bring it to the house tonight.'

Michael nodded. Like most telephone calls, business letters went to the factory. There might be a letter from one of his mother's friends in Sydney. If there was a letter from Jim, Mah would bring it down ...

Mah's bicycle flashed back down the drive again. She held a letter out, her face grave.

He ran down the steps. 'From Jim?' No, he thought, wrong-coloured envelope.

Mah shook her head.

He took the envelope. No postmark. Which meant this letter hadn't been through the Post Office and stamped at Gibber's Creek. Which meant it was almost certainly from Overflow, too far from town to have a phone. They'd have handed this to Mrs Flanagan, knowing that it would get to Drinkwater by mid-morning.

He said shakily, 'Thank you.'

Mah nodded, her eyes kind. She said, 'Tell your mother I'll be over later. Take care, Michael.'

He nodded, hardly hearing her leave. He sat back in his chair and opened the envelope. Good paper. A teacher's clear strong hand.

Dear Michael,

It is with a heavy heart that I must tell you we have had a telegram from Sydney. The Lady Williams was sunk in a bombing raid. The ships in its convoy picked up no survivors. Nancy's grandmother says that we must not give up hope, and of course we will hope.

The sentence ended abruptly, as if the writer wanted to say more, but couldn't. A new paragraph began:

The telegram arrived the same day as one from the army saying that Ben is 'missing in action'. 'Missing' may mean that he has been taken prisoner, or even been wounded and no one has recorded yet that he is in hospital, which is natural with all that is happening right now.

We will not give up hope for either of our children, but thought that you should know.

163

Please give my regards to your parents. Forgive my breaking the news to you like this, but my family needs me at home now, and I did not want to delay telling you what we knew.

Thank you for your friendship with my daughter. It meant a lot to her. Her happiness was ours.

Yours sincerely,
Sylvia Clancy

It meant a lot to her. She thinks that Nancy is dead, thought Michael, and her daughter-in-law and grandchild too.

No survivors. If there had been three … six … ten people who had escaped from the sinking ship … he might have hoped that she had been … mislaid … one girl among so many evacuees. But *no survivors* had the definite sound of finality about it.

No survivors meant dead.

He could not believe it. No, he would not — his mind accepted that it must be so. But his body felt she was alive. His eyes would not cry, nor his heart begin to grieve.

He had been so certain he'd know if Nancy died. Had thought that what she'd said, there at the cascades that early morning, more than a year ago now, had meant she thought that he would too.

He had been wrong. She was dead.

He had to go inside. Had to tell his parents. Couldn't.

Instead he walked, almost blindly, down the stairs, around the house and through the orchard. Sheba trumpeted at him from her paddock. He ignored her, slipping through the next gate then under the barbed-wire fence, down to the river across the hill and hidden from the house.

His spot.

Not hidden from the world like Nancy's. Just a place that was peaceful, without even sheep to overlook it, the redgums and the curve of reeds, the smooth face of the river.

He looked at the warm clear water above the sandy bottom, the darker water by the soil of the river bend, a pelican slowly paddling, dipping its head under as it fished. How long had his ancestors and hers watched this river? Tens of thousands of years? Hunted ducks or fished, and millennia later, used the water for their stock, to irrigate the lucerne his mother and old Mr Sampson had trialled, and that was now grown throughout the district?

My land, he thought. Her land. If she had to die somewhere — even at sixteen — and he knew that eventually, everyone must die — let it be here, where her bones would feed the trees, her spirit stay with the mountains and the river, where the black swans came in to land.

At first he thought it was a car horn, a honking far away. Then he realised it was coming from above.

He looked up.

It was a swan. It flew like an arrow across the blue, down to the river, landing heavily, gracelessly for such an elegant bird, before recovering and floating, neck arched, as if it had never been elsewhere than on this river.

The pelican watched.

His hands grew warm, and then his heart. He didn't know ...

And then he did. So deep it was impossible not to accept, to believe.

He watched the swan for one more minute as it ducked for food.

Then he strode up the paddock, to the house.

His mother was in the office. A pile of accounts sat on her desk, but her hands held Jim's last letter. It had arrived a week before and been read aloud at the breakfast table. It looked like it had been read many times since.

'Mum?'

She looked up at him. He felt the pressure on him to be two sons now, the slight hunger of her gaze. 'How are you feeling?'

'I'm fine,' he said shortly. He held the letter out to her.

She took it, read it, her face carefully not showing any expression till she had read it all. She stood, and put her arms around his waist. Her head only came to his shoulder now. 'Michael, I'm sorry. So very, very sorry.'

'Yes. But Mum ...' He bit his lip, trying to work out what to say. 'Mum, I don't feel she is dead.'

She nodded. 'I know what it's like. I ... I never told you ... I was engaged once, long before I married your father. He died in the Boer War. I couldn't feel he was dead either. Kept thinking I'd look up and he'd be riding up the drive ...'

No, she had never told him. One day he might ask more. Or wouldn't, perhaps, for it was as his mother he knew her now, needed her now, not the young girl she had once been. 'I don't mean like that. It's not a feeling. I ... I *know* Nancy isn't dead.'

'What do you mean? Have you heard something else?'

His mother had been the one to tell him about the pelicans.

He said flatly, 'I was just down at the river watching a pelican. A swan flew over and then landed on the river. And I knew. Nancy's alive, Mum. She's all right. For now, at any rate.'

Her face went blank, almost as if the real Matilda was far away. At last she said, 'Why do you think seeing a swan means Nancy is all right?'

'Because we talked about it, Nancy and me, down at the river. I told her what you told me about the pelicans. For her it's swans.'

Her look was hard to interpret. 'You remember what I told you about the pelicans?'

'Yes. It ... it works. Sometimes I see them and, well, I know. Her gran told her about the swans being hers. And just now, a swan landed on the river. And I knew.'

'Knew. Or wanted to think you knew?'

'Knew. I ... I'd been thinking she was dead. She didn't feel dead to me, but I've never known anyone who died. Mum ... I need to go to Overflow. Need to tell them.'

'Tell them you saw a swan? Had a feeling that Nancy is alive?'

It sounded stupid. But still he said, 'Yes.'

'Maybe,' she said gently. 'They have their own signs. If they believe in them.'

'Her gran does. I don't know about her mum and dad.'

'Neither do I. There are things that ... let's say that I couldn't have believed, if I hadn't known Auntie Love. Hadn't watched her —' His mother stopped. 'I don't know,' she said. 'It might hurt Nancy's mother even more. Give her false hope.'

'It's not false. And anyway, is any hope so bad?'

'No. Hope is good.' She took a deep breath. 'Any hope is good. I'll come with you.'

'You don't need to.'

'I do. You are going to be telling a mother her daughter is alive. A daughter you met properly only three times, more than a year ago.'

'I know Nancy,' he said evenly.

'And I'm a mother. Nancy's mother will need someone with her. I will be there.'

The Drinkwater gardens had been planted in defiance of the land around them, English trees proclaiming 'this land is mine'.

The Overflow homestead had no formal gardens beyond a row of roses next to the veranda, a wisteria tangled along its edges and a vast elderly mulberry tree with branches as broad as a horse's back. Paddocks out the back contained more fruit trees, but in no neat pattern, and more ordered fields of lucerne, corn, potatoes, tomatoes and other vegetables so necessary to feed Australia in this third year of war, and all produce possible to send to evade the German blockade of England or feed the armies.

There was no avenue of trees along the driveway here, to both welcome visitors and declaim the importance of those who lived beyond, only a strip of gums and wattles left outside the paddocks, of all ages, tall or little as they chanced to grow. The gate was an ordinary farm gate, except for the sign that said, in neat letters still wet from the paintbrush, *This house supports a prisoner of war.*

Ben, he thought. They would send cakes to the Red Cross, hoping that some, at least, would get through, if not to him, then to other prisoners. Like his mother, the women here would make jam, knit baby clothes, turn old curtains into toys, anything that could be sold to raise money for POWs. He wondered if Overflow, like Drinkwater, donated a portion of its income each year to the Families of POW Relief Fund. So much more support would be needed, he realised, now that Australians were being captured on yet another front.

The house was much as he remembered it from his previous visit, large, but not Drinkwater large, planned and comfortably imposing. This house had begun as the shack that was the shearers' cook shed now; had grown room after room as wives joined the clan, and children arrived, another cottage joined to the main house by a breezeway that was then enclosed into a veranda, which in time grew rooms behind. But the yellow paint was fresh, applied perhaps by a jackaroo off to war, leaving his mark upon the place like a wombat leaving its scent in its territory. Or maybe, thought Michael, kept freshly touched up from tins long stored in the shed, to welcome home the children.

Two children, both swallowed by the war. Ben missing. Nancy ...

Somewhere.

They dismounted, tethered their horses to a post. In the shade of the veranda a woman sat on an old armchair, two dogs at her feet. She must have been there as they rode in, but Michael hadn't noticed her in the shadows till now; nor had her dogs barked. Seventy at least, dark-skinned, white-haired, straight-backed, heavy around the arms and hips, a green dress and green flat shoes. She seemed older than the woman he had seen only weeks earlier, before Christmas. But she still looked as tough and comfortable as an old boot.

He saw his mother give the half-smile of sympathy. 'Mrs Clancy, I was so very, very sorry to hear about Nancy and Ben and his family.'

'Yes. Well. Thank you,' said old Mrs Clancy. Her face was impossible to read.

'You know my son, Michael?'

The dark-skinned woman nodded. 'We've met. How is your Jim, Matilda?'

'Good. Hates army food, which Tommy says is the normal reaction of any young man in good spirits. We had a letter from him last week …' She stopped, probably realising that mentioning a letter from her thriving son might not be tactful.

Mrs Clancy nodded, her face impassive. 'You'll be wanting to see Sylvia. She's been out checking the raddling harnesses on the rams. Won't be long. My son's down at William's. They're forming a local Volunteer Defence Corps, working out where to get the Japs if they try to come here. You should join it,' she said to Michael.

'I've joined the one at Gibber's Creek.' When I'm home in the holidays, he thought, not stuck with cadets and marching practice and maths homework while the rest of the world fights a war on my behalf. But he was glad Mr Clancy wasn't here, angry, perhaps, at what he might perceive as false hope given to his wife and mother.

'The Defence Corps is men only,' Mrs Clancy added to his mother. 'Though I reckon you or I could outshoot the blokes around here any day of the week. Haven't any of those blokes seen how a dingo protects her young? Ten times fiercer than a male and unpredictable with it. Come in and I'll put the kettle on.' Michael noticed she didn't ask why they had come. Nor did he think she had been crying.

The dogs stayed on the veranda, snapping at flies while keeping an eye on the newcomers.

It was cool inside the house, smelling of roast mutton, rosemary and pumpkin. Mrs Clancy nodded at the living room. 'Sit yourselves down there. Too hot in the kitchen with the stove on.'

'Can I give you a hand?'

Old Mrs Clancy waved his mother into the living room. 'You rest your feet.'

The living room was large, possibly the most recent addition, created for the extended family now flung far across the world. Two sofas with velvet roses, four matching armchairs; polished wooden floors with Chinese flowered silk rugs; a piano with too many photographs on top to see any but the front ones clearly: a young man in uniform, and Nancy.

It hadn't been there when he'd been in this room before. Nor was it the photograph she'd sent him from Malaya — in a white linen dress and white hat with blue ribbons, the one he kept in his wallet. Nor was she wearing the dress she'd worn the last time he'd seen her.

This must have been taken in Brisbane perhaps, or even Charters Towers. Nancy, in boots and jodhpurs and a man's old hat, on a horse among the gums. They were thin-topped trees, hot-country trees, not the trees of here or Drinkwater. But the photo still captured the heart of who she was. Nancy of the Overflow.

He looked at the other pictures. One of Ben Clancy, which had been here before, in a groom's morning suit with a laughing woman in white froth at his side. Moira, he thought, the woman Nancy had gone to help. Two more recent photos, one of Ben with a bald baby, the other a studio portrait of Moira holding the baby in a long white lace christening robe in her arms. This photo was surrounded by a black ribbon. The others were not. For Moira and Gavin had been declared dead. Ben was declared 'missing', and that could mean all sorts of things in the chaos of Malaya. But Nancy had been declared dead too.

Why was Nancy's photo bare?

His mother stood to help Mrs Clancy with the tray. He realised he'd been staring at the photo. He helped unload the tray: flowered china cups and saucers; a silver teapot, obviously kept for company; a silver sugar pot, the sugar lumpy from long keeping; a silver tea strainer; a milk jug that matched the cups; a flowered plate heaped with pikelets.

'Black, thank you,' he said at the same time as his mother. 'Three sugars,' he added.

Old Mrs Clancy nodded. 'That's the way I take it too. Still can't get used to milk in tea after the long paddock.'

He didn't say he'd never been droving the long paddock, never been out for more than a day rounding up stock; that he drank his tea black because the milk at school sat in the sun till the boys on duty lugged it in for breakfast, and so it had mostly gone and curdled like vomit in the cup.

He helped himself to pikelets, still warm from the pan — how had she managed to make pikelets so fast? — spread with melon jam. No butter. He supposed that was a habit of her droving days too.

'Dry up your way?' asked old Mrs Clancy.

His mother swallowed her bite of pikelet. 'Not too bad. Got twenty points last week. How about you?'

'Twenty-two.' Mrs Clancy's tone held the quiet satisfaction of any farmer who gets slightly more rain than her neighbours. 'But we're doing well enough. Every river channel here grows grass knee high, except when it's in flood.'

'What do you do then?' asked Michael.

'Wait it out. We get cut off for months sometimes. Get the stock up to higher ground. Always get plenty of notice when the river's going to rise.'

For a moment he thought she meant her family lore, the kind his mother sometimes talked about, explaining how it would rain after the termite queens flew. But then she said, 'Someone always rides down with a message from upriver. Takes about a day for the flood to reach here from Drinkwater, the way the river winds.'

He had nothing to say to that. Nor it seemed had his mother. He ate another pikelet to soak up the silence. It seemed wrong to speak of Nancy until her mother, at least, arrived.

'Heard that the Murphy girl from Riverbend is walking out with Terry Rogers.'

'More staying in than walking out.' His mother sounded relieved to be safely deep in gossip. 'Those Rogers boys could charm a kookaburra out of a tree. You remember his cousin, Ted Higgins?'

'Amy Higgins's third boy? No, I tell a lie, the fourth?'

'He joined up last month. Navy, can you imagine that? Never seen the sea in his life. He said, "Mum, I've joined the navy to see the world." And she said —'

'You'll see the sea.' Mrs Clancy completed the ancient joke.

A door slammed. A voice called, 'Mother?'

'In here.'

In the dark of the hallway, the younger Mrs Clancy looked like Nancy until she came inside — small-boned, brown from the sun — but her hair was red, not black. Michael stood up politely.

The woman looked tired; or rather as if life had been drained out of her, and she was forcing herself to continue. She froze as she saw them, one tanned hand touching her heart. She said breathlessly, 'Michael. Matilda. Has there been news?'

'No,' said his mother quickly. 'Not … not really.'

'What do you mean, not really?' Nancy's mother sank into one of the armchairs. Soldiers on leave, home after they'd been wounded, could bring back news the censors had forbidden in letters. Families passed news along. But not news like this, thought Michael.

For once Michael's mother seemed lost for words.

Get it over with, he thought. This is for Nancy …

'I saw a swan,' he said clearly. 'On the river at Drinkwater. We … we don't get swans there normally. Nancy said …' He took a breath, and forced himself to continue, no matter how stupid it sounded. 'Nancy told me the swan was a … a sort of sign for her.' He looked at Nancy's mother and her grandmother. 'I don't know exactly what the swan this morning means. But I know it means something. Means she is alive, at least, maybe thinking of home. And I had to come and tell you because …' He shrugged. 'Because.'

His mother sat quietly on the sofa beside him, her face carefully devoid of emotion. Old Mrs Clancy's face was expressionless too. Michael thought Nancy's mother's was as well, then saw the tears running down her face, untouched, unchecked.

Old Mrs Clancy reached over and took her daughter-in-law's hands. 'Means just what you think it means, I reckon.'

'I think … I know that she is alive.' Michael tried to sound firm.

'And Ben? Moira and Gavin?' Nancy's mother's voice sounded like a small nail scratching in a tin, her will to hold a piece of hope so strong, thought Michael, that she would clutch at any offering.

'I don't know. I'm sorry.' He felt helpless suddenly in a room full of so much hope and grief. He looked at old Mrs Clancy, impassive in her armchair. She gave him an almost imperceptible nod.

'And Nancy'll come home safe?' Nancy's mother looked as if anything he said would be as certain as an entry in an encyclopaedia.

Michael looked at his mother, her posture perfect, her hands in her lap. At old Mrs Clancy, watching him, and Nancy's mother, her face so eager it hurt. What I believe happened by the river either means everything or nothing, he thought. And either way I cannot tell these women a lie, give them comfort just to please them. For two of them at least would see the lie in his face, his voice. He suspected the third would too.

'I don't know,' he said honestly. 'I only know Nancy is alive now. Was alive this morning when I saw the swan. But I think … if … anything bad happened to her, I mean worse —' he couldn't use the word 'dead' '— then I'd know that too.'

'And we would too,' said old Mrs Clancy to Nancy's mother. 'You and me both.' She stood and hugged her daughter-in-law's shoulders hard, briefly. 'I'll make us a fresh pot. You can help me,' she said to Michael's mother. It was the first time Michael could remember anyone ordering his mother to do anything. But she stood, and followed the old woman.

The younger Mrs Clancy scrubbed her hand across her eyes. 'I … I don't know what to think. I want to hope. I so want to hope.' She looked up at him. 'Mother, well, she knows things. But this is more than if it's going to rain next summer. That's mostly just knowing the land well. This is ...' She shrugged, unable to find the words. 'It's not even about the land.'

'It's about someone who belongs to it.'

Nancy's mother shook her head. 'Predicting rain or bushfire or grasshopper plagues is a form of science. This ...' Again she shook her head. 'I just don't know. But you were sure enough to come and tell us. That mustn't have been ... easy.' She made an effort to change the subject. 'Nancy told us she was writing to you.'

'Do you mind?'

She stared at him, then gave a small incredulous smile. 'You and Nancy? You are a good young man. Kind. Courageous enough to come here today. You and your brother are also the heirs to the wealthiest estate in the district. In New South Wales perhaps. Drinkwater, the factories ... You must have girls lining up for you in Sydney.'

It had never occurred to him that the eager sisters of his friends might be influenced by his parents' money. 'None of them are Nancy of the Overflow.'

Mrs Clancy looked out the window. 'Nancy was born just after her grandfather had his first heart attack. We put her in his arms, all red and big, big eyes. She was with him six years later when he died. Out mustering cattle, with her on her pony. She said he just dropped to the ground. But he still knew her for a few seconds at the end. She was the last thing that he saw. She said he smiled as he died, old Clancy of the Overflow. It was my husband's idea to call her Nancy. "How about we call her Nancy, Dad?" he said. "Close as we can get to Clancy." And the old man smiled and smiled. Don't think that smile washed off for weeks. So the name stuck.' Her smile became almost a real one. 'Even though it's embarrassed her all her life. But that was what they called my father-in-law. Not Ned Clancy. Clancy of the Overflow.' She met his eyes now. 'Did she tell you about the letter?'

'The one written by Banjo Paterson? Yes.'

'Her father read it to me the night he asked me to marry him. Wanted me to know what the world might think, about a white woman marrying a half-caste. I've never regretted it. Regretted what people made of it, sometimes. But never for one second regretted saying yes that night.'

'You want to know if I would feel the same?'

She nodded. 'Nancy can pass for white. But people round here know she isn't. That'll mark your children, no matter how pale their skin turns out to be. Can you cope with that?'

'My children probably won't be any darker than me. My great-grandmother was Aboriginal too.' He hesitated, realising that his children might inherit darker skin from both sides of the family.

Children. He was sixteen years old, had only talked to the girl he loved, really talked, twice. And she was who knew where, only that it was away from him.

Nancy's mother blew her nose. 'She will come back. Thank you for coming. I didn't know till I said that about your children just now. But Nancy will return to Overflow.'

Chapter 19

Gibber's Creek Gazette, 30 January 1942

Highway Robbery in Main Street!

There was a 'hold-up' in Main Street last Saturday when a band of desperate-looking bushrangers held up passers-by, demanding their money or their life. Luckily for our citizens, they were pupils of Gibber's Creek Central School, raising money for the Prisoners of War Fund.

One of the 'victims', Councillor Bullant, congratulated bushranger Rodney Ellis (10), son of Councillor Ellis, on his clever disguise. Rodney replied that this was what he always wore on Saturdays, and said that his father had instructed him to say that a councillor's life was worth more than threepence, especially if they were fat.

The 'bushrangers' raised twenty-three pounds, four shillings and tuppence halfpenny.

Well done, Gibber's Creek Central School.

PULAU AYU, 30 JANUARY 1942

NANCY

'You will march,' said the translator.

Nancy felt the shock almost as strongly as the shot she had been expecting.

'You will not speak.'

'Where are we going?' The words were out before she knew she was going to say them. Her normal reaction at being told what to do, she realised as the guard's bamboo cane struck her across the face, was to do the opposite.

Her face stung as if a hundred wasps had bitten it. The translator looked at her impassively, his glasses glinting. 'You are being taken to a camp. A comfortable camp where you will be safe. Now you will march.'

They marched, even the elderly woman with her suitcase, or rather straggled, one of the guards in front, one behind, the translator walking more or less beside them.

More of the strange short trees laid out like a plantation. Chinese men chopping wood who glanced at them, then quickly, carefully looked away.

The air grew thick with moisture. Nancy's feet hurt, even though the road was mud, not rock. Moira hobbled, her feet bare too. Gavin began to cry, a thin wail. He needed a drink. They all needed a drink, a rest. But a baby would get ill, might die. She had to help. She couldn't help. She had to try.

'Please may we stop to give the baby a drink?' She waited for the cane to strike her again.

The translator glanced at the guard, gave an almost imperceptible nod. The cane flashed down again. But this time it landed on her clothed back, so lightly it hardly hurt at all. Another blow came, even softer than the first.

'You will sit. The baby will be fed,' ordered the translator.

They sat on the muddy side of the road, except for Nancy, who stood in front of Moira to give her privacy. Gavin whimpered, then was quiet. Nancy leant over her shoulder and was relieved to see he was feeding well, clapping his feet together in the way he always did when he was pleased with life.

On the other side of her the younger woman opened her suitcase. She pulled out a pair of golf shoes, well made of solid leather, and a pair of golfing socks. She passed them silently to Moira, glancing nervously at the guard.

Moira nodded her thanks. The shoes looked slightly too big for her. But better too big, thought Nancy, than too small. The younger woman gave Nancy a small shrug, as if to say those were the only other shoes she had. The older woman gave a small sympathetic nod as well. But if she had spare shoes, they'd be far too small for me, thought Nancy. Her feet might ache, but at least they wouldn't get blisters, which could so easily become infected.

At last Gavin finished. The guards and the translator stood. They too, it seemed, had been glad of the rest in the heat. They marched again, Moira holding Gavin over her shoulder to burp him.

Water, thought Nancy wearily. Please, please, a drink of water soon. A proper bed and food. Let the camp be around the next bend ...

Another bend. Another.

Then there it was.

She stared, her mind unable to accept it.

Two houses, one a comfortable-looking, verandaed dwelling, a plantation owner's or manager's, with a smaller house next door. A Japanese officer sat on a chair on the veranda, but made no sign that he had seen them. There were shrubs in front, bougainvilleas that sprawled over a stump. But behind ...

The area behind the houses had been fenced into a neat rectangle, enclosed in rolls of barbed wire, too tall to climb over, too wide to crawl through. Inside was mud, pale red mud, and three buildings. The first looked solid though small, two rooms perhaps, a bamboo frame and a proper suspended floor to let the breezes through and an outdoor kitchen next to it, the kitchen paved with rocks and a small awning above. A huddle of women sat around the open fireplace, intent on something on the ground, except for one large woman reclining in an incongruous green velvet armchair.

The next building was a storeroom, perhaps, with a tin roof, bamboo and thatch walls. The third might have been a garage, with thatch walls that didn't quite meet the bamboo frond roof.

A gate ... a quite substantial gate. One of the guards opened it and gestured them inside.

The guards left. The translator too.

The women stood there, unable to talk. Shock, weariness, disbelief.

'I wouldn't keep a dog in this,' said the older woman. 'Mrs Barry Harris,' she introduced herself. 'Mrs Deirdre Harris. This is Mrs Neville Montrain. Sally Montrain.'

'Pleased to meet you, Mrs Harris,' said Moira. 'This is my sister-in-law ...'

Nancy hardly listened to the introductions. The other women had seen them now. The big woman rose from her armchair. She was perhaps sixty, not just tall but so wide Nancy wondered how she had fitted in the chair, rolls of fat at her wrists, her ankles as thick as most people's knees above neat shoes and stockings ... real stockings. She even wore lipstick, as well as ropes of pearls, assorted brooches, bracelets, rings and what Nancy realised were more rings threaded on a gold chain about her throat.

The bejewelled mountain spoke. 'Good afternoon. I am Mrs Hughendorn. My husband and I own this plantation.' The voice was loud enough, the English vowels clear enough, to be heard a dozen paddocks away. She spoke in the present tense, not as if all she had — even perhaps her husband — had been taken from her.

'Good afternoon ...' began Moira.

Mrs Hughendorn held up her hand. 'I think introductions can wait for ...' she hesitated, 'after dinner. We are having a little trouble lighting the fire. You are in building number three.' She gestured to the shed.

'But ...' began Sally.

Mrs Hughendorn was examining Nancy, her eyes lingering on the black hair, brown eyes, newly tanned skin. She is wondering if I am Eurasian, thought Nancy. 'I'm afraid it is the only place left. There are already nine of us. There is no space in the other buildings even for a bed.'

Beds, thought Nancy. At least we have beds. She hoped they had not been relegated to the shed because of the colour of her skin.

'Put your things inside and join us.' Mrs Hughendorn lowered her voice to a clear, well-bred roar. 'Keep an eye out for the guards though. The taller one will steal anything. Even the blanket while you sleep.'

'They come in while you sleep?' asked Sally.

'Tie the blanket to your big toe.' It sounded so ridiculous, so impossibly regal coming from the large woman, that Nancy would have giggled, if she had not been so tired. Even her bones seemed tired, her brain wanting the blank of sleep or at least a rest from terror.

Mrs Hughendorn descended again into her armchair. The armchair seemed to sigh, but bore it dutifully. The four women trudged over to the shed.

A doorway. No door. Two rows of short, narrow bamboo beds, four in each row, with bamboo slats for a base. No mattresses, no bedding. Dirt floor. A faint smell of petrol. And another more basic stench from not far away.

'It's grim, isn't it?' Another woman had come up behind them. She held out a tanned hand to Nancy. Michael's mother shook people's hands, but this was the first time Nancy had seen any other woman shake hands. 'I'm Nurse Rogers. Elizabeth Rogers. There are three of us nurses in Hut Number Two. Australian. We ran an out-clinic from Singapore. Had the bad luck to be here when the Japs landed.'

'How long ago was that? I'm Nancy Clancy,' added Nancy. 'This is my sister-in-law, Moira Clancy, and her son, Gavin. We're Australian too. And this is Mrs Harris and Mrs Montrain.'

'Pleased to meet you. Though not under quite these circumstances. We've all been here just over three weeks, apart from you. You've got bedding?'

Sally and Mrs Harris nodded. 'Moira and I haven't,' said Nancy. 'And there's nothing for Gavin.'

Sally smiled and reached out for the baby. She examined him half professionally, half clucking as he grinned and pulled at her hair. 'You're quite a young man, aren't you, if you can smile at a time like this? Have you come from one of the other islands?'

'The ship we were on sank.'

'Any other survivors?'

'Not that I know of.' She didn't mention the bodies on the beach. The horror was too recent. Nor did she want to burden the others with the terror that death might come to them suddenly, at the whim of a Japanese soldier. Besides, if the Japanese knew that someone had witnessed the atrocity, they might decide to silence them — and anyone else who knew about it.

'We've got some spare bedding — they let us bundle up everything we could carry at the clinic. We looked like a row of porters, but it's been useful. There's mosquito netting for you at least, young man,' she added to Gavin. 'I'd better get back to what passes for dinner. If we can get the fire going before the rain arrives. Oops, too late,' as the air poured out its moisture, sluicing across the roof. Drips wriggled down the insides of the walls and a few heavy splodges on the beds.

'Buckets!' yelled Nurse Rogers into the deluge. 'Got to remind the others to put out the buckets when it rains.' She added more quietly to Nancy, 'We only get four buckets full, for drinking. Now at least you can have a drink.'

'Bathroom?' asked Moira hopefully.

Nurse Rogers pointed to a concrete channel at the edge of the compound that had once perhaps watered the servants' vegetable gardens. 'The guards pour a few buckets of water down that just before dark for us to wash in. It's pretty foul. I think it's the water they've already used for bathing.'

Nancy's skin itched again. Dam— *bother* it, she thought. She stepped out into the downpour, felt the fresh water drench her hair, her skin, her dress. It felt cold and fresh and wonderful. She held up her arms and let the water trickle down her skin.

'Nancy!' said Moira.

'Come on out! Bring Gavin! Get the salt off your skin. We'll soon dry off.'

Moira hesitated. Suddenly she grinned. She took Gavin from Nurse Rogers and stepped out into the rain. Gavin shrieked an objection, then stopped, puzzled at his mother's and aunt's grins. His fuzzy baby hair plastered itself to his scalp.

The downpour stopped. For a few seconds Nancy could see a white curtain sweep across the compound, then it was gone.

'Now we'll never get the fire lit.' To Nancy's surprise, Nurse Rogers sounded as though she was almost in tears. Surely a woman as capable as this wouldn't cry over one spoilt meal.

They trudged after her, through the mud, over to the outdoor kitchen. The other women huddled back, under the awning, except for two kneeling by the fire pit. Mrs Hughendorn, still in her armchair, put down an umbrella. She looked at Nancy and Moira disapprovingly. 'Miss Clancy, Mrs Clancy, I should make one thing clear. We may not have much here, but we do not let the side down.'

'Mrs Hughendorn, I'm so sorry,' said Moira. 'We have been in a shipwreck.' For a moment her voice shook. She visibly straightened herself. 'We were in the sea for many hours and we were just so desperate to wash off the salt. Particularly off Gavin.'

Mrs Hughendorn's gaze softened slightly as she looked at Gavin. She looked at Nancy again, and her eyes narrowed. 'Would you like to sit on the end there, Miss Clancy.' It was not a question. She gestured imperiously. 'Mrs Clancy, there is a seat up here, if you and your son would like to join me.'

'There' was at the far end of the line of blocks of wood, next to a Eurasian woman, perhaps thirty years old. Banished to social oblivion, thought Nancy, as she suppressed a slightly hysterical giggle. 'Mrs Thomas Addison,' said the woman quietly. She looked Chinese, thought Nancy, black hair drawn back into a neat French knot. 'My husband is with the Volunteers. He's the port agent here, for the gambir.'

'Gambir?'

Mrs Hughendorn interrupted her cross-examination of Moira to fix Nancy with a steely eye. She's even wearing fresh lipstick, thought Nancy half admiringly.

'Gambir is the major product of these islands. So useful for tanning, silk dying. The natives chew it too. My husband and I have owned the plantation here for the past seven years, though I am afraid the competition from the Chinese cartels,' the eye was now fixed on Mrs Addison, 'has made it less profitable than it should be. And we have a good acreage in pepper too, of course.' Mrs Hughendorn made it sound as if excluding pepper vines from one's plantation was a worse sin than wearing diamonds at a formal luncheon.

'Of course,' murmured Nancy.

Mrs Hughendorn's frown deepened. 'Enough of that. We need to get the fire lit. Now.'

One of the two women kneeling shook her head. She seemed close to tears. 'I'm sorry, Mrs Hughendorn. We've used ten matches, and there are only twenty left. It would just be wasting them to try again. You can't light wet wood.'

'Yes, you can,' said Nancy.

They all stared at her. She flushed.

'Well, you can,' she added.

'You sound very sure of yourself,' said Mrs Hughendorn. 'Unfortunately we can't waste matches for you to show us your, ahem, skill.'

'Half a match,' said Nancy. 'Do you have a knife? No? Doesn't matter. I'll use my teeth.'

She heard rather than saw Moira give a small sigh next to Mrs Hughendorn. She took the matchbox from one of the kneeling women, bit the wood end of the match in two, then peeled it carefully in half. She put both halves in the box for safekeeping.

Now, tinder ... She looked around. A pile of sweepings in a corner, leaves and flower petals, the usual compound accumulation of the day before, though this looked like it might be a full two weeks' worth. She hunted under the pile and found what she was looking for — dry leaves and twigs.

She examined the wood. It was unfamiliar and too thick to burn well, but as she thought, only the outside was wet. They'd have to split it to expose the dry part. 'I need a rock,' she said abruptly.

'Nancy ...' began Moira warningly.

She was going to alienate these proper mems. She knew it. But she was hungry. Gavin was hungry, despite Moira's milk. Moira might not be able to keep feeding him if she didn't have food. Now. And the night was going to be chilly. Despite her assurances that they'd soon dry, they needed a fire, Gavin most of all.

'A rock,' she repeated.

She looked down at the rock paving, used her fingers to prise up a stone, then struck it hard on the others. It split, just as she hoped. She held up a block of wood on its end, put the jagged end of the rock next to it, then used another block of wood to bash the rock. The wood split. She split that half into quarters, then the quarters into eighths. The rock's edge was almost blunt now, but she was able to cut up a second block.

She glanced around. The women watched her silently.

She parted the damp ash in the fire pit, made a small tent of split wood, filled it with dry leaves and twigs, then placed some of the larger bits of wood propped up against the tiny structure. She reached for the matchbox, sheltered the half-match with her cupped hands as she struck it against the box, next to the tinder. It flared, fast and hot.

'It will burn itself out, I'm afraid,' proclaimed Mrs Hughendorn.

Nancy said nothing. The fire continued to flare, higher and hotter, the flames biting into the larger hunks of wood now. She put on some larger pieces, watched them steam then catch alight, then hesitated. 'Do we have plenty of wood?'

'The one thing you do have on a gambir plantation is wood,' said Mrs Hughendorn, a new note in her voice now, and difficult to read. Perhaps Mrs Hughendorn herself did not know what was proper to feel towards a hoyden who could make fire from wet wood and a rock, but a fire they so badly needed. The big woman leant forwards and put her hands towards the blaze. Moira edged her block of wood towards the fire, the warmth of her body on one side of Gavin, the fire on the other.

Nurse Rogers silently handed Nancy the cooking pot. Nancy peered in it. Chunks of what looked like sweet potato, some sort of greens that smelt like rotten cabbage, a scatter of sago floating in the water. 'Nothing else?' she asked quietly.

'No,' said Nurse Rogers. The one word said it all. Explained why a woman might cry at the thought of losing even a few mouthfuls of warm food. 'This is what we've had for two weeks. Sometimes cassava, or more sago. A couple of coconuts. No fish or meat.'

'But ... but we can't eat this for three meals a day,' protested Moira.

'Two meals,' said Nurse Rogers expressionlessly. 'Breakfast after roll call. Make sure you bow low. You're beaten if you don't bow low enough. We've asked for more food.' She shrugged. 'That gets a beating too.'

Nancy put the pot on the fire, watched the edges of the water sizzle in the heat. Think of home, she thought, with a brief prayer of thanks to Mr Harding. Of Michael, laughing by the river bank as he fed Sheba apples. Of the wedge-tailed eagle, dark against the sky, the bleat of sheep from the far paddocks. Think of home and I will get there.

She looked through the rising heat shimmer at Moira and Gavin, huddled towards the fire. And my family will get there too.

Chapter 20

Gibber's Creek Gazette, 23 February 1942

Damage Still Unknown from Japanese Strike on Australian Mainland

There is still no update on the damage wreaked by the two
hundred enemy planes that attacked Darwin. The Prime
Minister, Mr Curtin, stated, 'We are Australians, and will
fight grimly and victoriously.'

On page 2: Australia refuses a British request to divert the
7th Division troops returning home to help defend Australia
to save Rangoon in Burma.

Australian Military Forces
District Records Office
RAS Showground, Sydney
27 February 1942

Mrs Joseph McAlpine
Moura
via Gibber's Creek

Dear Madam,
I have been directed by the Minister for the Army to advise you
that no definite information is at present available in regard
to the whereabouts or circumstances of your husband, Captain
Dr Joseph Alistair McAlpine, 8th Division headquarters AIF,
and to convey to you the sincere sympathy of the Minister and

the Military Board in your natural anxiety in the absence of news
concerning him.

You may rest assured, however, that the utmost endeavour
will continue to be made through every possible source, including
the International Red Cross Society. In the meantime it would
be appreciated if you could forward full particulars to this office
as quickly as possible of any information you receive from any
other source, as it may be of the greatest value in supplementing or
verifying the official investigation which is being made.

Yours faithfully,
(B.J. Smythe, Major)
Officer in Charge of Records

OVERFLOW, NEW SOUTH WALES, AUSTRALIA, 2 MARCH 1942

BRUCE CLANCY

Bruce Clancy stared across the paddock. Six hundred head of cattle gazed back at him hopefully. He wondered briefly whether they'd watch him so intently if he did a song and dance routine. No actor on the stage ever had an audience that watched you so attentively as a mob of Herefords waiting for their hay.

They still had grass enough, despite the drought. But the sky stared down at him, an unrelenting blue.

Yet why should the sky feel pity for the people below it? There was no malice in a drought. It simply was. He had a feeling the land — this land — was better for it, hard as it was to live through it. The weak died; the strong, the drought-hardy, survived. Leaves fell and made soil so new trees could grow.

Overflow's grass now was in the channel country where the river spread in a flood. If the cattle stayed in the channels too long, they'd compact the ground, sour it with their droppings. The hay was to lure them away from the river and its channels, to eat the tussocks here, after they'd had their taste of hay, drinking from the water trough, the windmill spinning away to fill it.

His mother had advised him to ride a drought like an eagle, letting the hot air carry him past it, watching, learning, but not letting the pain of what he saw hurt him. His father's response to a drought had been to head to 'the long paddock', taking their stock up to where the rain had been more kind, for months or years if necessary. Dad was happiest in the saddle, with the stars for a ceiling. But Mum belonged here. And Ben and Nancy for all their roving ...

The pain he had not let himself show to his wife and mother hit him like a ten-ton truck. He sat on the hard ground and let himself sob, deep, tearless cries. And the cattle watched, curious again, because this wasn't what humans did. They dumped hay from trucks or called, 'Houp!' and moved you on. They did not sit and make noises, or at least not by themselves.

The sobs finished. He stood, shaken. He had never lost control like that before. Had been the one who was sensible, who'd saved his pay and bought a farm, who'd built up the stock while Dad was off gazing at his stars and listening to the trees.

The protector. But he had failed to protect what was most dear, his daughter and his son. Ben had been so tiny when Mum had put him in his arms, red-faced and annoyed at what the world had put him through. He had expected the new baby to be a sort of cross between him and Sylvia, or maybe just a generic baby, a bit like a calf was just a calf, pretty much. But Ben had been an individual already.

And Nancy. You'd swear she was already gazing around with interest, taking it all in. For some reason he'd never worried about her, not when she jumped out of a tree and broke three toes, which taught her not to jump out of thirty-foot wattle trees; nor the time she'd headed off up the gorge to collect wild honey from a nest she'd seen as a surprise for her mum and gran. She'd been eight, and they hadn't been bees, but paper wasps. She'd come flying back stark naked as the wasps had been crawling all over her clothes, but not a single sting.

He hadn't even worried when she'd ridden off to Charters Towers. She had too much of the old man in her. She'd be back, like Dad was. Do wild things, but do them sensibly. If wasps attack you, cover your face and run, then take your clothes off …

Was Nancy dead? Mum said no. Sylvia said no too, but that was different. Sylvia would believe her daughter alive for the next twenty years, forty, however long they both might live, unless she saw her body. And that could never happen.

Did he have two children, or one, or none? He knew one thing and that only.

He had failed. For the duty of a father was to keep your kids alive; and happy and fulfilled. He'd thought he hadn't made such a bad fist of that bit.

But he was wrong. Nancy and Ben were gone.

'And when I'm gone you will be ownerless,' he said to the cattle. To the farm he had worked for, saved for, had ridden and fenced. All of it nothing if there were no children or grandchildren to love it after him. And there was nothing he could do. Nothing.

Except hang on. For Sylvia's sake. For Mum's. And for the flickering light of hope in the black blanket of the last few weeks, that all he did now, might still, please, he thought, please let it be for my children.

Chapter 21

Gibber's Creek Gazette, 5 March 1942

Aircraft Destroyed, Refugees Killed in Broome

A Japanese attack on 3 March on Broome in Australia's
northwest has destroyed aircraft and killed an unknown
number of refugees from the Dutch East Indies fleeing the
Japanese armies to the north, mostly women and children.
No further details are available. The number of those killed
may never be known as they were still on board ships that
had recently arrived with no passenger manifests.

PULAU AYU PRISON CAMP, MALAYA, 15 MARCH 1942

NANCY

Her bed was by the doorway. It meant less privacy, and more
splashes when it rained. But at night she could look upwards at
the stars. She might be trapped behind barbed wire, but as long
as she could look up, part of her was free.

When hunger ripped her stomach, too painful to sleep, when a
whimper from Gavin wakened her, alert till Moira soothed and
fed him, she could watch a star travel across the sky, and feel her
soul fly with it, into the endless black.

Morning began like all mornings these days, with yells of
'Tenko! Tenko!', two guards striding right through their hut, one

with a rifle with a fixed bayonet and one with a bamboo rod, long and thin and with a bite that ripped your skin. The one who carried the rod would tear your blanket off, if you didn't sit up fast, leering at whatever he could spy below.

The guards came in at night too, just as they also entered the latrine at will and leered at the women as they washed in their petticoats each afternoon.

There was no light in any of the huts — the light bulbs had been removed — but a ring of lights around the camp gave enough light to see dimly, even when there was no moon.

Only thirteen women still; one child. The spare beds stayed empty, except as a way to keep Sally's and Mrs Harris's possessions out of the mud, as water seeped under the thatched walls. No men other than the Japanese soldiers. The few European men who had still been on this island when the Japanese arrived had been taken to a camp elsewhere. Sally's and Mrs Harris's husbands were elsewhere too.

'Elsewhere', it seemed, was all that anybody knew.

'Tenko! Tenko!' The guards stamped through the hut a second time.

Nancy straightened her clothes and slipped her feet into the sandals she'd managed to make for herself out of slabs of wood, held on with ribbons donated by Mrs Hughendorn. The other women had been generous, as far as their meagre resources allowed: mosquito netting to keep Gavin safe from the small army of mosquitoes that invaded each dusk; a spare dress each for her and Moira, as well as hats; and the precious blankets because although the days were steaming hot, once the sun disappeared the nights rapidly grew chilly.

'Tenko!' The bamboo rod flicked at Nancy's arm as she shuffled out. She glanced at the mark. Just a bruise, thank goodness. It hadn't cut the skin. The wound in her side had scabbed over nicely, but Nurse Rogers had warned the women that any cut might become infected with only dirty water to wash in.

The morning 'tenkos' were the parades outside the huts, the women lining up for inspection by two guards. Nancy shuffled next to Mrs Harris, then bowed low.

'Say your names.' The translator was the one she had met the first day, with the soft hands of a city worker, not a soldier.

'Mrs Horatio Hughendorn,' said Mrs Hughendorn, as if announcing herself at the Court of St James.

'Bow lower!' A guard's hand came down, striking Mrs Hughendorn below the eye. A bruise, not a cut, thank goodness, thought Nancy again.

Mrs Hughendorn bowed lower, her lips tight, panting from both pain and the effort of bowing her bulk low.

The translator gazed at Mrs Hughendorn impassively. 'You will show respect for the Army of the Emperor at all times. Next!'

'Mrs Barry Harris.'

'Mrs Mainwaring.' Mrs Mainwaring also shared Mrs Hughendorn's house. In her twenties, she had evacuated from north Malaya where her husband managed a plantation to the supposed safety of the Singapore-protected south. She spoke little. This morning she looked like she had been crying in the night.

'Mrs Neville Montrain.'

'Nurse Williams.'

'Nurse McTavish.'

'Miss Edith Smith.'

'Miss Deborah Beatty.' Miss Smith and Miss Beatty had been retired governesses, living on their savings on the island, which Nancy assumed would have been even cheaper than the mainland, and far less expensive than life back in England. They were small and looked like sisters though they were not related, as though years of doing similar work had made them look the same too.

'Mrs Addison.'

'Miss Vivienne Crewlight.' Vivienne was in her early twenties, long nails with the red polish almost peeled off. She had been

Mr Hughendorn's secretary, though Nancy wondered how she had managed to type with nails as long as that. She had been relegated to Hut Number Two, with the nurses and Mrs Addison. Possibly expecting her to share with a Eurasian was a small revenge for Mrs Hughendorn, if her husband had cast too-fond looks towards his secretary.

Nancy waited for her turn. 'Miss Nancy Clancy.'

'Mrs Benjamin Clancy,' said Moira. 'Master Gavin Clancy.'

'Guggins,' said Gavin, as if recognising his name. He leant over to Nancy, his small arms out, his bottom bare under his wrapping of flowered cloth. It was impossible to wash nappies here. But he seemed to know when he could release his bowels onto the dirt, instead of soiling anyone who held him.

Nancy froze, waiting for the guard's stick to descend on him. But the translator merely nodded to her to take him. Gavin clutched her like a small koala, surveying the camp as if it had been designed for his entertainment.

'Nurse Elizabeth Rogers.'

Roll call was over. But still the guards kept them standing in the sun, staring straight ahead. Nancy flicked her eyes up, saw a heron fly towards the sea. A beetle buzzed about her nose, but thankfully didn't land. Brushing it off might get her lashed too.

At last the translator said, 'You may go.'

Nancy headed to the latrine with the others from her hut. They tended to go in a group, if they could. There was protection in a group. Perhaps.

The latrine was a trench, with a single plank suspended above it, its contents steaming in the heat, roiling with maggots and the occasional brown scurry that was a rat. Moira had vomited the first time she had seen it. Even Nancy had fought to keep her stomach contents in place. But there was nowhere else in their small camp to use. One of the other women held Gavin while Nancy and Moira used it, to stop any contaminated water splashing on him. Even if he didn't get any in his mouth, it might still cause a skin infection or fungal growth.

This morning the trench had half filled with water from the storm the afternoon before. The smell was less, but the foetid water so near to her buttocks made it hard to go at all. Finally she managed and wiped herself with one of the leaves that fluttered down into their compound each day.

Mrs Hughendorn had assigned each of the younger women jobs around the camp. No one objected — it made sense for the younger, fitter women to do the harder jobs. Nurse McTavish and Nurse Williams headed to the gate to fetch the two armfuls of firewood they were allowed each day. Sally began to sweep the compound, with an old twig broom that would have been a servant's in a previous life, pushing the wind-blown, sodden petals and leaves into a heap.

Nancy's job was to help fetch one of the four buckets of drinking water they were allowed after roll call from the well by the main house each day. She picked up the wooden bucket, and waited for Moira, Nurse Rogers and Mrs Mainwaring to join her. The four of them stepped up to the well. Nancy tied a rope onto the first bucket, and lowered it down till it splashed in the water below. She was glad the water level was high now, in the wet season. Moira had dropped a bucket into the well on their first day. They'd had to call a guard to retrieve it with a long pole.

They'd been beaten for that, three cuts across their bodies, and four for Mrs Mainwaring when she had cried out and tried to shield herself. But if the well had been deeper and the bucket harder to fish out, they might have been beaten more.

They waited till all four buckets were full, instinctively keeping safety in numbers even here, then carried them over to the outdoor kitchen.

Four buckets of clean water for thirteen women meant two mugs of water per day each, and four for Moira as she was feeding Gavin. That left just enough water to boil their cassava and cook their stews, though while the monsoon season lasted at least they were able to catch rainwater too.

The other women were already at the kitchen, sitting on their allocated blocks of wood while Mrs Hughendorn presided from her armchair under the awning. They each dipped their mug in the water, sipped slowly, making it last. There was no point leaving some to drink later — the heat evaporated the water during the day.

The door of the soldiers' house opened. The house had belonged to Mr and Mrs Hughendorn. The smaller house had belonged to Mrs Hughendorn's mother-in-law, until her death a year before. A guard whooshed out the food bin — what looked like an old pig's swill canteen on wheels. Nancy sniffed. Rotting cabbage again, she thought, as the bin drew closer.

It was — two native cabbages for the thirteen of them, each half slimy with rot, a small bag of sago, and chopped yams.

Nancy bent over the fireplace and pushed aside the dirt that she'd used to carefully cover the coals from the night before, to keep them alight and save their small store of matches. She added tinder, leaves and twigs. At last the fire flared. She added wood, then put on the pot, the sago and the yams in the last of the water. It seemed a sad waste of water to use it for cooking, but trying to eat the raw yams had made them sick.

The women almost unconsciously stared at the cooking pot, like snakes too fascinated by a snake charmer's flute to look away. White smoke began to filter across from the plantation, a scent so acrid you could taste it on your tongue.

'Ah, they are harvesting the gambir leaves,' said Mrs Hughendorn. 'Some plantations,' her voice made it clear what she thought of *those* plantations, 'only harvest twice a year. Mr Hughendorn found that with proper feeding we can get four cuttings, at least.'

'Why is there so much smoke?' asked Nancy. Not because she cared, particularly, but because when your world was mostly red dirt and barbed wire, anything new was interesting.

'The leaves and twigs need to be boiled. The men work in gangs of five. Two to harvest, one to watch and stir the pot, two to bring the firewood. The gambin looks a bit like treacle when it's ready to be dried.'

'How can you dry it in this weather?' asked Moira, watching Gavin bounce on Nurse Rogers's knee.

'We leave it in drums till the dry and finish it then. That's how we can get a better harvest than the Chinese.'

'It looks a bit like cakes of amber when it's dry,' put in Mrs Addison. 'The leaves are useful too. Good for dysentery, or as a lotion for burns.'

'Ah, yes.' Mrs Hughendorn carefully didn't look at Mrs Addison. 'The natives chew it too.'

Nancy wondered if there had been gambir leaves in the poultice the Malay woman had put on her side. But she didn't want to increase the tension between Mrs Hughendorn and Mrs Addison by mentioning it, nor spark too much curiosity about how she came by the wound.

Even here colour matters, she thought. And lipstick, though only Mrs Hughendorn used hers now. She suspected the other women were saving theirs for when they were rescued.

Ten minutes later she added the torn-up cabbage, as much slime removed as possible. Fifteen minutes later Mrs Hughendorn doled the food out, as dignified as if they were at a dinner party, a bowlful each.

No spoons. No knives. The women drank from their bowls, ate the sludge that was left with their fingers. Nancy supposed there were spoons still in the houses. Was this a deliberate attempt to humiliate the mems, making them eat like animals? Or did the guards simply not care to give more than the minimum required?

But they ate, the mems who only months ago had been served by butlers and 'boys', had small boys to pull the fan above their heads as they dined; had major domos to market for them, to bring them their early-morning tea and toast, their breakfast, their morning tea and luncheon, tiffin and evening drinks then dinner and a supper perhaps, if they were entertaining.

They had all journeyed a long way in their short time within the barbed-wire enclosure. But they were alive, and that was what was important. If we are alive, thought Nancy, we can hope.

All she had to do was live, and one day she'd be back at Overflow.

The area around the fire was silent; they were each trying to make the gruel last as long as possible. Hunger battled with repulsion at the smell. Nancy glanced around the circle of women, Mrs Hughendorn grimly doing her duty to absorb calories, Moira's worry tinged with despair that Gavin might reject the only food they had. It was far away from her last proper breakfast, the porridge, the omelette at the Raffles.

A giggle bubbled up inside her. 'Let's pretend,' she said suddenly.

Mrs Hughendorn transferred her disapproval of the gruel to Nancy. 'What *do* you mean, Miss Clancy?'

Nancy held up her bowl. 'This only looks like dog vomit.'

'Nancy!' protested Moira.

Mrs Hughendorn cleared her throat meaningfully. But Nancy thought she detected a crinkle of laughter about the piggy eyes.

'We can take turns to say what we're really eating. I mean, this *can't* be breakfast, because one doesn't eat dog vomit for breakfast. So it has to be porridge, then lamb's fry with onions and Mum's gravy and fried tomatoes …'

'Eggs and bacon,' put in Nurse Rogers. 'With black pudding and maybe a sausage, and baked beans …'

'Oh! Crab omelette,' said Mrs Addison dreamily. 'With mango sambal, and proper rice, a pile of it, all fluffy …'

'It sounds terribly fattening,' said Vivienne. 'I just have toast for breakfast. No butter, of course, and black tea.'

The group was silenced. Mrs Hughendorn looked at Vivienne with a carefully neutral expression, as if she did not deign to discuss the concept of 'banting' when they were close to starving. She turned to Nancy, her expression the most amiable it had been. 'It sounds an excellent idea, my dear. Shall one of us choose what each of our meals will be? I shall go first.'

Of course you will go first, thought Nancy, both amused and grateful.

'This morning we are eating kedgeree,' proclaimed Mrs Hughendorn. 'But made the proper way, none of this lentil business. I always inspect the new cook boy's work every day of his first week in my kitchen. The best white rice, and Keen's curry powder — it must be Keen's — the onions sautéed in butter then added to the cooked rice, flaked salt cod, then hard-boiled eggs scattered over the top. No cheese paring with the butter either.'

Mrs Hughendorn looked down at the bowl in her hands with a small smile. 'Coffee, not tea, two spoonsful of sugar and a dash of condensed milk. And then toast.' She flicked Vivienne a look. 'At least four slices. Thick ones. Served hot, so the butter soaks in. I always ask the boy to bring me two lots of toast. Toast gets cold so quickly. Butter right to the crusts, plum jam — my dear father sends it from home. Ninety-four last birthday, but he still insists his housekeeper makes enough jam every autumn for our household as well as his. And then perhaps a sliced mango ...'

Nancy shut her eyes. She could almost taste the old woman's words. She lifted the bowl to her lips, eyes still shut. Yes, that was plum jam, deep red, solid with lumps of fruit but light enough to spread, the crunch of toast, the tang of melted butter spreading across her tongue ...

The bowl was empty. She opened her eyes again.

Mrs Hughendorn looked at her empty bowl too. 'I must say, that was a definite improvement. But I fear that the effect on the digestion will still be the same ...' Her voice trailed away.

Nancy grinned. Ladies did not speak of digestions. But she knew what Mrs Hughendorn meant. They all did. Their bodies revolted at the scarcity of their diet. Some had only used the latrine to urinate.

'I think we need to get used to it,' said Nurse Rogers. 'There's no point hoping they'll feed us more once they have got the area properly under control.'

'Could we grow vegetables?' suggested Nancy. If the locals could grow most of their own food, why couldn't they? But she doubted this would be a tactful way of putting it to the women assembled here. 'Your servants had a vegetable garden, didn't they? Hens. Do you think they'd let us keep hens?'

'What would we feed hens?' asked Moira.

'Good point,' said Nancy. 'But we could grow vegetables.'

Vivienne looked at her nails. 'If you think I am going to go grubbing in the dirt ...'

'Nonsense. There is nothing wrong with gardening as a hobby,' said Mrs Hughendorn.

Nancy looked at her in surprise. She had expected the mem to have had nothing to do with manual labour.

'You should see my father's rose garden at home. Papa won't let anyone else prune his roses. And his asparagus ...' Mrs Hughendorn looked as if she was tasting the spears. The first true smile Nancy had ever seen her give touched her lips. 'We must ask that translator fellow if we can get seeds and roots. If we can get a note to one of our servants, I'm sure they will help us get seeds and tools and cuttings. They are all terribly loyal to me.'

'You might be putting them in danger if they help us,' said Nancy.

'Ah. You may be right there.' Mrs Hughendorn nodded. 'We shall have to test the lie of the land first. Softlee softlee catchee monkey. Perhaps we should ask the translator if we might buy seeds from the villagers. And spades and garden forks. If he accepts that, we might push it a bit further.'

'You have money to buy tools and seeds? What about food? Proper food?' asked Vivienne.

Mrs Hughendorn did not reply.

'We've got a right to have proper food.' Vivienne looked sideways at Mrs Hughendorn. 'It's your fault I'm here anyway. I should have taken a job on the mainland. Somewhere with a proper club. A golf course.'

And have been on an evacuation ship that was torpedoed, thought Nancy.

'It's up to you to make sure I get treated decently! All of us,' Vivienne added quickly, glancing around.

'I think we should pool any money we have,' said Nurse Rogers. 'Use it for the most important things.'

Vivienne looked righteous.

'What do you think is important?' asked Moira, lifting the bowl of gruel to Gavin's lips again. They made his food more liquid than their own, partly so he could eat it without teeth, but also so that he spilled less of it. Food was too precious even for a few drops to fall on the ground. He slurped it eagerly, waving his arms and legs as if hoping to catch some more.

'Medicine,' said Nurse Rogers crisply. 'Quinine in case we get malaria. Sulphur, if there is any to be had in the village. If we buy things like food, well, we may be here for years. We'd need a lot of money to buy food for that long.'

'Surely it won't be years,' said Mrs Addison. 'The Allies will have retaken the islands by next Christmas. And we'll all starve if we don't get more to eat.'

No one spoke for a minute. Was it because Mrs Addison was Eurasian and kept slightly but subtly an outsider, or because they, like Nancy, were less than sure that they would be rescued by Christmas?

At last Nurse Rogers said, 'A garden would still be useful. Just in case.'

'I think,' proclaimed Mrs Hughendorn, 'that we can safely leave decisions about how to use the money wisely to those who own it. But we should ask about garden tools and seeds.'

Which means you do have money, thought Nancy. Possibly Mrs Hughendorn had even travelled to the bank at Singapore to draw out cash, as many people had immediately after the invasion, in case the banks closed. To her surprise, the Japanese guards had neither searched them nor demanded they hand over any valuables, as she knew had happened in German prison camps in the last war. The thefts that had occurred had been minor. Possibly the guard responsible might even be disciplined if the camp commandant knew what he'd done. Which meant that Moira's pearls and brooch, and whatever money the others had, were still safe — if they were allowed to spend it.

She didn't contribute to the argument. Alone of all the women here she had nothing, neither money nor jewellery that might be sold for money. But I can grow things, she thought, though she doubted anything would grow much in the dry season. Even if they saved the dirty water they were allowed for washing, it would not be enough to keep vegetable gardens watered.

She looked around the camp restlessly. She had thought school was bad. But at least school finished at three o'clock. Things happened at school. Here they just sat, apart from their camp jobs, the women who had known each other before gossiping, the others trying to find acquaintances or experiences in common. A rectangle of dirt, barbed wire and years of it, maybe. One year at least ...

'Rats in the cupboard,' muttered Sally. That was their code for Japanese soldiers approaching.

It was the translator. They stood, bowed. Mrs Hughendorn now wore the green and purple bruise across her face.

'There is news for captives of the Emperor,' said the translator. 'Item the first. Japanese soldiers march in triumph through the streets of Singapore.'

'No!' said Mrs Addison. 'Singapore is impregnable.'

'The sons of the sun will always triumph,' said the translator. He is reciting from a radio broadcast, thought Nancy. 'Item the second. The imperialist armies have surrendered. All ships trying to escape have been sunk.'

Moira gave a small cry. Sally gasped, biting her lip. Her husband too was with the local Volunteers. I don't believe it, thought Nancy. Not every ship. But that was probably what the translator had heard on Nippon radio. She remembered how the BBC had refused to admit the British losses in Malaya. Why should the Japanese be any more careful with the truth?

'Item the third. All white imperialists will stay in camps. All will work.'

'What sort of work?' demanded Mrs Hughendorn.

The translator blinked. Even he can't see Mrs Hughendorn chopping firewood to boil gambir leaves, thought Nancy.

'Work will be found. Japan will be generous. Till you work you will be given food.'

'We need more food,' said Nurse Rogers. 'Vegetables. Fish and meat. Fruit.'

The translator ignored her.

'If we can't have more food, could we have seeds and cuttings to grow our own? Spades and garden forks?'

'No tools for prisoners.'

'Do you really think we might attack the guards with spades and garden forks!' cried Nurse Rogers.

I might, thought Nancy. And if Mrs Hughendorn sat on a guard or two, they'd never get up again.

The translator went on as if Nurse Rogers hadn't spoken. 'Item the fourth. All Asian races are now freed.' He looked at Mrs Addison, and then shot a less confident glance at Nancy. 'You may leave. Now.'

'I can go? Go where?' asked Mrs Addison, her voice suddenly tremulous.

The translator again had no reply. He turned, and stepped neatly back past the sentry at the gate, then across the veranda into the house.

'I ... I had better get my things.' Mrs Addison carefully didn't look at the others. Nancy followed her. She sat on one of the other bunks as Mrs Addison folded a dress into her suitcase.

'Where will you go?'

'I have friends in Singapore. If I can get there, I can stay with them.' She stopped, looked at the dress in her hands, then held it out to Nancy. 'Here. You need another spare dress. And my shoes should fit you.'

'Thank you. It's incredibly kind of you.' It was. Mrs Addison might be free, but Nancy suspected that there would be few new dresses available even in Singapore for some time to come.

'Miss Clancy?' Mrs Hughendorn's bulk darkened the doorway.

'Yes, Mrs Hughendorn?'

Mrs Hughendorn said nothing as Mrs Addison moved towards the door. 'Good luck,' said Nancy.

'Thank you.' Mrs Addison stood aside as Moira came in, her arms empty of baby. As the only child in the camp, Gavin now had twelve aunts, none with anything better to do than play with an eight-month-old child. No, eleven aunts now, thought Nancy.

'Miss Clancy, I hope you don't mind my mentioning it,' said Mrs Hughendorn, with all the tact of a tiptoeing elephant. 'But with your ... tanned ... skin, I think the Japanese might accept that you were Eurasian too.' She held up her hand as Moira began to protest. 'Yes, I know you are not.' She carefully avoided looking at Moira. She knows I am not truly white, thought Nancy. 'But if you were to wear a sarong, perhaps — I have one I use as a bedspread — and tie your hair back, I think the Japanese would accept that you were Straits born.'

'She's right,' said Moira.

Nancy sat on her bunk. She had thought of escape. She had thought of an Allied landing, the ships that *had* to come to take the armies from Singapore, just as the armies had been rescued at Dunkirk, stopping at all the islands to rescue all the Japanese captives.

But if the translator was right, there had been no Dunkirk for Singapore. She thought of Mr Harding and his belief that the British commanders were incompetent, despite the men under their command outnumbering the Japanese. How many men were in camps like this? Was Ben?

If she could get out of here, she might be able to find out. Surely someone on the island other than the guards had a short-wave radio that might get news from the BBC or Australia, or even a local newspaper. Prisoners of war taken by the Germans were listed in the newspaper, so maybe those taken by the Japanese would be too.

Or would they? What exactly was in that Geneva Convention that Mr Harding had talked about? She should have asked him more questions. And loaded herself with jewellery and coins … and probably sunk under their weight.

She looked at Moira, carefully expressionless, at Mrs Hughendorn, ludicrously formal in her rings and pearls, diamonds at her ears, her lipstick and stockings and sensible shoes, even if her dress was becoming grey from repeated washings in muddy water, both waiting to hear her answer. If she was free, or at least out of the camp, she might even be able to persuade one of the fishermen to take her to the next island towards Australia. Then another fisherman to take her to the next and the next …

Or she could stay on the island, try to get food to the inmates. But would the islanders shelter her? Would they risk their own lives if they took a stranger in?

Freedom. Free of a hut that stank of sewage and a touch of despair; of this miserable blank rectangle of ground with its single tree; be able to breathe and move, even if she had to work as someone's servant in exchange for food. She didn't mind working. She *wanted* to work. To see the sea and trees. Even birds avoided the camp, as if they knew there was neither food for them there nor shelter. She needed to walk. To walk and keep on walking, the wind in her face. If her grandfather hadn't been suited to the office, as the poet had claimed, then neither was she suited to sitting still. Not when she could be free …

'Will you go?' asked Moira quietly.

'Do you want me to?'

'That's up to you.'

'Mummmll ffop,' said Gavin, suspended in the doorway between Nurse Rogers and Sally, his tiny bare feet just touching the ground.

'Look!' said Sally. 'He's walking! Tell Mummy how well you can walk, Gavin.'

'Maaaaaaahstpt!' said Gavin in delight.

'See,' said Sally. 'He can say Mummy. Now say Auntie Nancy.'

Gavin's small face broke into a grin. 'Gibba!'

'Near enough,' said Sally.

Nancy bent and picked him up. He pulled her ear lobe and stared at it, fascinated, as if he had never really noticed ears before.

'No,' Nancy said to Moira. 'I'm not leaving.'

'Good show,' said Mrs Hughendorn. She nodded approvingly at Nancy.

Moira said nothing for a moment. Nancy wondered if those were tears at the edges of her eyes. But all she said was, 'I'm glad.'

Chapter 22

Gibber's Creek Gazette, 17 April 1942

General MacArthur Arrives to Take Command!

Heroic American General Douglas MacArthur has taken
control as Supreme Commander of Allied forces west
of Singapore. 'All Australia welcomes the hero of the
Philippines,' said Councillor Bullant at last night's Council
meeting ...

ST ELRIC'S SCHOOL, SYDNEY, NEW SOUTH WALES, AUSTRALIA, 31 MAY 1942

MICHAEL

The classroom smelt of old wooden desks and chalk, long-boiled
school lunches and the indefinable scent of caged teenage boys.
Mrs Glokerman tapped on the door during maths. 'Headmaster
would like to see Andrew Taylor in his office, please.'

Michael glanced at Taylor. A year ago a summons to the
headmaster's office might mean you'd been caught smoking
behind the tennis courts. Now Taylor's two soldier brothers were
somewhere in the Middle East. His father was in Malaya. A
summons might mean many things; nearly all of them were bad.

Michael gave Taylor a sympathetic nod as he passed.

He tried to focus on the textbook in front of him, while
Mr Fothergill dozed at his desk. Old Fothergill had been retired

for nearly a decade, but the shortage of teachers since so many had enlisted meant he had come back. He wasn't a bad teacher, when he was awake.

A shadow behind him: Taylor returning. Mr Fothergill gave a grunt and opened his eyes. His smile showed long yellow teeth, like a walrus's. 'Taylor. Good news?'

If it had been bad news, Taylor would not have returned to class; would have been allowed to join his family, his mother might already have been waiting in the headmaster's office.

Taylor nodded. 'Good news, sir. A phone call from my mother. My father's made it back.'

'Jolly good show,' said Mr Fothergill. 'I think a prayer of thanksgiving is in order, don't you, boys?' He put his hands together and shut his eyes. 'Oh, heavenly Father, we thank you in our hour of need for protecting Captain Taylor. We thank you for ...'

Michael looked at Taylor through his half-shut eyes as the prayer rumbled on. Taylor's hands trembled. Suddenly he put his head on his desk, sobs erupting even though he tried to choke them off.

'Amen,' said Mr Fothergill, opening his eyes. He looked at Taylor, his head still buried in his arms, his shoulders heaving with the effort of suppressing his sobs. 'I think you boys could all do with a bit of exercise. Twice around the oval. Chop, chop. Taylor, you will stay behind.'

Michael ventured a pat on Taylor's back as he passed him. But Taylor did not respond.

The wind from the south was cold as they jogged around the oval, compulsory gas masks flapping at their belts — even if you got up to the toilet in the middle of the night, you had to take your gas mask — avoiding the air-raid trenches at the edges of the oval, the walls of sandbags the boys had filled last month. A small plane circled them briefly, then vanished towards the sea. The bell had gone by the time they'd finished. Michael trotted

back to the dorm to change. Cricket practice, then dinner —
stew tonight and frog's eggs, tapioca — then prep.

The sirens came just as prep was over, the sound shuddering
between the buildings. For a moment Michael thought it was
another drill, then realised that no one had warned of air-raid
practice today.

This was real.

'To the shelters,' said Mr Fothergill, who had been supervising
prep that evening and was suddenly very awake. 'You two,
Taylor and Thompson, go and fill the baths.' Sydney residents
had been instructed to do this at the first sign of a raid, in case
the pipes were bombed and broken and Sydney's water supply
disrupted. Michael wondered how long six bathtubs of water
would last twenty boys ... 'No running!' Mr Fothergill shouted.
'Brisk walk. Now!'

'Sir, should we take our prep with us?'

'Sir, can I get my ...'

'Go!' shouted Mr Fothergill.

Michael and Taylor broke into a run as soon as they were out
of sight, over to the boarding house and into the bathrooms,
hopping from foot to foot as they filled. Thunder boomed, over
towards the harbour ...

Not thunder. He looked at Taylor.

Taylor's face was white. 'Bombs,' he said.

Michael nodded. No time to run for the shelters now. Visions
of the dust and shreds of blitzed London flashed before him.
Would that be Sydney tomorrow morning? He could hear the
sound of an aircraft's engine. Ours or the enemy's?

'Under the stairs,' he said. They dived for the space and sat
together as an explosion, louder now, shook the timbers above
them. He tried to listen for more aircraft engines, but all he
could hear was Taylor's breathing and his own.

It was stuffy under the stairs. Stuffy and quiet. No point
keeping his eyes open in the dark ...

'Thompson?'

Michael opened his eyes. Mr Fothergill's teeth loomed above him. It was daylight. He had fallen asleep, leaning against the wall. It was now early morning. Taylor yawned behind him. 'Sorry, Mr Fothergill. Didn't hear the all-clear.'

'There wasn't one. Bad show all round.'

'How much damage, sir?'

'Don't know yet. Wireless reports say that a ship's been sunk in the harbour. By Japanese submarines.'

'Submarines? Here?'

'Apparently.' Mr Fothergill's mouth tightened. 'Chapel in twenty minutes. Better get yourselves tidied up.'

'Chapel,' said Taylor disgustedly, as Mr Fothergill hurried away. 'You'd think they'd give us the morning off after this.'

Michael said nothing. The war is here, he thought. Enemy submarines in our harbour ...

Was Sydney about to fall to the Japanese too? Impossible ... but that was what they had been told about Singapore, until the very end.

He followed Taylor to the showers, felt the cold water sting his body. Stupid, to be here at school, when all he loved was being threatened. But what could he do at sixteen? Enlist in the navy, but not without his parents' permission, and he knew they'd not give that. Nor would he be allowed to go on overseas duty until he was twenty-one and in the regular forces, or eighteen if he joined the militia.

Two years, he thought, till I can do anything worthwhile. Two years of parading with cadets, learning semaphore, bayoneting dummies slung between the gum trees. At least at home he'd be able to train with the Volunteer Defence Corps, though he suspected that he'd be doing much the same as they did at school cadets. He could already march, and a fat lot of good that would be against the enemy. Could already pot a rabbit in the dusk so quietly it never knew he was there; clean a rifle or a shotgun; even make his own ammunition, though he doubted the army would require him to do that. What more did he need? Would the ability to shave every day instead of twice a week make him a better soldier?

English boys could join the merchant marines at fourteen, would face the enemy at sea as they brought desperately needed supplies through the U-boat blockades. Now that Australia was under direct attack, would they change the age limit here?

He grabbed a towel and began to dry himself. Chapel, he thought, to pray for victory. That was all he could do now.

Chapter 23

Gibber's Creek Gazette, 6 June 1942

Citizens of Melbourne are working hard to dig an air-raid trench for every household. Melbourne parks and gardens are ringed by trenches now, even around the Shrine of Remembrance.

The Gibber's Creek Council is divided on the issue of digging trenches in our own fair town. According to Councillor Bullant: 'If General MacArthur says we need to dig trenches, then that means we have to dig in Gibber's Creek too. We have got two important factories here. We're kidding ourselves if we don't think they can be targets too.'

Councillor Ellis commented: 'If Councillor Bullant and General MacArthur want to dig trenches in ground as dry as my back paddocks, I'll lend them a mattock.'

> *Mrs Matilda Thompson*
> *Drinkwater Station*
> *via Gibber's Creek*
> *7 June 1942*

To the Editor
Gibber's Creek Gazette

Perhaps if your worthy journal spent less time eulogising General MacArthur and more time championing our own troops' achievements, our district would be better informed. What of the many Australian fathers now fighting for their country, the fathers working in our fields and factories as their sons fight overseas?

Is the editor aware that General MacArthur has decreed that any Australian victories should only be referred to as 'Allied victories' with no mention of our forces? Is he also aware that only official communiqués are allowed to be posted by journalists attached to headquarters or in the field? If Australians wish to know about our own forces — or any information not pre-digested for the American public — they must go to the British or even foreign-language papers for information.

I am not denying the sterling, or even corn-fed, worth of General MacArthur, nor the debt we owe America and the American forces. But Australians too have a right to know of the successes for which we have all sacrificed and turned our shoulders to the wheel. It is to be hoped that in future editions this paper might do more than ponder these questions, and give the people of Gibber's Creek the standard of journalism they deserve.

> Yours faithfully,
> Mrs Matilda Thompson

A note to the editor: please do NOT put my name as Mrs Thomas Thompson. Proud as I am of my husband, I do have a name of my own, as do the other women working so hard for the war effort in our town.

PULAU AYU PRISON CAMP, 7 JUNE 1942

NANCY

Nancy watched old Miss Smith and Miss Beatty and Mrs Hughendorn trudge back down to Hut Number One from the Japanese quarters. Each day the three women were assigned to scrub floors, with a bucket of water and a scrubbing brush each. Nancy suspected it was no coincidence that the most proper of the 'mems' had been chosen for the most menial of jobs. It was a way of saying, 'We are your masters. You must not only bow to us, but bend.'

They scrubbed. No work, no food. Nancy worried the older women might have a stroke with the unaccustomed work. But there was no choice, not here, not now. So far no jobs had been found for the other women in the camp. Nancy hoped that perhaps she might eventually be sent out to work on the plantation. She could at least pick leaves, skinny as she was. She looked down at her chest in disgust. It had taken sixteen years to grow a decent bosom, and three weeks to lose it. Even Mrs Hughendorn's skin hung in loose flaps about her chin now.

'Tenko!'

Not another roll call! They came at all hours of the day lately. How hard was it to keep track of twelve women? She sighed, and got up from her bunk, where she had been playing clap hands with Gavin. He could manage to meet her hands almost every time now, grinning with delight as he did so. Somehow, miraculously, Moira was able to continue to feed him, despite the meagre diet.

Soon the food bin would trundle down again, with the evening's offering. Last night it had been a mush of cassava and a single coconut, not even any vegetables. But that was better than the days when no food arrived at all, not as a specific punishment — or if it was, they were not told of the transgression — but as a sign of power. We give food, or not, to you, as we choose. They kept a little cassava or sago each night now, in case there'd be no more the next day. Adults could survive a day or longer without food. Gavin might not.

At least near starvation meant that she no longer had to worry about her periods. Nurse Rogers had told her privately that none of the women were menstruating, nor were they likely to without more food.

Food! It was the focus of their days. Last night's cassava mush had been roast beef, Yorkshire pudding, roast potatoes, fresh peas and cauliflower cheese — Mrs Harris's choice — followed by Miss Beatty's favourite dessert of trifle: 'Sponge cake and strawberry jelly and stewed peaches and custard and cream. May we be very naughty and soak the cake in sherry?'

It was Mrs Mainwaring's turn to choose the breakfast menu today. Even when there was no food, the pretence continued.

Nancy hoisted Gavin onto her hip and headed out into the compound, dust now, instead of mud, and the incessant stench of wood smoke from the gambir pots. Moira lined up next to her. 'Will I take Gavin?'

Nancy shook her head. Moira looked more fragile than ever, her hands almost transparent. 'I like to hold him,' she said truthfully.

'Me too.' Sally smiled at them both, then quickly bowed as a small line of guards appeared, the commandant at the front.

Nancy looked at the commandant sideways as she bowed low. The commandant rarely came out to the prisoners' compound. Nancy suspected his more important duties lay with the rest of the island and its plantation. He was in his fifties, perhaps, his uniform always freshly ironed, his face smooth and clean-shaven. Even without his uniform it would have been impossible to miss his officer's bearing. This was the first time she had seen him close up.

He stood and looked at them, then said something quietly to the translator.

'Women stand straight,' barked the translator.

They stood up, Mrs Hughendorn and Miss Smith with audible sighs.

'Silence.' A guard lashed a bamboo cane against Miss Smith's arm. She bit back a cry.

The commandant watched impassively. He nodded to two of the guards. They marched back to their living quarters and brought down a table.

What is going on? thought Nancy.

Away they marched again, as if on parade. They came back almost at once, this time carrying a brown Bakelite wireless, its cord trailing back to the house. They placed it on the table and stood to attention on either side.

The commandant nodded again. One of the guards leant over and switched the wireless on.

The radio gave its preliminary whine. A voice spoke, a man's voice, in English with an Australian accent, so clear that Nancy jumped. It sounded as if he was standing nearby.

'In place of the news commentary this evening, it is our pleasure to convey to you a special message of cheer to the families of those Allied soldiers now in prisoner-of-war camps. It is a message of good cheer.'

The Australian voice sounded relaxed and confident. 'From my personal experience of living as a prisoner of war in these camps, I can tell you that our men are being treated considerately by the Japanese. I have personally been shown so much kindness by the Japanese that this is an opportunity for me to repay that kindness. There is one place I know of where civilian prisoners are interned. Regular concerts are held and there are no restrictions on internees going for walks, unescorted, through the countryside. Some suffered from the Eastern diet of rice at first but now thrive on it, milling the rice and baking cakes with it, with very good results. Sentries insist on compliments being paid to them, but they never fail to return them, so there is no problem on that score. When your men return to you I am sure that they will agree with what I tell you tonight, and express their gratitude for the compassion and kindness shown to them by those who were, a short time ago, their enemies.'

Nancy kept her face still. Impossible to smile, to laugh, even snort to show contempt. This was just another humiliation to accept.

The voice changed. It was a woman's now, soft and melodious, with a slight American accent. 'In other news, Australia today is almost totally under Japanese domination, with our aircraft sweeping down as far as Port Hedland in Western Australia, our bombers reaching into the very centre of Australia and ships shelling north of Newcastle and Sydney on the east coast. Supplies from Britain and America have now been completely cut off. Australia today is the orphan of the Pacific. Military collaboration with America is impossible.

'Today the Australian Prime Minister banned the manufacture of all swimming costumes and announced a day of prayer. Australia has no choice now but to accept the friendly hand of Nippon, as offered on so many occasions by Premier Tojo —'

Nurse Williams gave a small cry beside her, hurriedly cut off.

Was it true? It couldn't be! Or not the whole truth. The BBC World Service had not told the truth either. But she suspected the BBC's lies had been smaller than the Japanese ones.

She bit her lip. She had to believe, believe no matter what, that Overflow was safe, her land still hers. She knew it was a lie that civilian internees could go for walks and were baking rice cakes. Bombers reaching to central Australia must be a lie too. It must *all* be a lie ...

And yet ...

She closed her eyes. And suddenly there it was: Overflow, its channels dry now, the grass brown, but safe, serene, sheep nibbling at the earth, no helmets and no war.

She opened her eyes again as the translator shouted the order to bow. I would know if my land was taken, she thought. Surely I would know.

Chapter 24

ST ELRIC'S SCHOOL, 8 JUNE 1942

MICHAEL

He was asleep when the explosions came again, the booms loud enough to wake him. He was already hauling on his dressing gown when the siren went. He grabbed his gas mask, the flask of water and box of food they kept by their beds now, and hurried with the others to the trench shelters the boys had dug behind the oval.

At least the air was fresh here. You could see the stars, with so many lights blacked out. He wondered if he would see a torpedo or bomb as it fell on them. Only if it came straight down, he thought. The 'air-raid shelter' was a joke anyway. As if a trench could save you from a plane's bomb or a submarine's torpedo. The most the trench would do would shield them from debris if the school buildings were bombed. Buildings would be more of a target than trenches and an oval ...

Part of him wanted the school to be hit — it would provide an escape from maths and Latin grammar while the world suffered and fought. He had left nothing of value in the buildings to lose; even the photo of Nancy was as usual in his wallet, in his dressing-gown pocket. But if the school was to go ... To his surprise, he felt a sudden affection for it. It was like winning a game of rugger: ultimately completely unimportant, but a symbol of the strong teamwork that made it happen. If the Japanese bombed his school, then that would be a victory for them, and a theft from his life.

No more, he thought. They have taken Nancy. They had Ben and Dr McAlpine, had killed Bluey White who worked in the Gibber's Creek butcher's shop, and Anderson's dad. They will not take my school now. Though he ruefully admitted that if a bomb was dropped or a torpedo shot from a lurking submarine, he knew no way to stop them.

I'm a 'gunna', he thought. Gunna stop the Japanese, while doing nothing about it.

He heard the noise of a plane, chugging through the air. Ours or theirs? Another roar, closer now, so near he could hear the clatter of falling rubble, women screaming, a man yelling, 'Watch out! Turn off the gas.' If the gas mains had been broken, any spark would make them explode too …

He waited; he felt the others around him wait too, no whispering or even movement. The second attack in a little over a week … How many submarines were out there, beyond the Heads? How many planes waiting to attack? The bombing of Darwin and Broome had seemed remote, so far north and west as to be almost another country. But if Sydney could be bombed, then nowhere was safe.

There were no more explosions. He leant against the rough dirt wall, angry, tired, helpless.

Helplessness was worst of all.

Chapter 25

Gibber's Creek Gazette, 18 June 1942

General MacArthur Named Father of the Year

Heroic General MacArthur has just been named Father of
the Year. The new Father of the Year breakfasts with his
son Arthur each morning before heading out to the day's
command. The General states that his son is the only one
who can tolerate his singing, and they sing duets together.

PULAU AYU PRISON CAMP, 20 JUNE 1942

NANCY

She couldn't sleep. It wasn't just the heat, which sucked at her
bones despite the sea breeze that grumbled around the bamboo-
leaf roof. It was hunger, deep sinew-weakening hunger, as if her
body had used up almost its last reserves.

She stared at the gecko on the ceiling, almost invisible in the
moonlight. In the bunk next to her Moira lay with Gavin — he
at least still looked, not plump, but not gaunt either. Moira was
still feeding him, and was thinner than anyone else in the camp.

They had asked again for more food. Vivienne had even cried.
The translator had watched with emotionless contempt. Nancy
was good at reading the emotions on his almost expressionless
face now.

'No more work, no more food.'

'But we don't have any other work to do!' said Nurse Rogers.

The translator looked her up and down. 'Will you work for Japanese soldiers in the Japanese hospital?'

'No, of course not. You can't ask prisoners of war or internees to work for the enemy army. It is against the Geneva Convention.'

Which the Japanese didn't sign, thought Nancy, remembering what Mr Harding had told her. She wondered if Nurse Rogers knew that small but possibly important detail. But Nurse Rogers had known one of the nurses bayoneted by the Japanese when they'd taken Hong Kong. Perhaps she suspected that Australian nurses would be no safer in a hospital controlled by the Japanese. So many atrocities, Nancy thought, as the nightmare bodies on the beach seared across her mind again. But here we are at least alive.

'No work. No food. Nippon soldiers are kind to give you food at all.'

Vivienne had bribed the guard to buy a chicken — half the money to the guard, half to buy the chicken. But when she realised that the other women expected her to share the food equally among them, she bought no more. A week after that Sally had become feverish. The quinine Mrs Hughendorn had bought — the guard again pocketing half the money — had worked. No one else was prepared to buy food now. Not yet.

No more work. No more food. Why feed mems who could not contribute to the war effort?

No extra food until the war ended. If it ever ended. Sometimes Nancy lay and watched the sky. But the only planes were Japanese ones, and those infrequent, as if there was no need for planes now to capture Malaya.

No extra food forever then. How long was forever?

Hunger nibbled you, like a mouse inside. Hunger made you listless, so you couldn't think. Hunger was turning her wits to chicken bones. Hunger would kill her sister-in-law, this small courageous woman she now knew she loved, was not just bound to by duty.

Something moved in the shadows of the hut. Rat! Few rats lived in the camp — there was no food for them here — but the stench of the latrine attracted them, and bamboo walls and thatch would make good nesting places.

A memory floated into her brain: Gran, sitting still while a goanna lumbered past; her fingers flicking, suddenly, crushing the goanna's head down. 'Bush meat' she had called it, cooking it on a fire by the river for lunch, never taking it back to the kitchen she shared with her daughter-in-law. Nancy wondered if Gran had ever cooked 'bush meat' in the kitchen even when the house was solely hers and Granddad's.

Goanna, black snake, echidna — echidna tasted of ants — the bush rats that weren't rats at all and had small sharp teeth and devoured insects, the small hopping creatures that were almost rats as well ...

She raised herself slowly on the bed, noiselessly. The rat didn't seem to see her, too intent on scratching out a cavity in the wall. She stood, again so slowly as to be almost motionless. One foot, and then another, making sure her shadow stayed behind her. Six feet away, then three.

Her hand flashed down. The rat wriggled, tried to bite. Her hands twisted. It lay limp in her hands.

One dead rat.

She looked at Moira, Mrs Harris and Sally, all still asleep. Would they eat rat? She looked up at the ceiling, at the gecko. May as well be hanged for a sheep as a lamb. She climbed up onto the bunk and grabbed.

The gecko didn't stand a chance.

She took the booty out into the moonlit night. They had no knives. She found a rock by the barbed-wire fence, chipped it against the stone paving of the outdoor kitchen, and then used her teeth to make a blade, like Gran had shown her. One small cut to the rat's anus, then she sliced through the fibres up between the flesh and skin. Another cut. The guts spilled into her hand. She threw them into the latrine and began to skin the gecko.

There wasn't much meat when she had finished. A few spoonsful each. But a few spoonsful of meat every few days might make the difference between life and starvation. And there were more rats and lots of geckos.

She headed up to the well to get one of their buckets of water. They were allowed more now, in the dry season. The guard glanced at her, but didn't yell at her to go back. Dawn was coming. She filled the pot with water and set the meat to cook. The scent of it as it heated almost made her faint.

She felt an instinctive urge to pull out the half-cooked meat, to gorge on it. She almost hoped the others would reject it. She could feast by herself. And feed it to Gavin too: he was too young to have learnt prejudices about his food.

The meat was shreds now. She added some of the cassava from the night before, let it bubble to the normal gruel, slightly browner now and dappled with the meat, then let the fire die down, covering it with green wood to keep the coals alight until supper.

Sally came out, yawning. 'How long have you been up?'

'A while.' She waited as Sally went to the latrine. Moira woke next, at the cry from Gavin that announced he was hungry.

Mrs Hughendorn emerged, adorned with rubies, emeralds, and dressed in yet another suit, of which she seemed to have an endless supply, though they hung lower and lower on her legs as she lost more weight. She sniffed, then came over and peered into the pot. She looked sharply at Nancy.

'The guard gave me some meat,' said Nancy. 'I added it to the cassava.' She tried to keep her voice even, her cheeks from blushing. She had never found lies easy.

'I ... see,' said Mrs Hughendorn. She looked at Nancy's hands.

Nancy glanced down. Red fingernails. Rat's blood, or lizard's. There was no way to clean her hands till the afternoon's washing water was released.

Another gecko scuttled past. Food, thought Nancy.

Nurse Rogers emerged. 'Has anyone got a ribbon they could spare? My hair keeps getting in my eyes. Do you think Tojo would cut it for me?' She too sniffed, came over and gazed down at the pot. 'Don't tell me we've got meat! What is it? The bones are too small for chicken.'

Mrs Hughendorn glanced at Nancy, then at Nurse Rogers. 'Island rabbit,' she said clearly. 'We used to eat it now and then.'

She knows, thought Nancy. Some of the others may suspect, but they'll follow her lead. This is 'island rabbit' as long as Mrs Hughendorn says it is.

Moira came out, with Gavin on her hip. Nancy smiled at her. 'There's meat for breakfast. Not much. But at least it's meat.'

And somehow the wind from the sea seemed to breathe Australia, the scent of gum leaves, the scent of Overflow.

Chapter 26

Gibber's Creek Gazette, 30 June 1942

New Proprietor for the *Gazette*

Your editor is delighted to announce that the *Gibber's Creek Gazette* is under new management. Proprietor Mrs Matilda Thompson said today, 'We hope that the people of Gibber's Creek will continue to subscribe to the district's only newspaper, and find in its pages inspiration and information and the standard of journalism that all Australians should expect as we fight together to win this war.'

Your editor wholeheartedly endorses Mrs Thompson's words, and looks forward to a stimulating, prosperous working relationship.

MOURA, NEW SOUTH WALES, AUSTRALIA, 30 JUNE 1942

BLUE

The breeze dusted the river as Blue McAlpine bicycled back along the road from the factory, borrowing some of its coolness as it gusted across the paddocks up to Moura, sheltered in its hills. She and Mah had extra petrol rations for the factory, but it would be a pity to waste petrol when they could go by bicycle. And, in truth, she welcomed the ride — the quietness, seeing the sheep on the side of the road, the crepe myrtles growing in the gardens nearer town. Trying to keep herself focused on today, because thinking of last year, or even next year, hurt too much.

She stopped at the letterbox, tried to slow her heart as she reached in, as she did every day.

Nothing. Nor had she expected anything. Business letters came to the factory; the monthly letter from Aunt Daisy had come the previous week, complaining about the butter ration, the sugar ration, the behaviour of men in uniform with their *brazen hussies, not at all like in the last war, my dear.*

But she had hoped ...

She wanted ... anything, except an empty ten-gallon drum pretending to be a letterbox when it couldn't even produce one page of mail. She shut her eyes. A letter from Joseph, saying he'd been wounded and evacuated with the fall of Singapore to hospital in Darwin, too badly hurt to write to her till now, his records mislaid somehow in the army system, but he would heal and he'd be home with her next week. That would be the most perfect letter of all.

Second best: a Red Cross postcard saying her husband was a prisoner of war. Even, she thought, trying to swallow the agony, even a telegraph boy with a yellow scrap of paper, saying Joseph had been killed. At least then she would know, would not wake at two am with nightmares of horrors the man she loved might be facing now. She could mourn, as she could not mourn now, for that would be betrayal if Joseph was still alive.

But there was nothing. Had been nothing since the letter from Singapore dated January 1942 that had arrived soon after the army informed her he was missing, swallowed up by Malaya after the fall of Singapore with the 9th Division ...

Their army shouldn't have been lost! Not even lost — handed to the Japanese. The British government had assured them that Singapore could not fall. That Australia could and should send its men, its planes, its tanks to the Middle East and North Africa to defend England against the German armies, in the security of knowing that Singapore would hold the Japanese back.

And yet it hadn't. There had been no Dunkirk-like rescue of troops, just a few who managed their own escape, hiding and island hopping. The Red Cross had notified many families that their men were being held as prisoners of war.

But Joseph had vanished.

His hat hung on the hat stand. His favourite plum sauce was on the table. She had even put away his summer clothes and got out his winter suit. These objects were talismans assuring her that he was alive, that he'd be back with her.

Once she had wanted many things: a factory empire greater than the one her grandfather had built, burning a spot upon the world that said, 'I may be just a girl but I can leave my mark, and it will be etched deeper than yours.' She would swap it all now for that one thing — her husband's arms about her in the night.

Now she was just a woman, not even quite a wife. To be a wife, you needed your husband there, or at least the promise that he would be. Nor was she a mother ...

Why had they waited to have children? Mah hadn't waited: she'd had a boy and a girl within three years of marrying Andy. When the war was over ... when Joseph came back to her ... she would have a thousand children, as many as the stars. If she only had a baby now, a warm child to cuddle, because when you had a baby your arms always had something warm to hold, not like the cold nights now ...

A child was life. When there was life, new life, then you had beaten death. Death might march the world, she thought, but we women will fight back. We'll give you life. We are the uncounted army.

She squinted at the sun, still an inch from the horizon. She'd chop firewood for half an hour, till dark. Supervising the factory, doing the accounts, managing the army paperwork was no substitute for physical work, the kind she and Mah had shared with Gertrude, Fred and the others in the circus, exercise that left you sleeping deeply and with sweet dreams.

Though her dreams were not sweet now, and wouldn't be, no matter how much firewood she chopped. But fires were warm, and she craved warmth now. Fires, blankets, feather quilts, draught excluders at the door, as if by keeping out the cold she could make a small safe hole into which somehow Joseph might creep back.

She opened her eyes at the sound of a car. An emergency? Most cars were up on blocks in these days of petrol rationing. The driver came around the corner in a cloud of dust. Mah. She pulled up at the gate. Blue ran to meet her. What was so important that Mah used a car, not her bicycle?

'What's wrong? Has something happened?'

Mah held out a letter mutely. Blue took it, recognised the copperplate hand, the only gift of the orphanage where Mah and Fred had spent their early years.

Dear Cousin Marjory,

How are you all up in New South Wales? Just wanted you to know that your old cousin has joined up. I thought they could run the war without me, but it seems they can't, even though I've been sending them instructions every week. So it's time to put on the uniform and get them doing it properly. I'll be a General by next week, or at least by Christmas time. It'll shorten the war by two feet six inches, you'll see.

Give my regards to that husband of yours and a hug to the nippers. One day you might just see me turn up for Christmas with a teddy bear for them.

Here's looking at you, kid. Don't you go worrying about me. Just thought you should know, you being my only family and all, and I have listed you as next of kin, because I had to put something in the space on the form, or they mightn't have let me in, and then who knows what our boys would do, without your loving,

Cousin Murgatroyd

'Fred.' Blue handed it back.

Mah nodded. Blue watched her hold the letter to her cheek as if it was the brother she hadn't seen in eight years.

Fred, he'd called himself, in the days when they were all in the circus together. But his name was really Robert, and he was on the run from a bank robbery gone wrong. When the police had begun to nose around the circus he had scarpered.

He'd been in love with Blue. Or had he? He'd said he was, but it was hard to know with Fred. He'd said he'd left her for her own good, and Mah too. Hard to know if that was true either. She thought it was, but Fred could have you believing a kangaroo could win the Melbourne Cup.

'He's found out I'm married to Andy. And about the kids.' Mah looked at Blue appealingly. 'You haven't been writing to him, have you?'

Blue shook her head.

'He doesn't know anyone else here who might have told him. Except Sheba.'

The old elephant seemed as intelligent as a human sometimes, but even Sheba, thought Blue, would find it difficult to wield a pen or send a telegram to tell Fred the news.

'You know Fred,' she said instead. 'Probably made ten friends at the pub on the way out of town. Or more likely reads the *Gazette*,' she added.

She and Mah appeared in the local paper several times a year, under the paper's policy of mentioning everyone in town at least four times per annum and not just in the hatch, match and dispatch notices. And when you owned one of the town's biggest employers, the biscuit factory, and were members of the CWA, the Red Cross, the Literary Institute, and with Mah teaching at the Sunday school, and both of them riding Sheba in the War Bonds parade, well, Cousin Murgatroyd could learn a lot about his sister and her friend, especially now another woman owned the *Gazette*, and made sure women's activities were given due prominence.

'Murgatroyd?' said Blue.

Mah's worried face lifted in a smile. And suddenly they were both laughing, though there were tears there too. Fred could do that, thought Blue, wiping her eyes. Even with a letter he could make them laugh.

Keep him safe, she prayed. For Mah's sake, and for mine. Keep Fred safe. And bring my Joseph home to me.

Chapter 27

Gibber's Creek Gazette, 2 July 1942

Children's Evacuation Preparations

Council met today to discuss arrangements for all children in the district in the event that evacuation to Alice Springs is ordered by the State Emergency Council. In that event, all children are to assemble at the school with two labels, one with his name and other particulars and another for his luggage. A circular will be given to each parent, giving information regarding luggage, clothing, food and other requirements. With regard to the evacuation of aged persons, cripples and invalids, forms are now available at the Town Clerk's office.

Councillor Bullant stated yesterday that any person who wished to discuss these preparations might call upon him at an early date. Councillor Ellis replied that if the government wanted to take his kids, they could send a search party to get them. He reckoned neither the government nor the Japanese could find his children if they didn't want to be found, and suggested that instead of evacuation all children should be sent to pot rabbits to improve their target practice.

NANCY

She was dreaming, and knew that she was, the dream too good to let go, even though she could still hear Gavin's fretful cry, Moira's soothing voice as she settled him to feed, Nurse Rogers and Vivienne arguing in the next hut, the sound of chittering from unfamiliar insects, a yell and a response in Japanese.

No. She was in the mountain paddock, rounding up the steers. The noises were the cicadas in the trees, pulsing, swelling, the lowing of the first beast as it saw her and swung away.

She was seven perhaps, because she was small and the steer was very large. But there was still that magic moment when it thought, human, and obeyed, swinging around as she yelled, 'Hyah!'

And then they all moved, the mob like one multi-legged beast, while a small girl with a stick walked after them, one yell and a sweep of her stick now and then all that was needed to keep them moving. She felt power, and happiness, but couldn't have named either. This was just how the world was, would always be — the sweet sharp smell of cattle dung, the cicadas drumming, dust puffing up behind the herd, the thud, thud, thud of hooves.

Thud, thud, thud …

Nancy opened her eyes. The thuds were the translator's boots on the hard-packed ground. His face seemed to swim in the heat-soaked air as he bent his head and came into the hut.

'We need a lock on the door,' said Mrs Harris, as she clambered up off her bed to bow.

'We need a door,' muttered Nancy.

She scrambled to her feet and bowed too, next to Sally and Moira, who was holding Gavin awkwardly as she bent her face to the ground.

The translator's face and voice were impassive. 'Japanese officers need company at the officers' club tonight. Four women. One woman from each house. Two from one house.'

'This isn't a house,' said Mrs Harris. 'It's a hovel.'

He ignored her. 'One woman from each house.'

'Company?' said Mrs Harris. 'I have another word for it.'

She means sex, thought Nancy blankly. She had thought of many things they might face in the next few months before they were freed or found a way to escape. Not this.

Moira heaved Gavin higher on her shoulder. He clutched her hair, staring at the man in uniform. 'None of us,' Moira said, each word distinct. 'Not a single one of us will keep your officers company.'

'One woman from every house, two from one house. A total of four women. The women will be paid in food or money. If there are not four women, there will be no food for anyone.'

'You can't do that!' cried Nancy, then wished the words unsaid. Of course they could do that. They could do anything to the women in this camp. Anything at all.

'Very well,' said old Mrs Harris crisply. 'Your officers shall have me for company tonight.' She looked the translator straight in the eyes. 'I hope they enjoy my ... conversation.'

'One *young* woman.'

Me or Moira, thought Nancy, feeling sick. Or Sally.

'None of us,' repeated Moira, 'are going anywhere near your officers. Or their club house either.'

'No women. No food.' He turned and left.

They met at the latrine, despite the stench, one woman from each house, no more than three at a time, two leaving one behind to tell the next two what had been said. If they tried to all talk together in one of the huts or in the yard except at mealtimes, the translator yelled, 'No consorting!' and the bamboo rods lashed down. The guards would be especially watchful now.

Nurse Rogers joined Nancy from Hut Number Two, then Mrs Hughendorn from Hut Number One.

'No one from our hut is going,' declared Mrs Hughendorn, her bosom still impressive under its ropes of pearls. 'We'll show them what British women are made of.'

'Vivienne wants to go,' said Nurse Rogers flatly.

'How could she?'

Nurse Rogers shrugged. 'She says the Japanese only want what every other man does. Says we'll starve if we don't get more food. I told her if she tries I'll cut her hair off, then no one will want her anyway.'

'What will you cut it off with?' asked Nancy. None of them had knives or scissors.

Nurse Rogers grinned. 'She's too dumb to think of that. Believed me anyway. For now.'

Nancy walked slowly back to the hut. Moira propped herself up on her elbows. Her ankles were swelling, and she was out of breath. Over on the other bunk Sally played Peepo with Gavin.

'What did the other huts say?' asked Moira.

'Nothing doing.'

'If we all stand firm, they can't make us,' said Moira. She seemed almost to believe it.

They can make us do anything, thought Nancy. Anything or die.

There was no cassava, sago or yams at dusk. No vegetables. Not even a coconut.

'They'll see we mean business,' said Mrs Harris.

Moira nodded as Gavin began to wail.

For the first time the pretence of food — Mrs Mainwaring's cheese on toast — petered out. Perhaps it was just that cheese on toast was uninspiring. But this was the first time the absence of food was due to their deliberate actions.

Gavin was still crying with hunger deep into the night. The others pretended to sleep while Nancy and Moira took turns to walk him around the compound. At last Mrs Harris came out, brushing the mosquitoes from her face. 'I'll take him for you for a while, darlings.'

Moira nodded, beaten. 'Thank you. I ... I'm sorry. He must be teething.'

'He's hungry,' said Mrs Harris bluntly.

We are all hungry, thought Nancy. Hunger was a small rat inside her, eating her innards. The twice-a-day gruel had been just enough to just keep going. Already the lack of it made her head swim. The lack of sleep didn't help.

'I'm feeding him as often as he wants ...' began Moira.

Mrs Harris glanced fleetingly at Moira's chest. Her thin chest, gone from slender to bones in a month. 'Time to wean him, love,' she said tactfully. 'You can't give him what you haven't got.'

Gavin had fallen asleep on Mrs Harris's shoulder. Perhaps he too had finally accepted there was no food to be had. Or perhaps he had no more strength to cry.

They sat at the cook pit the next morning. No one even suggested a breakfast menu today. Gavin cried fretfully, small bubbles of complaint, lying like a toy doll against his mother.

'We have to give in, don't we?' Mrs Hughendorn put into words what they had all been thinking. The guards had shaken their heads when Nancy had knocked on the door to fetch the water earlier. Nor had the food bin appeared.

'Yes,' said Nancy. They could survive a while without food. But without water in the constant dry heat they would die in days. Moira today, perhaps, or tomorrow. Or Gavin.

It was agree to their demands or die. You could throw away your own life for honour. But not Moira's life, and not Gavin's.

It was as simple as that, she thought. If we do not agree, then Gavin dies.

The translator's boots thumped again at midday. Thud thud, thud thud, into the hut ...

They bowed.

'Four young women, tonight.' His voice was expressionless.

Had he rehearsed the words? thought Nancy. Did he have a textbook that he studied every night? It was impossible to know how much he understood of what they said.

'There will be a young woman,' said Mrs Harris. 'If you give us the food we should have got yesterday and this morning, tonight.'

'You will get supper.' Was he refusing or agreeing?

'More supper? If we do not get more food,' said Mrs Harris clearly, 'this young boy will die. We need food for him now too.'

'You will get supper. I will take the women before supper. The women will get supper at the club. A very good supper.'

'Water?' asked Moira, her voice a hoarse whisper.

The translator looked at her, at Gavin, lying white-faced on the bed, his arms and legs slack, as if in sleep. But he was not sleeping, had not slept since early morning, his eyes open, far too large for his small face.

'The guards will bring water now.' The translator turned, and marched between the shadows to the next hut.

The silence filled the hut. Nancy waited for Sally to volunteer. She didn't.

Moira didn't look at any of them. 'I'll go.'

'No,' said Nancy.

'Nancy, darling, I ... I'm married. I know what to expect ...'

From men like that? thought Nancy. Men who would force a woman by threatening to starve her and her friends?

'I will go,' she said. 'Because I could never face Ben if you go in my place. Or Mum or Gran. Never.'

She sat on the dirt floor and waited for Moira's arguments. There would be an afternoon of arguments, she knew, surfing back and forth as supper and dusk approached. But when the translator returned, she would be the one going with him.

Four women, from three huts. Herself, Vivienne, Nurse Rogers and Mrs Mainwaring. None of them looked at each other, as they waited in the shade of the Number One tree. Mrs Mainwaring had been even more quiet the past weeks. The other women spoke of the families they longed for, fears for their families. Mrs Mainwaring had never spoken of either. Nancy wondered if she knew — or feared — her husband was already dead. She stayed silent now, her eyes empty.

At last Nancy said, to break the silence, 'Nurse Rogers, I'm worried about Moira. Her ankles are swelling.'

'Scurvy,' said Nurse Rogers. She looked relieved to be back in professional territory. 'Or beri beri,' she added. 'Vitamin deficiency. We need to ask for more vegetables.'

'We have asked. They won't give them to us.'

'But they have to —' Nurse Rogers stopped, accepting once again that their captors did not have to do anything, except what their own honour required.

'Those bushes in the garden out there — they look a bit like hibiscus. Back home, my gran told me you could eat the flowers and buds of the Australian hibiscus. She said they were good for you — I think she meant they had vitamins. Could we eat the flower buds?'

'We could. And they might kill us,' said Nurse Rogers dryly.

'One of us could try it. Me,' Nancy added. 'I know what the ones at home taste like.'

'It's worth trying,' said Nurse Rogers, just as the translator arrived.

They bowed.

'Sensei,' said Nancy, not sure she had got the honorific right but hoping her willingness to try might move him, as well as their presence here tonight. 'We need vegetables. We are getting sick because we don't have any.' She pointed at the bushes. 'May I go outside each morning to pick the buds and flowers to eat?'

The translator looked at her, at the bushes, then back at her. 'They are food?'

'Full of vitamins,' said Nancy, hoping it was true.

'You will pick them for the Japanese too.'

Nancy bowed. If I live through tonight, she thought. I can pick flowers for the Japanese if I can get through tonight. And if the flowers poison me, then they'll kill the lot of you too.

The 'club' was the front room of the officers' house, still furnished as it must have been when Mrs Hughendorn's mother-in-law lived there. Floral sofa, four chintz-covered chairs, even two family photographs, a woman with two small children and a young man who might have been Mr Hughendorn, before acquiring Mrs Hughendorn and the moustache that adorned the face in the photograph Mrs Hughendorn kept tucked in the armour that still served as her underwear, although no longer needed to rein in her bulk. The photos sat on the ledge that might have been a mantelpiece, if a fireplace had been needed. A portrait of the Emperor hung on the wall above it.

Four men sat in the armchairs, including the commandant, all in uniform, the youngest one in his early twenties perhaps. He was the only one who smiled. The others neither moved nor changed their expressions.

The translator bowed, then left. The door shut behind him.

Vivienne stepped forwards. She smiled at the youngest officer. 'I'm Viv,' she said.

They can't speak English, thought Nancy. We can't speak Japanese. She stifled a hysterical giggle. How are they going to tell us what to do if we can't talk?

Except, she realised, the married Mrs Mainwaring would know what to do. Vivienne too, she suspected. And Nurse Rogers? Did they teach *that* to nurses? Her own animal husbandry knowledge probably wasn't going to help her predict the behaviour of Japanese officers.

She tried not to think of Michael. Trying not to think of him made her think of him even more. Could she marry him after this? Would he even want her, if he knew she had ... been with ... a Japanese man? An enemy? And not from choice, but for food and water?

Yes, she thought, Michael will forgive. Though perhaps she would not be able to forgive herself. No, she told herself.

Whatever happens tonight will be done to you, as a soldier might be wounded in war. You will let it slide away from you, leaving you untouched. Just Nancy of the Overflow.

I can do this, she thought. No matter what. I can do this.

They stood there, silent, even Vivienne. The men regarded them. The commandant stood. He nodded to Nancy, then walked towards the corridor.

He expects me to follow him, she thought. He is the highest-ranking officer here, so he gets first choice. I should be flattered.

She could refuse to follow. I have no choice, she thought again. No choice. No choice.

She followed.

Down the corridor. The commandant stopped by a door, obviously expecting her to open it for him. She did, standing back to let him walk through. She wondered for a moment if she should leave it open, so she could call for help perhaps.

But who would help? Or if they did, at what cost?

I can do this, she thought. I *can* do this.

She shut the door. She waited.

There was a bed — a single bed, with an ornate bedhead and a flowered bedspread. The commandant sat on the bedspread. He nodded to her to sit next to him.

She couldn't. She knew she had to but she couldn't. Her feet were lumps of flour, her heart was trying to choke her. It was all she could do to stand there and not cry, or urinate like a scared puppy when a big dog barked. She wished she had not bitten her nails because then she could have dug them into her hands and that pain might drive out this other one ...

The commandant regarded her, much as he had in the front room. He reached over to the bedside table, opened a drawer. He drew out a black-and-white photograph. He held it out to her.

She found that she could take it, her fingers hardly trembling.

It was a girl. A girl about my age, she thought. A girl with shiny black hair gathered up about her face and wearing a kimono with a pattern of leaves. The girl did not smile at the

238

camera but she looked happy. Above her a tree seemed to be in bloom, though without colour it was hard to tell if they were flowers or strange leaves.

Was this his mistress, back in Japan? A young girl like her? Or was this photograph the Japanese equivalent of a poster of Bette Davis, illustrating his idea of beauty?

But the girl was not particularly beautiful. Pretty, but nothing dramatic.

The commandant pointed to himself, then to the photo. He took it from her hand, then looked at it, his face gentle.

She understood. 'This is your daughter?'

He said nothing. She guessed he had as little English as she had Japanese. He studied the photo, then lay back against the bed.

She tensed as he began to speak.

It was not directed to her, but to the photo. To what it represented, perhaps, to his family, to his home. His voice continued, tender, sometimes laughing, once almost in tears.

She stood. At last she sat on the floor, letting herself slide down the wall. She sat cross-legged, as she might before a campfire, and waited for him to stop talking, to order her to the bed. Finally he stopped speaking. He looked at the photo for some time more, then opened the drawer, and hid the photo away again. He looked at Nancy.

'Watashi no musume,' he said.

Was he asking her to undress? She didn't move.

'Watashi no musume,' he repeated and then, 'Musume,' again.

Oh. It was a language lesson.

'Musume,' she said slowly.

He nodded, smiled. He pointed to the bed. 'Shindai.'

'Sindoi.'

'Shindai.'

'Shindai,' she said.

Ten words later he seemed to have had enough. He lay there, looking at the ceiling. He consulted a pocket watch. Later — much later — he stood up. He nodded to the door.

It was time to go.

Once more she understood what he was trying to tell her. Understood it all: that he was protecting her; that she must not say, even to the other women, that nothing sexual had happened here tonight.

Had he protected her because she reminded him of his daughter? Or because he was a basically good man, whatever the war had brought to him, who would not take a woman against her will, even if he had not the courage, or perhaps even saw no need, to protest when it was done to others?

'Thank you,' she said.

He stood. For the first time he smiled at her, not at the photo.

'Arigato,' he said.

'Arigato,' she repeated.

'Sayonara.' He opened the door and walked back down the corridor.

The front room was empty. Empty of humans anyway, for the sofas and fat armchairs still sat invitingly. How long had it been since she had sat in a chair? And there on the table ...

Food. Real food.

Rice balled together somehow, held in place by a strip of something black. She hadn't eaten rice since they'd arrived — it wasn't grown on the poor soil of the island. Fried fish, small and brown and crisp, piled on a platter. Slabs of the baked plantain she had become familiar with in Malaya, as well as strange fat dumplings, shiny and white, again piled high.

The translator had promised them supper.

She wanted to eat. Needed to eat. She also wanted to curl up behind the door and cry, because whatever hadn't happened to her tonight might still happen, and was happening to Nurse Rogers and Vivienne and Mrs Mainwaring.

She did not cry. She was Nancy of the Overflow, and if she ate here tonight she need not eat at all tomorrow, so there would be more for the others to share.

So she would eat.

She still hesitated. There were bowls, chopsticks. She couldn't use chopsticks. If she tried to learn how tonight, she would go hungry. Perhaps she was meant to wait, and the four women were to eat with the officers.

Four bowls. Four sets of chopsticks. Just for the women then.

She picked up some of the dumplings and rice balls, and stuffed as many as she thought she could get away with into her bra, to share with the others. The fish looked oily, and she dared not risk getting oil stains on her dress that might be noticed.

She began to eat, fast, resisting the instinct to cram food into her mouth with both hands. Rice balls first, using her fingers — Mum had once told her and Ben that rice lined the stomach when they'd eaten too many green apples. Then, more slowly, because if she was sick after eating too much rich food when she was so very hungry, then the food would be wasted. She ate a fish, a plantain, hoping it was high in Nurse Rogers's vitamins. She was nibbling a dumpling, even more slowly, when she heard a door open. Nurse Rogers walked stiffly down the corridor and into the sitting room.

For a moment they looked at each other in silence. Then Nancy said, 'I think this is for us.'

'Good,' said Nurse Rogers, in a voice that said, do not ask me, and I will not ask you. 'Don't eat too much too fast,' she added.

'I'm not.'

Nurse Rogers picked up a bowl and manoeuvred the chopsticks easily. She glanced at Nancy. 'One of the nurses at the hospital was Chinese. We'd go to her parents' place sometimes. Chopsticks aren't hard when you get used to them. I'll show you.' She seemed relieved to talk about the normality of food.

Nancy let herself be shown. It was something to speak about that wasn't unspeakable; and she had eaten enough now to know that she needed to slow down. Managing chopsticks meant careful eating. She had just manipulated a piece of fish into her mouth when Vivienne came out. Her lips looked puffed and red.

'That wasn't too bad,' she said.

The others stared at her.

Vivienne shrugged. 'Don't expect me to go into a maiden's faint. I expect you've done it before,' she added to Nurse Rogers.

Nurse Rogers didn't reply.

'It's not something any woman likes doing, no matter who it's with. But if you want to get a man to do something for you ...' She shrugged again. 'What about you?' she asked Nancy.

Nancy said nothing either.

'As long as they didn't knock you around.' Vivienne helped herself to fish and rice, using her fingers. 'Here,' she added. 'Show me how to use the chopsticks.'

'Why?' asked Nancy, though she had been willing to learn herself.

Vivienne sat back, stabbing a rice ball using her chopstick like a dagger. 'Because the Japanese are winning the war.' She looked up at their silent faces. 'You don't really believe that we can win, do you? You've seen what the Japanese did in Malaya. Thailand. Singapore. The entire American Navy is sunk. Yes, I know the precious mems back there,' she nodded in the direction of the huts, 'want to pretend that the British Empire has to win. I'll pretend all they like. But we can be honest here. Can't we?'

'Why?' asked Nurse Rogers.

'Because ...' Vivienne's voice trailed off. She looked at them. 'If you don't think they're going to win, why did you volunteer for this?'

Because no matter who wins, it was the right thing to do, thought Nancy, for her and Nurse Rogers and Mrs Mainwaring.

'Where's Mrs Mainwaring? She should be out by now.'

Even as Nancy spoke a man yelled at the rear of the house. Boots sounded outside, familiar footsteps. The translator appeared, glanced at them, then stepped down the corridor. He reappeared seconds later, beckoning to them to follow him.

Nancy looked at Nurse Rogers enquiringly. She shrugged and began to follow him. They walked down the corridor, Vivienne trailing behind. Nurse Rogers paused at the door. She gasped, then pushed Nancy back. 'Don't come in here.'

'Why not?' Vivienne pushed past her. 'Oh. I'm ... I'm going to be sick.'

The translator's voice came from behind them. Nancy could feel his anger now. 'You take her. You bury her. All of you. You do it now.'

She stepped into the room. Blood stained the wooden floor, the pale blue counterpane — blood from Mrs Mainwaring's wrists. A broken sake glass lay on the bed beside her.

Nancy turned to the translator in fury. 'You did this!'

The man stared at her. 'I did nothing. I was not here.'

'The man she was with!'

'She asked the Japanese officer for sake. The Japanese officer gave it to her, one, two, three times. He left. I saw she was not with you so I came here.'

'She died of shame,' said Nurse Rogers softly. 'She knew someone had to go. So she sacrificed herself.'

'Better all of you die of shame. Japanese women would not be taken by the enemy. Japanese women would kill themselves first.'

Nancy gaped at the translator. 'You think we should all kill ourselves because we have been taken prisoner?'

'English women do not understand honour.' The translator looked around the room, the blood, the woman on the bed. 'Maybe this one did. You dig a grave for her. You bury her.'

'What if we don't?'

'The guards will put her body outside for the dogs.'

The guards gave them three shovels. The other women peered at them from the huts, but the guards gestured them back.

It was almost morning by the time the grave was deep enough. Nancy had expected Vivienne to complain, but she scraped at the dry soil as diligently as the other two. She was pale, shivering now instead of confident.

Two guards watched them. As they stepped back, one nodded for them to follow him to the officers' club.

The body lay where they had left it. At least it is night, thought Nancy. At least there are no flies ...

'We'll wrap her in the bedspread and sheets,' said Nurse Rogers.

'Maybe they don't want us to use them —' began Vivienne.

'Too bad,' said Nurse Rogers.

Nancy bent to the dead woman. Mrs Mainwaring looked ... not peaceful exactly, but the lips almost formed a smile. Oh, yes, she thought, English women know about honour. This woman had the honour to volunteer, to save her friends.

Would she have done the same as Mrs Mainwaring, if her commandant had wanted more than her attention?

No, she thought. We all have our own codes. And mine says that I must live to care for those I love. Gavin and Moira belonged to Overflow. She would take them back for it, for Ben. And for herself.

She had expected an adult body to be heavier, but Mrs Mainwaring had starved with all of them. The guards stood back as they carried her down the hall, across the main room, out into the night. Nancy could hear the sea muttering beyond the bushes. The waves must be high tonight. The stars peered down at them, strangely familiar stars in this all-too-strange land.

They leant down as far as they could, but the body dropped the last few feet. Nancy and Nurse Rogers reached for the shovels, to fill in the dirt. Vivienne held back, still shaking. 'I'm going to ask the translator if the other women can come to say goodbye. We need a ceremony.'

Nancy looked at her, surprised, then nodded wearily. 'That's a kind thought.'

'I ...' Vivienne stopped whatever she had been going to say. 'We have to do what they want,' she whispered. 'Don't you understand? We will die if we don't. A worse death than this. Those men in there can kill us. But they can save us too. Nancy ...'

'What?' asked Nancy tiredly, not looking at her. Her body and mind felt as bruised as if she too had been assaulted.

'Nothing,' said Vivienne. 'I'll get the others while you fill in the grave. I ... I'm sorry.'

Thunk. Thunk. The soil thudded into the grave. Impossible to think that the woman under the dirt, within those sheets, had been alive only a few hours before.

Thunk. Thunk. It was far faster to fill in the hole than dig it. Slowly, one by one, the other women came out, the guards surrounding them. There was no sign of the officers who had sought their company.

Mrs Hughendorn lifted her hands in prayer. 'Our Father ...' she began.

The others prayed with her. Sally was crying, and Mrs Harris. There was no sign of Vivienne. Suddenly Nancy sensed movement at the huts. She looked over her fingers. The young secretary slipped through the shadows, her suitcase in her hand.

What else had Vivienne said to the translator? wondered Nancy, as Vivienne walked swiftly not to the house where they had been 'entertainers', but to the Japanese living quarters. The door opened. Vivienne shot a haunted look back at her camp companions, then vanished inside.

'Dear Lord, please care for our sister,' said Mrs Hughendorn. 'Deliver her from the pain she suffered in this world, into Your love and mercy in the next. Amen.'

Deliver us all, thought Nancy, from those who think we have no honour because we choose to live.

They trooped back in silence to the huts. No one asked her what had happened in the house. No one spoke at all till they reached Hut Number One. Mrs Hughendorn paused, then embraced Nurse Rogers and then Nancy. 'You are the bravest of the brave,' she said. 'We owe our lives to both of you.'

It seemed Nancy had not been the only one to see Vivienne go.

Moira hugged her back at their hut. 'Thank you from me too,' she whispered. 'And Gavin. They gave us chicken tonight. Chicken! And rice and pumpkin and a whole lot of greens. Darling, are you all right? Can I help with … anything? Will you … will you have to go again?'

'Probably. Moira …' She *couldn't* let Moira think that she had been used as Mrs Mainwaring had been used, no matter what she had been instructed. 'The man I was with — the commandant. He didn't touch me. Just talked to me.'

Moira's face relaxed into so much relief that Nancy understood the horror her sister-in-law had been trying not to show. 'Thank God.' It was a prayer. 'What did he say?'

'I don't know. He spoke in Japanese.'

'What about Nurse Rogers?'

Nancy shrugged. Tomorrow and tomorrow, she thought, we will have to go back there. What if the commandant changes his mind? What if another man asked her to go to his room?

Suddenly she remembered her store of dumplings and rice balls, all squished together now, but still food. They could stay where they were in her bra till breakfast, she thought. At least they'd be safe from rats.

Would they ever see Vivienne again?

Chapter 28

Gibber's Creek Gazette, 1 August 1942

New Speed Limit

A speed limit of twenty miles an hour has been set by order
of the premier during all blackouts and brownouts. It will
apply between sunset and sunrise. In addition, at all times
and places headlights must be effectively screened.

According to Councillor Bullant: 'Council-appointed
officers will be ensuring that all motorists keep to the advised
speed limit at all times.'

Councillor Ellis commented: 'If the premier thinks he
can drive at more than twenty miles an hour on some of the
roads around here, I'd like to see him try.'

PULAU AYU PRISON CAMP, 1 AUGUST 1942

NANCY

The cramps hit her at dawn, so bad she doubled up in pain. She
glanced over at the next bed. Moira had vanished, presumably
to the latrine, leaving Gavin sleeping on the narrow bed, arms
sprawled.

She hobbled out to the latrine. Moira was crouched on the
plank above the trench. Mrs Hughendorn trudged quickly
behind her, and then Nurse Rogers. The four of them crouched,

like chooks perched in the henhouse, trying to ignore each other's sounds.

'Dysentery,' said Nurse Rogers at last, as they staggered weak and dizzy back towards their huts. 'Gavin ... is he all right?'

'I think so.' Moira's face looked even paler.

'He was still asleep when I left,' said Nancy.

'Thank goodness. It's not the food then.' Gavin only drank the thin stews they boiled morning and evening. 'Must be the well water. Better boil it ...' Another spasm hit her. Nurse Rogers ran for the latrine again.

It passed. Days of agony every time she swallowed, trying to keep the boiled water down. Somehow one of them managed to boil enough for the next day for the others, make a soup of whatever food they were given. Gavin ate it eagerly; Moira was no longer able to give him any nourishment at all. Her body had grown skeletal, her eyes like dark-rimmed moons.

'Drink,' urged Nurse Rogers, and they did, in sips, as small as possible, for any larger swallow brought the spasms on.

Nancy recovered first. Because I'm younger, she thought. Or because my body got used to bad water on the way to Charters Towers? After a week, she was the one to light the fire, to boil the water, to feed Gavin, to watch him crawl about in the dirt, his hands and knees becoming crusty, for she did not have the strength yet to wash him as well as do the other chores.

'At least,' said Nurse Rogers, taking her ration of water mixed with a little rice gruel, 'the officers won't want us to entertain them now. Not and risk catching something from us.'

Nancy nodded. Nor, she thought, could any man want their company now. Even the floor scrubbing had been stopped, for fear the women might infect their guards. Nancy looked at the others: thin to hardness, eyes well sunk into black shadows, hair filthy, smelling of the latrine. Even Gavin was thin now. Vegetables alone were not enough for a growing child, and she hadn't had the strength to catch 'island rabbit', or to ask again if she could go out and pick hibiscus flowers.

At home Mum would make sure he drank a glass of milk with every meal. He'd be eating meat and vegetables, chopped fine, stewed apple, grated pears, mashed banana …

She looked at him, slouched in the dirt as if too tired to crawl. 'Nanna?' he said. He lifted his arms to her.

'Nancy,' she said softly as she picked him up.

'Nanna,' he agreed. He burrowed into her like a baby wombat seeking its pouch.

She took him into their hut, put him next to Moira. Her sister-in-law rolled over, still half asleep, and wrapped him in her arms.

For a moment Nancy stared at them. She stepped wearily to the 'dressing table' — a block of wood where Mrs Harris had put her brush and comb for them to share. Mrs Harris was asleep too, the skin of her face drooping like sheets of paper, her breathing harsh.

Nancy brushed her hair, stripped off a shred of bamboo to tie it back as smartly as she could, and changed her dress for her one clean one, already fraying at the edges.

That was as respectable as she could make herself, she decided. She walked, telling herself that her trembling was from illness, not fear. She knocked at the door of the officers' club.

The youngest of the officers opened it. He stared at her as she bowed, as low as she could, then shouted down the corridor.

She rose from the bow. She stood there, waiting. The same men who had been there the night of Mrs Mainwaring's death sat in what had been Mrs Hughendorn senior's armchairs. The commandant sat there too, a glass of what looked like tea in his hand. He neither looked at nor acknowledged her.

'What do you want?' It was the translator.

'The little boy needs food,' she said. 'We are all sick. We need medicine.'

'Japanese soldiers have been generous to give you food. No medicine.'

'We can pay for the medicine! Please!' She was sure Mrs Hughendorn would agree; she was as sick as any of them.

The translator looked back. The commandant gave an imperceptible nod. 'If you give me the money, I will see if I can buy medicine.'

'Thank you.' She bowed deeply again. She hoped this man would not take half the money for himself. 'Please, may we have more food for the little boy?'

'If you can pay for medicine, you can pay for food.'

'But ... but Japan is defeating the British Empire. We will be here many years. Won't we?'

The translator gave no answer.

'We cannot buy food for that long. Please, food for one small boy. And some seeds? So we can begin to grow our own?'

'You have food —' began the translator.

The commandant said something to the translator, not to her.

The translator looked startled. He turned to Nancy again. 'There will be food for the boy. No seeds. Gardens need tools.'

'Proper food?'

'Do not question Japanese officers.'

A guard approached, with his bamboo rod at the ready. She bowed again hastily. 'Thank you. Arigato. I thank the honour of Japanese officers, to help one small boy.'

'Go,' said the translator. Nancy went.

The translator was with the guard when he delivered the sago the next morning: two coconut shells full, for the eleven of them. The guard also gave her a hand of bananas, a dozen of them, not much longer than her finger.

She gazed at them, hunger growling like a dog smelling roast lamb. It was the first fruit she had seen since they had been interned.

'For the boy,' said the translator, as if he suspected she might eat them herself.

'Nanna?' Gavin crawled from the hut towards her. I really must wash him today, she thought. And catch rats early tomorrow.

'Come here, darling.' She lifted him onto her knee. Even that was an effort. He clung there, waiting for the sago to cook.

She shook her head. 'Look what Auntie Nancy has for you. Bananas.'

He opened his mouth, a small starved bird, as she fed him tiny chunks.

Chapter 29

Gibber's Creek Gazette, 29 August 1942

Australians Hungry on Kokoda Track

Reports from letters home suggest that Australian troops are going hungry as they battle along the Kokoda Track since the destruction of the RAAF 'biscuit bombers' in an air raid at Moresby.

See page 4 for 'How to Pack a Long-Lasting Fruitcake for the Front Line' and other recipes suitable for food packages, provided by Mrs Mah McAlpine.

ST ELRIC'S SCHOOL, BLUE MOUNTAINS, NEW SOUTH WALES, AUSTRALIA, 30 AUGUST 1942

MICHAEL

The phone call came at prep. He was supposed to be working on his Latin grammar. He had been daydreaming about Nancy instead, that last morning by the creek, the words she'd said to him, trying to ignore the chill of the mist seeping in around the rattling window frames. Since the school had moved up to the Blue Mountains, partly for safety and partly because its school buildings were requisitioned by the military, the cold attacked him every time he sat down.

He missed the old ivy-covered buildings down in Sydney. He missed the river more. No rowing up here in the mountains. No pelicans either.

He didn't want to be here. Boarding school was what one endured, even if parts of it were good. Every classroom seemed a prison, walls enclosing him when he wanted paddocks and hills, or the challenge of army life, despite its dangers and hardships.

His parents longed for the best for him — all that they'd never had. He even accepted that at some stage he might want to go to agricultural college, and to do that he must finish school now. But he also wanted the chance to succeed that they'd had, on his own merits. Mostly he wanted to choose his own future. To be part of the world, now. Australia needs you, the posters said. He needed to be part of that too.

'Thompson. Phone call for you. Your father.' Wilkins looked sympathetic. Phone calls these days were rarely good news — like parents in town unexpectedly, offering you dinner, an aunt who'd like to visit with a spare five-pound note.

'Thanks.' Weird that his father would call, just when he'd been thinking about him, then with growing terror: something has happened to Jim, or Mum. Nancy! They've found her. She's coming home.

He hugged his arms around himself, his blazer too thin to keep out the chill. He'd put on every singlet he had. He would have asked Mum for thermal underwear like Taylor had, but she'd used up the last of his clothing coupons on his school uniform. There had been no choice, the way he was growing, his trouser cuffs heading up to his knees, and Mum would never go black market, like the parents of some of the students here.

The single phone was in the headmaster's office. 'Sorry to disturb you, sir.'

'Quite all right.'

The headmaster left, though Michael knew he lingered just outside the door.

Michael picked up the receiver. 'Hello? Dad? Is everything all right?'

'Yes. Just thought you'd like to know. The news came through from Radio Tokyo last night. Ben Clancy is a prisoner of war.'

'Oh, Dad, I'm so glad. Will you pass on my best wishes to the Clancys? I'll write to them of course. No news of Joseph?' Or Nancy, he thought. But of course if there had been any news at all of either, his father would have told him without prompting.

'No.' His father's voice was gentle. 'How are you keeping, son?'

'Another three minutes?' It was the operator.

'Yes,' said his father. 'Anything you need? You know Mrs Mutton is about to send another fruitcake.'

'I'm fine. Well, actually, if you have any spare singlets, I'd love them. It's cold up here.'

'I can do better than that. I've got the long johns I bought when we visited England. Haven't worn them since. If you don't mind your dad's cast-offs.'

'I'd love them,' said Michael, wondering how he'd fit his six-foot-two body into his five-foot-nine father's not-so-very long johns.

'I'll get Mrs Mutton to lengthen the legs. I've got half a dozen pairs, which should make three at least for you. Here's Mum.' There was a hesitation, then, 'All my love, son.'

'The same to you, Dad.' Dad rarely said the word 'love', thought Michael, but I've always known it was there. He's a canny old bloke. He knew news of Ben would make me think of Nancy. 'Mum?'

'Michael, darling, how are you? Not getting a chill up there?'

'Mum, stop fussing. I'm fine.'

'I've been knitting you a jumper. I pulled apart a couple of old ones of mine.'

Just what he needed — one of Mum's knitting attempts, more holes than jumper and sleeves that might fit the Hunchback of Notre Dame. 'Thanks, Mum.' At least diverting her knitting to him meant saving a couple of soldiers from trying to fit their feet into lumpy socks with a heel close to their toes. The poor blighters had enough to cope with without Mum's socks.

'Another three minutes?' asked the operator.

'Of course. Michael, I wish you'd been here yesterday. Mountain Lass had the most lovely foal. A filly, dark grey, like Snow King used to be. And the CWA finished six camouflage nets last week, our personal record. There's the Red Cross Bazaar next Wednesday ...'

It was the same news she'd written in the letter he'd got yesterday. But he didn't mind. It was good to hear Mum's voice, see home in his mind's eye. See Nancy, sitting by the river, her eyes laughing at him. One day, he thought, she will be there again.

Chapter 30

Gibber's Creek Gazette, 10 September 1942

Australian Victory at Milne Bay

Australian forces have won a victory at Milne Bay in Papua, pushing a Japanese landing force back to the sea, the first major victory against Japanese forces. According to a letter home from a soldier whose name we cannot give here in case the censor turns his attention to his letters, Milne Bay would have given the Japanese a vital point from which to bomb mainland Australia.

On page 5: Daffodil Fair makes one hundred and sixty-five pounds for the war effort. See the winners and runners-up in all categories, including Largest Bloom and Best Collection Under Ten Years Old.

On page 6: Cricket results, Gibber's Creek thrashes Yass.

PULAU AYU PRISON CAMP, 15 SEPTEMBER 1942

NANCY

Mrs Harris died in the night. Old Miss Smith collapsed at tenko. Nurse Rogers bent to tend her, despite the slash of the guard's bamboo rod. But Miss Smith was dead as neatly as she had lived, her hands and feet tucked under the small starved body.

'Heat perhaps,' said Nurse Rogers tiredly, rubbing at the welt left by the bamboo on her cheek, and then remembering not to touch it in case she broke the skin. They had recovered, more or less, from the dysentery, though every bowel motion was now painful and slightly liquid, and even walking too fast brought on dizziness. 'Perhaps her heart gave out. Or starvation. Dysentery. Scurvy ...'

We need hibiscus buds, thought Nancy wearily. She had forgotten the hibiscus buds. She explained about them again to Nurse Rogers.

The woman shrugged. 'Like I said before. Might work. Might poison us too.'

'I'll try them first.'

'You're immune from poison?'

'No. But my grandmother showed me ways to see if something is edible.'

Gran had also impressed on her that the tests weren't fool proof — that some people could tolerate foods that would make others sick, and that domesticated fruits were all bred from the same trees by cuttings, but that wild ones varied. A fruit that had been safe to eat from a tree on one hill might kill you if you ate another from a hill nearby.

But Moira's wrists were swelling now, as well as her ankles. Mrs Hughendorn too looked nearly as fat as when they had arrived. But this was a different kind of fat: fluid had pushed up under her skin like a blown-up balloon.

Nancy tried to smile at Nurse Rogers. 'I'll be right,' she said.

She waited till afternoon roll call to ask the translator. As usual the women lined up at the call of 'tenko', bowed as the guards walked along their line. Nancy wasn't sure why the roll-call ritual was so important. There were only nine of them now, including Gavin, so it would be easy enough to see if anyone had escaped. But perhaps this was in the soldiers' rule book: 'Prisoners must assemble twice a day to be counted.'

The translator waited in the shadows, as he always did during roll call. As soon as the guard had nodded that they might leave, she walked up to him, bowing even more deeply. 'Translator-san, please may I collect the flower buds that I told you about before the illness?'

'You will pick them for the Japanese too?'

'Yes, Translator-san.'

He considered. 'No guard can be spared to watch you.'

'I will stay near the bushes by the fence, Translator-san. Where I can be seen. I will not try to escape. You have my word.' Please, she thought. We will die on what you are giving us now. But she didn't want to say that. Perhaps it would suit the guards if the women did die. They might be transferred to work they thought more honourable than guarding mems who had let themselves be taken prisoner.

At last he said, 'You may go after roll call tomorrow. Half for women, half for Japanese soldiers. If you try to escape, one woman will die. You understand?'

'Yes. I understand.' She tried to keep the anger from her voice. 'Arigato, Translator-san.'

It was strange to walk out the gate, holding one of Mrs Hughendorn's baskets; strange not to have a horizon of barbed wire. She wanted to run, to see the sea, to feel just a little free, to go beyond the rat-trap of the camp.

She didn't. Couldn't. She didn't have the strength to run. And even if she was only gone from sight for a few minutes, the translator might make good his threat.

She looked at the bushes. The flowers did look like the hibiscus in the bush at home, but these were larger, and their flowers a different colour. She sniffed them. The smell was slightly different too. She snapped one off and, remembering Gran's words, broke it in half and sniffed again.

No scent of almonds — an almond smell meant there was a good chance a new fruit or seed was deadly. No white sap that could burn your mouth, throat and insides, killing you more slowly but just as surely.

She rubbed the juice from the flower bud on the tender part of her inner arm, waited to see if it left a red mark. But it just felt slightly sticky.

Time to taste. She nibbled, let the stuff lie in her mouth, then swallowed.

Waited.

It tasted slightly sweet, a bit mucilaginous, but otherwise tasteless, much as the flower buds she had known had tasted too, though they had grown sweeter and more flavourful when they were dried and made into a tea.

She ate the rest of the bud, then began to pick. The wild hibiscus she was used to put out new buds every day during warm weather, the flowers only lasted a day too. If this was going to work, this bush would have to flower just as frequently. The basket was soon full.

I shouldn't have picked so quickly, she thought. If I'd been slower, I could have stayed out here longer. She turned to go back to the gate.

'Shh. Mem!' It was a woman's voice, accented, unfamiliar.

She froze, carefully not looking around. 'Are you from Mrs Addison?' she whispered. She had wondered if the woman who had been allowed to leave might try to help them.

'Mrs Addison sail away.'

'From Vivienne?'

'Sorry, mem, do not know Mrs Vivienne. Mem, I leave parcel in bush. You take it to Mem Hughendorn?'

'Yes,' she whispered, trying not to move her lips, or look like she was talking. She heard another rustle, then footsteps, fast, heading away. She picked another few buds, slowly, as if looking for the fattest, then moved over to where she had heard the voice.

Nothing. No cloth-wrapped bundle. No basket ... Then she saw the little package, wrapped in banana leaves, almost the same colour as the bushes. She moved slowly, trying to look as if she was still picking. She bent down and picked up the bundle, about the size of a sandwich, and thrust it deep under the flower buds at the bottom of the basket, then straightened.

Should she really try to smuggle it in? What if the guards searched her basket? How else to carry it?

She bit her lip. Leave it, or take it? Such a small decision, but it might be life or death.

She didn't know.

Walking back through the gate, onto the hard-packed dirt of the prison compound, was one of the hardest things she had ever done. The closest guard beckoned to her. She walked towards him, trying to keep her breathing steady and unconcerned.

'Nanny!' No, she thought, as Gavin toddled towards her. He had just begun to walk, lurching from one handhold to another. As she looked, he dropped to all fours and began to crawl along in the dirt again.

Please, she thought, someone take him back. Keep him away from me. Because if the guards find the package and want to punish me, Gavin will be within reach too ...

'Nanna!' Gavin grabbed her legs. She picked him up, because to do otherwise would seem strange. The guard nodded at her basket. She gave it to him. He thrust his hand down among the flower buds.

Seconds passed. Gavin wound his fist in her hair. Every time he did that some strands fell out. Everyone's hair was growing thinner now. Nurse Rogers had said it was their bodies, craving protein.

The guard removed his hand from the basket, waved her towards the guards' living quarters. She bowed. 'Thank you, sensei.' She was still not sure this was a polite way to address a Japanese man, but Nurse Rogers had heard it used in a moving picture and none of the Japanese had objected. She picked up the basket in her other hand, and walked to the Japanese living quarters, still holding Gavin. She knocked on the door and waited.

A woman opened the door — local, with shadowed eyes. Nancy hadn't seen her before, and hadn't even known there were other women working in the camp. Was this woman just a cook? Willing, or forced?

She saw a bruise on the woman's face. Not willing.

'Half these are for the guards,' she spoke slowly, hoping the woman understood.

If she did, she made no sign. But she had obviously been expecting the flower buds. She proffered another basket, waited while Nancy tipped half the buds into it and then shut the door.

Once again Nancy tried to keep her expression calm as she walked back to the cooking fire, put the basket in the shade, then casually carried Gavin to Mrs Hughendorn's small house. She knocked on the doorframe. Her knuckles made little noise on the bamboo, but it was a small gesture towards courtesy nonetheless. Keeping up standards, as Mrs Hughendorn would say.

'Come in.' Mrs Hughendorn looked up from her bed, her room hot and airless despite the open window. They all spent as much time as they could lying down now, weak from the dysentery and starvation, as well as the oppressive heat. Nurse Rogers sat next to her.

'Excuse me for not standing, my dear,' said Mrs Hughendorn.

'I've brought the flower buds. I hope they'll help. We'd better wait till tomorrow before anyone else eats them though, in case they don't agree with me.'

Nurse Rogers raised an eyebrow. 'I thought that you would know if they were safe.'

'Just to be sure,' said Nancy. She had a vision of herself, dead in her bunk the next morning. Of all the guards dead too, because they had eaten toxic flower buds. Would the others be better or worse off if that occurred? Any freedom would be short-lived. They might even be blamed for the deaths of the Japanese and executed.

'Do sit down, my dear,' said Mrs Hughendorn. She reached over and passed Nancy a shell of boiled water. Their allowance had been doubled since their dysentery. Not quite enough. Never quite enough. But they could now drink during the day. The water tasted of coconut and wood smoke and entirely wonderful. She put it back on the shelf and sat on the edge of Mrs Hughendorn's bed. She spoke as softly as she could, 'Someone gave me something for you.'

'Who was it?'

'I couldn't see.' She reached into her bra, grateful that she had thought to wear it, a ridiculous celebration for going outside. She pulled out the parcel. Mrs Hughendorn took it in trembling hands. She unwrapped it and stared.

'Oh, how wonderful,' she said, as though she had been given a bunch of roses.

They were dried fish, a dozen of them, brown and straight and thin, hard as rock but far more pungent.

'Protein,' said Nurse Rogers softly.

Mrs Hughendorn picked up a note, greasy from the fish. '*Will bring more.*' There was no signature. 'I told you they were loyal to me,' she whispered. 'They all loved me like a mother.' She began to cry, long gulps she tried to hide.

'Shh.' Nurse Rogers leant down and held her close. 'It's food. One of these a day for the next week and the flower buds for vitamins and you'll feel a new woman.'

'No. We eat them all tonight, in case they are found. Everyone must have one,' said Mrs Hughendorn.

'But they are meant for you —' began Nancy.

'You are my family. We are all family,' said Mrs Hughendorn. 'Will you pick more of the buds tomorrow?'

Unless they've poisoned me, thought Nancy. Aloud she just said, 'Yes.'

Mrs Hughendorn wiped her eyes. 'I knew they wouldn't let me down.' She managed a weak smile. 'I think we might even live now, my dears. I think we have a chance to stay alive.'

Chapter 31

Gibber's Creek Gazette, 22 October 1942

Volunteer Defence Corp Meeting

Two-thirty to six-thirty Council Chambers.

The afternoon's work will consist of Lewis gun instruction followed by a description of a Molotov cocktail. Every able-bodied man should take the opportunity to take this instruction. Please bring a pannikin as it is hoped tea will be served.

CWA Meeting

Two-thirty to four-thirty CWA rooms.

Mrs Thelma Ritters will give instruction on the blanket stitch, followed by instruction by Mrs Matilda Thompson on construction of a Molotov cocktail and underwater spear gun, based on the diagrams in the recent book published by Angus and Robertson, available at Lee's General Stores. Please bring a plate.

KOKODA TRACK, NEW GUINEA, 22 OCTOBER 1942

FRED

The wooden box with his sister inside lay open on the trestle in front of him, ready for him to saw her in half. Mah smiled up at him in her blonde wig, her frothy skirt that made her slenderness look larger. As soon as Fred put the lid on, she'd scrunch up, so when he sawed the box in two she'd be curled up in one half, safe.

Around him the circus audience breathed the scent of hot peanuts over the top of the tang of elephant dung.

Over at the performers' entrance the mermaid blew him a kiss, her blue spangled tail glittering in the circus lights.

He lifted up his saw and began to cut. One stroke, two …

Blood spurted from the box. Red blood. He tried to yell, 'Mah!' but no sound came, just blood.

He opened his eyes. The blood was his, staining his shirt, as he dozed against the tree. Or, he admitted to himself, looking at the redness of his shirt, had lost consciousness, briefly.

But he was back, now. Back to New Guinea mud, air that smelt of mould and flowers, where any tree could hide a snake or sniper.

His name was Fred Smith. He had not been born Fred Smith, nor Cousin Murgatroyd. The police hadn't put out a warrant for a Fred Smith either, after the jewellery hold-up had gone wrong in Brisbane. And that was almost twenty years ago now. He'd been fourteen, and hungry. But two men had died. He'd been on the run ever since.

Not that there'd been much running. A running man attracts attention, that's what Madame had taught him. Her circus had sheltered him. Had sheltered Mah for a while too, the only time he'd spent with his sister since the orphanage where they'd grown up. He had met Blue there. He'd loved her too. Blue was a joy to love. And then he'd left, left Mah, because Fred Smith was on the run again, and his name was no longer Fred Smith.

He'd been George, and Marmaduke for a while, for a joke, a new name for each new town or property. He called himself Alby when times were good, earning a few quid and sleeping in a clean bed; and no one called him anything when they weren't, and he was pinching a clean shirt off a washing line and trapping bunnies.

War had been good, at first, most of the young men gone and jobs aplenty to fill. Farming was a reserved occupation, so no one asked why he wasn't in uniform instead of mending fences and baling hay. What had Australia ever done for him that he should risk his life to defend her? Starved him in an orphanage, then tried to imprison him in a cold cell where he'd have been starved of light and freedom.

He hadn't thought twice about joining up till that weekend in the big smoke when he bought a serve of chips and potato scallops, wrapped in newspaper. And as he ate the thick potato slices in their crisp batter, he read.

Doctors bayoneted in Hong Kong when the Japs took the hospital. Nurses bayoneted too. And worse, before they died. He'd moved into the shade, startling a dog sprinkling the dust with drops of gold, and read the article again, and then the pages on both sides too.

The Japs were coming here. And suddenly it hit him. Those nurses might be Mah and Blue. And something more ...

This was *his* land. Never mind the wardens at the orphanage, or the coppers. They were merely ants, crawling on top. They'd never trudged towards the horizon, week after week, seeing termite mounds grow to mountains then leaving them to dwindle behind. They hadn't seen the bunnies cluster, deeper, thicker every night at a drought-shallowed dam, till one day the water had gone and the rabbits had died in the mud.

Like he and his mates were going to die here. Fred looked at the blood oozing from the rough bandage on his chest. He'd refused to be evacuated down to the dressing station at Templeton's Crossing. A wound like this meant back to Port Moresby, or even to Aussie. It might mean contacting his next of kin too, or attracting other official attention that might make the authorities look too closely at 'Fred Smith'.

Besides, the boys needed him.

'Know what I'd like now?' The voice next to him was quiet. You never knew where the enemy was in country like this, two yards away or two miles, halfway up the next cliff or twenty ridges away. Bert had been a farm boy, dairying, grew up potting rabbits. Tough feet, like Fred's, even when his boots rotted. Knew which way was north as well as he knew his own hand, which meant that Bert might even get them back to the rest of the platoon, now that the lieutenant had stopped trying to lead them in the wrong direction.

'Six pints of beer and a roast leg of mutton. Extra gravy,' suggested Fred.

'How'd you guess?'

Fred grinned, flapping at the clouds of gnats or whatever the bloodsuckers were, clustering about him. 'Me too. Make that eight pints of beer.'

'When I get home I'm going to drink me beer out of Jap skulls.' Big Bob smiled. Big Bob was small, like a bit of twisted fencing wire, and his eyes glowed too blue in his brown face. Big Bob had been smiling when he'd cut the throat of one Jap sniper while Bert had shot the other two. He'd smiled when he'd looked at their bodies too.

Fred had seen smiles like that before. Hadn't liked them then. Didn't like this one now, not in the jungle with the leeches as thick as lizards and the mud waiting to rot your leg off after a single scratch.

'Going to have a whole line of skulls, I am, along the mantelpiece.'

'A skull won't hold a pint of beer,' said Fred shortly.

'Tried drinking out of them, have you?'

Fred said nothing. He'd seen a human skull, back at the circus. Clean, it was, yellow with age. And loved. He'd seen half-rotted skulls along the tracks here, the meat eaten away by what you hoped were animals and insects, not men. But most of the skulls he'd seen were what a bloke in the bush saw: attached to the bleached bones of wombats, roos, or last year's roast mutton, gnawed by the dogs. He wondered if Big Bob really would try to get hold of a skull, dig one up perhaps, that might be halfway clean and not stink too much, so he could sneak it back on a troopship. No, he thought. They were too close to being skulls themselves just now for even Big Bob to think of that.

Fred looked at the lieutenant, leaning against a tree, his eyes still closed. Fred reckoned the lieutenant had been trying not to cry since the snipers got Billo and Greg. Probably been trying not to cry all the way up the Kokoda Track too, ever since he left his mum and teddy bear behind.

But he *hadn't* cried yet. Which was good going, Fred reckoned. 'How about you?' Fred wasn't going to call the lieutenant 'sir'. Fred hadn't joined up to start calling blokes 'sir'.

The young officer shrugged.

'Go on,' urged Fred. The bloke had been too quiet for too long. 'Tell us what you really want.'

'Tell us what you really, really want,' mimicked Big Bob, his mocking voice high and feminine. Fred ignored him.

'You really want to know?'

'We really, really want to know,' said Big Bob.

'A Vegemite and lettuce roll. That's what they gave us every Tuesday at the school tuck-shop. And then to spend the afternoon teaching Grade Three how to draw a map of Australia.' The lieutenant's voice was a challenge: laugh at that.

No one laughed. Fred said, 'I want you to promise me something, mate.'

'What's that?'

'If we get captured by the Japs, don't teach *them* how to draw a map of Australia.'

He wanted to make the lieutenant smile. Wanted to make them all smile. It worked. The lieutenant said, 'I'll tell them Australia's next to Africa. They're in the wrong place. We're all in the wrong place ...'

The smiles died. Bert said, 'Yeah, well, you've got that right.'

The flies, mosquitoes, whatever they were, buzzed.

Fred pushed himself upright, then spoke to the three lads still sitting. 'Time to go.'

'That way,' said Bert. They didn't argue. No point saying, 'Are you sure?' 'That way' was as good as they were going to get.

Downhill, now. That was the problem with climbing mountains. Downhill was worse than uphill. Better aching legs from climbing than broken ones. Bush bashing, except this wasn't bush. Fred was used to trees with decent trunks and leaves that didn't sprout till they were way above your head.

A stream half seeped, half flowed along the gully at the bottom. Water stopped hunger pains. For a while. The platoon had been on quarter-rations for three weeks, as no supplies had come up the line. Since they'd been separated from the main group, there'd been no food at all.

They stopped to drink, taking turns, the others keeping lookout. Though all they could see was more green and more mud, and if anyone had spotted them they'd be dead now, rotting back into this soil like the tree limbs and the vines.

Suddenly, deeply, Fred did not want to die here. Yeah, he had to die sometime. But he wanted his bones to sit properly in good dry soil, where they'd lie a while before they turned to dirt. Maybe a wombat would dig up his skull and leave it lying so some kid could pick it up, take it to school to scare the girls ...

Fred grinned, then stopped himself. He was light-headed from lack of food. And loss of blood. No proper sleep since, well, he hadn't counted. No point counting nights now.

Bert started up the opposite slope. They followed him. Up, up, ankles aching, even though they'd been doing this for three months now. Mist trickled down from the high ridge. Air turned liquid, making Fred's shirt damp. Or maybe that was blood too.

The air was white up on the ridge top, mist so thick they could only see each other's faces, as though they were floating, separated from their bodies.

Bert pointed. 'Reckon we need to go over there.' He shrugged. 'Or if we wait here long enough, they'll come to us. The boys have got to be heading this way.'

Made sense to Fred. Eventually this whole small hell of gullies, valleys and mountains would be crossed and re-crossed by Allies and enemy alike. All they had to do was sit down and put their feet up.

And starve.

'Along the ridge,' said Bert. 'It'll be easier going.'

It was — not easy, but not as bad as the terrain they had been walking through. Rocks like flint, no mud, mist that was almost too dense to breathe. No mosquitoes or leeches though, which was a plus. Just silence, not the rustles and squeaks and squelches of down below. No sound at all.

And then there was.

Voices, easy sounding, blokes having a chat.

Four blokes speaking Japanese. Not that Fred could speak Jap, except for three words, nor even Chinese, for all he looked it, and the locals spoke more languages than you could poke a stick at. But he'd heard enough Jap now to know what it sounded like.

The others caught it too.

Bert's whole body seemed to focus. The lieutenant flinched. Fred pretended he hadn't noticed. Big Bob's smile seemed suddenly painted on.

The mist began to lift, like a giant hand had twitched the curtain. Fred pulled the lieutenant onto the ground just as Bert hissed, 'Down.'

A handkerchief of blue shone above, the mist eddying as the clouds sucked it up.

A hollow in the ridge in front of them, the size of a football field with just enough soil for waist-high grass to grow. The sun glinted on two machine guns, each almost hidden in the trees. If it hadn't been for the voices, they'd have walked right onto them. Beyond the grass the ground rose in a bald knob, then fell down a slope that'd foil even a rock wallaby, but this route was more passable than any mountain around.

Fred heard his breath, tried to silence it. They were sitting ducks here. Make that lying ducks, pressed to the ground.

Those four Japs were waiting. Waiting for the rest of the platoon to come up one of these slopes. Waiting above them, to pick them off. Two machine guns could get the lot of them, if they had enough ammunition.

Were they a lookout? An ambush? Were more Japs heading their way? Possibly not, he thought. The Japs they'd come across had been starving, in a worse state than them. Were these scouts or snipers? Maybe like them they'd been separated from their platoon.

It didn't matter. Two machine guns in the right spot could pick off fifty men. Hundreds maybe, taking down one lot, then waiting for the next to come along unawares. Impossible to tell where shots had come from in country like this. The echoes bounced from one crag to another, each echo repeating a dozen more.

He flicked his eyes towards Bert, the lieutenant, Big Bob. If any one of them moved, they'd have them all.

He felt his heart rate slow as he began to think. That's what living hand to mouth did for you. He was at his best in a tight corner.

Two options. They could wait till dark, or for the mist to fall again, and creep off, the way they'd come. Or they could fight it out.

He reckoned the lieutenant was frozen with terror. Chances were he'd make it till dark without giving them away. Bert could sit like a stone for hours, waiting for a bunny for his pot. So could Fred, for that matter. Big Bob would be right too. They could slink off through the trees, down the ridge, back to the gully. Hide among the trees. Wait for reinforcements to make it as far north as them, because eventually the Allies would have to beat the Japs. Another week or two of going hungry and then …

No, he thought. Another week or two of hearing machine-gun fire, the screams of dying men. A week or two of knowing they had let their own blokes climb up a hill and die.

Which left fighting it out.

Fred considered that too.

Four blokes versus four men. Fred reckoned he could take down two himself, with his bare fists, even if he hadn't had his knife. But it didn't work like that. It wasn't man versus man up here, but two machine guns facing three Lee-Enfield .303s because the lieutenant had lost his.

Back in Australia they said that one Aussie was worth six of the enemy. They didn't say that on Kokoda. Here the greatest enemy was the land itself, and if you survived that, well, the Japs had survived it too. They'd been at war for more than ten years now. He and the others after their few weeks' drilling were powder puffs compared to that.

Stop right there, he told himself. Think defeat and we will lose. Back in the golden circus days, Mrs Olsen had told him how you kept smiling up on the trapeze. You don't let yourself think that you can fall, she said. Your body obeys your mind.

So. Four Aussies. Three rifles. If they stood suddenly, all together on the command, they'd ...

He tried to think of four Japs falling as the bullets flew. It wouldn't work. The circus taught you realism too. Those four were behind the trees. They might get one, or two if they were lucky. Then they'd be in the open with no cover. Dead.

Two snipers with machine guns could do almost as much damage to troops below as four.

Something niggled at him. Circus, he thought. Madame, the old woman who had taken in a fourteen-year-old boy with his armful of stolen gems, the blind fortune-teller who had told fortunes and created them too. He could hear her voice in the whisper of the trees in the valley, the cry of some unknown bird. 'Think circus,' the air about him breathed. 'The punters see what they want to see. It is up to us to make sure they do.'

Think circus.

What did the snipers want to see? Mates, he thought. Reinforcements. Japanese men like themselves, short, wiry, bodies all bone and sinew from climbing up and down cliffs and starvation. Dark hair. Like his. What most Aussies called 'slant eyes', but which weren't really slanted. Eyes like his, inherited from the Chinese father he'd never known.

He'd kept his hair dyed blond, mostly, so as not to look Chinese. It had been cut short and had grown out black now. He had his mother's build, short but stocky. He reckoned he was starved enough to pass as Japanese now.

Uniform? His boots were Aussie boots. Some of the Japanese wore them after they had pulled them off corpses, as their own boots had rotted, but best to take them off. He used the other foot to ease them over his heels and toes, and then socks. Then the shorts. What did Jap soldiers wear under their uniforms? He reckoned not white cotton underpants. He slipped them off, felt Bert's glance, and a lifted eyebrow. The lieutenant was still hugging the ground, Big Bob lying relaxed, saving his strength for creeping out tonight.

Fred glanced up. Yes, the mist was falling again. Good.

'What you plannin'?' Bert's voice was an almost breath.

Bert would come with him. The lieutenant couldn't. Big Bob wouldn't. He'd enjoy the killing, risk his life to do it. But he wouldn't put himself in the way of certain death.

Certain. Death. 'Nothing is certain,' came Madame's voice. 'Yes, death, perhaps, but when? And love lives after death. I know.'

Love. His love for Marj. Another sort of love for Blue, the kind you keep in your pocket and look at wistfully and it makes you think, what if? And something for the land he'd walked on, so deep and so diffuse he wasn't sure if it was love at all.

He wasn't letting these bastards put their feet on it. If he could saw his sister in half four times a week for nearly a year, he could do this.

He moved one hand, slowly, slowly. Undid his shirt, smeared blood across his hand and then his face. Slid the knife up his sleeve, holding it by the hilt, blade hidden. His rifle rested in the dirt. He hated to leave it there, but it too would give him away.

A drop of water slid down his face. For a moment he wondered if he was crying without realising it, then realised it was the mist again. A clammy, wonderful shield of mist.

Sound carried in mist. He made his voice softer than a breath. 'Don't move. No matter what I do, don't move.'

Big Bob looked at him. He mouthed, 'Yeah.' The lieutenant managed a puzzled nod. Bert whispered, 'I'll go round behind.'

Bert'd worked out what Fred planned to do. Maybe Big Bob had too. 'Ain't no behind to go round, mate. They'd see you. Give the game away.' He took a breath, felt its sweetness in his throat, then said, 'My sister's Marjory McAlpine, Drinkwater Station, Gibber's Creek. Give her my love, and Blue, and Sheba.'

Bert gazed at him for ten heartbeats. He said, 'Yep. Good luck, mate.'

'Yeah,' mouthed Fred. He shut his eyes, imagined himself yelling one of his three words of Japanese, then opened them. Time to give the punters their show. 'Here I come, Madame,' he whispered. 'The biggest Galah of me life.'

The scream came from the mist: 'Tasukete!'

A figure staggered through the white: a man of mud and blood. 'Tasukete!' he screamed. 'Tasukete!' Help. Help.

The Japanese soldier held his machine gun ready, waiting for other figures to appear too, enemies chasing, shooting the staggering, blood-streaked man. The seconds passed, two, three ...

But there were no shots, no chase, just the staggering figure, his hands clawing at his face. Mutilated? Bitten by a tree snake ...?

The soldier stepped out, reached to help. The stranger's knife thrust in and upwards. He managed a gurgle, lost in the bloody figure's cries of 'Tasukete! Tasukete!' Saw the stranger strike his companion, another quick blow in and up. The mist filled his body.

Then the black.

─❦◎

Two down, thought Fred. Could he reach the second machine gun before they worked out what had happened in the mist a short distance away? Already the soldier across the rocks was yelling, jabbering stuff he couldn't understand, him with his three words of Japanese. He used one of them again, 'Tasukete!' and ran forwards.

The men were wary now, peering into the mist. One of them ran towards him, bayonet in hand. Then Fred was on him.

In. Up. Old Jim had taught him this, back when he was riding the rattlers as a kid. Jim said he'd learnt the technique up on the Somme, but more like in some back street.

This one did not die cleanly. He called out, even as the blood bubbled from his mouth, was mumbling even as his eyes opened, never to close again.

Fred let the body slump onto the ground. The fourth man must have heard it. Where was he?

Trickery would not work now. He pinned himself against the tree, hoping it would absorb the bullets. They didn't come.

Bastard was waiting then. Waiting for a clear shot.

Let him wait.

A bee stung his leg. The venom trickled down; no, not venom: blood. He looked at it with curiosity. No fear. He had said goodbye to his body, to his life. This was just a leg that must be used. He'd better use it then, before it gave out.

He waited till a thicker finger of mist waved between him and the fourth soldier with the machine gun. And then he charged.

Lunge right, left, then right, right, then realised it didn't matter, the sweep of the machine gun would get him anyway.

It did.

He felt it, not pain, just blows. Blows to his chest again, his side, his arm. Left arm, knife in his right. A blow to his leg, the one that had been hit before. Hard blows not hard enough to stop him.

He was running for his country now, for Mah, for Blue, for Sheba, for anything he had ever known that was good. He was running for Bert and the lieutenant and Big Bob, for the hundreds of blokes who might come up this hill. He was running for them all.

He was nearly there.

More blows. He saw the surprise on the shooter's face. Saw him reach for his own knife. But the security of his powerful gun and hidden position had made him leave it too late. The eyes knew it too. Brown eyes, so like his own. Was there pity and admiration in them, as he thrust the knife in and up? Was there pity and admiration in his own too?

He knew nothing. Nothing to know.

Just, at last ...

Nothing.

He woke. A fire burnt his leg, his chest.

Couldn't be a fire, 'cause it was raining.

'Get his pants on, Bob.'

'Why? He's done for.'

Privates on parade, thought Fred, somewhere down a far-off tunnel.

''Cause he wasn't in uniform. And when we get his body back and tell them what he done, we ain't saying how he done it. All right?'

A pause. 'All right.'

The fire flared again. Big Bob said, 'He's breathing.'

'What?'

More flames, hands tying string around him.

Then Bert again. 'All right, lieutenant. If we get back ... when we get back — you're going to tell them about this. Tell him how he should get a medal. The Victoria Cross. And we're going to go through it time after time till you get it right.'

'No need.' The lieutenant's voice. When had the boy grown up? 'He charged two machine-gun positions single-handed. Despite injuries, he carried on. He saved the three of us, and who knows how many others too.' A pause. More hands, but the feeling was flowing from his body now. The world was supposed to be turning black, but it was green, dark green. The lieutenant's voice came faintly, from very far away. 'That sound right to you?'

'It'll do,' said Bert.

More green. The flames vanished into cold.

Time. No body. No thoughts. Just knowing that time had passed. He supposed he should be dead. But he'd never practised dying, only living. Maybe he didn't know how to die yet. More time. More noises. Noises that slowly turned into the King's English, or at least an Aussie version of it. The unmistakeable smell of disinfectant.

A first-aid post. He managed to move his head enough to see white bandages, with only a small amount of mud and blood. Dressing station then.

'Here he is, sir.'

A face bent over him. Officer's cap. Officer's voice too. 'Good to see you're still with us, Smith. Soon have you down to Myola. Then Port Moresby and home.'

Where was home? Not the orphanage, long past. Not with Mah. The circus vanished. Repairing a fence, maybe, the plain stretching into blue-grey distance.

'Captain Southam is recommending you for a Victoria Cross. Well done, soldier.'

The face vanished. The voice said something indistinguishable, which ended with, 'Think he'll survive?' More words, among which were 'he might'.

At first he just felt shock — life, when he had expected none. Joy, seeping through him just as the pain began to creep too, as if his body had decided it might belong to him again.

A Victoria Cross for Fred Smith! His lips began to grin.

Stopped. Victoria Cross winners — or even those with lesser medals — got their photos in the paper. One photo and Fred Smith would be Robert Malloy, wanted for armed robbery and murder.

Prison? Maybe not, or not for long. Because he hadn't killed that bloke, hadn't even touched the gun that did, and the robbery was decades ago. But it would mean ... fuss. Would mean that Marjory McAlpine would be pointed at not as the sister of a hero, but of a crook. And at worst it might mean a cell instead of the blue sky.

He had to escape. He found a smile somewhere. Finally, safe at last, a hero, and he had to escape. Into the jungle, first chance he got. They had to put the stretcher down sometime. He'd crawl, crawl so they couldn't find him, might think other stretcher-bearers had picked him up. No one would expect a wounded hero to desert.

And then? Death, probably. It would find him even if he'd refused to look it in the face. He had no illusions about how badly he was hurt. 'Might make it' depended on nursing care, hospitals.

'Only one thing I can do for you now, Marj,' he whispered.

Vanish.

Chapter 32

Gibber's Creek Gazette, 15 December 1942

Fashions for Victory

The new fashions for Victory show that there is still plenty of
scope for attractive dressmaking under the new regulations.
    Five buttons are allowed for fastening.
    Tucking and shirring are allowed if used for shaping.
    Tailored frocks for everyday use may have a flared skirt
and a belt no more than two inches wide.

GIBBER'S CREEK, NEW SOUTH WALES, AUSTRALIA, 19 DECEMBER 1942

THOMAS THOMPSON

Thomas Thompson looked at the paperwork on his desk. It had
seemed so simple in *The Boy's Own Annual* adventures he'd
read as a kid, back at the library in Sydney. Invent something
brilliant and needed and you'd end the war.

In reality it made you rich. It also gave you paperwork, at least
a ton of it each week, and the war ground on, because all sides
had inventors just as good as him.

He looked out the window at the factory floor below, conveyor
belts, the foremen in their grey dustcoats, the women in white.
Before the war the only women in the factory had worked in
the lunchroom. He'd never thought of employing women, despite

being married to a wife who managed half the district. It had taken the example of Blue and Mah McAlpine as well as a war to show him that women were not only as capable of the technically difficult assembling but often more reliable employees, less likely to blow their wages on grog and vanish for three days on a spree. They worked, went home to their families and, if the kids were sick, got their mum or auntie or the woman next door to mind them so they could still turn up at work.

He looked at the paperwork again and made a bargain with himself. One-third of the pile and he'd go home for the day, put his feet up and not even turn on the wireless for the news. Talk to his wife, his son, back from boarding school, take a walk down to the river with peaches for Sheba. Neither he nor Matilda had meetings or plane spotting tonight. A good thing too. She had been looking tired lately. Forget the war for a whole night ...

'Mr Thompson.' Mrs Jamieson, his secretary, opened the door. 'There's someone to see you. Mrs White. She's been working down in the carpentry section for the last ten days.'

'Tell her to come in.' It meant a few minutes away from paperwork, at least. 'Yes, Mrs White? Come in and sit down.'

She stood, despite his invitation, twisting her white cap in her hands. Her face was a queer mixture of nervousness and something else that he couldn't quite identify.

'Excuse me, I'm sure, Mr Thompson. I'm not one to put myself forwards. But in days like these you got to, don't you?'

'I'm sorry, Mrs White. I don't know what you mean.'

'Them nasty Nazi spies. Told us on the radio they're everywhere, ain't they? Got to look out for them. A place like this would be just what they'd like.'

He pushed his chair back, looked at her more closely. Spite, he thought, that's what I'm seeing, and pleasure in it too. She's enjoying this. But she was also right. The factory work was top secret, one of the reasons he'd chosen this of all his factories for the production. Everyone knew everybody in a country town. A stranger would not just be noticed, but the neighbours would know his grandmother's name and what he liked for breakfast before teatime.

'You think there's a spy here?'

'I know so. Sir,' she added.

'Who?'

'That George Green. That's what he calls himself anyway. His real name is Jürgen Grünberg.'

Tommy looked at her, the malice, the self-importance. 'How do you know this?'

'His parents live in Rocky Valley, same as my hubby's parents. Grünberg they were before the last war, then all at once it was Green. But they was still German. Still are. The old woman still calls herself by a German name.'

'That doesn't mean he's a spy,' said Tommy quietly.

She looked at him shrewdly. 'Bet he didn't put down his real name on those forms we had to fill in to work here, did he? Bet he didn't say his German cousin came out here, year before the war. Stayed with the family and everything. Bet there's lots of things he didn't tell you.'

Tommy wondered if he'd have had the courage to make known his German heritage, if he'd had one, on any official forms at times like these. But this woman was right. The young man should have done so.

'Very well. Thank you for bringing this to my attention. I'll take care of it.'

She stared. 'Is that all? Aren't you going to call the police? He should be in prison. Passing secrets on. Whole lot of them should be interned.'

'I said that I'd take care of it. Please don't mention it to anyone.' He gave her the blank stare he knew was more effective than any anger. 'This is now a security matter, Mrs White. You too may be prosecuted if you speak of it to anyone at all. Thank you, Mrs White.'

'Well, I just did my duty, same as anyone would have. No thought of a reward neither.'

Good. Because you're not getting one, thought Tommy.

He shut the door after her, and sat at his desk to think. George Green. He knew the lad vaguely. Not in the carpentry section either, nor in the loading bays, but in the design department, worst of all. Few if any of those who put his machines together knew the whole design. But George Green would. Or Jürgen Grünberg.

A quiet lad. Well groomed, handsome even. Well spoken too. He'd done engineering at night school, been working at the factory for almost a year before the war broke out. Reserved occupation, which was why he wasn't in uniform — though Tommy had never put any obstacles in the way of any man who really needed to fight physically for his country, despite the value of the work they were doing here for the national war effort.

The woman spoke from malice, he had no doubt. But there might be some substance to her allegations.

What should he do now? Nothing in a hurry, he thought. These were people's lives he was dealing with. The last design change had been almost four months ago — if George Green was really a Nazi spy, he'd have had plenty of time to pass it on. Tommy felt slightly sick at the thought of his plans, so laboriously thought through and rethought, tested and retested, handed on a plate to a German factory, then built and used to kill Australians, not to save them.

No, he needed to talk this through with people he could trust. His wife ... he hesitated ... and his son.

Dinner was Irish stew, a good one, onion and carrots among the potato, gravy and mutton chops long simmered till they were tender. Green peas, home grown, tomato salad, the tomatoes grown by the Gibber's Creek Central School and sold to raise money for the war effort, which meant they had tomatoes at every meal as Matilda could never resist a child's road-side stall. Grilled for breakfast, in sandwiches for lunch and a salad with dinner. Tommy didn't mind. He liked tomatoes.

He waited till Matilda and Michael had taken out the plates — Mrs Mutton only worked half-days now — and brought in stewed peaches and custard, home-grown fruit, milk and cream and eggs from the property too, the peaches sweet enough to need no rationed sugar. We do well, thought Tommy; the shortages hardly touched them here at Drinkwater. They had always lived mostly on what they grew anyway, not from lack of money, but because it was the only way to get fresh food.

He took a spoonful of stewed peaches. His hand was almost steady these days, despite the stroke ten years earlier. He swallowed before he spoke. 'There's something I'd like your opinions about. Classified,' he added.

Matilda raised her eyebrows. 'Do we have to sign the Official Secrets Act?'

He gave a slight grin. 'Even more secret than that.'

Michael laid down his spoon. He looks like his mother, thought Tommy, with a good bit of his great-grandparents too. There was intelligence in those brown eyes and, he reckoned, compassion. Pride in his son was so strong he had to put his spoon down. 'A Mrs White came to me with a tale today.' Briefly he told them what the woman had said. 'The question now is what do I do?'

'You could fire him,' said Michael slowly. Tommy noticed that his wife had held back to allow their son to speak first. 'But if you do that, the police probably would arrest him, and maybe intern his whole family.'

'Not good places, internment camps,' said Matilda. Tommy didn't ask how she knew.

'But, equally,' Michael seemed to be treating the matter like a maths equation, 'you can't risk her story being true. Or at least you can't risk the part of her story about being a German spy to be true. Is there any other proof that he might be sending messages? Has he any real links or loyalty to Germany beyond this cousin? If the cousin really was German,' he added. 'You know what gossip is like. Flinty would know.'

Of course. Flinty Mack had lived her whole life in Rocky Valley. She'd know the Greens, or Grünbergs. She'd know more about them than the police could ever find out too. More even than her brother Andy, their manager, who'd been away from the valley all through the last war, and most of the post-war period too, first droving and then working here.

'We'll drive up there tomorrow.' Matilda began to clear the plates again. 'It's urgent business, so we can use the petrol for this. We can't wait till we see them at the Christmas party. We need to get it cleared up fast. Either the woman is a troublemaker, in which case we need to stop her before she does any real damage, or ...'

Or all my security precautions of the last three years have been for nothing, thought Tommy, and the Germans have everything I have created.

Matilda waved Michael back into his chair. 'I'll wash up tonight. You stay and catch up with your father.'

'Leaving us men to our port and cigars?' asked Tommy dryly.

It was a joke — even in the old days Drinkwater people had never gone in for the formal routine of ladies retiring and leaving the men to discuss important manly matters over their port.

'A cup of tea. Fresh too, not stewed — Mah got the rations this morning. And Mrs Mutton made stuffed monkeys.'

'Can't do much better than a stuffed monkey,' said Tommy. Though the biscuits were made without sugar these days, they were sweet enough with a filling of home-dried plums and peaches and apples.

Michael sat back in his chair. He's grown again, thought Tommy. How had he and Matilda had such tall sons? But then who knew how tall he and she should have been? They'd both been half starved as children, working in the jam factory where he'd first met her when she was a child of twelve — a little skinned rabbit of a thing but, oh, she'd had courage. His ma had made sure he had enough to fill his belly, but it had been mostly bread and jam or treacle duff — tummy stuffers, and not the milk or meat or fresh vegies that gave his boys their height. Not to mention feet like a kangaroo's.

'Dad?'

'What? Sorry, I was far away. Back when I first met your mother.'

Michael nodded. He and Jim knew the story of the jam factory, just like they knew the tale of their grandfather, the striking shearer turned swaggie at the billabong whose death had inspired Banjo Paterson's 'Waltzing Matilda'. But they only know them as stories, thought Tommy, romance, not the anguish it was then. And the joy. The excitement of simply being young ... 'Sorry, Michael,' he said again. 'What did you say?'

Michael gave a half-smile very like his mother's. 'How proud I am of you. I ... I know it can't be easy, being a civilian just now.'

Which means some of the boys at school have been ragging you about having a father not in uniform, thought Tommy, though he said nothing. Even if his war work wasn't vital, no army would have accepted him, not at his age and after the stroke that had half crippled him for a while, and still left him weak on one side. Even before that, the dreadful burn that had ended his career as the jam factory's odd-job boy had damaged his arm too much for him to be accepted into active service. 'I'm proud of you too.'

'And I'm proud of the lot of us.' Matilda carried in the tea tray. 'Up ourselves, aren't we?'

Tommy smiled at her, his beautiful wife. His handsome son. People of integrity. People who cared enough about a man they hadn't met, and his family, not to condemn him out of hand. Good people. I have been blessed, he thought. So blessed, a family and a job and a land to love.

Chapter 33

Gibber's Creek Gazette, 20 December 1942

Shire engineer Mr Bill McIvor has informed the *Gazette* that the new Gibber's Creek air-raid siren is now ready for testing. It should be heard within five miles of shire offices. Mr McIvor says that Hurricane air-raid sirens powered by compressed air will be sent to all churches in the local area, with air-raid wardens appointed to sound them in the event that enemy planes are spotted. Residents are reminded that they can obtain forms showing the silhouettes of enemy and Allied planes from Council offices, nine-thirty am to four pm Monday to Friday, to avoid mistaken identification.

ROCK FARM, ROCKY VALLEY, NEW SOUTH WALES, AUSTRALIA, 20 DECEMBER 1942

FLINTY MACK

She found Sandy cleaning the shotguns in the room where the firearms were stored, off the veranda.

The shotguns didn't need cleaning. Sandy and the other men of the valley hadn't wasted ammunition since Pearl Harbor. They had trained, twice a week, down by the schoolhouse, where Sandy and her brothers had enlisted with the Snowy River men a war, a depression and nearly thirty years earlier.

One brother had returned. The other hadn't. And Sandy had come back so damaged in mind and body it had taken years to get him to admit to the scars that made him doubt his capacity to be a husband.

She leant against the door, and watched him. The last war had left him hard of hearing too, from shells screaming past his dugouts. But the years of their marriage had been the most fulfilled of her life: three children, a man who shared her joy in the roos grazing on frost-tufted grass, the mist that eddied and twisted snake-like about the gullies and the vast flat rock that gave the farm its name.

Sandy managed the farm. She wrote her books. The farm made a profit — just — but it was the books that paid for the children's high schooling in Sydney, for her youngest brother to go to medical school, for Kirsty to learn to fly. More precious was their financial security: drought, flood or snowstorm could destroy a farm's income for years or decades. Books didn't depend on the weather. The worse it was, the more material she could write about. She smiled at the idea of blizzards as a crop, like lucerne or potatoes …

Sandy turned, and smiled. 'What's so funny?'

'Not funny. Just happy.' And a little worried, she admitted. Sandy'd had nightmares again last night. Nor had they had word of Joseph, still missing after the surrender in Malaya. There had been rumours about horrors in the prison camps, of torture, even ritual cannibalism, the eating of parts of the bodies of captured men.

For the first time she wished they had more than a weekly mail service, or even access to daily newspapers. She'd never minded the isolation of the farm before. The nearest phone was an hour's ride from the valley, so two hours from here. She had grown up with the rhythm of the mail once a week (as long as there was no flood, snow or bushfire), and telegrams.

But a telegram can reach us almost as quickly as a phone call, she assured herself. And with the kids away she could pore over their letters every day. You couldn't replay a phone call.

The isolation that made the war strangely far away was both a blessing and a trial. She suspected that Australia could be invaded and their valley be missed; that Sandy and Dave White and other men could march and find vantage points among the rocks to foil the invaders while life here would go on untouched ...

If only they could hear that Joseph was safe, in a prison camp. If only the war ended before either of her boys was old enough to enlist. If only Nicola didn't end up marrying a Yankee soldier and becoming a war bride, sailing to another land just when everyone else was coming home.

She looked at her husband again; he was back cleaning a shotgun. No, the war was here, in the frustration in Sandy's eyes that he could do no more than exercise with the local militia, which was also essentially the local volunteer bushfire brigade and the progress association and the school committee.

'Where are the boys?'

'Potato digging,' she said succinctly. Her father-in-law had put most of their lower paddocks into potatoes — the ground up here was too rocky for them. Ever since the school holidays had begun, Jeff and Rick had been down there most days, digging and packing the spuds in hessian bags before the sunlight turned them green. The boys'd be back at dusk, racing their horses up the track to the house despite the hard day's work. If only Nicola was with them. But she was enrolled in occupational therapy next year and was spending these holidays as a full-time volunteer down at 'the 13th', the repatriation hospital that tried to give injured soldiers the skills they'd need to cope with life beyond its walls.

'They like Mum's lunches.'

'You complaining about the tucker here?'

He grinned — the old Sandy grin. 'You know what I mean, love.'

She did. She was a good plain cook, but old Mrs Mack was an artist, with a dining table almost as long as the room it was in, piled with food for husband and son and grandchildren, at least a dozen sitting down at every meal: just the way she liked it.

'Speaking of lunch,' she said, 'it's ready when you are.'

'What is it?'

'Delicious leftovers.'

She followed him to the kitchen, began to dish out the reheated rabbit stew, thick with onions and carrots from the garden, and the Macks' potatoes. Stew was always better the second day; she was glad the boys hadn't wolfed down the lot last night. She stopped mid-ladle. 'Car coming.'

She hurried along the corridor and looked out the front door down the valley. It had been months since they'd heard a car engine up here. Even the post came by horseback again these days, and the boys had ridden up the back way from Drinkwater when they came home from school for the holidays, borrowing Drinkwater horses and camping out overnight on the way. You really knew you'd left school behind, Jeff said, with a night under the Southern Cross before you arrive home.

'The Thompsons' car,' said Sandy, coming up behind her.

Something's happened to Andy, Flinty thought, as Sandy put his arm around her shoulders protectively. Or Mah or Blue. Or Blue has heard that ... She could not even let herself think the words. Blue has had ... news ... about Joseph, and Matilda and Tommy want to tell me in person ...

Bad news was usually brought by someone you knew, friend or clergyman. Good news was sent by telegram. She clenched her fists then unclenched them, placed a welcome smile on her face and stepped down off the veranda to meet them. Matilda and Tommy and Michael, she thought. It *is* bad news ...

'Flinty, you look wonderful.' Matilda stretched up to give her a kiss. 'It's all right. It's not bad news.'

'You've heard from Joseph?'

'No. Nothing about the family.'

Flinty let go of the breath she hadn't known she was holding. 'Come in. Have you had lunch? I'm just dishing it out. Michael, you've grown another yard at least. Bend down so I can kiss you. Tommy, you're looking well ...'

She led them in, chatting. What could be so urgent as to bring them up here now, when they'd be seeing each other at the Christmas Eve party in a few days?

Matilda placed a pie on the table. 'Don't worry, it's not one of mine. From Mrs Mutton.' It was only manners to bring food when you came calling unannounced at mealtimes. 'Turkey and vegetables. Andy let us have one of the Christmas ones early.'

Tommy added a large tin. 'These are from Mah. A new biscuit she's trying. Fig and walnuts, grown locally. Got a mob of Land Girls picking them.'

Sandy — brought up on his mother's jam drops, pikelets and scones — looked wary at the mention of figs.

'They're actually quite good,' said Michael. 'I tried some when she brought them over.'

He pulled out a chair — no ceremony at the McAlpines — and looked at the stew with enjoyment. Mrs Mutton didn't like cooking rabbit — too many bones, she said, and too much cleaning for too little meat — which meant that the Drinkwater bunnies went to the kitchens of the workmen.

'Tuck in,' said Flinty, helping everyone to a slice of pie. 'Dry down your way?'

Matilda nodded. She looks older, thought Flinty. Not just the grey in her hair either, or the laugh wrinkles at her eyes. 'A good wind'll blow away half the paddocks, but I don't want to reduce the amount of stock, not with the meat needed for the army. We've got enough sileage still to see us right for a while. Everyone well up this way?'

'Yes, fine. How about at Drinkwater?'

'Not bad,' said Tommy. 'Blue's holding up well. She's upped production at the factory. She and Mah will be feeding half the Pacific fleet biscuits soon.'

Keeping herself occupied, thought Flinty. She knew the feeling well. Courtesies over, she lifted an eyebrow. 'What brings you up here? Not that we're not delighted to see you …'.

'But you don't waste petrol these days on social calls,' Matilda completed Flinty's sentence. 'And it's not a social call. Tommy?' prompted Matilda.

Flinty listened while Tommy explained. 'You see,' he finished, 'I don't know what to do next. Is it true the Greens are really Grünbergs — or at least they were?'

'Yes,' said Sandy slowly. 'But they're as dinkum as you or me. Been here since the turn of the century. Couldn't want better neighbours either. When Flinty was in trouble, well, they stood by her.'

As had everyone in the valley, even the Whites.

Tommy looked relieved. 'So do you think she's just making trouble?'

'Maybe not,' said Flinty quietly. 'They did have a cousin out here visiting in early '39. Didn't like the look of him either. Kept talking about how much better things were done in Germany. Even wanted to have a meeting down in the schoolroom to show slides about the wonders Hitler had done for their country. Sandy put paid to that,' she added.

Sandy grinned. 'No electricity, so no slide show. Didn't tell him about the generator.'

'Did George ... Jürgen ... seem to agree?'

'I don't know. He was already at Gibber's Creek working for you, remember.'

'Then he probably had little to do with his cousin.'

Flinty looked even more uncomfortable. 'Except that the reason the cousin was here was because George had been to Germany to catch up with the family there.'

Tommy laid down his knife and fork. 'Ah,' he said.

Flinty nodded. 'There's more. Worse.'

'George is a ham-radio buff,' said Sandy. 'Couple of the lads around here are too. Had to hand in their equipment at the start of the war. But who's to know if they handed in everything.'

Flinty stood and collected the plates, put a strawberry pie

wordlessly on the table, added the billy of cream from the Coolgardie safe on the veranda and plates to eat it from.

There was silence as they bit into their pie. 'Better than Mrs Mutton's,' said Michael.

'But not as good as Mrs Mack's.' Flinty looked around the table. 'So, what are you going to do now?'

'Talk to him,' said Michael. 'It's the only thing to do,' he added, as the others stared at him. 'You can't condemn a man without hearing his side of the story.'

'He's not going to admit he's a German spy, son.'

'No. But you're a good enough judge of character to know if he's lying. Or even deliberately not telling you something.'

'And if I think he's lying?'

'Then tell the police,' said Michael.

'No. Please,' said Flinty. 'It would half kill the Greens if their son was arrested. And if he's arrested, they might take the whole family too. You know what it was like in the last war.'

'Then what do I do with him?' Tommy's voice held a hint of exasperation. 'I can't risk him working in the factory. Can't send him out to get a job in munitions or ship-building where he might find out even more. Or to the army.'

'Send him here,' said Sandy. 'He can dig potatoes. He can't do any harm here. It's a reserved occupation, so Manpower will have to leave him alone. If he's been up to any nonsense, we'll sort it out.'

Flinty was suddenly glad that there were no security implications in either books or potatoes. One fed morale, the other fed your belly, and the Nazis were welcome to anything they wanted to know about either of them. And, come to think of it, her apple and potato cake recipes had been German, given to her by Mutti Green, years ago ...

Tommy considered the pie on his plate. At last he nodded. 'Fair enough.'

But is it? thought Flinty. This is war. How much chance does fairness have in war?

The talk meandered after that, from Sandy and Tommy talking cattle prices to ways to fix pumps when you couldn't get spare parts.

'Thought about putting in for Land Girls yet?' asked Tommy.

Sandy laughed. 'Dad's keen on them. Mum's not so sure. Says she's not having her men distracted by a row of young women bending over in tight jodhpurs. But we'll need the extra hands come harvest.'

'They're not bad workers ...'

Matilda said nothing. Flinty watched her across the table. When she'd first met Matilda she'd seemed ageless, as full of energy as the wind.

She's tired, thought Flinty, not just 'need a good night's sleep' tired. She's working all hours, and Tommy too. Not that she and Sandy didn't work till late, but nor did they have the responsibilities of so many families depending on them, on whatever Tommy's factory was making now — she was pretty sure it wasn't just wirelesses — on the meat and wool and other crops from Drinkwater and the properties it had absorbed over the years.

Flinty stood. 'You all go out to the living room. It's too hot in here with the stove on. I'll bring tea out there.'

'I'll give you a hand,' said Matilda, as Flinty knew she would. Women got the tea while men talked. She supposed they always would while there were women, men and teapots.

She moved the kettle from the side of the stove to the hot plate. It wouldn't take long to boil now. She reached up for the old cake tin and took out this week's apple teacake. Mutti Green's recipe, she thought again, with the apple grated and stirred through so you didn't need to use much sugar. How apt.

'Milk still in the Coolgardie?' Matilda asked.

Flinty nodded. She waited till Matilda came back from the veranda, the billy of milk in her hands. 'Are you all right?' she asked bluntly, putting the tea cloth on the tray.

Matilda looked up from pouring some of the milk into the jug. 'Tired.'

'I can see that. Worried?'

Matilda gave a small smile. 'Aren't we all worried these days? You have a brother away.'

'Yes. But I've been through it before. Grew up with it, in a way, during the last war. It must be new for you.'

'Not really.' She looked out the door, to where the mountain rose glinting in the afternoon sun behind the horse paddocks. 'There was a war before the Great War. The Boer War. I lost my fiancé.'

'I'm sorry. I didn't know.'

'Ancient history. But I know what waiting is like. It's funny: I don't just worry about Jim being hurt. Dying ... I can even say the word. I'm worried about the war changing him like it did Sandy ...' Matilda's voice trailed away. Tommy and Sandy talked on, out in the living room, about gas-powered vehicles versus charcoal burners, oblivious.

'The war changed Sandy. Changed Andy. But in a funny way it didn't really change them at all. I think maybe it helped them to come back to what they loved.' It was true, she thought. Sandy's scars, his nightmares ... nothing had changed the true Sandy, deep inside. It had made him more protective of her, the valley, even of their country, knowing what it was like to see women, villages, farms, countries destroyed. But he was still the boy she'd loved when he came back a man. Though it had, she admitted, taken him a good while to see that for himself.

Matilda placed the cups and saucers on the tray, too carefully.

Flinty said quietly, 'Sometimes I used to look at Sandy and think, he killed men. And they tried to kill him too. It seemed so far away from anything I'd known.'

'Used to?'

'Not since the night they bombed Darwin and all those refugees at Broome. When we turned on the wireless the next morning I had a vision of bombs falling here. I thought, if they come here, I will kill them. I didn't know I could kill another person till then. Not deliberately, if I had a choice.' She made her voice go light. 'Though if we were to be invaded, I expect the Japanese won't even find us here for a couple of decades.' Flinty looked at Matilda directly. 'It's good to have someone to talk to. There's never been another woman my age in the valley. And just when Kirsty grew old enough to really yarn to, she moved away.'

'How is she doing?'

'Fine, I think. She says if she can't be flying, then working up north is as good as anywhere. She only writes once in a blue moon, and then just tells me everyone is well.' She shook her head. 'Maybe she thinks deep down she's still a little girl, and I'm her big sister who'd forbid her to do anything dangerous.'

'Would you try?'

Flinty grinned. 'With Kirsty? No. Gave up on that years ago — but I don't think she's noticed yet. Matilda, do you have people you can talk to down at Drinkwater?'

Matilda looked at her hands. 'Lots. But I don't, for some reason. Well, for many reasons. They've got their own problems.' She shrugged. 'People depend on me. Got to keep up a good front. Keep calm and carry on and all that.'

'You can always talk to me,' said Flinty softly. She bent over and gave the older woman a hug. Her shoulders felt bony. Who could ever have thought that Matilda might get old?

'Thank you.' Matilda shook her head sharply and moved to wipe away what might have been a tear. 'I might take you up on that.'

'Always here,' said Flinty lightly. 'Stuck to the mountains like the rock, that's me.'

They carried the tea tray into the living room.

Chapter 34

Gibber's Creek Gazette, 21 December 1942

Empire Biscuit Factory to Make Beefless Meat Pies

Now that beef supplies are being kept for the armed service,
the Empire Biscuit Factory has developed a new line in beefless
meat pies. According to proprietor Mrs Blue McAlpine, 'Our
pies are made with local mutton and local mutton suet, with
a unique flavouring developed in our test kitchens. A penny
from every pie sold will go to the Comforts for POWs Fund.'

The new pies can be bought at the Bluebell Tea Shop,
the Royal Café, the Shearer's Arms and the Gibber's Creek
Hotel.

PULAU AYU PRISON CAMP, 26 DECEMBER 1942

NANCY

They had turkey for Christmas dinner at the prison camp. Nancy
had a feeling it was really Boxing Day, but Mrs Hughendorn's
calculations said it was the 25th, and the others accepted her
judgement. It was good to celebrate. Malaria and its delirium
came and went, and dysentery too. But here — now — they
were alive.

So their evening meal was turkey and roast potatoes and
roast pumpkin — only Nancy wanted the roast pumpkin (cattle
food, Mrs Hughendorn called it) but they indulged her. Brussels

sprouts and new peas. Plum pudding and mince pies and custard and brandy butter and trifle with red and green jelly and pavlova, which Nancy had to explain too, the meringue crisp on the outside and soft in the middle and the cream and sliced passionfruit and strawberries. And giblet soup to begin with and a fruit cocktail and devilled eggs to Sally's mother's recipe and fruitcake.

It was still cassava, of course, with a few shreds of carrot and some of the bitter greens that Nancy now collected with the flower buds, as well as a couple of especially fat 'island rabbits'. But it was what you called it that mattered. And today, Christmas Day, it was turkey with all the trimmings.

They sat around the cooking fire. Their dresses were tattered now, even Mrs Hughendorn's. She had been generous with her spare clothes, but after a year of washing by hand in not enough water, and the ever-present dirt and heat and no way to dry anything properly in the wet, and with no needle and thread for darning, the fabric was rotting through.

Gavin wore a length of material wrapped around his waist. Moira had refused to let him wear a pair of Mrs Hughendorn's knickers, tied up with grass string. A sarong might be 'native' but it was better than ladies' bloomers.

They had managed Christmas presents for him, and one of Mrs Hughendorn's remaining stockings to hang up for Santa to put them in: a ball, woven out of sticks and grass, the sort Gran had woven sometimes at the Christmas week picnics by the river; a 'new' hat, padded to make it small enough to stay on his head; a cricket bat made from a flattish hunk of firewood with cloth wrapped around the end for a handle. 'It is high time he learnt cricket,' Mrs Hughendorn had proclaimed. 'Every young man needs to be able to play cricket.'

They had taken it in turns to throw the ball to him, to show him how to hit the ball with the bat. He could catch, laughing at every throw, but hadn't managed to hit the ball with the bat yet.

'Maybe by the time he's two,' said Moira, smiling.

Now he sat with the women on the benches, eating his cassava mash with every sign of pleasure. He knows no different, thought Nancy. She blinked sharply, refusing to cry today, even at the thought of all that Gavin had missed, not just food but proper beds, clothes, other children. But extra food still came for him every day, usually bananas but sometimes a precious egg, or a bowl of cassava mash, leaves and root together, or chunks of roasted breadfruit.

And he still laughed as they played with him, or told him stories. He was their miracle: a child who laughed.

Sally put down her bowl. '*O, little town of Bethlehem,*' she began. Her voice was high and sweet.

'*How still we see thee lie,*' Mrs Hughendorn joined in.

'*The hopes and fears of all the years,*

Are met in thee tonight.' They all sang now, even Nancy in a sort of tuneless hum below the others.

'*Away in a manger, no crib for a bed ...*'

Gavin crouched in the dirt at their feet, looking around at the singing women with joy. Moira had given up trying to keep him out of the dirt. Dirt was what they lived with.

We should sing more often, thought Nancy. Sing the night terrors away. Sing away fear for themselves, for Ben, for what was happening on the battlefields. The Japanese radio broadcasts from Tokyo Rose that they were made to listen to once a week said that the Japanese Imperial Army would soon conquer the whole of Australia.

We will fight, she thought. Even Gran will fight. But she didn't want to think of Overflow battling invaders. One invasion is enough for a thousand years, she thought. She wanted to think of home as she had left it, a place of peace and grazing sheep, with a wedge-tailed eagle soaring overhead.

'*We three kings of Orient are*

Bearing gifts we travel so far ...'

What gifts were being exchanged at Overflow? Mum always gave books at Christmas. Dad had plaited her a whip one year —

she had been so jealous of Ben's, and Ben wouldn't lend her his, said girls didn't crack whips. A new saddle another year, new boots. Gran gave chocolates and big jars of boiled lollies, or conversation lollies with their engraved sayings like *I love you* or *Kiss me quick*, all the treats she had never had until she was an old woman, with the postman to bring packages from Gibber's Creek.

And Santa Claus still came, of course, even to Mum and Dad and Gran that last year at home, because she had the remainder of her wages in her pocket and because she had missed them more than she could admit, more than she could bear to think of now ...

'*Silent night, holy night,*
All is calm, all is bright ...'

Someone moved behind her. Nancy turned.

They were all there, the guards, the officers, the translator, the commandant, also thinner than they had been nearly a year earlier, even gaunt. For a moment Nancy thought they were going to be beaten for singing, that it was against some rule. But then she saw that the soldiers were listening, watching. That they too were remembering home, somewhere beyond this place of stink and mud where there was beauty and love.

'*Round yon virgin, Mother and Child*
Holy infant so tender and mild ...'

So not like Gavin, she thought, smiling at Gavin's dirty face.

'*Sleep in heavenly peace ...*'

It was the translator's voice, a tenor descant, surprisingly tuneful. The women stopped, startled, then joined in again for the last line.

'*Sleep in heavenly peace.*'

Chapter 35

Gibber's Creek Gazette, 24 January 1943

Victory at Guadalcanal: Allies Retake Solomon Islands

In a stunning victory, Allied forces have retaken the Japanese garrison at Guadalcanal. According to Colonel Angus 'Mattie' Matherson (retired), of Skye Station via Gibber's Creek: 'This gives the Allies a base from which they can take Japanese stronghold Rabaul. If the Japanese thought they'd crippled America at Pearl Harbor, this victory shows them they were wrong.'

GIBBER'S CREEK, 24 JANUARY 1943

MICHAEL

Michael sat in the armchair in his father's office often, partly flattered by his father's need for his company, partly disturbed. He had been at school through the worst of his father's recovery from his stroke. He'd assumed that his parents were ageless. But he and Jim were his father's second family — their half-sister, Anna, was down in Melbourne, married to a banker, neither of whom had enough of a taste for country life for them to holiday at Drinkwater. Dad was in his sixties now; and Abercrombie, his foreman for decades, was like Mr Fothergill back at school — past retiring age and still working only because of the war.

For the first time Michael realised that there would come a time when he was the protector of his parents, not the other way around. And earlier than for lots of the chaps because his parents had been older than most when they'd had himself and Jim. Not yet, perhaps, or never entirely. But today, at least, his father relied on him enough to delay his going back to school.

What would Dad think, he wondered, if I suddenly told him: I want to leave school now? Work at Drinkwater till I'm old enough to join the AIF ...

A sharp rap at the door interrupted him.

'Come in.'

George Green was tall with light brown hair and blue eyes. He still looked pale. According to his landlady, he had been ill with bronchitis since before Christmas. 'You wanted to see me, sir?'

'Sit down.'

George sat on a hard chair opposite the desk. 'Is there a problem with the trials for my new secondary valve? I thought the results were good.'

'No. Not about the valve. Mr Green, I won't beat about the bush. Your family name is Grünberg, isn't it? Not Green.'

A moment's stillness. The man looked from his boss to Michael, then back again. 'It used to be Grünberg,' he said carefully. 'My grandfather changed it to Green at the start of the last war. But we are loyal Australians.'

'Ah.' His father seemed slightly flummoxed by the man's evident sincerity in the last statement.

'But what does being a loyal Australian mean?' asked Michael. This matters, he thought. The Nazis lumped anyone who wasn't white, and a certain kind of white at that, together as enemies of the state or even as sub-human. We are better than that. Aren't we?

'I suppose ... doing what's best for your country.'

'Australia is your country?'

'Yes.'

That sounded honest too, thought Michael. But there was another tone beneath the words.

'What do you think is the best future for Australia then?'

Another pause. 'You know I've been to Germany then.'

Michael nodded. His father said, 'Yes.'

'I won't pretend to you. Hitler's done a lot that I admire. National socialism — it's good for workers to have a say in how the factory in which they work is governed. The Jews have too much power, and the old guard too. Those who inherited money or position, but who didn't earn it.' Michael wondered if he was imagining the hint of a German accent now.

'You would like to see this for Australia?'

'I should lie, and say no. But, yes, I would. The socialists say every man is as good as another. National socialists say that is nonsense. *You* know it is nonsense. Why should a man of intelligence, or education, have no more say than a fool who drinks his pay? But that is the system we have now.'

'You admit you're a Nazi?' Thomas Thompson's face showed his horror. 'Well, you can get out. Now.'

'No,' said Michael. 'Dad, please. George isn't saying that, are you?'

'No. I am being honest. You wanted honesty. I could have told you I want none of these things. But I want Australia to choose them, not because a foreign power says we must. I don't want German overlords here, nor Japanese ones. You think I'm a spy for Germany? No. Never. I love this country as much as you. I want the best for it. And when your country is at war, you do your best for it. As I do my best here.' He looked at his boss now. 'How much overtime have I put in and never charged for? How often have I come in with new designs on a Monday, after working during the weekend? Even when I was sick I was sketching, planning.'

'And your ham radio?' Thomas kept his voice neutral.

'I handed it in, like all the others. You can ask the police to search. I expect you will. They will find nothing.' There was slight contempt in his voice now.

No spy would hide a transmitter in his own home, thought Michael. Not with a thousand miles of bush to hide it in. 'You like to walk on the weekends?'

George looked at him warily. 'Is that a crime? Yes, I like bushwalking. It keeps me fit. Helps me to think. I haven't been for a walk since I was sick though.'

Michael exchanged a glance with his father. His father nodded slightly, as if to say, up to you.

'Mr Green, what would you say if we told you that you have been accused of being a spy for Nazi Germany? But rather than report you to the police — as probably we should do — instead we are offering you the chance to go back to Rocky Valley. To work at the Macks' farm.'

'Digging potatoes? I'd say you are a fool. Both of you. Your factory needs me. Our country needs me. It needs the new valve I'm working on too. I'm an engineer, not a potato farmer. Australia has all the potato farmers it needs, but not enough engineers.'

His face was flushed. From anger, thought Michael, then realised that it was humiliation. George Green was his valley's success story, along with Joseph McAlpine, the only two in their community to go to university and work with more than their hands. For the first time Michael accepted finishing school as a privilege, one that he would be stupid to turn down. Now George Green would be returning to dig potatoes.

And Australia desperately needed engineers.

'How about this then?' suggested Michael slowly. 'You say you are working on a new valve. No, don't tell me more,' he added, as the man began to speak again. 'I don't need to know about it.' Nor would I understand it, he thought. Jim, with his love of all things mechanical, should be doing this. 'Can you work on it at Rocky Valley?'

The man still looked at him warily. 'Yes. I have tools at home. I can work on the design there. If I have to.'

'Then tell your family part of the truth. Tell them that for security reasons you need to work on this valve of yours away from the factory. Say there is a danger of security breaches here. We'll pay, say, half your salary.' He looked at his father. 'Is that OK, Dad?'

His father nodded.

'But you'll also dig potatoes, or whatever else is needed.' And Sandy and all the others can keep an eye on you, he thought. Put one foot out of line — try sneaking away to transmit messages — and you'll find you have as many eyes on you as a flock of cockatoos.

The young man considered it. 'I've no choice,' he said at last.

'No,' said Thomas Thompson. 'Under the circumstances we have been generous. We don't want to see you or your family interned unnecessarily.'

'You think you are generous. But I'm the one who is the loser.' He took a deep breath. 'Mr Thompson, Mr Michael Thompson — what happens when the war is over? Will you give me my job back then?'

'If the Nazis win, they might give you the factory,' said Thomas Thompson dryly.

'They won't win. We'll beat them,' said George Green and, for the first time, Michael knew that he did tell the truth now, or at least what he believed. 'We'll beat the Japanese too. When that happens, will you take me back?'

Michael didn't look at his father. 'Yes.'

'Even though my beliefs are not the same as yours?'

'Yes,' said Michael again. 'That is part of what we are fighting for, isn't it? The right to free speech.' Even as he said it, he realised it wasn't true. It was a good propaganda slogan, but not the truth. They were fighting to keep their country their own, no more, no less.

George Green — or Jürgen Grünberg — stood up. 'I'll pack my things. I'll send a report on my work to you,' he nodded to Thomas Thompson, 'each Monday.' He raised his chin and looked at both of them. 'And if the Japanese ever land on Australian soil, I will fight against them as hard as either of you.'

He shut the door behind him.

Chapter 36

Gibber's Creek Gazette, 20 February 1943

Japanese Plane Over Sydney

A Japanese plane over Sydney yesterday caused the city to
be blacked out again and anti-aircraft batteries to be on full
alert ...

PULAU AYU PRISON CAMP, 2 MARCH 1943

NANCY

She dreamt, though she was still awake.

Bogongs, with velvet wings that still left you itchy when
they brushed against your cheek. Hills by starlight, red-tinged,
blood country, star shadows, purple, green, rocks that sat
like humped sheep and sheep that sat like rocks. Black-frost
night. No white rims on the gum leaves but in the morning
they would be frozen. Odd but if she leant against the tree, it
would be warm: bee warm, honey warm, scent of sweetness.
The little black bees wouldn't sting you, most like, Gran said,
but take care. The natives bred with the new bees, bees that
did sting. You couldn't be sure now if a hive of wild bees were
stingers or not.

Like me, she thought. Black bee, long yellow bees, Gran and
Granddad marrying, Dad marrying Mum and here I am, not
quite a native bee. One that didn't used to sting but now ...

Ancestors like strings in the night, stretching up and far away. Two strings for parents, four for grandparents, then eight, sixteen, all strings leading to me and Ben. Another string to Gavin, leading to the future, a small strong string from Ben.

Where was Ben?

She called, but made no noise. Ben? Ben?

Somewhere outside the dream the women spoke. 'She's been like this for over an hour.' Moira's voice. But Moira should not be here, not in the land of rocky, bony hills. My bones. My ancestors' bones lie here. Not hers. Suddenly, deeply, she knew that Moira would never be buried in these hills.

'Don't think it's malaria. Some other fever. Try the quinine.'

'I didn't know we had any.'

'Miss Beatty bought some.'

'Doesn't she need it?'

'She died an hour ago,' said the voice. 'Wherever she is now, she doesn't need quinine. There's some native stuff too. Smells like wormwood, but it's worth a go.'

'Go fetch wood,' said Mum, wood shaped like snakes and snakes like wood.

She'd run screaming from a big brown snake, but Ben laughed. 'It's a stick. Not a snake at all.'

She'd stared, not admitting she'd been wrong. 'It's a snick then.'

'Ah,' said Ben. 'You have to be careful of those snicks. Dangerous creatures. Snicks pretend they are a snake, then when they've got you scared, pretend they are a stick.'

'Where is Ben?' This time it came out aloud.

Someone took her hand. Moira, who was here but not here. Moira crying.

'Yes,' whispered the not-Moira. 'Where is Ben? Ben? Where are you, Ben?'

Chapter 37

Gibber's Creek Gazette, 9 April 1943

Petrol Warning

Those using their cars for purposes not on their licences will be prosecuted. There will be no more warnings, stated the Chairman of the Gibber's Creek Fuel Control Board, Councillor Bullant. 'Travel from your place of work to your home does not come under the category of "business licence".'

According to Mrs Councillor Ellis, there may still be a problem with the licensing scheme. 'I am happy to go back to teaching, but when I applied for petrol to get from Sevenoaks to the Gibber's Creek Central School I was told by the Board that teachers are to "catch a train to their respective schools". The Board do not appear to realise there never has been a train from Sevenoaks to Gibber's Creek.'

Mrs Ellis's son, Rodney, told the *Gazette*, 'Mum can ride on my horse with me, but she's heavy so school might have to start later.'

AERODROME LABOUR CAMP, MALAYA, 11 APRIL 1943

BEN

Ben bounced on his heels, fists out, his eyes on his opponent, blood dripping from his cheek. The flesh about his eye was swelling. He ignored it.

He swerved as a punch hit him in the gut, let himself sink down as if it had winded him, then lashed out. One blow to the nose, the other to the stomach, two more to the shoulders. His opponent fell gasping.

'One. Two. Three! The winner!'

Ben let the referee lift his arm in triumph, enjoying the cheers. The Japs might have beaten him, but here in the boxing ring he was the champ. He grinned, wiping the blood from his face, then bent down to Corporal Martin.

'You all right, mate?'

'Should have known better than to take you on. You've got hands like pumpkins.'

'And feet like a kangaroo's,' Ben added for the benefit of anyone listening in the crowd as he helped Martin towards the medic hut. But the blokes were tallying their bets.

He hadn't bet on himself — that would have been bad form. But the Japanese camp captain gave a basket of fruit to the winner of any of the sports the men organised. Just a way to see who was fittest for the work parties, Ben knew.

As an officer, he wasn't required to work, but those who did got ten cents a day. You could buy a turtle egg for a cent or a coconut or a few small bananas. Add that to their rations, as well as the vegetables from the gardens, and Ben reckoned he was eating better than when he was part of the Australian Army. And the work wasn't too crook: an eight-mile march in the heat to what was going to be an aerodrome. But he was used to heat. Days of chopping back the jungle or old rubber plantations, wheeling barrow-loads of gravel to fill in the swamp. If you worked hard enough, you got a cup of coffee as well as lunch. They even had breath to sing on the way home.

Ben deposited Martin, then ambled over to the outdoor kitchen. It was growing dark. The generator began to thud. Lights glowed around the barbed-wire camp perimeter. Ben picked up a pannikin, then stood in line for stew.

'How's your face?'

'Probably looks worse than it is.'

'Nah. Anything makes your ugly mug look better.' Curly bent his head and whispered, 'Cockatoos in place.'

Ben nodded. Cockatoos were lookouts, in case any of the Japanese guards approached. But they rarely did after dark. The shadows of the many men and their chatter were an effective cloak over what was really going on.

He took his stew — dried fish boiled up with rice and vegetables; Cookie was no chef — and sat on one of the blocks of wood, carefully chattering to Curly, their ears alert for any sound inside the hut.

And then it came. A hooting whistle and then a plummy English accent, quiet but clear on the radio waves: '... and then manure the cucumbers well for a good crop. To ensure each flower is fertilised ...'

Someone called out, 'I'll fertilise him.'

'Shh.'

The chatter rose again. The sounds inside the hut changed to a whistle, a lower voice, and then more clearly, 'The BBC World Service ...'

'Rhubarb, rhubarb, rhubarb,' Ben said softly to Curly.

'Rhubarb, rhubarb, rhubarb,' answered Curly. All around them men spoke similar nonsense as they listened: '... where General Bernard Montgomery is sweeping to victory at El Alamein ...'

'Good old Monty,' whispered Curly. The Australian 9th Division was fighting under Montgomery.

'... in the biggest raid in Italy so far the RAAF has ...' The radio sank to an indecipherable mutter as the power level fell. Ben could hear the men who helped Ah Chee pile more wood in the boilers.

'Wish they'd give us some Aussie news,' said Curly.

'It's the BBC. They think all that happens down this way is cricket. If we're lucky, they might give us the scores.' Or perhaps events were too bad for the British public to stomach. Ben suspected that just as the bulletins delivered by Tokyo Rose only gave news of Japanese victories, the BBC carefully selected its news too.

The one hard fact was that in their months here they had neither seen nor heard an Allied plane, or even the sound of bombing. Which meant that this part of the world must be surely under Japanese control, the war itself moved elsewhere.

South.

Australian iron ore was desperately needed for the Japanese war effort. Australian coal was essential to smelt the ore, as was Australian copper for wiring, and Australian labour to smelt it, just as the 9th were already labouring for the Japanese. Australia, where Moira and Gavin and Nancy must now be back home at Overflow. He'd heard they'd gone south with time enough to get out. Moira and Nancy would have got Gavin on a ship home even if they'd had to cling to it with their fingernails. But if the Japs were coming after them, then ...

... he could do nothing. Sit here, eating fish stew, listening to a secret radio cobbled together from bits and pieces bought from the locals ...

Ben stopped eating. 'Curly?'

'Mmm?'

'If we can build a receiver, we can build a transmitter.'

'What, and tell the cheese and kisses you're fit and happy?' They had been allowed to send one Red Cross postcard to their families. Ben hoped his had got through.

'Tell them what Japanese planes fly over. How many guards. Ah Chee might know more. You never know what bits the blokes in Intelligence can put together.' Better yet, thought Ben, see if Ah Chee could put them in touch with Malay traders heading to other islands. There'd been rumours that not all the Malays had accepted Japanese rule. If they could smuggle in arms, they could break out of here. Join local guerrillas ...

Nah, I'm dreaming, he thought. Or that blow to the head has given me concussion.

But the seed was there. Escape. And fight.

Chapter 38

Gibber's Creek Gazette, 14 April 1943

No Hot-Water Bottle for Winter?

Shortages of rubber from the Malay plantations have meant that Lee's General Stores are unable to acquire hot-water bottles. Try a brick or a large clean rock heated in the fire, suggests Mrs Matilda Thompson of Drinkwater, but be sure that it is dry or it may explode if heated too long. Wrap well in an old blanket and it will keep its warmth.

With coffee, potatoes and prunes now reserved for the armed forces, and tea rationed, Mrs Thompson suggests planting a crop of potatoes now for early-spring eating, and a further crop in spring. 'There is no reason why any home should not grow all its own potatoes. As for prunes, they are simply dried plums, of which Gibber's Creek and the local fruit bats have no shortage at all.'

Mrs Thompson did admit that 'nothing can really replace a good cup of tea' but reminded us that our boys overseas face far worse than an empty teapot.

PULAU AYU PRISON CAMP, 17 APRIL 1943

NANCY

Nancy looked around the outdoor kitchen. The armchair stood empty, mildewed now and tattered at the edges. 'Where's Mrs Hughendorn?'

'Having a rest,' said Nurse McTavish. Nurse McTavish had moved into Mrs Hughendorn's empty second room now, while Sally had moved in with Nurse Rogers and Nurse Williams. Moira and Nancy had refused beds in the more sturdily built structures. They might have been more waterproof, but they were also hotter. At least their hut let in every breeze, and they welcomed the privacy. 'It's all right,' added Nurse McTavish. 'I looked in on her. She's just tired. I promised to take in her stew.'

Too tired to preside over the evening gathering? To make sure no one discussed religion, politics, business or any of the other socially unacceptable subjects Australian nurses — or farm girls — might bring up?

'I'll take it to her. Sure she's not sick?'

'She says not.'

Nancy carried in the bowl. At least the flower buds and greens gave it some bulk as well as vitamins and minerals, though she hadn't managed to provide any 'island rabbit' today. She knocked on the bedroom door.

'Come in.'

Mrs Hughendorn sat up in bed. A nightdress, thought Nancy, trying not to smile. How long since she'd seen a nightdress? The other women slept in their clothes — less revealing for the guards' night patrols. But Mrs Hughendorn had a door, and to get to it a guard would have to step over two other beds jammed into the tiny living room. Perhaps they didn't bother.

The nightdress was pink, with lace; or rather grey-pink, after many washings in muddy water. Mrs Hughendorn had a pillow behind her. A real pillow, not rolled-up cloth. 'I was worried,' said Nancy. She held out the bowl.

'I ... I'm just tired.' Mrs Hughendorn took the bowl without looking at her. 'Thank you, my dear.'

It was a dismissal. Nancy didn't go. Instead she sat on the end of the bed. It wasn't much of a bed, no wider than hers. But it still almost filled the room, already crammed with a wardrobe and a pile of trunks, presumably hauled down from the main house when the Japanese took over.

'Really, I am quite …' Mrs Hughendorn broke off. She put her bowl down on the bed and stared out the window, its bamboo shutter open to let in the breeze. If there had been a breeze.

'What's wrong?' asked Nancy softly.

'Nothing, my dear. Really.'

Well, she'd never been good at being tactful.

'Of course there are things wrong. We are imprisoned. Starving. Filthy. I've got mosquito bites on my mosquito bites, and I'm sure that the one on my leg is a flea bite …'

'My dear, one doesn't …'

'Talk about flea bites?'

'One doesn't. Although you do,' added Mrs Hughendorn dryly, a little of her spirit back.

'Something is bothering you. Not just fleas and …' Nancy nodded to the bowl '… slush for dinner.'

'It's Mr Hughendorn's birthday today,' said Mrs Hughendorn suddenly.

'I … I'm so sorry.'

'There is nothing to be sorry about. It … it didn't seem to matter last year. I was so sure I would see him soon again. But I won't, will I?'

'No,' said Nancy.

Mrs Hughendorn laughed. 'You should have said, "Of course you will."'

'Of course you will. But it won't be soon.'

'No. Not soon. I … I always used to make a ceremony of his birthday. I never gave him a child, you see. He never reproached me but … well, I could give him a birthday party. In Singapore, at the Raffles. Once a trip to Scotland. Back home several times. Chocolate birthday cake, his favourite.'

'Then that's what this is.' Nancy nodded at the slush. 'Chocolate cake. With candles.'

'Oh, not candles. Not and tell everyone his age!' The eyes had a definite twinkle in them now. Her expression sobered. 'That young woman made a play for him, you know. His secretary. She thought I didn't know. Fluttering her lashes at him. "Oh, Mr Hughendorn. You ARE funny, Mr Hughendorn." I don't think he even noticed. She could have given him children, perhaps, but we were happy. So happy.'

'You will be happy again. But to do that you have to live.'

Mrs Hughendorn looked at her shrewdly. 'And to live I need to get out of this bed and stop feeling sorry for myself?'

'I couldn't have put it more tactlessly myself,' said Nancy.

Mrs Hughendorn nodded. 'You are a good girl. Tell me, while we are being tactless, what is your background?'

She wasn't asking about Overflow, or Ben. Nancy had shared that with them all, as they too had shared much of their former lives, as much to fill empty days as with friendship ... but the friendship was there too.

'My grandmother is Aboriginal.'

'Ah. So you are a quadroon. That explains your ability to get a fire going ...'

'No, it doesn't. Any bushie can do that.'

'Bushie?'

'Someone who lives in the bush.'

'Ah. I was thinking of men with bushy beards.'

Nancy grinned. 'Some of them have those too.'

'You don't think your ... heritage ... matters then?'

Nancy considered. 'I don't know,' she said honestly. 'I think ... Gran taught me to see things.'

'Like "island rabbit" as potential meat? And flower buds and green leaves to try to keep us alive?'

'Yes. Maybe. But that's knowledge, I don't think that's inherited. Or maybe it is. Who knows.' She looked at Mrs Hughendorn directly. 'Does this make any difference? My being quarter Aboriginal?'

'To our select social club at the Pulau Ayu Prison Club? No, my dear.'

'I'm glad,' said Nancy lightly. 'I wouldn't want to miss sharing the chocolate cake. Without candles. What does Pulau Ayu mean anyway?'

'Pretty Island,' said Mrs Hughendorn expressionlessly. 'And it was, you know. So pretty. Still is, perhaps, outside.' She swung her legs out of the bed, mottled, the ankles still thick. 'I'll just get dressed, then meet you outside. Chocolate cake should not be eaten by oneself.'

'Of course not,' said Nancy. She reached up and kissed the woman's drooping cheek. 'We need to sing happy birthday, dear Horatio Hughendorn, too.'

'Thank you, my dear,' said Mrs Hughendorn quietly. 'And if ... when you see your grandmother, could you give her my thanks too?'

Chapter 39

Jim Thompson
AIF
20 August 1943

The Thompson Family
Drinkwater Station
via Gibber's Creek

Dear Mum and Dad and Michael and whoever else you read this out to,
It was grand to see you all last month. Sorry I haven't written before, but they always seem to move us before we can get to a post box and no one has been collecting mail. But Wilton will make sure this is sent off.

Did I tell you about Wilton? He is my batman! One of the perks of being made an officer. Could have used him in the Middle East but am dashed glad that promotion has meant I have him now. He knocks on the door and brings me tea in bed each morning — well, it's not quite a bed and nor is there a door on the tent but it IS tea. And then he brings me my shaving water and my uniform all pressed and socks inverted for putting on. He has even found a clean hessian sack to give me a 'bedroom' carpet. He has scrounged me more blankets and two nights ago I even had a hot-water bottle, though I think medical must since have snaffled it to use as an enema bag. Pardon the gruesome details there. I am still learning how to be an officer and a gentleman.

Anyhow, New Guinea isn't going to be too bad at all if it has early-morning tea and hot-water bottles, not to mention no blinking sand. I don't ever want a holiday at the beach again.

Love to all,
Jim

Gibber's Creek Gazette, 21 August 1943

Mrs Councillor Bullant thanks all involved in the magnificent costume ball last Saturday. First prize was won by Mr and Mrs Andrew McAlpine, in their gorgeous outfits as trapeze artist and circus strongman. Mr McAlpine's leopard-skin garment was much admired by the ladies. The door prize of a leg of lamb and a pumpkin was won by that lucky Land Girl, Annabelle Strong. Strong by name, strong by nature!

The ball raised five hundred and seventy-six pounds and six shillings.

Where the money went:

Red Cross POW Fund
Australian Comforts Fund
Material for CWA needle and wool work
Books for soldiers' children
Bombing for London Relief
Mobile education unit
YWCA for accommodation for single munitions workers
Greek war victims
Two pianos for the army

AERODROME LABOUR CAMP, AUGUST 1943

BEN

The troops came at midday, bayonets ready, helmets down. Most of the POWs were away finishing the road to the aerodrome; only the sick and those on camp duties were left. Ben had taken a turn in the medical hut. He half carried, half supported a one-legged man — the amputation the result of a tropical ulcer gone gangrenous, but healing surprisingly well, thanks to medical supplies they'd smuggled in.

The POWs stood in the shadowless sun outside the barbed wire as the troops took the huts apart, pushing down the bamboo walls, ripping apart the thatch, turning over bunks and tables.

'Think they're going to find it?' whispered the man he was supporting, his face grey with heat and pain.

Ben shrugged.

Six hours later, as the work party marched back, the troops had still found nothing.

'You!' The camp commandant pointed at Captain Grey. The commandant spoke English, and well. 'We know you have a radio.'

'We have no radio.'

The commandant hit him three times, under the chin. Captain Grey just stood and took it.

'Where is the radio?'

'We have no radio.'

The commandant grasped the sweat rag around Captain Grey's throat. He pulled it down, then twisted it. Tighter, tighter. The captain's face grew red, then purple. He dropped to his knees.

'Cripes,' said the man Ben was supporting. 'He's going to kill him.'

Or kill us all if they find out half of what we've done, thought Ben. Only he and a few of the men knew they had a transmitter now, as well as the receiver; had been able to pass on information about the landings at the aerodrome, estimates of troop numbers; had even been able to get enough information to plan an escape. Ben and Curly were lined up to try to get on a Malay boat and island-hop down the coast of Java to Timor. If my ancestors could do it, so can I, thought Ben.

Or might have done, till now. He suspected that at best the camp's easy discipline would be tightened after this. At worst ...

'Where is the radio?'

'There is no radio,' the captain gasped.

The commandant kicked him. 'Where is the radio?'

'There ... is ... no ... radio ...'

The commandant nodded. Two Japanese soldiers with bamboo rods began to beat him. *Slash. Slash.*

'Where is the radio?'

'There ... is ... no ... radio ...'

Shadows became night. The lights flicked on, showing nothing but the barbed wire, the sentry posts, the man lying on the ground, the commandant, the troops. The prisoners knelt or lay in the shadows, forbidden to move. No water. No food.

Someone groaned. Was it the man who now lay beside him? Ben's gaze was fixed on Grey.

A soldier approached, with a plate of what looked like rice and a shred of meat. For a moment Ben thought they were going to tempt their prisoner with food, before realising that the rice was raw.

A soldier pulled the captain up, opened his mouth, shoved in the raw rice. The captain gagged, then swallowed.

Another soldier, with a hose. They thrust it into the captain's mouth. He convulsed, choking, as the water splashed over him, choked him. Finally he lay, gasping on the ground.

The commandant picked up the shred of meat, placed it carefully on the end of a bayonet, then thrust it into the captain's ear.

The captain screamed. His scream went on and on.

At last it died away.

'Where is the radio?'

This time there was no reply, though the captain still lived, his eyes still open.

The commandant turned to the men kneeling on the ground. 'There will be no food, no water, until you give us the radio. Where is the radio?'

The captain gasped something. Ben tried to hear. 'Under ... Hut ... Two.'

Not the cookhouse, where the radio sat. Not the hospital hut, where they had the transmitter. Hut Two's hidden pit had only spare valves, spare wire and tin foil in it. Would the Japanese think that they were assembled to make the camp's radio?

Night turned to day. They waited as the soldiers ransacked Hut Two, thorough as a careful housewife hunting every cockroach. The sun glared at them, slowly moving through the sky. The captain began to scream. The raw rice inside him was swelling up. His body arched, over and over. He screamed again.

One of the Japanese called from inside the compound. He held up the spare valves, the wire and tin foil. The commandant nodded. He turned to the prisoners. 'Look at this man. You will not see him again. Japan has been lenient with you. Now you will pay.'

Two soldiers carried the still-screaming captain away.

The barbed wire was doubled around the camp. There were double sentries now too. Double guards who marched the work parties to the work site, refusing to let the men buy coconuts or fruit. Dogs were placed in the camp each night; dogs that bit, dogs that fought you for the half-rations that were poured into a trough each night. Every man in camp had dog bites now.

A starving man can fight a dog, and win.

Beatings every day. Beatings if you did not work fast enough, or hard enough. Beatings anyway: beatings with bamboo rods that knocked out eyes, opened flesh down to the bones.

If you did not work, if you did not bow each time a sentry passed, you were beaten; if you tried to swap a watch with one of the locals for quinine for malaria, you were thrust into the ishu cages. These were made of bamboo and sat on stilts about a yard off the ground, a yard high, too low for a man to stand, no room for him to sit or lie down. You knelt, in the glare of sun, your sweat mingling with that of those who had gone before you, till your body grew too water-starved to sweat at all and you slumped, held up by the bodies of your companions.

You might be caged for hours, for days, for weeks. Ben was thrown in there one afternoon. He had not noticed the commandant pass. He had not bowed.

He straightened himself on the bamboo bars and knelt, taking up the smallest amount of room he could, apologising to the men he'd landed on. Three of them, for 'crimes' committed today too. He didn't know their names, though their faces were familiar, like everyone's in camp. None were Aussies, though few in the camp had recognisable uniforms now. They all wore shorts and a scrap of shirt, or even native cloth wound into a sort of nappy that hung between the knees. Boots had worn out with work and socks were just a memory, rotted in the heat and damp.

Ben glanced over at the next two cages. The men in the far cage had been there over a month. Most were still alive. The blokes in the next cage to his had been there just over a week. You never knew how long you might be caged. That, thought Ben, was the worst of it.

It wasn't.

They continued kneeling. Lice circled over them, from one man to the next. The fungal infection on his legs itched. Impossible to scratch. His legs and back ached; then screamed at him. He shut his mouth hard to stop from crying aloud.

The afternoon heat closed its fist about him. He was used to heat, but not like this, the heat of four men together. No water. No shade. They knelt, heads bent, smelt the food poured into the nearby trough, longed even for the jostling with the dogs, for at least then your limbs could move.

Night, a blanket of dark. They weren't allowed to speak, but they could whisper. 'How you going, mate?'

'All right, mate. All right?'

'Yeah. I'm all right.'

Another day. A night. Day. It was better now. He was so dazed he could not think or feel.

Shadows that must mean that night was coming again. More shadows. Men. The guards. The cage door opened. He let his body go limp, knowing what would happen now. Dragged onto the ground, kicked and punched, while about him the three others were beaten too. Water, held to his mouth. Drank, and drank. He tried to stop. They poured the water in. At last he lay, gasping and gagging on the ground. He felt his body as if it was far off, felt it lifted, thrust back into the cage, felt a bayonet point on his back till he found the strength to kneel once more.

Somehow they slept that night, all leaning against each other. Morning came in a blaze of pain and light. A guard approached. He opened the door. He left it open, opened the next cage too, then walked away.

Ben couldn't move. If he couldn't move, none of them could get out, for he was by the door. But there were Curly's hands, hauling him out onto the ground, already back, helping the others too.

He looked towards the third cage, its door still shut. Saw the men inside look at him, no envy and no hope.

He tried to stand. Couldn't. He staggered, bent over, to his hut. For three days he tried to straighten up and each time it was agony. On the fourth day he managed to stand, holding a stick.

That night after the radio broadcast he risked the dogs to stand by the cage, holding his stick to keep them off, and whispered news to men who didn't answer, perhaps could not even hear now or understand. 'The Yanks have landed in Italy, at Anzio. Russians have smashed the German lines at Leningrad. Anthony Eden was talking about Jap camps on the BBC tonight. They've picked up some Aussies who were on a Jap ship, torpedoed by a submarine. Left to drown — they kept the hatches locked — but our blokes got to them in time. Three Yanks who escaped from the Philippines have told their stories too. Bad as here, I reckon. Starved. Some poor blighters buried alive. Know what old Eden said?' He'd memorised it.

There was no reply from above.

'"Let the Japanese reflect that their war record will not be forgotten." The world knows about us, cobbers. Our side is on the move now. They're coming to get us. Any day now they'll be here.'

At last a whisper from the shadowed cage. 'And miss our holiday camp here? They'll have to drag us out.'

And that, thought Ben, as he staggered back, lifting his stick at an approaching dog, might well be true.

The days dragged on; the weeks, the months. Still no one came, not even a change of guard. No Allied planes. No Aussies marching down the road with the tramp of boots, the sound of 'Waltzing Matilda'.

No medicine either. No way to buy it now. Malaria and cholera, gasping above the latrine trench while your insides slid out, left you so weak you crawled on your stomach back to your bunk.

Men died.

Ben lived. For now.

Chapter 40

Gibber's Creek Gazette, 10 September 1943

Sugarless Desserts for Sweet Tooths

Fruit Salad in Jelly

Prepare two thinly sliced bananas sprinkled with lemon juice in a mould and cover with the pulp of four passionfruit. Dissolve a dessertspoon of gelatine in a cup of hot water. Add the juice of a lemon. Pour into a fluted mould and allow to set. Unmould by running under the hot water for a few seconds. Arrange on a plate and decorate with fresh passionfruit.

Contributed by
Mrs Councillor Bullant

Easy Desserts for Busy Women

Get the kids to dig a strawberry patch. Ask Gran for some strawberry runners. Send the kids out to pick berries after dinner. Tell them to pick some for their parents while they're at it then ask the cow for cream.

Contributed by
Mrs Councillor Ellis

BLUE

The man was waiting for her in her office, a stranger in a blue suit — the wrong kind of blue — and brown shoes. No gentleman would wear brown shoes with a blue suit. Why isn't he in uniform? wondered Blue.

'Can I help you?'

He grinned, showing a gold tooth. 'It's me as can help you, little lady.'

'I am not little, and I am the owner and manager of this factory.' Blue tried not to let her anger show. 'But I am a lady, so I will ask you again, politely. How can I help you?'

'You won't be like that when you hear what I've got to offer you.' The man oozed confidence. 'What would you say to another four gallons of petrol a week, eh? Might be useful to a businesswoman like you.' He took her shocked expression for acceptance, and winked. 'Could throw in a pair of silk stockings too. Might even be able to get me hands on some lipstick.'

She made herself smile politely. 'How would you manage that, Mr ...?'

'Just call me Sport. Always like to be a good sport, especially to pretty girls.'

I am twenty-seven, thought Blue. And I have earned the right not to be called a girl.

'Anything else?'

'Like what? Reckon you don't need butter nor sugar here. Can help yourself from the supplies for the biscuits, eh?'

Blue squeezed her palms together so he wouldn't see her anger. Rob men who were fighting a war for them all? But she knew what he wanted from her now. She forced her voice to be friendly. 'I was thinking about a few yards of silk, Mr, er, Sport.'

'Tell you what, I'll make a bargain with you. You get me, say, ten pounds of butter a week and ten pounds of sugar. Won't even be missed in a place this big. Just make your bikkies a little less sweet, eh? And in return I can get you petrol and all the pretties you want. Maybe even a ham at Christmas.'

'That is an interesting proposition, Mr Sport.' She gave him her best 'fool the punters' smile, well practised from her days with the circus. 'Why don't you sit here and I'll get my secretary to bring you in a cup of tea?'

'Wouldn't mind one of your biscuits too. Heard they're real good.'

They are, she thought. And they are for the army, not for you. 'Of course. I won't be long — I just need to tell my partner. She'll be as interested in your offer as I am.'

'Chinese lass, ain't she? Ah, you ladies will do anything for pretties.'

Blue stood, shut the door behind her and turned the lock. Tea! She wouldn't waste even the dregs on that man in there. As for a biscuit ...

He was bashing at the door by the time she returned, Mah at her side. 'You let me out of here! One more minute and I'll break this door down!'

Blue turned the key and opened the door.

He stopped, his fists still in the air. 'What the flaming hell —?' he began.

'So sorry to keep you waiting. It took a while to get hold of the sergeant. But he should be here any minute.'

'Sergeant! What do you think you're doing?'

'Stopping a black marketeer. He should get five years for this, don't you think, Mah?'

Mah nodded.

He gazed from one to the other, furious. 'If you think I'm waiting here for any sergeant, you got another think coming. I'm getting out of here.'

'Oh, no, you're not.' He found himself gripped by four strong hands. How did women get hands like steel?

'We were trained by an expert,' said Mah calmly, as if she knew what he was thinking. 'Exercise every day. Somehow never quite got out of the habit. Never know when you might need to stand on your hands again.' She glanced out of the window. 'Yes, that's the police wagon now. He's mostly on his bicycle these days. The wagon is specially for you.'

She looked at him steadily, her hands still gripping like iron. 'My brother died up in New Guinea defending this country. Blue's husband is a prisoner of war.'

Blue shut her eyes. Please, she thought, let Joseph truly be a prisoner ...

'What I'd really like to do is kick you where your mother never kissed you. But I was taught to be a lady by an old woman who was most respectable. So instead I'm handing you over all in one piece.'

Mah turned and smiled at the sergeant who had appeared in the room. 'Sergeant, he's all yours. And I wish you joy of him.'

Chapter 41

> *Jim Thompson*
> *AIF*
> *3 October 1943*

The Thompson Family
Drinkwater Station
via Gibber's Creek

Dear family,
Excuse this, must write it in a rush. There may be a gap in my
letters for a while, so don't want you to worry. All is fine and will
be fine, but expect mail services will be few and far between.
Wilton sends you his best wishes, and wants to know if there
might be a job as a shearer's cook after the war. I said you'd
probably snap him up!

> *Love to all,*
> *Jim*

PULAU AYU PRISON CAMP, OCTOBER 1943

NANCY

'Wire,' said Sally.

Gavin looked out the door at the barbed-wire fence, rusty brown after two wet seasons. 'Vire,' he said.

Water from the late-afternoon storm dripped through the roof. It was impossible to keep anything dry; impossible to keep anything damp free from mould. Rope was forbidden to them, but every day when she picked the basket of hibiscus buds, Nancy managed to gather some of the long tropical grass too, then plaited it into string the way Gran had shown her.

Washing lines now stretched from hut to hut, festooned after every storm with their blankets and clothes, steaming gently in the sun.

'W. Wire,' repeated Sally.

'Wire,' said Gavin. He gave her a cheeky grin, as if he knew he'd got it right that time.

'Very good!' Nurse Rogers clapped as well as Sally and Moira. Nancy smiled as she twisted more string. Gavin might have no proper toys, no playmates his own age. But he had six aunties and a mother lavishing him with love and attention.

'Green tree,' said Sally. 'Green bush. Blue sky. Blue dress.' Gavin stared at Sally's dress, vaguely puzzled. Its cloth was a long way from sky blue these days.

Nancy looked back down at her plaiting. The string was strong, but rotted as fast as cloth in the heat and the wet. Gran had shown her how to run stringybark rope through a fire to make it waterproof, but when she'd tried that with the grass string it simply frizzled and burnt. Which meant she had to make new string every few weeks.

A shadow made her look up. The translator stood there, the commandant behind him. She stood hurriedly with the other women and bowed.

The translator made the signal to rise. Nancy looked from him to the commandant. Even now they no longer had dysentery — more or less — neither she nor any of the other women had been called to the officers' house again.

The commandant held out a small packing case. Nancy took it automatically.

'A present from a Japanese officer to the child,' said the translator. For the first time he looked at his superior uncertainly. 'The commandant says that it is International

Children's Day. It is proper for children to get presents on Children's Day.'

Nancy had never heard of International Children's Day. Nor had there been presents or any celebration the year before. She met the commandant's eyes. He looked at her, his mouth stretched in an emotion impossible to read. He said something briefly to the translator.

'The commandant says to tell you he must leave the island now. He says he has left orders that the food for the child will come every day. He wishes you and the child a good life.'

'Where is he going? Will we get another commandant?' All at once she realised that life in the camp could have been far worse, with a crueller man in charge. They had not been beaten in camp, except the odd flick with the bamboo poles, which hurt enough but weren't life threatening. Other than that one night there had been no demand for company. She tried to thrust away the memory of the grey bodies on the beach. That could have been all of them, with another man in charge.

We are alive, she thought, despite being nothing more than a nuisance at best, at worst an insult to honour. And if we have far too little food, our gaolers are almost as thin as us.

'You must not ask Japanese officer questions,' said the translator.

'I ... I apologise. Please, thank the commandant.' Nancy nodded to the box, wondering what it contained.

The commandant spoke before the translator could say anything more. 'Sayonara,' he said.

It was one of the words he had tried to teach her, that night she tried to forget.

She looked at Gavin perched on Sally's hip, this little boy who lived because this man had perhaps broken rules from headquarters to give him extra food, had perhaps broken other rules to let her pick flower buds and the grass for the string — and therefore secretly bring in the small parcels that still appeared in the bushes every few days, sometimes dried fish or a sweet potato. It was not much. But combined with the flower buds, with the meat from a rat or lizard once or twice a week, it had kept them alive.

She looked back at him. For the first time her bow was genuine. 'Sayonara,' she said. 'Arigato.' She hesitated. This man had also starved them, allowed his men to strike them, steal from them; crimes that in normal life, if there was ever normal life, would have meant years in prison. But every man should have someone farewell him when he went to battle. 'May you travel safely, sensei,' she added softly.

She gestured to Sally, to Moira. They bowed again. The other women did the same. They kept the bow as the commandant walked back to the officers' house.

She thought, as she looked at him from under her eyelashes, that there were tears in his eyes. But perhaps it was just the glint of the sun.

She opened the box in the hut she shared with Moira and Gavin. For some reason she didn't want the guards to see what was in it, though surely the commandant would not have given her or, rather, Gavin, anything the guards would object to.

She drew the objects out, one by one. A book. A book written in English. Not just in English — an Australian book, *The Magic Pudding* by Norman Lindsay. It had pictures too — Gavin would love the pictures, even if the book was a bit too old for him. But she could use it to teach him to read. She could read it herself, over and over, dream of an Australia where the mornings smelt like Pears soap and there was always pudding to eat, no matter how much of it you'd consumed the night before.

There was a small cloth bag too. She opened that, and stared. Small wrapped lollies, in bright paper. Her stomach cramped with longing. But these were Gavin's. Nurse Rogers said it was important to give anyone with dysentery sweet and salty things, to keep up their strength. She must keep these for an emergency. Dysentery could kill a child far quicker than it could an adult.

A bottle. She looked at the label, which was in English, not Japanese. Quinine tablets. Enough for several cases of malaria. She was glad that the guards hadn't seen her with those.

A can of cheese, again with an English label. Gavin needed the calcium. A can of bully beef. What soldiers' rations, she wondered, had the beef and cheese come from? A packet of Empire Rich Teas. Also known as squished flies.

And suddenly she was crying, gazing at the biscuits made so far away at Blue and Mah McAlpine's factory, at Gibber's Creek. I will keep the packet, she thought, after Gavin eats the biscuits. Because that packet had come from home, had been touched by people from her land. She would tell him the story of how the circus came to Gibber's Creek too, how its mermaid and magician's assistant had stayed, in the country they had recognised as home.

She wiped her eyes before Gavin saw she was crying — he got upset too when anybody cried, so they all kept careful smiles on their faces when he was near. And then she saw it.

Sitting at the bottom of the box was the photograph of the girl her age, sitting facing the camera. She picked it up, and gazed at it.

Had the commandant put the photo in the box accidentally? He had held it like it was the most precious possession he had.

And that is why he left it, she thought. Whatever he was going to, he wanted that photograph to be safe. Not buried in mud, or blown up at sea. The commandant had no need to look at it; had gazed at it for a thousand hours perhaps. But he loved it too much to risk it being destroyed. Was his daughter still alive? Perhaps this was the only image of her that remained. She could never ask him now.

Was he a good man? She didn't know whether he was good, but she did know that he was not bad. Had he fought battles to keep them alive? Or had he simply done his job, not caring much, till ordered to another battlefield, one with more honour for him than this one. But she thought, perhaps, it was the former.

Sayonara, she thought, then called Gavin over to feed him squished flies, and read the most precious book in all the world.

The car came for the commandant the next morning. Nancy assumed it had come from a ship, as they had heard no car engines until now. As far as she and the other women knew, there were no cars on the island, only bicycles, now all commandeered by the Japanese. Mrs Hughendorn had burnt their own car, just as she had ordered the burning of all machinery and the stores of rubber, before the Japanese arrived.

No new commandant came, nor did new guards.

'You know what that means,' said Sally, as they sat around the cooking fire one evening. There had been a small packet of spices in the bushes that afternoon. The camp smelt of mould and latrines, but their nightly sago was now fragrant, mixed with the flower buds, and the small, green kidney-shaped leaves that Nancy had thought looked like ones Gran sometimes picked and ate at home (they tasted like them too), and an 'island rabbit', caught by the latrine and given an extra-long boiling.

'What does it mean?' demanded Mrs Hughendorn. She had regained much of her strength, perhaps as much from the knowledge that the islanders she had known had not abandoned her as from the food they left. She now sat erect again on their only chair, her skin hanging in long flaps from her jaw and arms, and swaying as she sipped her stew.

'It means the Japanese need every man they can get. They don't have any spare soldiers to come here and watch over a bunch of women and a child.'

'Or maybe the opposite,' said Moira quietly. 'Maybe they feel confident that the island has settled under Japanese occupation. Maybe they have Papua under control now too and are fighting in Australia.'

'No!' The cry came before she realised it came from her. Nancy bit her lip. 'We'll beat them off.'

'Of course we will, dear,' said Mrs Hughendorn quickly. 'You Australians are splendid fighters.'

Nancy said nothing. That was what everyone had said about Malaya, about Singapore. That they could not be taken by the Japanese either. Australians had fought there as well, in a combined force that far outnumbered the Japanese. And they had lost.

She ate her stew in silence.

Chapter 42

Gibber's Creek Gazette, 1 December 1943

School Bonfire Success
By Elaine Sampson, aged eleven and a third

Last night our school had a bonfire night. We made a big scarecrow called Hitler from Joey Marshall's dad's old trousers and shirt and lots of straw. We used black paper for the moustache and hair and flour-paste glue. We all brought sticks from home.

We each paid a penny to take a ticket to see who would light the fire and Sharon Adams won but made a mess of it so Billy Bloggs did it for her. It took half an hour for Hitler to burn and we all cheered and roasted potatoes. Today anyone who gets kept in after school has to rake away the mess.

We raised two shillings and ninepence for the war effort, and Councillor Bullant said, 'Well done, Gibber's Creek Central School.'

DRINKWATER, 24 DECEMBER 1943

MICHAEL

Santa arrived in a dusty ute and with three days' dark stubble below his white beard. He'd been dagging sheep for the past week, and still smelt slightly of sheep bums and lanolin.

Kids and their parents gathered in the shade of the oak trees as Santa handed out the gifts, one to each child, not just for those whose fathers were overseas or serving elsewhere, but a special hug for them. Good gifts too. Toys were as scarce as zippers and knicker elastic, but his mother had hired old Stumpy Farrel to make wooden rocking horses, cricket bats, tricycles and wagons for the children to pull. Anything that could be made of wood, cut from the farm, mostly she-oak with its red-gold sheen from up the gullies, soft enough to work with, hard enough to take rough use. The curtains from the spare bedrooms had been sacrificed to make dresses for the older girls, created by Mrs Barrington on her treadle sewing machine, inspired by the latest photos in *The Sydney Morning Herald*.

There would be no party tonight. No dancing. His mother had made the excuse that it was too hard for many of the families to get to Drinkwater and back at night, with petrol rationing, too late for kids to ride ponies or bicycles. Which was true, but Michael suspected the heart of her decision was the deepening grief and worry of their family and friends. It was easier to turn the annual Christmas party into a children's afternoon tea than smile and dance.

But the trestles were still covered with the Christmas cloths, the silver still shone, the punch bowl was full. The plates were filled with afternoon tea: scones and pikelets, with sugarless jam from home-grown strawberries and peaches, cakes sweet with fruit too, fairy cakes with home-churned cream under their wings, thick-cut mutton and chutney sandwiches, corned mutton sandwiches, chicken and lettuce, and mock chicken, the egg and tomato and onion mix that didn't taste like chicken at all, and that the fellows at school called 'train smash'. The big CWA teapots were kept filled beside the rows of teacups — his parents and Mah and Blue had saved their tea rations for months.

Michael sat on the veranda. Around him, men talked stock prices or how to keep pumps going when there were no spare parts, comparing rainfalls, pitifully small. Michael glanced up at the sky, hoping, yet again, to see thunder clouds climbing over themselves on the horizon. It was bare of all but the silhouette of cliffs and trees.

But a prickle between his shoulder blades still said a storm might be building. He peered down at the ants that usually scurried between the veranda pot plants. None to be seen. Which meant they might, hopefully, be barricading their holes against the water to come ...

'Looking for the ants?' Mr Clancy sat heavily in the squatter's chair next to him.

'Yes, sir.'

'No need to "sir" me, son.'

'Thank you.' What was he to call him then? Mr Clancy didn't say. Instead he moved restlessly in his chair.

'Feel like a walk?'

Michael nodded. He followed the small dark man down the steps and around the Santa-less side of the house. For a moment he wondered if Mr Clancy would head down to the river, to check perhaps if the swan was there. It was, along with some of its offspring from the year before too. Michael suspected that with inland lakes drying up, the swan preferred the security of the backwaters of the river. Which did not affect its link with Nancy. Or that was what he told himself.

Instead Mr Clancy strode past the shearing shed, over to the horse paddock. He leant on the gate, watching Snow King's great-great-grandson canter along the fence line, excited by the scents and sounds of other horses and strangers.

Michael leant next to him. Surprisingly the silence was companionable. Mr Clancy yawned. 'Sorry. Long days. Too much to do and not enough hands to do it. You know how it is.'

Michael nodded, aware as he did so that he did not really know, but only guessed at the edges of the reality, insulated as he was at school for so much of the year.

'You don't have any Land Girls?'

'No.'

The word was curt. Of course not, thought Michael, feeling he had put a size-fourteen boot in his mouth. Young women about the farm would only remind you all too much of Nancy.

'We're only staying for tomorrow, then I'd better get back to it. Need to lay pipe down from the creek up in the hills. The windmill shaft broke in the wind a fortnight ago and I can't get the necessary parts.'

'Would you like me to come over for a few days to give you a hand?'

The look on Mr Clancy's face told him the answer, despite his careful, 'You're not needed here?'

They manage without me during term time, thought Michael. 'They can spare me for a week or so. That'd be enough time to get the pipe laid?'

'I reckon. Thanks.'

'Maybe Dad could have a look at your windmill too.'

'Your father?'

Michael laughed. 'Dad was a pretty good bush mechanic before he became the industrialist, Mr Thomas Thompson. He fixed Mah's washing machine last week.' Someone at the factory could probably either fix or replace the shaft too, he thought. But what went on at the factory was classified, not even to be mentioned to Mr Clancy.

'Thanks,' said Mr Clancy again, still looking at the horse, not at Michael.

I'm doing it for Nancy, thought Michael. Then, no, not for Nancy. Even if he'd never met Nancy, he'd have made the offer. The man was a neighbour. He liked him. You stood by your own or laid pipe with them. This was simply what you did, as Mr Clancy would help in his turn, if he could.

'Look.' The older man pointed at the ground, at an ant's nest, now covered with shreds of bark. 'Thunderstorm's coming. And rain with it. Hope we get it down our way too. Come on, the wife'll be wondering where I've got to.'

They turned back. We haven't mentioned Nancy, thought Michael, unsure whether to be relieved or saddened. But we have spoken of Overflow and ants. In a way he could not explain, that felt like they had talked about Nancy too.

Chapter 43

Gibber's Creek Gazette, 5 January 1944

Red Cross Donations for this Week

Mrs H Bullant: 14 prs socks; 5 cakes soap; 2 prs bootlaces;
    2 pyjama coats; 2 parcels old linen

Mrs H Ellis: 16 prs socks; 6 face washers

Mrs Lee: 1 pr socks; 2 prs comforters; 2 prs bootlaces;
    2 shaving cream; 12 cakes soap

Miss Anita Bevedge: 4 prs socks; 1 hot-water-bottle cover;
    3 singlets; magazines

Mrs M Thompson: 6 face washers; 50 cakes soap

Mrs B McAlpine: 7 prs socks; 6 hot-water-bottle covers;
    20 shaving cream and brushes; 14 fruitcakes

Mrs M McAlpine: 12 prs socks; 12 plum puddings

Miss Beverly Bridges: 3 prs socks; 6 pillow slips

PULAU AYU PRISON CAMP, JANUARY 1944

NANCY

Christmas departed: 'roast goose', which was really a small boiled python Nancy had caught and killed as she picked hibiscus buds, then wrapped around her middle to smuggle it into camp. Her dress was so loose now she could have hidden a medium-sized crocodile.

Malaria came again. While they had access to quinine, at least, they survived. Mrs Hughendorn's hands were bare of rings. Nancy didn't know if it was because they had grown too thin for the rings to stay on, or if she had sold them all in exchange for the drugs that kept them alive. Rain came, solid water from the sky, or sudden windstorms sweeping, roaring, chewing their roofs and spitting them out.

The rations had changed: less cassava, more sago. But she was able to catch 'island rabbit' nearly every night now, crouched by the latrine, ready to pounce. And bananas still came each morning for Gavin. He was thin, his legs like sticks, a small potbelly she knew was not fat. But he still had the energy to catch his 'ball' when the women took it in turns to throw it to him; still snuggled up to her in the heat of the afternoon to listen to *The Magic Pudding* and stories of Overflow, far away.

But there would be no stories this afternoon, not over the clatter of rain in the wet season, with only half a roof left from the previous night's storm, and the clouds building up again.

The translator had grown even thinner, she realised, as she stepped up to him head down in a show of respect before she drew close enough to bow. His uniform hung off him now. The cuffs were tatty, his cap stained with sweat. His posture was still erect, but she thought his expression was softer these days, especially when he looked at Gavin.

'Please, Translator-san, may we cut more palm thatch to mend the roof?'

'No knives for prisoners.'

'Oh.' She hadn't thought of that. 'But perhaps the wind blew down palm fronds, Translator-san. We could pick them up.'

He considered, nodded. 'I will go with you.'

The statement surprised her. He had never gone out of the camp with her when she had picked hibiscus buds. Perhaps, she thought, he is as tired of this compound as we are, though he probably spent most of his time at the plantations, translating for the workers there, or for the fishermen who spoke more English than Japanese. Perhaps that too had now changed, as the people of this land once again learnt a victor's language.

'Please, Translator-san, may the other women come too? And the little boy? He has never seen the sea.'

Yes, the translator's look did soften when he looked at Gavin. 'You and one other woman may go. And the boy.'

She bowed low again. 'Thank you, Translator-san. You honour us prisoners.'

He didn't smile. He knows I am lying, she thought. Knows I am trying to please him to get what I want. But it is worth it.

The sand steamed that morning, as the sun sucked back the rain. Moira and Nancy held Gavin's hands as the little boy stared at the unimagined endlessness of the sea. 'Why does the water go back and forwards?'

'I don't know ...' Nancy had started to say, when the translator spoke from behind them.

'The wind blows the water one way and makes a wave, then the water rolls back and feeds another wave, which rolls forwards.'

Gavin frowned, trying to work it out. 'If we push the waves, can we make them all roll back?'

'No,' said the translator. 'Sometimes the wind makes great waves, taller than the tree. Sometimes there is a big shaking of the earth, under the sea, and a big wave comes then too.'

Gavin stepped back, his hands clutching their fingers tighter. 'Will it do that today?'

The translator smiled. Nancy realised that she had never seen him smile before. 'No. The sea is happy today because the storm is over. Come.' To Nancy's amazement, he took the boy's hand in his. They walked down to the water, the translator picking up bits of debris, seashells, pointing to a crab for Gavin to laugh at.

'Wonders will never cease,' said Nancy. 'Moira, what is that?'

Moira held up something — it was small, almost blue-white. 'An egg.'

'It must have blown down from a nest.'

'Not hard-boiled it didn't. Look.'

Nancy looked. In the fork of nearly every bush was a tiny egg, the kind laid by the local hens. Someone — perhaps many someones and not just the person who left the food packages — must have watched her pick buds here, at the same time every day; have put these eggs here for her to find before they could go bad in the heat. She gathered them quickly, sticking them down her blouse before the translator saw. But he had caught a crab between two sticks and was holding it up for Gavin to see.

So many eggs. Twenty, twenty-two ... it would be a feast. It had been more than a month since they'd had an egg, and that was just one shared between them all.

This was more than kindness, she thought. The local people would be punished, beaten, perhaps even killed if the guards discovered they had helped the prisoners. But still the parcels came, and now the eggs. Maybe several people had pooled their eggs to give to the prisoners, hard-boiling them to keep them from going bad ...

Something moved out on the sea. She covered her eyes, to shield them from the glare. It was a native fishing boat, the triangular sail catching the wind.

A boat ... and the three of them outside the camp, with only the translator to guard them. And local people willing to help ...

She had abandoned any thought of escape not long after they were first imprisoned. But now she knew there were people who might help them. Now Gavin was older. Now the guards trusted her enough to go beyond the compound, and Moira and Gavin too. The three of them could vanish. Moira still had her pearls to trade ...

Excitement rose like the giant wave the translator had talked about. Not today, she thought. We can't escape today. We have to plan, to gather stores. Ask Mrs Hughendorn to write a note to leave in the bushes. Make sure a fisherman will help us get off the island, to another without Japanese guards, where we might sail to another island, and another ...

342

Perhaps they could all go …

The sun shone brightly against the blue. The whole world seemed brighter. Escape, thought Nancy. We can do it. Leave the compound. Leave the island. Leave the Japanese behind. And one day, across the islands, get back home to Overflow.

She looked across the sea again.

Escape …

Chapter 44

Gibber's Creek Gazette, 20 March 1944

Farmers Urged to Produce Charcoal for Victory

With fuel supplies needed for the war effort, all farmers are
being urged to turn wood into charcoal. The only equipment
needed is a large pit and ...

FAIRHILLS STATION, NORTHERN TERRITORY, AUSTRALIA, 20 MARCH 1944

KIRSTY

She wasn't going to knit. Or join a RAAF typing pool.

Kirsty McAlpine rubbed the sweat from her forehead,
narrowly avoiding knocking an eye out with the pliers she still
had in her hand. Clouds piled up on the horizon; clouds that
refused to rain, as though they were waiting for someone to say,
'The wet season hasn't finished. Time to rain!' and fire a starting
pistol. She eyed a buzzard, lazily circling her, and made a face.
'Buzz off,' she told it. 'And no need to be so smug. I can outfly
you any day.'

Except she couldn't. The Swaggie sat in the Fairhills shed, with
the last of the cans of gas. This was as far as she'd got, back from
Europe after winning the Zurich to Milan air race, and in record
time too. She'd barn-stormed her way back, stopping wherever
there was a chance to buy gas and a flat place big enough to

land — which for the Swaggie was an incredible hundred and fifty-four feet, the shortest runway required by any competitor. She was light too, just over a thousand pounds, eighty-horsepower motor, two-blade tractor propeller, maximum speed ninety-six miles per hour, or better with a tail wind, stall speed a fabulous thirty-four miles per hour — she could balance her craft in a breeze and she would stay up like a cloud. Plywood skin, wooden frame, steel twine struts braced with piano wire. Best of all, she was light on fuel: one tank would take her a thousand miles, depending on wind and altitude and weight carried, which in her case was eight stone twelve pounds, measured exactly so she'd know whether she could get over the Alps in safety.

She'd been flying solo by then. Johnno had wanted to get married after the Dover to Paris race. But marriage meant children, cooking dinner, sitting at home while your husband challenged the eagles. And no matter how much Johnno protested, that's what'd happen, just as it had to Flinty back at Rock Farm.

Not that Flinty minded. Rock Farm and her family were her life, interspersed with the novels that brought in enough to keep the family prosperous and, if Kirsty was honest, keep her in the air, because the prize money from the air races only went so far, and that wasn't to Dover or even the Giro Aereo D'Italia.

Flinty was a good sort; hadn't kicked up a ruckus when she'd learnt that Kirsty had been flying, not studying Arts like a good girl at Sydney Uni.

If she'd known that the RAAF was going to put its collective head in the sand like an ostrich, she'd have stayed in Britain. At least there women could fly aircraft from the factory to the bases, even fly cargo, although they weren't allowed on combat missions. But here — ha! All the RAAF wanted its women members to do was type. Or chauffeur officers in cars. Let anyone with a bosom get within sneezing distance of an aircraft and the RAAF had pink kittens.

She could fly rings around them. And under and over them too, like she'd flown under the Sydney Harbour Bridge that long-ago night for a dare. But no matter how many air miles, or wins, or air-mile lines across the world map she could show them, flying was lost to her for the duration.

Sometimes she felt that she'd rather lose her arms than her wings.

She'd landed here two months after war with Germany had been declared. Gas was already in short supply and going to Rock Farm, even if she'd been able to find the fuel, seemed suddenly less attractive. She'd be back to being younger sister Kirsty, peeling potatoes, planting potatoes, knitting socks on the veranda with Flinty ...

No, she was not going to knit.

So she knocked on the homestead door and got a job. They were easy enough to come by, what with all the station hands galloping off to Darwin to sign up. There were worse places to spend the war than this. Admittedly the heat struck you like a fist at seven am, and if she had to stare at one more steer's backside she'd scream. Breakfast, lunch and dinner were a tough steak with an egg on top if you were lucky, and boiled greens that she'd been careful not to ask Cookie to identify. But she could do the work with one hand tied behind her back. All right, not without both hands, not fencing, mile after mile of it; nor building stockyards for the yearly muster or shelters for the bulls so the bally animals didn't get sunburnt. Crikey, if only they'd farm roos in this country instead of bally cattle ...

Even Greta was tired on the way back to the homestead. Kirsty brushed the flies from her eyes as they turned the last bend in the track. The heat built up each day, not so much hotter as heavier, as if eventually the air might crush you to the ground. No wonder the poor southern bulls needed shelter.

A jeep sat in the sun by the veranda. All at once the weariness left her. Johnno! She urged Greta to a reproachful canter around the back, unsaddled her and watered her, then let her into the house paddock. She climbed the kitchen steps. But the kitchen was empty. 'Cooee! Where are you all?'

'In here.' It was Marg's voice.

Kirsty pulled off her boots and padded down the corridor. 'What do you want to take this great mug into the living room for? Kitchen's good enough for him.' She lifted her cheek for a kiss.

Johnno smelt of salt and wilted starch from his uniform. He was tall, but skinny as a post-and-rail fence, which had been good in his flying days — less weight meant less fuel and more speed.

'Why didn't you tell me you were getting leave, you great galoot? We'd have killed the fatted calf. Or at least shoved another buzzard in the stew. How can they manage the war without you?'

'Left instructions. Can't stay — I have to drive back tonight.'

'What? You won't get back till the small hours. Probably get lost on the way.'

'Nah. Keep my back to the sunset and follow the searchlights to the base.'

Sudden panic hit her. 'You've heard something about Joey?'

'No, I'm sorry.' His voice was gentle.

'There's nothing wrong at home? Flinty?'

'Keep your hair on, darling. It's nothing like that. This is work, not family.'

She smiled in relief. 'Just as long as you remember I'm not your darling.' And not for want of trying, she thought. He'd kissed her once, after that win in Milan. Well, all right, she had kissed him too. The kiss had shaken her like a hundred-mile-an-hour headwind. She'd been careful not to repeat the experience. Too many kisses like that and who knew where she'd find herself? Or rather, she knew too well, and each scenario led to her marching up the aisle. Except ladies didn't march. She wouldn't even be allowed to wear boots under her wedding dress ...

Marg stood — tall, sun-streaked hair and skin toughened by three decades at Fairhills, managing it with her husband after her parents died and now with Kirsty since he'd joined up, though 'managing' a property up here meant both less and more than it did down south. There were few fences, except around the house, sheds and yards, and you had to bring in a new bull or six every few years and cull the older ones. The real work was rounding them up over a thousand square miles, then droving them to Darwin. 'I'll get fresh tea. Johnno has something he needs to tell you.'

'Yeah, he's been trying to tell me that for five years.' She looked at him with affection. 'And I'm not buying it.'

'I think you need to hear this,' said Marg quietly. She left to get the tea, which would not be a fresh brew, but this week's ration stewed for the fifth time, last week's bread, no butter, tough meat sliced thin enough to chew it.

Kirsty sat down, and put her feet on the table. 'I'm done in. All right for you in your nice office with your fan.' Ten years of flying and the RAAF had stuck Johnno in a Darwin office, which was the RAAF all over, just because he had a heart murmur. Couldn't send a man out to die unless he's a hundred per cent fit.

But she was glad. Glad that Johnno was safe, or as safe as you could be with Jap bombers overhead, even though their raids on Darwin and Broome barely made the newspapers. Glad, in a way, that she needn't be jealous of him, up in the sky while she was stuck here, looking at cattle bums.

'Wish I'd never told you about that fan.' Johnno looked at her steadily.

'All right, what is this you need to say to me?'

'Can you keep it quiet? I'd probably be court-martialled if anyone knew I'd told you this.'

'Who am I likely to tell? The goannas?' She looked at him more closely. 'You're absolutely serious about this, aren't you?'

He nodded. 'I've never really told you what my work is.'

'Paper shuffling,' she quoted promptly.

'It's what's on the paper that matters. I ... coordinate reports, from all across the Top End. Some from the north too.'

'Papua? New Guinea?'

He didn't answer. 'Ham-radio operators mostly. They can warn us that Jap planes are coming in. Some are up on mountains with good visibility to look out for ships. And sometimes ... other things.'

She nodded, aware that there was much he wasn't telling her, and she was careful not to ask for more. Was the real reason he was at a desk not a heart murmur? Perhaps there wasn't anything wrong with his heart at all, but he'd been chosen because he'd flown over this country, knew it from the air in the way it would take someone a lifetime to know it from the ground. He had dropped in — sometimes almost literally — on villages all over Papua, New Guinea and northern Australia.

'You want us to watch here?' She shrugged. 'If we ever see a Jap, I'll let you know.'

'No. That's not why I came. Kirsty, a report came in yesterday. And this is the top-secret part, because if word got out we were even getting a message from this area, it might mean the death of the bloke who sent it.'

She took her feet off the table, nodded. 'I'm listening.'

'He's a padre. Church of England. Good bloke. When the Japs invaded Papua most of the Anglican missionaries chose to stay with their flocks. They said that their church expected it, that Jesus would have expected it, that their own consciences said they must do it — not abandon the members of their church as the enemy approached. So they stayed.'

The simple story touched her so much it was hard to ask, 'Are they still alive?'

'Some of them. Had to leave their churches, of course. Go into the jungle. Their mission people, those they'd converted to Christianity, protected them, mostly at any rate. Others went over to the Japanese. When that happened ...' He shrugged. 'Well, the missionaries didn't live long after that. Sometimes it was a native axe. Sometimes the head was brought to the Japanese for the reward. But the bloke I'm telling you about, he's still there.'

'And he's one of your watchers.'

He nodded. 'He says there's nothing in the Bible against sending information to those who can do good with it. He's got a radio. He's given us some good stuff. But yesterday ...' He searched for words. 'Reception's bad most of the time. He can't say much either — the longer he broadcasts, the more likely it is that the Japs will pick up his signal and work out where it's coming from. He has to keep moving. So all I can tell you is what he told us yesterday. "Mrs Overflow shot last Wednesday."'

She sat frozen on the couch. Nancy of the Overflow, the laughing girl of so many Christmas picnics. Missing for two years, presumed dead, but only because her body hadn't been picked up from the sea.

What if she'd survived? Not just survived, but managed to get to Papua?

It wasn't impossible. Neither she nor Nancy's family had been told where the ship had been when it went down. Maybe it had been closer to Papua than Singapore. If men could escape after the fall of Singapore, wangle their way onto boats to get across the Straits and bush-bash their way across country, then Nancy could do it too. Of all the people who might be able to get to Papua, she'd put the girl she knew towards the top.

'Mrs Overflow?'

'It might have been "Miss". As I said, the reception wasn't good.'

'Not Nancy?'

'No. Just what I told you. Nothing but that. But we don't have any record of a woman called Mrs Overflow in the area.'

And Nancy, she realised, shot, delirious perhaps, might well have whispered, 'Nancy of the Overflow,' instead of her real name.

'Where is she? Yes,' she added impatiently, 'I will keep it secret. And if you're not going to tell me, why do you have a map in your hip pocket?'

He drew it out, spread it on the table. 'There.'

About a hundred miles from the coast. High country. She had a memory of dark green mountain ranges, a sea of trees below her, cliffs that reared nearly vertically from river valleys below, mountainsides swimming in clouds as thick as snow and just as deadly, ready to sink on you in swirling clouds that were blindingly thick one moment and vanished the next.

'You have to get her out. Where are the Allied forces now?'

'I can't tell you that.'

'Can't, or won't?'

'Won't. But I can tell you there are none of our forces near enough to get there. And even if they could,' he looked at her again, 'it would take weeks to get her out of there on foot.'

'Not worth it. She'd be dead,' said Kirsty flatly.

'You can't redirect the war for one girl,' he said softly.

'No. Johnno, I'm sorry. Of course you can't. You or anybody else.' She sat back. 'Why did you tell me?'

'You told me about the Overflow girl, how much she means to everyone ...'

'I don't mean that.' She fought down what might have been tears, a blooming great lump in her throat. That poor girl, a stranger in strange hands, dying, so far from home. 'If there's no way to help her, why tell me? I can't tell her family this. That she might possibly be alive, possibly somewhere deep in Papua but possibly dying too, and there's nothing we can do.'

'Nothing I can do. Nor the army or the RAAF.'

The way he said it implied that someone else might. 'I don't understand.'

He took a deep breath. 'We need to get someone up there. Someone who knows the country, someone who's younger than the bloke who's there now. Someone to report on ... well, that doesn't matter. Or rather it does matter, but it's on a need-to-know basis. If someone were to fly up there — unofficially — carrying a passenger, then bring one back but not necessarily the same person ... Well, unofficially — totally unofficially and we'd deny it if you had to land or were captured, if anyone heard about it at all. But strictly hypothetically, we could make sure that no one from our side at least intercepted you. The bloke you'd be taking up there could tell you where to go. We could give you weather forecasts, though you know as well as I do how much they're worth — conditions up there can change in minutes.'

'You'd help me to fly up there?'

'Yes. Get you whatever fuel you need. I can even help you check Swaggie over.'

And he was a damn good bush mechanic too. As good as she was. 'Because you need someone dropped off?'

'And to rescue a girl — or a woman, if it isn't the girl you know. Yes.' He met her eyes. 'You wanted to fly, my dear. I'm giving you back your wings.'

'Unofficially?'

'Totally unofficially. You need to understand that if you're taken, we can't protect you. Can't even acknowledge you. You might be shot for a spy. You might be shot for no reason other than that you are white and you are there. You might be met by a pack of blokes waiting to hand you in for a reward, or just hand in your head.'

'Why don't you take this bloke in yourselves?'

'We could try to parachute him in, but that'd be like sending a great white flag saying, "Look over here," to every enemy within a hundred miles. Our craft are too big to land up there anyway. There's about fifty-two yards of jungle clearing. The only craft I know can do that is yours. It needs someone who can fly close to the tree line, in the edge of the clouds if she can.'

Flying in cloud in country like that meant risking a mountain meeting you head on. And Johnno knew it.

'You make it sound so tempting.'

He grinned. 'That's my girl.'

'Not yours, and not a girl.'

'Yes. Well. One day we need to talk about that.'

'Nothing to talk about. Can you really see me as a dear little wifey in an apron?'

He smiled. 'Has it ever occurred to you that if I wanted a dear little wifey in an apron, I wouldn't want you? Have I ever given you an apron? Or a bunch of roses?'

'The only thing you've ever given me was an adjustable shifting spanner that time in Turkey, and even then you wanted it back.'

'Not true. I've given you something else now — a chance to risk your neck.'

She looked at him. It was a strange way to say, 'I love you.' More, perhaps, a way to say, 'I know you, I accept you, and love you enough to let you risk your life.'

Women were expected to wave goodbye with brave smiles when men risked their lives for their country. But a man who'd not just let his wife go into danger, but offer her the way ...

'Come to dinner when I get back,' she said suddenly. 'A nice tough steak and boiled pumpkin greens. We can talk about it then. Can you wangle a few days' leave?'

'If you can pull this off, I reckon they'll owe me a few days' leave.' All joking had left his eyes now. 'You'll do it?'

'What, fly your mission or marry you?'

'Either. Or both.'

'I'll fly your mission,' she said slowly. 'And then we'll talk about marriage. Really talk. I mean it.'

'Can't we talk about it now? We could start up a transport company, you and me after the war. Fly freight across Australia. No aprons involved, or not on you.'

She liked the sound of it. They might even make a go of it, both the company and the marriage. 'In a hurry, aren't you?'

'This is war, my love,' he said lightly. 'You might not come back. Or I might not, if the Japs have better aim tonight.' There was no laughter in his eyes at all now. 'Give me a few hours at least when I can dream.'

'All right.'

He stared at her. 'You mean you will?'

'I said all right.'

'That has to be the most unromantic response in the history of marriage proposals.'

'If you wanted romance, you should have gone down on one knee. And brought me the roses.'

'Would you have said yes if I'd gone down on one knee?'

'Probably not. But I wouldn't mind the roses.'

'Roses are a bit in short supply up here.'

'Fair enough. But I'm warning you: you bring one apron into this marriage and you'll be the one wearing it.'

'You can give me one for a wedding present. You ... you won't change your mind?'

'No.' Ten minutes ago she had liked him, more than liked him, known he was her best friend, a mate. And now ... Could you fall in love in ten minutes, all because he'd given you back your wings?

No. But you could because you had found out how deeply he understood you needed them. And she'd always known if she'd ever said yes to Johnno, there'd be no going back. Twenty thousand feet and a hundred-mile-an-hour wind behind her, gusting a bit, but true.

'Kiss me, you fool,' she quoted.

'Kissing's allowed now?'

'I reckon so. You can even say you love me, if you like.'

'I love you.'

'Love you too.'

They grinned at each other foolishly. He bent towards her.

'Tea,' said Marg, plonking down the tray. She looked at Kirsty, then at Johnno. 'Not interrupting anything, am I?'

Johnno drove the boy to Fairhills before the dawn — for he was still more boy than man, at twenty years old at most, with a pimple on his chin and round shoulders, not the warrior she'd been expecting.

All the better, she thought. More weight meant more fuel used. And they'd need to conserve all the fuel that they could in case there was a storm and she needed to detour, or if the map was wrong and the mountains were higher than expected so they had to go around, or they had to fly into a headwind — that used up fuel like a steer gulping water on a hot day.

Johnno swept his long legs out of the jeep, and kissed her, not a romantic kiss so much as a 'Hello, world, this is the woman I am going to marry' kiss. She accepted the declaration, enjoyed the kiss.

'This is Brownie. Brownie, this is my fiancée, Kirsty McAlpine.'

'Pleased to meet you, Miss McAlpine.'

'Call me Kirsty.' The boy wore khaki trousers, a khaki shirt, and carried a kit bag not much bigger than a lunch box over one shoulder, a Tommy gun and a knife shoved in his belt and a rifle over the other shoulder. He didn't look like he could use any of it.

Was Brownie his real name? Or a nickname in case they crash-landed and survived, or she was captured but he escaped — so she couldn't tell the enemy what she didn't know?

'All ready to go?' Johnno asked.

She nodded. They'd been over Swaggie a dozen times. They'd even taken her for a test flight about the property, scaring the steers so they ran towards the river. Might be a good way to round up stock after the war, she'd thought. Much quicker and more fun than in the saddle.

'I brought you something.' He reached into the glovebox and handed her a rose.

It was just a bud, short-stemmed and very slightly wilted. But she could smell its scent when she lifted it to her nose. 'Where the heck did you get this?'

He grinned, proud of himself. Worried too: she could see that in his eyes. 'Mate flew up from Brizzie yesterday. I put in a special order.'

She stood on tiptoes and kissed him again, swiftly, because the boy was looking, because there wasn't much time, not if she was going to get there and back in daylight — the only lit landing strip was at the base and she had a feeling they would not be happy if she tried to use it.

'I'd offer you a cup of tea. But we'd better make the most of the daylight.'

She put the rose in the top buttonhole of her jacket, hoping the wind would be kind to it, and led Johnno and the boy behind the shed. If the boy was shocked by the tiny, tinny-looking craft, he didn't show it. 'Do I sit in the front, or back?'

'Front. It has twin controls, but you won't need to use yours.' Unless they shoot me, she thought. But I don't have time to show you how to bring the plane down yourself if that happens. 'I won't be able to hear you, so you'll need to signal where to go. Like motorcar signals. Hand up to stop. Right hand out to go right, left to go left. Down for down.'

'And up for up?'

'I'll know about the up bit. She's a tougher craft than she looks,' she added.

He nodded, either because he accepted her word or because there was no choice but to accept it.

He's accepted death is a possibility too, she thought. For surely he must know he had little chance of surviving this expedition if any tiny thing went wrong. He might send signals for weeks, or months perhaps. But one day, unless the Allies pushed the Japanese out soon, they'd track down those signals and find him. She supposed once you had accepted that, then death in a small plane was a minor thing, a nuisance that meant you could not complete your mission — or even begin it. Though death was the final arbiter of every mission, in the end.

He said, 'I hope we find your friend.'

'Thank you. I hope … I hope your mission goes well.'

He smiled at that. 'Dad was an actual missionary. He wanted me to be one too. Seems right to hear you call it a mission now.'

'Was?'

'He died.'

'I'm so sorry. When?'

'Don't know. We don't really know he's dead, for that matter. But he stopped transmitting more than a year ago.'

One of the ones who stayed, Kirsty realised. 'You must be

proud of him. Australia would be proud of him, if they knew … if they were allowed to know.'

'He did the right thing,' said the young man who called himself Brownie. 'That's what would matter to him.'

'We'd better get going.' She showed him how to get up, to strap himself in, and helped him with his helmet.

'Good luck,' said Johnno quietly. 'Come back safely.' He hesitated. 'Haven't even got you an engagement ring yet. Or don't you want one?'

'You're not getting out of it that cheaply, mister. I want a sapphire. Might even wear a dress when you put it on me too.'

'A sapphire it is then. And I'll be waiting for that dress.'

She'd loved dresses once, in the days before she'd had to prove herself ten times better than a man to be allowed to fly at all. She realised that after doing something this insane she could wear all the pretty dresses she liked and no one would question her qualifications.

She had a feeling that Johnno might like that too.

She fastened her own helmet, tied a scarf around her neck and secured it safely, belted herself in. Normally she'd have turned the propeller herself, but this time Johnno did it for her. Nothing happened. The engine caught the second time.

Johnno gave her the thumbs up. She returned the gesture, then blew him a kiss. Swaggie ran lightly across the stony ground, then leapt towards the sky.

We are beating the sun up, she thought, the old excitement thudding in her. Up into the greyness, the horizon not even flushed with the coming dawn. Feeling the cold bite of air, the taste of warm air currents where the eagles flew.

This is my world, she thought. Not with eagle wings, but with an engine beating like my heart.

The day lightened about them as they flew. She had forgotten the sheer speed of flight. It was green below them, the dry land still soaking up wet, and then the sudden shock of blue. Rich blue sea here in the north, sea that almost glowed, edged with green, the too-white sand.

Islands, white-fringed, rock-fingered, grey-brown or green; more sand, then more sea ...

Cold air. Fresh air, no smell of steers or hot grass. It was so good to have cold air in her lungs again. I am a mountain girl, she thought. No: I belong to the sky.

She glanced at the compass, but was reasonably sure still where they were, where they were meant to be. Yes, there was the promontory just like on the map. There was the wide beach like a smile. A hill, shaggy with grass, the sea again. And then the land. Sand and grass then jungle, rising swiftly, looking more black than green.

And no one had shot at them yet, neither enemy nor ally. Johnno had been as good as his words. This route was as safe as it was possible to make it.

She kept low, skimming the trees, then turned towards the east, drove at the sun, half blind, her goggles half shielding her from the glare. And there was the mountain range.

My word, she thought, that's not a mountain, it's a wall. What her mind had known her imagination hadn't seen. It was like a green wall that just went up and up, vanishing into white so it might keep rising up forever.

A hand came out in front of her, pointing left. And, yes, there was the gap, like a pulled tooth, cliffs among the green. She flew under the cloud, then into it, flying almost blind, visibility measured in yards, at most, as slow as she could make it. A second the fraction in the wrong direction could kill them now.

She hoped he didn't know it.

The mist thickened. For a moment she thought they'd have to pull out of the cloud, go back, and then, miraculously, it lifted, like a hand had picked up a tablecloth or twitched aside a curtain. She had only a second to correct their flight: she shot away from a waterfall, a thin trickle down the rock, wondered if it was indeed a miracle, if the man in front of her had prayed, because if the fog hadn't lifted they would be scattered in wreckage at the bottom of the cliff by now, brief flames among the green.

The chasm curved; she swerved with it.

Then they were out. Another slope to their left again. He pointed right, then suddenly his hand went up in a 'stop' sign. He pointed down.

She saw it. A pale green slash among the darker green, with what looked like bananas at the far end. The strip was as long as a cricket pitch perhaps.

There was a difference, she realised, between landing in fifty-two yards on a wide oval, and having only fifty-two yards to land in before you crashed into trees or a cliff. But if she could do the one, she could do the other.

And take off again. She hoped.

Down. Down. I am a bird, she thought. I am the heron, I am the eagle, I am the seagull landing on the soft green sea. The plane bumped once, almost clipping the bananas, rolled then stopped.

The clearing was empty.

Had they come to the right place?

She lifted her helmet off. The air hit her like a fist, humid and cold at the same time. She climbed stiffly out onto the wing and jumped down. He followed her, shivering. I should have warned him to put on three pairs of thermals, she thought. 'What now?'

'They'll have seen us if they're still here. We wait.'

Kirsty wondered who else might have seen them. There had been no sign of humanity below them. But there must be villages in under the canopy; could be the entire Japanese Army, for all she knew, invisible beneath the thick cover of trees.

She'd give her right-hand propeller for a cup of tea and a cheese sandwich. Well, maybe not a propeller, given the circumstances, but her sugar ration for the next month.

Something moved in the shadows of the trees. Two men emerged. One was dark-skinned, and bare-chested despite the cold, with a pair of ragged shorts and frizzy black hair. He supported another man, one leg wrapped in bloody rags, the other smudged with blood and mud under a pair of shorts as ragged as his companion's. His skin had once been white. Now his face was clay; clay-daubed, deliberately she thought, not the kind of dirt from sliding down a mountain.

The black-skinned man said something softly. The other nodded. The black-skinned man slipped back into the shadows of the trees.

The other limped forwards. He was dressed in what had been army uniform, though what he mostly wore was mud. Under the clay his face had the pallor of pain, illness and exhaustion. 'Adam Ansover?' The voice was breathless too.

'Brownie' glanced at Kirsty, shrugged. 'That's me. I'm supposed to meet the Reverend McPherson.'

'I'm sorry. We haven't had a chance to call in. He died three days ago. No, not the Japs. Malaria, I think. His boys buried him. Marked the grave too. You've got the radio?'

Brownie — Adam Ansover — tapped his swag.

'Good. The reverend's is on its last legs. The boys are waiting for you. There's a cave —' He stopped as Brownie indicated Kirsty. The man blinked. 'You're a woman.'

'Last time I looked,' said Kirsty.

'I didn't know a woman could fly.' His voice was strangely flat, all emotion worn away.

'You and the entire air force or most of it.' She knew the near miracle of flying she'd done today. Not just the luck of the fog lifting when it had, but matching the plane with the wind, manoeuvring among the clouds. She hoped she didn't spoil her good impression by crashing on the way back.

She glanced up at the sun, automatically checking the time by that, rather than her watch. You could forget to reset a watch as you crossed time zones, but the sun never let you down. 'I need to get back. Where's Miss Overflow? How is she? The message said she'd been shot.'

He stared at her, almost too tired to take her words in. He shook his head. 'I'm sorry. When I said "shot" I meant she'd been killed. They threw her body in the water.' Still no emotion in that tired voice. 'Her husband died two nights later. Grief as well as illness, I expect.'

'Her *husband*? Nancy is — was — *is* — seventeen. No, eighteen.'

'You must be thinking of someone else. Mrs Overflow is ... was in her forties. Good woman.' Again, the flat voice. 'She was Reverend McPherson's sister. Most of the wives evacuated back in '41. She stayed put, and her husband too. Think that was how they could transmit for so long. Lots of folk respected them for that, staying with their flock.'

'I ... see.' She felt curiously empty. All this for nothing. But she had known it was a long shot at best, hoping that a girl could find her way from island to island, evading capture both by the enemy and local men. And yet it had not been for nothing. For who knew what Brownie would report back, how many lives would be saved with the information he'd transmit.

She was glad she hadn't told anyone at home about this, raised hopes that would now be flattened.

The man swayed, his fists clenching as though with the effort to stay upright. 'Can you take a passenger?'

'What? Yes. You?'

He nodded.

'What do you weigh?'

'No idea. Used to weigh eleven stone six, but that was a year ago.' He looked down at his leg. 'I can cut this off now rather than wait for them to do it in Darwin if that would help.'

She felt sick; tried not to show it. 'We'll be right.' Even if they couldn't make it back to Fairhills, Swaggie was amphibious. She could land on a river if need be, though the sea would be better, near a nice calm beach. And with no crocodiles or sea snakes. And a chauffeur to meet us with cheese sandwiches and a tea urn, she thought, while I'm putting wishes in.

The man said evenly, 'I'll be back if ... when they've patched up my leg. Or given me another one. In the meantime I can make a map of where the others need to go. Fifteen men with Tommy guns could stop the enemy from crossing this range, if we could get them in here, and if they knew where to go.'

'Give me a bigger craft and I'll fly you all. Or bring you one by one.'

For the first time emotion showed, a tiny curl of a smile. 'I believe you would. But it's going to be hard enough to convince the brass to give me fifteen men.'

Fifteen men, she thought, to hold an army back. 'Better not try for the impossible as well: getting them to admit a woman can fly. Hop aboard.'

She turned to Brownie. 'Good luck.' She almost said, 'Send me a message to say how you're going,' but of course he couldn't. She hoped Johnno would at least let her know if he lived or died. She hesitated, then gave him a kiss on the cheek. 'There. You won't get that from any other pilot. Good luck, mate.'

'Good luck getting back. And thank you.' He gave the thumbs-up sign. He still looked stooped and office pale. But there was a confidence about him now. As she watched, he strode off, towards the trees.

She thought she saw the black-skinned man meet him, but perhaps it had just been the flickering of shadows.

She handed the stranger the helmet. Hoped she could find the way back; looked for the images in her mind and knew she could. Born in mountains, raised in mountains. Mountains were as good as a map to her now, once seen never forgotten, recognised again no matter what angle she approached from.

Kirsty turned to the stranger. 'I'll get the crate turned round and we can be off. No, I can manage it alone.' She was afraid his leg would give way if he tried. 'Can't land you on the base, I'm afraid, but there'll be a jeep waiting for you.'

To take Nancy to hospital, she thought. Pity for the dead woman, the unknown Mrs Overflow, flooded her. A brave woman, with a brave husband. She deserved more than a whisper of regret that she wasn't Nancy Clancy.

'We'll be home by suppertime,' she said, as she hauled the plane around to face back down the small strip. 'How does a nice tough steak sound, and a plate of bitter greens?'

'I'd rather have a beer.'

'You might have to settle for a pot of stewed tea. Black, no sugar.'

Nancy, she thought. Dear Nancy. Where are you, child?

Chapter 45

Gibber's Creek Gazette, 24 March 1944

The Gibber's Creek Volunteer Defence Corps was called out today when a plane spotter reported men in shorts running along Gibber's Creek. Assuming the Japanese had landed, the corps turned out in force, but soon discovered that the 'aliens' were Gibber's Creek students on their cross-country run. Several of the pupils lost time while being 'interrogated' so the result of the race is inconclusive.

PULAU AYU PRISON CAMP, MARCH 1944

NANCY

Nancy lay on her bamboo slats and stared up at the starlight through the gaps in the roof. She had felt strangely well all day, as if she could reach up on her tiptoes and dance across the camp. And plan escape.

She'd picked greens and flower buds this afternoon — no parcel to collect today. But Mrs Hughendorn had scratched a message with a piece of charcoal on the back of one of the old notes to their unknown local friends, a careful message, referring to *that lovely picnic we had before the war* and wondering if they might do it again.

The picnic had been on the next island, an hour's sail away, but the Japanese weren't to know that. It was a small island, no plantations, no one living there except fishermen camping now and then, so it was unlikely to have Japanese guards. No water either, so whoever went there would have to take enough to survive there for a few days until, possibly, hopefully, their local helpers could get word to someone from a nearby island to pick them up, to take them to another island, and another ...

They couldn't decide whether they should all try to leave at once, or alone, or two at a time. One or two would be easier, but those remaining would be punished, perhaps even killed, in retaliation. Perhaps they could make it seem as if there had been an accident. Get permission to clean themselves in the sea, pretend two of them had been eaten by a shark ...

Which almost certainly wouldn't work. But at least the women had hope now, something to talk about, to plan, as they sat around the cooking fire, instead of just rehashing memories and dreams.

Nancy felt ... odd. The day's euphoria had given way to something else. She probably needed to go to the latrine, and now she'd thought of it she couldn't go back to sleep till she had. There had been no severe dysentery again, but all still suffered from loose bowels either as a residue of the infection or because of the low-protein diet of gruel and vegetables.

She slipped out of the hut, the lights around the perimeter enough to see by, then stopped, staring at the crumple of cloth halfway over the edge of the hole.

It wasn't cloth. It was a woman. She bent to pull her up, dragging her by her thin ankles, scraping the muck away from her face with her hands, trying not to gag at the stench. 'Mrs Hughendorn!' She was so used to thinking of Mrs Hughendorn as large. Even thin, her very presence made her imposing. But this was a skeleton.

She bent, and heard breathing. Thank goodness. Just a faint, perhaps ... they often felt faint after going to the latrine. She needed to fetch Nurse Rogers, but Mrs Hughendorn would hate anyone to see her like this. She ran to get the bucket of dirty water they had used for washing earlier. The ground swam and wandered beneath her ... Something's wrong with the lights, she thought vaguely. They keep flickering on and off ...

The bucket seemed three times as heavy as usual. But she managed to wash the putrid mess off Mrs Hughendorn's face and from her hair, thin and straggling across her scalp, and even get most of her dress clean.

She sat, suddenly unable to stand again. 'Nurse Rogers,' she called. Her voice was faint, and hardly hers! 'Nurse Rogers!'

'What is it?'

Nancy relaxed at the sound of the nurse's voice, shut her eyes against the lights around the barbed-wire fence. The guards must have new lights, for these were far too bright. That must be why they flickered. The ground lurched ...

An earthquake? she thought muzzily. But the huts didn't shake, nor did the palm trees beyond the camp sway ...

Nurse Rogers appeared, still wearing only her slip. 'Mrs Hughendorn!' She knelt, felt the woman's forehead. 'High fever. Help me get her back to her hut.'

'I ... I don't think I can.'

Nurse Rogers looked at her sharply. 'What's wrong?'

'I'm feeling ... the world is feeling ...' Black, she thought. Then nothing.

She woke a minute later. It had to be only a minute, for there had been nothing, not even dreams, just a quick walk along the river, holding Michael's hand. The native chooks had darted in and out of the reeds, and then the swan had sailed out, leading her cygnets ...

She blinked, and realised it was day. Moira sat by her side. 'Nancy? Oh, Nancy, thank goodness. No, don't try to sit up.' The dear thin arm held her head, pressed white tablets to her mouth and then a coconut shell of water. 'Drink,' she ordered.

Nancy drank, and swallowed, the tablets harsh against her throat. 'What ... what happened?' That husk wasn't her voice. What had happened to her voice?

'You've been sick, darling. Here, try to swallow this.'

More liquid, warm this time, in a spoon. It tasted of chicken. What miracle had brought chicken? And a spoon!

She blinked. Something was different about Moira. Not thinner, not browner. Her pearls: that was it. No pearls at her throat, no earrings. Even her wedding ring was gone.

Had the Japanese confiscated them?

'Your jewellery,' she whispered.

'Never mind that now. Try and sleep. Nurse Rogers says that you need sleep.'

'I'm sick?'

'Three weeks,' said Moira, and Nancy heard the strain now, the throat hoarse from crying. 'We don't know what it is. Nurse Rogers thinks cerebral malaria perhaps, but it could be all sorts of other fevers. Thank goodness the tablets brought the fever down.'

'Tablets? Your pearls ... they bought my tablets? And the chicken?'

'Shh. It doesn't matter now. Nothing matters except to get you well.'

It took the rest of her strength, but she had to ask. 'Mrs Hughendorn? Gavin?' Please don't let me have given him my fever, she thought, thinking of the kisses she shared with the small boy.

'Mrs Hughendorn is recovering too. Gavin is fine. Mr Shigura is teaching him how to use chopsticks.'

'Mr Shigura?'

'The translator. He ... he has been very good. He gave us the full price for the jewellery, arranged for the drugs. From Singapore: that is why they were so expensive. Everything is in such short supply, even for the Japanese. Sleep now, Nancy. Sleep.'

She slept. She woke to find another figure by her bed. The translator. Mr Shigura. It seemed strange to think of him with a name now, a person, not just a function.

'I … I'm sorry. I can't stand to bow.'

'It is no matter. I am glad you are recovering.'

'My sister-in-law says you have been kind.'

He said nothing. Had he broken regulations to help them? Who was this man? She had never even wondered where he had learnt English so well.

'Your English is so very good, Mr Shigura,' she said tentatively.

'I learnt in Japan, then came to Malaya. I worked as a barber, wrote reports of what I saw, what I heard. English customers meant my English becomes like theirs.'

'You were a spy?'

'I gathered intelligence. For my country, for the Empire of the Sun.' He met her gaze properly for the first time. 'The English took from Malaya, from Thailand, from India. They gave nothing back.'

'We've given them …' she tried to think '… buildings. And education …'

He gave a short laugh. 'You gave education, but no jobs. All managers had to be English. Now Japan makes local people managers. They govern themselves now.'

Was it true? How could she know, lying back here? She was too weak to think, much less find an adequate reply.

'Thank you,' she said again. 'For all you have done, Mr Shigura. You have been kind.'

He looked at his shoes for a moment, then at her. 'English mems are lazy. They spend their time at parties, ordering servants. At home my wife works in a factory. My daughters too. Two hours at school, eight hours in the factory. English mems are like fleas on a dog.'

'That's not true! I work … or I did work, back home. My mother teaches school, my grandmother has worked all her life.'

'You are different.'

'No. The nurses work, did work.'

'You and the nurses then. The others?'

She said nothing, had nothing to say, no energy even if she had.

'You sleep,' he said, 'get well. Your nephew needs you. He is a good boy.' He hesitated. 'When the war is over, perhaps you will go home. Your nephew will speak excellent Japanese by then. It will be useful for him.'

You have been teaching him Japanese, she thought, not knowing whether to thank him or protest.

'He may be a manager one day, under the Japanese Empire. By then mems may have learnt to work.'

'We would all have worked, and gladly, if you had given us work to do,' she whispered. But would they all have worked if it hadn't been forced upon them? She didn't know.

'There is no work now,' said Mr Shigura. 'Now you must rest.' He bowed, the first time he had ever bowed to her, and left.

It was another three days before she could sit up, a week after that before she could stumble to the latrine so Moira no longer had to hold a coconut-shell bowl underneath her, and clean her with dried leaves and water. It was two weeks before she could sit on a block of wood by the evening cooking fire. Mrs Hughendorn sat in her usual chair, pale and even thinner, the skin drooping from her chin onto her neck. Moira sat beside her and Nurse Rogers, with Gavin on her lap.

'Where is Sally? Is she sick too?'

'Sally died four weeks ago,' said Moira quietly. 'And Nurse Williams and Nurse McTavish. It was the same fever you had. The medicine didn't come in time to save them. Nurse Rogers was sick too.'

'Luckily not till after we had the medicine,' said Nurse Rogers. 'Whatever it was didn't hit me too hard.'

Nancy looked at the fire. Four of us left, she thought, and Gavin. Three of us too weak to walk further than the latrine, and Moira not much better. And there will be more illness, as long as we are starved, and live with mosquitoes in the dirt. Four left from thirteen. Seven of us dead. Perhaps Mrs Addison and Vivienne dead by now as well, in whatever was happening beyond their barbed wire.

She thought of the translator — Mr Shigura — the thinness of his face too. Had war taken so many men, destroyed so many crops, that there was not enough food for anyone? When would the guards finally decide that there was no point wasting any food on their useless charges?

She didn't know. She sat, trying not to cry — it still seemed important not to let the guards see any of them cry, and Gavin too. She sipped her soup, with no flower buds or greenery or 'island rabbit' in it now — nor would there be till she had more strength.

But she knew one thing, clear as the moon bouncing on the cloud above. Four weakened women and a child could not escape, no matter how much help the local people might give them. They must stay and let the war buffet them, the guards command them. There was nothing else to dream of now.

Chapter 46

Jim Thompson
AIF
23 September 1944

The Thompson Family
Drinkwater Station
via Gibber's Creek

Dear Mum, Dad, Michael, Gussie, Bonkers, Sheba and assorted sheep,
All well here but we could do with some of your drought. Any chance, Dad, that some of your mates in the War Office could arrange a rain exchange?

Have been climbing up and down a mountain all day and believe me, down is worse than up in this country. The Japs have been dive-bombing us like mosquitoes. We'd get up ten yards and have to slide back down into the jungle again.

We got to the top after five hours and were jiggered so decided to have a sleep for a while. A native boy brought us water, coconuts, bananas and a paw paw each. Lay down to sleep then heard tramping through the jungle. We grabbed our gear right smart and got ready to have at them, and then heard the swearing. Only Aussies can swear like that. The native boy brought us four more paw paws and a coconut. He is a good sort. He said he'd show us the back tracks away from the roads, ones the Japs don't know about.

Don't know how much of this the censor will leave in but hey, mate, every bit of jungle looks the same up here and this letter

371

won't be of any use to enemy intelligence. Whoever designed this jungle isn't intelligent at all.

Give my love to everyone, sheep included, and especially Sheba. Tell her we could do with an elephant here. She'd have all the bananas she wanted to eat and could carry our gear down these damn hills. Or we could sit on her back and just slide her down the mud.

Jim

SYDNEY, 23 SEPTEMBER 1944

MICHAEL

Michael hefted his overnight bag as Skimmer put his key in the door of the Point Piper house. He could hear music and the chatter of voices.

The door opened in a gust of perfume: frangipani flowers, brandy fumes and something that was almost like the whisky he was familiar with from home, but not quite ...

'Bertie, darling!' A woman ... girl ... floated down the hallway towards them through a crowd of men in the tailored beige of American Army officers. There were a few dark blue uniforms of the RAAF, one grey-blue of a New Zealand airman, but otherwise the guests were all young women in floral dresses: red hair, dark hair, blonde. This one wore a short blue silk skirt, silk stockings — how did anyone manage to have silk stockings now? Even Mum drew seams down the backs of her brown legs, keeping her one remaining pair of stockings for an 'emergency' — her hair was blonde, in short tight waves; her lips were a vivid red; and there was a drink in her hand. 'Have they let you out of school?'

'Just for the weekend. Thompson, this is my sister, Eva. You met each other at the picnic races.'

'Of course,' Eva said vaguely, glancing back at the throng spilling out of the doorways on either side and sipping from her drink. Suddenly she looked back at Michael. 'I do remember you! Drinkwater, isn't it?'

'Yes,' he said shortly. Now that he'd noticed the appeal his parents' estates held for these girls reared to find a good husband, it seemed inescapable. And for that matter, maybe it had even made a difference at school, where he suspected he'd have been liked well enough anyway — pleasant chap, handy with an oar, not bad at rugger. But the Drinkwater/Thompson fortunes eclipsed anything he might achieve himself.

'Come on, honey bear.' Her accent had a haze of American about it. She waved her drink casually. 'Put your stuff in a bedroom and let me introduce you.'

'Your parents ...?' Michael asked delicately.

Eva laughed. 'Darling, they shot off as soon as the Japs hit New Guinea. They're snug up in the Blue Mountains now.'

'They left you here alone?' Eva was a year older than him, he remembered, had left school at sixteen.

She fluttered dark eyelashes at him. 'Rarely alone, honey bear.' He wondered quite what she meant, but she added, 'Mrs Murphy is off tonight.' Housekeeper, thought Michael, as Eva added, 'Besides, I'm needed in Sydney.'

'You're working?' It was difficult to imagine this young woman as a Rosie the Riveter, welding ships out at Cockatoo Island, or labouring in a wool or munitions factory.

'Eva and her chums raise money for War Bonds,' said Skimmer.

'You should buy a ticket to the orphans' ball.' Eva smiled up at him from her glass. 'Two tickets.'

'Which orphans?'

'Darling, does it matter?' She shrugged. 'Belgian. No, British Navy orphans. Now isn't that worth two tickets? Only two pounds each and I promise you a dance. Two dances. Do you still have those wonderful Christmas parties at Drinkwater? They say everybody goes. I'd love to come to one of them.'

'Yes. We still have them. You must come one time.'

The words were automatic, because that is what you said when people asked for invitations. But the parties she was thinking of did not exist, not just in these war-straitened times but ever. While the neighbouring squatters came to Mum and Dad's party, so did everyone else: factory workers, station hands, shearers sleeping in their swags in the men's quarters, young women crammed in makeshift beds upstairs, and boys in tents down by the river, sometimes even rolled in blankets in the hall.

He felt at once desperately homesick but, just as desperately, not wanting to be home, the world where his parents had dictated he remain a schoolboy. At this party, at least, he was a young man, though he was embarrassed by his lack of uniform.

'Come on, bedrooms are this way,' said Skimmer.

'Help yourselves to drinkies,' said Eva, as she turned back towards the doorway and the music. 'There's a buffet in the dining room too.'

Two hours later the house was even more crowded, the music louder; his head was buzzing with the noise and two drinks of what he knew hadn't been whisky. He had eaten, but not enough: oyster patties, a prune wrapped in bacon, asparagus vol-au-vents, crustless ham sandwiches, rich after the austerity of school and even the rationing back home. Drinkwater's house cows gave them more butter than the ration allowed and the hens gave eggs, but not black-market ham or bacon or the luxury of oysters so far inland.

Michael sat awkwardly on a sofa. At the other end a young Yank lieutenant gazed soulfully into the eyes of a girl who was perhaps eighteen. 'I'm going north tomorrow. You're not the kind of dame that would let a fellow be alone on his last night in Sydney, are you?'

The girl giggled. An older girl in a hennaed pompadour, her lipstick smudged, leant over the back of the sofa. 'Don't believe him, honey. He's a shiny bum over at headquarters. Tells the world how the Yanks are winning the war.'

The lieutenant grinned. 'Got to keep the Corn Belt interested. But we do admit you fellers give us a hand too ...'

'Michael, darling, I've been looking for you everywhere!'

She hadn't. He'd last seen Eva jiving with an RN captain over by the gramophone. There was no sign of him now.

'All alone?'

He nodded. Skimmer had vanished somewhere with a girl in green.

Eva reached out a hand and pulled Michael to his feet. 'Dance?'

'I'm no good at it. Not jitterbugging anyway.'

She smiled from under her eyelashes. 'I'll put on a slow one just for you. Come on, drink up.'

He heard someone mutter behind them, 'The Drinkwater property. Father's making a fortune in military contracts too.' He swallowed the liquid in his glass, then wished he hadn't. Black-market rotgut could send you blind. Or kill you. But he didn't know how to refuse. 'Who were you dancing with?'

'Jealous? Captain Mulholland. He's on the ship that brought out German POWs from England.'

And that is classified information, he thought, not knowing if it would be useful to the enemy or not. But it wasn't for either of them to judge. His father had impressed on him the need for security. In a war where you were outnumbered and poorly equipped, knowledge could win a war. Nor had he been jealous, just trying to make conversation.

Eva paused at the pile of records by the gramophone.

Michael tried another topic. 'I thought the Manpower regulations meant that all unmarried women have to have a job. Though I'm sure your War Bonds work is wonderful.'

Her smile was all lipstick and straight white teeth. 'I'm on the payroll of Daddy's factory. Secretary.'

'Really?' He couldn't imagine those long nails typing.

'Darling, I've never even seen the blasted factory. But what can one do? Every girl I know has to do something like that,

375

or be hauled into some ghastly munitions factory. Seriously, can you see me in munitions?'

Seriously, he couldn't.

He wanted to ask, 'Do your parents know about this party? Do they know you live like this?'

As though she sensed his thoughts, she said gaily, 'Live for the moment, darling. That's what this war has taught us.'

She selected a record, dropped it onto the turntable. The music softened; it was Irving Berlin's 'Cheek to Cheek'.

Somehow he was holding her and they were dancing. Eva murmured the words just below his ear, her own cheek on his shoulder. The whispers, the music, the scent of her all swam together.

Other couples swayed about them. Older, assured men who were doing something, even if it was just writing dispatches at headquarters, girls who were ... well, at any rate, they weren't working as the women he knew were used to doing, even in peacetime. Except at pleasure.

And this was pleasant, though curiously remote as well. Eva was soft and smelt of gardenias and face powder and the scent of woman, even more intoxicating than whatever had been in his glass. Her silk legs rubbed against his ... Nancy was far away ...

Nancy. He pulled back. Eva pushed herself closer again. 'The song's not over yet.'

His head buzzed with whatever he had drunk. He couldn't embarrass her by leaving. Didn't want to go. For Nancy *was* far away and the world was too uncertain. Yesterday and tomorrow might be hard, but here tonight a young woman whispered in his ear, '... a private party. Just you and me. Somewhere quiet ...' He felt light and somehow not here at all. Quiet. That's what he needed. He let her take his hand again and lead him down the corridor, into a room. It wasn't until she pulled off her dress in one smooth move that he realised it was her bedroom, pink silk and white lace.

She wore brief silk French-cut knickers, a matching brassiere, a silk suspender belt holding up her stockings. He could see a hint of white flesh under the brassiere. The rest of her skin was tanned, almost polished, the tan from a beach. Nancy's tan had formed a V, from her shirt, the tops of her arms in her mother's old party dress far paler than her forearms.

Nancy. He broke away.

'Lover, what's wrong?'

'Sorry. I'm going to be sick.'

It was no lie. He staggered down to a bathroom, vomited neatly twice, then sat on the cool of the bathroom floor till his head steadied.

He had been half afraid Eva would follow him, but perhaps she was put off by the sound of retching. When he went outside the corridor was empty.

He found his bedroom again, picked up his bag, headed for the kitchen, through a small throng of uniforms examining bottles and labels, then out the service entrance, down the steps, through the lobby and into the cool and blessed night.

He walked. The streets were so dark he could almost imagine he was home. But above him planes roared, heading to Richmond, and the beams of searchlights tore up the high dark sky. The music faded behind him. An army lorry passed, and then a taxi.

He should have hailed it; gone to a hotel. He had money; didn't need to be back at school till Monday night. Instead he walked, almost instinctively, towards the light, the rattle of trams. Far off he heard the faint roar of an electric train.

He was there before he realised where he had come. Bayswater Road, Kings Cross. Suddenly it was night no longer. Light spilled into the road. So did people, the pavement as crowded at midnight as during the day.

Men lounged in doorways: American, Australian, British, New Zealand uniforms. Sailors in striped vests and pompommed hats gazed at women swaying their hips, smiling or too carefully ignoring the stares, women in clothes like Eva's but shorter, tighter, hair a little brighter, rouge as well as lipstick and strangely dark eyelashes, like film stars', hair piled high, flowers pinned to their shoulders, and again the overpowering scent of gardenias and frangipani.

Shops were open even now, ham and beef shops whose smell made him queasy again; plate-glass windows with spotlit dummies in silk dresses; flower shops, their baskets spilling out onto the footpath.

Taxis hooted, crawling in a steady stream, passengers sitting, or leaping out and thrusting money at the driver while the taxi still moved, others crowding in. A police car inched among them, its loudspeakers booming out some vice squad warning impossible to make out among the noise.

He glanced down a dark laneway. A couple gasped and grappled. He forced his eyes away; his legs kept going.

Was this truly Australia? Was this the price of war too? Not just the men lost, the families torn apart, Mum working in the paddocks like she was twenty again, Dad's shadowed eyes at the factory.

The plane trees rustled above him, scattering shadows across the footpath. A sailor clutched a girl against a trunk, mouth to mouth and hip to hip, so flagrant that he wondered if they were drunk, not to see the others on the footpath. He glanced around. It was as though he was the only one who saw.

This is everyday to them, he thought. The grappling, the desperation. Eva's words came back to him: 'Live for the moment.' Could he really blame them, these men who might have days or weeks left, or else were headed for a long life, blighted, blinded, legs blown off, like so many from the last war, living in pain and poverty. Women like Blue, a war spent working, waiting. Had she kissed Joseph like this, on his last leave when he came back from the Middle East, knowing he would be sent north after a brief home leave? And how would *he* have kissed Nancy, if he had known of the years that would part them, instead of weeks?

But that was love. This was passion used like the 'whisky' back at the house, not for itself but to dull desperation.

Down another alley a man leant against a dustbin, moaning into his mouth organ, while a couple jitterbugged, imagining brightness from the melancholy tune. Dance, he thought. Make sunlight from a shred of moon.

A street, with dark houses, a sketch of gardens at the front. He turned, and went on walking. At last the sounds behind him ebbed. A baby cried, its mother hushing. A normal sound. Or was it? Where was that child's father? Fighting overseas? Dead? Captured?

For the first time in his life he felt that those of good heart might not always triumph. There had been a darkness in that Kings Cross light that he had never seen before; he hadn't even seen the darkness in the world he knew either. For the first time he felt, not that Nancy was dead, but that he had lost the certainty that she was living.

He walked. Hour upon hour. He walked.

At last there was water, deep and black, shimmering and sliding in the starlight, only one streetlight faint behind him. He walked along the jetty, sat and looked at the blackness of the harbour, the million starlights of the shore now the blackout regulations had been eased. Almost possible to believe that two hundred years ago there'd been no Sydney here at all. But there'd have been campfires in place of these window lights, fires like Nancy had slept beside on the track to Charters Towers.

He hadn't forgotten her tonight. He was generous enough to himself to have known that he had neither been unfaithful to her, nor meant to be. His mistake had been in drinking when he did not want to drink; in accepting an invitation from Skimmer because Taylor's brother had been killed a fortnight ago, and so he hadn't wanted to intrude to stay at their place, as he usually did, when school breaks were too short for the journey home.

He had not danced with Eva because he thought Nancy was dead. Nancy was alive and she was coming home and one day

Australia would be free and they would be together. That was so much the foundation of his being that there was no questioning it.

'Excuse me.'

The woman had nearly tripped over his bag in the darkness of the jetty. He stood up and moved it. 'My fault. I'm sorry.'

She smiled, accepting his apology. She was somewhere between his age and his mother's, bundled in a shapeless coat and scarf. It must be later than he'd thought, if the first ferry was due.

'Coming home from work?' he asked. She looked tired.

She shook her head. 'Early shift.'

Which meant a factory. He didn't ask what they made. Loose lips sink ships. Instead he asked, suddenly lonely, 'Do you enjoy it?'

She stared. 'Enjoy it? You're joking. Two quid ten shillings a week for six days' work and overtime and no pay rise neither, because we don't come under the new regulations for working women. My hands got so cold last winter I nearly lost a finger. Girl down the bench next to me did.'

'Can't you get another job?' Australia had changed, even in his lifetime, from a place where men queued, desperate for any work. Now even at Drinkwater one man ... or woman ... had to do the work of three.

'Reserved occupation. Manpower won't let me go.'

'I'm sorry.' It was inadequate, him sitting there in his good wool coat, straight from a school that, if not comfortable — comfort for some reason not being something that turned a boy into a man — was expensive and, he supposed, did in fact give the students the education and valuable business and political contacts for which it was well known.

He caught the glimpse of her smile. 'It's not so bad. Mum minds the kids. Living with her I can save most of my pay, and my allotment too. Not that we have much choice. Not a room to be had in the whole city with the Yanks and Brits here. But Mum's a wonder. Keeps us all going on the smell of an oily rag.'

'Your husband's in the army?'

'Navy,' she said with pride. Again he neither asked nor did she offer details. 'We're going to have ourselves a garage after the war. Out Frenchs Forest way maybe. He's a real good mechanic. Fresh air for the kiddies. He says he's going to make sure it's not like it was after the last war, the men just tossed out on the scrap heap. I'm saving every halfpenny. It'll be worth it in the end.'

'Yes,' he said. 'It will be worth it.'

The waves lapped at the jetty, rocking them like a baby in a cradle. 'I'm still at school,' he offered at last. 'I'm enlisting in a couple of months, as soon as I finish school.'

'Good on you.' She didn't ask which service he'd enlist in. If he joined the regular forces like Jim had, he wouldn't be sent on active service overseas till he was twenty-one. If he wanted more than office work or guard duty, he'd have to join the militia, the 'Koalas', never meant to be exported, now fighting in New Guinea.

'You haven't got the time, have you?'

He looked at his watch. 'Quarter past five.'

'Thank goodness. Thought I might have missed the ferry. Our clock at home is always on the blink. I like to get here a bit early. Only quiet time to think, what with factory work and the kids.'

He stood. 'I'll leave you to it.'

'I didn't mean ... You're not catching the ferry?'

'No.' He'd get a taxi. Go to a hotel. Buy a bunch of flowers tomorrow, and take them to Taylor's parents, to show his respect. They wouldn't want a houseguest this weekend, but a visit was different. Taylor would probably want to talk too, away from eavesdroppers at school. A bloke couldn't cry at school. Not openly. He had a feeling it might do Taylor good to cry with a friend. 'I hope you buy your garage. Maybe one day I'll be a customer.'

He was suddenly conscious that the money in his pocket was more than five times her wages. What he would spend at the hotel this weekend might be enough even to lease a garage. How much did a garage cost? Would it insult her if he offered her money?

She had given up so much already he suspected she might have given up pride at being helped by strangers too.

He fumbled in his pocket for his wallet, drew out six five-pound notes. He held them out to her. 'I hope you don't mind. Please take it. I ... needed ... to talk to someone tonight.'

She took the notes between two gloved fingers. For a moment he thought she would let the wind take them, then she stuffed them into her big handbag, without counting them. 'Thank you, sir.'

He flushed. Money had severed the partnership of darkness, made him a 'sir'. He wanted to say that she was the one who should be revered, not him. Not just because of her work, the children, keeping the worry she must feel about her husband tucked away, but because of her post-war dreams, as solid as his own. But he had no words to say it, or rather, had the words but too much embarrassment to let them out.

He lifted his hat to her instead. 'Good evening.'

'It's morning,' she said, smiling at the grey-edged sky.

'You're right. It is.' He walked along the jetty, the sea at his back, the greying ocean that ... somehow, somewhere ... connected him to Nancy.

Chapter 47

Gladys Ellis
Parramatta, Sydney
1 November 1944

Councillor and Mrs Ellis
Gladacres
via Gibber's Creek

Dear Dad and Mum,
Well, we have done our Land Army training and you wouldn't
believe it. The training lasted eleven days in a big old home. You
could smell the mice as soon as you opened the door. The stove
was a wretched old thing and we all had to take it in turns to
cook breakfast and one girl couldn't even make porridge or boil
eggs. Then we were taken out and shown how to milk a cow on a
wooden cow with a rubber glove for teats. I've told the other girls
that if we ever do meet a cow when we are sent out, I'll show them
how to really do it, and how to dig as well. At training they just
gave us a trowel and got us to dig weeds out of the flower garden!
I think we are going to be sent to pick fruit though. I hope it is
apples or peaches or cherries and not lemons or plums for prunes.
Give my love to everyone at home. Tell Rodney if he borrows
my saddle, I'll clip him one.

Your loving daughter,
Gladys

NANCY

Several of the familiar guards had left. They only realised it when two new ones appeared at roll call the next morning.

'Not more than twelve years old,' whispered Mrs Hughendorn to Nancy.

The young guard's bamboo rod slashed down, striking the old woman in the face. Blood dribbled down onto her neck, bare of pearls now, the folds of skin like patterns of lace.

He is trying to show us he's strong, not scared, thought Nancy. The other guards hadn't struck them for months, longer perhaps, and never as deeply as this. There had almost been the feeling in the past year that they were all stranded here together, guards and prisoners both.

Mr Shigura stepped towards the boy, said something softly in Japanese. The young man stood stiffly. He gave the translator a short sharp bow.

Mr Shigura nodded to the women. 'You may go.'

The women straightened. Nancy glanced towards the guards' quarters. The food bin hadn't come out at all twice in the last week. She hoped it would come today.

At least there would be hibiscus buds and the wild greens. There were fewer 'island rabbits' now, in the hot lead-up to the wet, as though they were waiting like everything else to breed.

She bowed to Mr Shigura. 'May I go to pick the buds now?'

He nodded, said something to the young guard. The boy followed her out of the gate and sat by a tree with his rifle in his arms while she picked.

Only a few cupsful today, and half of that went to the guards. Not enough to fill their bellies, nor substantial enough to live on. Please, she thought, let there be sago or cassava today. Let there be a packet of dried fish from the villagers ...

But there was none. The islanders too must be hungry, she thought, in this barren time, their gardens stunted and shrivelled, waiting for rain. At home the hens had often gone off the lay in mid-summer. She supposed they did the same here.

The once-moist soil near the beach was too dry for greens too. She found a handful; didn't dare pick too much in case there wasn't enough of the plant left to regrow when rain finally came. Let it be soon, she thought. I don't mind being wet. Just give us rain soon, so there are buds, and cassava in the gardens ...

Time to go back. There was no more food to find, and anyway, her legs felt like marshmallow and her head swam. You need food to find food, she thought vaguely.

She looked for the young guard, expecting him to have followed her. He still sat under the tree. At first she thought he was asleep, perhaps had even fainted.

Then she realised he was crying long silent sobs that shook his body. She looked at him for a minute, at his face turned from her in shame. He cannot cry in the camp, she thought, not with the other men to see him. It must be here, with only me to see his distress. A girl. A prisoner with no honour. A person who doesn't count.

He was a guard, a bully who had struck Mrs Hughendorn across the face and made her bleed. It was a cut that would take weeks to heal in their starved state; it might not even heal at all, or it might become infected. Would leave her with a scar, perhaps, even if it did heal, if the war did ever end, if they ever left this place for another where things like facial scars might matter ...

He was a boy, away from home, who cried.

She knelt by him, slowly, waiting for him to strike her. He didn't. She put her hand on his arm, and then her arm around his shoulders.

He didn't look at her. He leant into her shoulder, like Gavin might, sobbing. At last he quietened. She felt him pull away and stand, quickly, before he had to meet her eyes. She turned and pretended to pick another hibiscus bud, then, still slowly, moved towards the gate.

This time she heard his steps behind her.

They have sent boys to war, she thought. Did it mean that Japan was desperate, even retreating from the land it held? Or were all nations in this war desperate now? Did boys from Australia, England, America, face the enemy?

She didn't know. And that, she thought, is the hardest thing of all. Starvation not just of the body, but also of the mind.

Chapter 48

Flinty Mack
Rock Farm
Rocky Valley
4 November 1944

Matilda Thompson
Drinkwater Station
via Gibber's Creek

Dear Matilda,

I hope the dry isn't affecting you too much. Sandy has the syphon going from the creek, but we are down to an hour's watering a day, or rather night. Sandy gets up at two am and turns the water on the potatoes. The creek has dried up entirely down the other end of the valley so despite the slope we are putting in all we can up here. It will be corn next, as much as we can manage.

George Green is working out well. I think he has been surprised at how much he enjoys being up here and his grandparents enjoy having him at home. He's been giving lessons in chemistry and physics and electronics at the school on Friday afternoons, which is a great success, and he has joined the bushfire brigade.

But I must tell you something. It is so funny. You know all his talk about the 'Jewish conspiracy'? Well, he tried that on Mutti Green and she fixed him with her eye — Mutti is good at that — and said, 'Your great-grandfather, the rabbi, would die of shame to hear you talk that way.' Her mother was Jewish! Anyhow, it has knocked the wind out of his sails a bit, but on the other hand he is chuffed because he was able to fix the pump on the fire truck when no one else could. He is talking about setting up a steel-fabricating works after the war, making prefabricated sheds. I must say I can't see how that would work — aren't all sheds prefabricated before you put them up? But Sandy says he may be onto something.

Do give my special love to Blue, and hug her for me? I know you will anyway. I do wish she was closer, but then I'd probably fuss and drive her mad, bringing over apple pies and generally reminding her of Joseph when she doesn't need reminding, just getting on with work and life the best she can. But I still worry.

Do give my very best to Jim and Michael when you write to them. Sandy sends his best too.

Love from us all,
Flinty

DRINKWATER, 20 NOVEMBER 1944

MATILDA

She knew when she saw the mail cart drop him off at the front gate, knew as her son walked down the drive carrying his suitcase, instead of staying safe at school in the Blue Mountains. Two more weeks of school, she thought. Couldn't he at least have finished his last two weeks of school?

If only Tommy had been home. If only Michael had gone to the factory first, then they could have both come home together. She could have smiled easily then, with Tommy at her side …

She had to smile now. She stepped onto the veranda, the smile in place, made herself say, 'Hello! Shouldn't you be at school?'

He stepped up beside her, bent to kiss her cheek. He had stopped doing that in public when he was twelve; began again at fourteen. She'd asked him, 'Why?' and he'd said gruffly, 'I'm bigger than them now.'

Yes, he was tall, this clear-eyed son.

He straightened, then hugged her, after the kiss. 'Don't worry. I've got my Leaving Certificate all right and it's in my case. They coughed up for it early.'

'Come inside. You must be parched.'

'It's dry all right.'

He plonked his case down in the hall and followed her to the kitchen. It was empty, thank goodness, Mrs Mutton at her afternoons at the factory. She took a jug of cordial from the Coolgardie safe — petrol was too valuable to use the generator now, except for shearing, and kerosene almost impossible to get — poured him a glass and reached for the cake tin.

'Any chance of a sandwich? I'm starving. Had nothing since leaving Sydney last night. They don't run the buffet car any more.'

'Of course.'

Cold meat, bread, chutney. She buttered great slabs, piled on meat, watched him sink his teeth into them. She noticed the chipped tooth he'd got playing football when he was fifteen ...

He demolished the third sandwich. 'I've enlisted.'

'I guessed. Militia?' Please, she thought, let it be the AIF. Let him stay safe in Australia for three more years. He can do his bit in the AIF ...

'Yes.'

Matilda looked at him, her clear-eyed son. He took her hand. When had his hands grown so large? But they had always been big, she remembered, even that first day as a baby, eyes glaring towards her voice as though demanding where he was and what this world was like.

'Mum, listen. I'm not going to die. You understand?'

She nodded.

'I'm not going to die. And Nancy hasn't died either. She's alive. We're coming back here. Both of us, when the war is won.'

'Michael ... you're not going to find her. You know that, don't you?'

He almost laughed. 'Mum, what do you take me for?'

Eighteen, she thought. Eighteen and a man. I never realised …

'I expect they'll send us to New Guinea. Doesn't matter. Whatever is needed.' He met her eyes. 'All right, I'm doing this for Nancy too. The sooner the war is ended, the sooner she'll be home. The sooner we get the Japs, the sooner you'll be safe, and every other woman —' He stopped, as if he'd said too much.

'If they invade, we'll stop them.'

He grinned. He was the baby, the little boy, as well as the young man. 'With bayonets made out of brooms and carving knives, like in *The People's Manual*?'

'With the guns your great-great-grandfather left in the back room,' she said. 'We could arm half of Australia with what's in there. Though half of them might blow up if anyone tried to fire them.'

'It won't come to that.'

And for the first time she knew with certainty, no, it won't.

Chapter 49

Matilda Thompson
Drinkwater Station
via Gibber's Creek
21 November 1944

Jim Thompson
c/- Australian Infantry Force
New Guinea

Dear Jim,
All is well here, dry but I've known it worse. That sounds cheery,
doesn't it? But truly, we do very well: the windmills are going at
full bore and your dad is a wizard at keeping the pumps going.
I took a photograph of him yesterday in his ratty paddock hat,
covered in grease. I felt like sending it to The Sydney Morning
Herald — *'Industrialist Mr Thomas Thompson at Work'.*

I'm mostly writing to let you know that Michael has joined up.
I'm sure he'll write to you himself and he may already have done
so, but I wanted to tell you in case his letter hasn't reached you yet.
He is hoping to be sent to New Guinea after basic training, which
I gather is pretty basic indeed these days. So if you see a bloke with
feet the size of Belgium and a look of your father about him, it's
your younger brother, now grown up.

There isn't much other news. The Clancys received another
postcard from Ben yesterday, a Red Cross one that just said, 'I am
well and thinking of you.' But at least they know that he is safe for
the duration of the war. No, that is not your mother fussing that

you are up there facing the enemy. I am proud of you, and you know I am, and I would not have it any other way. Besides, I'd worry about you just as much if you were in Sydney. You might get run over by a tram. Unpredictable things, trams.

Hope the socks enclosed fit you. I know they are a bit wobbly at the heel, but I'm sure that after you've worn them for a few days they'll fall into shape.

Speaking of falling into shape, I'd better go out and show the Land Girls how to dag a sheep. Or rather, 1,492 of them. I know the girls signed up for whatever work was going, but I have a feeling they hadn't thought of 1,492 maggoty sheep bums. They are grand girls, only one a whinger. They've taken over the shearers' quarters — they'll move into tents when shearing comes around — can't see the shearers giving up their beds for the ladies. Your father is enjoying having them here very much indeed, especially the display of undies on the line every Sunday, and their singsongs at night. Though I doubt they'll feel like a singsong tonight. 'Click Go the Shears' it won't be.

Your father sends his love, and may even get round to putting pen to paper one of these weeks. You know your father.

All love from me, always,
Mum xxxxxx

DRINKWATER, 2 DECEMBER 1944

MAH

There are certain benefits to having a husband so much older than you, thought Marjory McAlpine, as she slid the roast into the oven, then wiped away the sweat. One was that her husband was too old to go to war, even if he still had nightmares from the last one.

And Andy treated her like a princess. Other men might spend their pay on beer and cigarettes. Andy had given up the grog, except when someone shouted him a pint, and he'd never smoked. He bought her something special with every Christmas bonus, from the emerald brooch to the radiogram or the electric fan that blew hot air from the kitchen table. No one else in Gibber's Creek had an electric fan, though she hadn't been able to use it since the petrol rationing.

Mah looked at her kitchen with satisfaction. All her life she'd dreamt of a kitchen like this — plain blue-painted walls, blue and white cupboards, lino all blue and white flowers. Lace curtains at the window, a wood stove and a gas one, though there'd been no gas for it, or the gas refrigerator or steam iron, since the war.

But it was a room that said plenty of money, from Andy's wages and bonuses as the manager of Drinkwater and from her own income from her half-share in the biscuit factory.

Plenty of food, even with rationing — meat from Drinkwater sheep and cattle, hens' eggs, milk, cream and butter from the cows, vegetables and fruit from the gardens. With sugar now rationed, she used pumpkin to sweeten the cakes, or even stewed prunes. The one thing she really missed was tea. Six cups a day, strong enough to bend the spoon, a habit she'd got into in service as a kitchen maid, when only tea got you through the early rising, sweeping, water-carrying until breakfast, and on through the cycle of the day when tea kept you bright till late at night.

It was a long way from orphanage bread and scrape or eating on the back steps because Cook didn't want to eat with a 'heathen Chinee' girl. Let Gertrude keep her movie stardom. Mah had the Drinkwater stars at night, and a husband warm in her bed, and the kids to cuddle when they jumped into bed with them each morning.

Mah looked at her wristwatch — a birthday gift from Andy. An hour to put her feet up and go through the accounts before she had to pick up the kids from Blue.

She stopped as an engine put-putted down the road from the main house driveway. Not a tractor engine, nor the station generator, rarely used now with petrol shortages. Even Andy's precious Model-T was up on blocks for the duration. Thank goodness Matilda had kept the horses.

She peered between the curtains as the engine stopped. A motorbike and uniformed dispatch rider — you saw them sometimes on the way to the factory, where men worked on something never mentioned that Tommy had invented, but which everyone suspected must be an improved version of the wirelesses he had been working on for twenty years. But this rider had a passenger who was now stepping off the bike — young, tall, fair-haired, in the blue uniform of a wounded soldier. He sketched a half-salute to the rider. The bike puttered back up past the house.

She moved through the house, her hall with its Persian runner, its painting of the mountains, the bookcase with Andy's sister's books, and opened the front door just as the soldier limped up onto the veranda. He used a cane, and when he took off his hat she saw the red scar in place of his little finger.

'Mrs McAlpine?'

'Yes? Can I help you? Please, come in out of the heat.' Impossible to say otherwise to a man in uniform, especially one who had been wounded.

'Thanks.' He stepped inside. 'It's hot enough to melt a dog out there. My name's Thornton. Private Bert Thornton.'

She led the way into her living room — blue-and-red Persian rug, dark leather sofa and chairs, the big gold-and-white pot with *Souvenir of Gundagai* written on it that Blue had given her as a joke when she and Andy got married (the joke being that neither of them had ever been to Gundagai) that had lost its tackiness when she'd filled it with tall fronds of dried pampas grass.

'Tea? Or a cool drink? Or both?'

'A cool drink would be bonzer.' He sat, looking like he needed to.

The tank-water was cold. She added a slice of lemon and a sprig of mint to two tall glasses, filled the jug, placed slices of pumpkin cake and apple tarts on the flowered plate, along with cake forks, and carried the tray into the living room. He took the glass gratefully, downed the lot, then nodded when she offered him more.

'Bonzer,' he said again, then, 'Ta,' as she handed him a plate with both cake and apple tart on it. He used the cake fork properly, she noticed. Some mother had taught this boy well.

She sat back and tried to calm her heart. She knew why he was here. Only one reason why a soldier — especially a wounded one — might be at her door, asking for her, not Andy. But she still repeated, 'How can I help you?'

'Mrs McAlpine, you're Fred Smith's sister, ain't you?'

'Yes. You knew him?' Of course he knew him. This was what men did, visited the next of kin after their friends had died. She'd known that as the men came back there'd be a visit one day, ever since the local padre had arrived with the telegram, one sheet of yellow paper, to say her brother was no more.

'Yeah. Not for long. About four months. Long months, but.'

She tried to find words, one word. None came. She nodded.

'He saved my life.'

She had expected that too. A letter from his commanding officer said that Fred — or rather Robert Malloy, for it seemed the authorities had found out about the deception — had been recommended for the Distinguished Conduct Medal.

'I'm glad. That your life was saved, I mean.' The words were meaningless, polite. She did not know this boy; barely knew her brother, only the early desperate years in the orphanage until they were chucked out at the age of twelve and from that one year together with the circus, before he'd run off again. What difference did his removal from her life mean, beyond the loss of a postcard every few months, each bearing a different postmark, and signed off with a different name. *I'm enjoying the apple picking. Your affectionate Uncle Perce.*

Except that the loss was like a black hole in her heart. Not what was gone, but what now could never be. The kids laughing in their uncle's arms; showing him her factory and their bathroom, inside toilet and all; Christmases after the war with all of them — Blue's Joseph back, Nancy and Kirsty, Matilda and Tommy's boys returned, the combined McAlpine and Thompson families gathered around her plum pudding and custard … She wrenched her mind back. 'I'm sorry, you were saying?'

'Before he took out the machine-gun posts, he told me to tell you he loved you. You and Blue and Sheba.'

'Sheba?' Despite herself, she smiled. 'He sent his love to Sheba?'

Private Thornton frowned. 'Isn't she one of your sisters?'

'She's an elephant,' said Mah dryly. 'Blue, well, Blue is like a sister.' But she knew that wasn't why Fred had sent his love to her. 'We were in a circus together,' she added, because he was obviously wondering where an elephant could have joined her life, or Fred's. Funny, she thought of him as Fred, perhaps because that was how Blue had known him. Blue was the only person with whom she could share memories of Fred now. Except for this boy here.

'I thought … maybe you'd like to know about what he did.'

'The captain wrote to me.'

'Not the true story,' said the boy.

She stared. And she found she was smiling and crying at the same time. No story with Fred at its centre could ever be simple. 'Tell me.'

'He pretended to be a Jap. Took off all his clothes except his shirt. Ran in screaming, yelling this Jap word. That's how he got to the first machine-gun post, and partway to the second too before they realised he was one of us.'

She could see it, the green mountains and Fred's bare buttocks. Trust Fred, she thought, to go out in one great Galah.

'And then they killed him.' Her voice wasn't shaky, though she realised her hands were.

'Maybe.' The tone was cautious.

'I … I don't understand.'

He put his plate down carefully, still obviously unused to the balance of a hand without a finger. 'We got him down to Templeton's Crossing dressing station. Took us three days before a patrol found us. He was alive then. Breathing. Two bullets had gone through his chest and out again, broken a couple of ribs but nothing much worse, I think, or he wouldn't have made it that far. Leg and shoulder hurt too. Shoulder was pretty bad.' He saw her flinch. 'I'm sorry. Just trying to tell you how he was.'

'Thank you.' She managed to add, 'It is ... good ... to know exactly how he died.'

'But he didn't. I mean, we don't know that he did.'

Again, all her words had vanished.

He looked at her steadily. 'He never got to Myola dressing station, that was the next one down. They never found his body neither. Said he must have crawled off into the jungle, but you can't crawl far banged up like that.'

'But that is what must have happened,' she whispered.

'Maybe. If that was all it was though, I wouldn't be telling you this. The captain got a letter, just before I got this.' He nodded at his leg and his hand. 'The letter said that Private Malloy — not Smith — was recovering in Australia, would soon be rejoining his regiment.'

'I ... I don't understand.'

'Me neither. When they shipped me back I got one of the doctors to try to find out. There had been a Private Malloy in hospital in Darwin, for a while. Then he vanished too. Both Private Malloy and Private Smith have vanished, Mrs McAlpine. And seeing what your brother did that day, and what I saw with my own eyes, well, like I said, I just don't know. But I reckoned I should tell you about it.'

A dog barked in the paddock behind the house. Andy, coming home. Dear safe Andy. Suddenly she wanted his arms, warm and close, around her. Wanted him on the sofa next to her while she explained that one day — maybe, just perhaps — one day there'd be a postcard, from Uncle Perce, apple picking in Tasmania.

Hope, she thought. That is what we live on now. We hold it close like a hot-water bottle.

Now she had hope too.

Chapter 50

Gibber's Creek Gazette, 15 January 1945

According to a government spokesman, one thousand five hundred Australian war brides have already set sail for America and their new families, while another ten thousand war brides wait for passage to be reunited with their American husbands. Every transport ship provides berths for a handful of lucky brides.

Wife of the Prime Minister, Mrs Elsie Curtin, yesterday told a press conference she was worried that some of these young brides had very little idea about the life each would be making. Many expected to live in New York City or Hollywood or places they had seen in the movies, but instead most are destined for the '... backblocks. If they are city girls,' she commented, 'they will have a rude awakening.'

It is evident that many of these marriages were hasty and even ill-considered, with young women sympathetic to the young men so soon to face the Japanese and help our country. But second thoughts are too late once you are married. It is believed that a new bill will soon be presented to the Australian parliament to allow war brides to divorce under Australian law, so that they need not go to America to dissolve a union that was too rash.

But for Gibber's Creek's only war bride, Dahlia Polanski (née Bullant), life in America is 'grand'. In a letter to her parents last month, Dahlia says, '... there is a wireless in

every house in the street and a new movie at the pictures
every week. They have this wonderful store called the
Piggly Wiggly, where you can buy ice cream and stockings
and all the bacon you want. Last night we went out after
dinner and had an ice-cream sundae with hot fudge sauce.
I had two!'

PULAU AYU PRISON CAMP, 15 JANUARY 1945

NANCY

'Nanna! Tell me story! A Ben and Nancy one.'

Nancy settled Gavin on her lap as she sat on her bunk. Outside,
the wind muttered and tore at the roof. The bed was damp. She
was damp. But at least it was warm damp, not cold. A small pile
of smouldering coconut shells warded off the mosquitoes, a gift
from Mr Shigura.

'Once upon a time there was a bunyip! A big hairy bunyip
that lived in the waterhole at the place called Overflow. It used
to call every night, when the moon shone, "Ooooerrrrrrrrrrr".'

Gavin giggled.

'"Never swim in the waterhole by the big rock," Gran told
Ben and Nancy. "The bunyip who lives under the waterlilies
there will drag you down."'

'What is a waterhole?'

She stared at him, this child who couldn't remember a world
beyond the hard-packed rectangle of dirt and huts. 'It's like a
bucket of water, but big ... bigger than the whole camp!

'One day Ben had an idea. He said, "Let's make the bunyip
happy. Then we can catch fish in the waterhole."'

'How do you catch fish?'

'I'll show you one day.'

'Tomorrow?'

'Maybe not tomorrow. Ben decided that they should give the
bunyip everything they liked best. They brought a teddy bear ...

That's a soft thing you cuddle,' she added, forestalling the next question. 'They brought food too.'

'Cassava and nanas?'

'No cassava and no bananas. They didn't have any bananas then.'

'Coconuts?'

'No coconuts.'

'What did they eat then?' asked the boy who had eaten cassava and bananas for as long as he could remember.

'A big plate of mutton and pickle sandwiches. Half a watermelon. Buttered scones and pikelets with jam, and lettuce with salad cream and pickled beetroot. They're good things to eat.'

'Really?' Gavin was not convinced.

'Really. One day you'll eat them too. Ben said the bunyip wouldn't like pickled beetroot, because Ben hated it, but Nancy said she loved pickled beetroot, so they left it in. And they had apple pie and cold roast chicken with lemon stuffing and roast potato and roast pumpkin ...' She realised that Nurse Rogers had stopped to listen, and Moira too, gazing at her, their minds far away, in the world where there was so much food you could give away a picnic to a bunyip.

'I think the bunyip would like cassava and nanas best,' said Gavin. 'But not dried fish.'

'Dried fish is good for you. Ben and Nancy put out all the food by the waterhole. And the next morning what do you think they found?'

'The bunyip didn't like it.'

She grinned. He grinned back, so like Ben she nearly cried. How could a smile be Ben's, and hers and Gran's, but all his own too? Did all three-year-olds talk as well as Gavin did? Was he brilliant? Well, of course he was brilliant, but perhaps it was the company of so many doting aunties too: he spoke like a child who'd never played with another his own age.

'The bunyip loved it! All the food was gone.' Eaten by a wild pig or possums, most likely, she thought. 'And Ben said,

"Hooray! Let's fish in the bunyip pool." So they threw in the fishing lines.'

'Didn't they want the fishing lines any more?'

'No, they held onto one end and a great big fish grabbed the hook at the other. And Ben pulled it up and took it home and they all had roast fish for dinner.'

'I'd rather have nanas,' said Gavin decidedly.

Nancy laughed. 'Ben's family wouldn't. They said he was the best fisherman in the world. And do you know who Ben is now?'

'My daddy!' yelled Gavin, bouncing on his grubby knees.

'That's right. And one day we are all going to Overflow. Me and you and Mummy and Daddy.'

'And Auntie Rogers and Mrs Hughendorn and —'

'Everyone who wants to come.'

'But not men with sticks.'

'No. Not men with sticks. We will never see the men with sticks again. And we'll eat apple pie and roast lamb and your daddy will say, "You are such a fine big boy, the best big boy in the whole wide world."'

A cry was muffled across the hut. Nancy saw Moira bury her face in her hands.

She quickly kissed Gavin's cheek. Despite the lack of water, the dirt, the stench of the latrine, the too-fragrant dried fish, Gavin always smelt sweet. 'Now you go and ask Mrs Hughendorn if she'll play Old Maid with you.' The older woman had made a set of cards from dried bamboo leaves.

'Moira? Are you all right?'

'Yes. I'm sorry. Stupid. Just being stupid. I just miss him so.' She raised a tear-reddened face. 'Will we ever see him again?'

'Yes.' Nancy had to believe that. It wouldn't be fair to have gone through all this, and not to see Ben, and Overflow, again.

'What is he doing now, do you think?' whispered Moira. 'If only we knew. Is he a prisoner? Did he escape?'

She carefully didn't add the other all-too-real possibility: Is he dead?

'I bet he's having a right good time,' Nancy said, equally carefully cheerful. 'You can always trust Ben to fall on his feet. Bet he's living the life of Riley right now.'

'Really?'

Nancy nodded, imitating a conviction she didn't feel.

It was funny. Overflow was in her heart. And Gran and Michael, Mum and Dad. It was as if she knew they were where they should be, knew they were waiting for her. She just had to live long enough and she'd see them again.

But Ben?

She didn't know. Had never been able to feel her brother, the way Gran said she could feel both of them. Ben was ... Ben. He was his own person. Not hers. Moira's and Gavin's perhaps. She loved him, deeply, dearly, but he was not hers to keep.

'He'll be right,' she said again. She put her arm around Moira's thin shoulders and hugged her sharply. 'He'll be right. You bet he will.'

Chapter 51

Blue McAlpine
Moura
via Gibber's Creek
6 February 1945

Flinty Mack
Rock Farm
Rocky Valley

Dearest Flinty,

It is sweet of you and Matilda to worry about me, but truly, I am
quite all right. You would be proud of me — I knitted a whole
cardigan last week, holding the wool in my overall pocket as I went
around the factory. We have a new biscuit, 'Aussie Crunchies: a
tough biscuit for a tough land'. They've got chunks of choko stewed
with ginger, honey, thinly sliced then dried and chopped. It tastes
just like dried pears. Well, it doesn't, quite, but it doesn't taste of
choko. Though of course chokos don't taste of anything, much.

Really, my life is not just work! I even went to the dance last
Saturday, though with all the Land Girls we women outnumbered
the men nineteen to one. I counted! I trotted around the floor with
old Dr Archibald, then danced with Andy. It's very useful having a
resident brother-in-law at times like these.

It was a wonderful spread, quite worth the two shillings we paid
for supper. It is amazing what women can do with no eggs or butter
or cream. I made a pavlova with my sugar ration and Drinkwater
cream. Mah and I get so sick of the smell of sugar in the factory

that I never seem to use all of it for myself. It was a fine pavlova, if I say so myself, and filled with cream and strawberries it looked a treat.

It was a worry to see Dr Archibald so tired, but there is no possibility of getting anyone to help him. There has been a bad measles outbreak. Two girls have died and a boy left deaf, and it still hasn't run its course. I'm glad Mah's two got it so lightly before the war, as they'll have immunity now. Dr Archibald says it's a very virulent form of the disease.

Sorry, I meant to be telling you about the dance, not going on about measles. I even dyed my legs and put a seam up the back to look like I was wearing stockings. Thank goodness it didn't rain till AFTER the dance, as within ten seconds my legs were streaming brown!

Give my love to Sandy and to the boys and to Nicola, and truly, don't worry about me. I am fine.

Your loving sister-in-law,

Blue

DEATH MARCH, MALAYA, FEBRUARY 1945

BEN

The Allies bombed the camp one morning — American planes, appearing over the island's hill. Craters burped dust. Bullets scraped along the ground.

Ben grabbed a forty-four-gallon drum, hauled it inside their hut near a wall and crouched down behind it. 'Over here!' he yelled.

Others followed his example. It was the only shelter they could make.

'Haven't the Yanks seen the POW sign?' muttered someone in his ear. Curly, still alive too, a stick of a man with enormous green eyes.

Ben didn't answer. The sign must be impossible to miss.

But still the bombs dropped.

At last the planes vanished.

'What do you think?' Curly heaved himself onto Ben's bunk. 'Think our lot is going to take Malaya back yet?'

'Don't know.' They still had the radio, despite the danger; still heard the BBC World Service most nights, the sentries leaving guard duty to the dogs after dark. Dogs could not tell anyone they'd heard a radio. The POWs knew the Allies had landed in Burma, that the Soviet Red Army was winning on the Russian front, sweeping through the Crimea, Bucharest and Poland. On 6 June the previous year, Allied forces had stormed the beaches of France in 'D-day'. Rome had been liberated, Belgium, Paris; the Americans were surging across the Pacific — even Japan itself was bombed.

But here each night the day's dead were placed on the top bunks, safe from dogs; buried in a single trench come morning, with brief prayers and a salute. Men more skeletons than men, dead of malaria, infected ulcers, diseases, all compounded by starvation.

'Can't get much worse than this,' said Curly. 'Means it's gotta get better. Don't you think?'

Ben said nothing.

'Don't give up, matey. You just keep thinking of that home of yours. Your missus waiting, and your nipper. What's his name again?'

'Gavin.' He knew what Curly was doing, what they all did for each other now. When a mate gave up he died. So you got him talking about home. Talk about home and think that he could live.

He should talk to Curly too. Curly came from Brisbane. Ask him about hunting prawns on a moonless night, down at Moreton Bay. Joke with him about his kilt — back at home Curly played bagpipes in the Brisbane Pipe Band. Talk to him ...

He didn't.

The next morning Curly was dead.

The soldiers burnt the entire camp that day, after the work party had staggered out. No warning, just the torches biting at the bamboo walls and thatch. The sick escaped out onto the road. Mostly. Running, being carried.

There was no chance to grab their meagre possessions, not that there was much to take — a few blankets, pannikins, the precious radio and transmitter.

The Japanese pointed, shouted. The men marched along the roads, and then through swamps. If a man fell, he was shot where he lay or bayoneted. There was no food, or not for them. The Japanese had supply camps, with bags of rice. The prisoners scavenged bamboo shoots, banana shoots, and once a python the guards let them cook in return for half the meat.

The guards were hungry too. Gaunt. Not starving. Yet.

This land could not support so many people, and so much war as well.

They marched at night and through the day, stopping only when the guards needed a rest. Those who did not get up after the stop were shot, if they were lucky; bayoneted if they were not.

Another camp. Ben felt a flare of hope. Food? A bed? But even as he watched, the huts in front of them erupted into flame.

More prisoners stumbled out towards them, starved, naked apart from scraps of rag.

A guard thrust a pack at him. Ben tried to lift it, couldn't. One of the prisoners from the new camp helped him. They managed to carry it between them, along a road now, white in the night.

'Thanks.' He could manage one word. And a step. Another step. Another.

The man said, 'I know you.'

Ben glanced at him — brown face, no whiskers, a coolie hat he must have woven himself from straw, some shreds of shorts — finally found the face he'd known. 'Dr McAlpine?'

Memories. The last Christmas party at Drinkwater before he left for the new job. The tables laid with food: roast turkey, hams, corned lamb. His mouth was suddenly flooded with saliva. Salads in great big heaping dishes and loaves of bread. Butter. Cheese. Jam rolls and whipped cream.

He thrust the memory away and found another: Andy McAlpine introducing his kid brother, Joseph McAlpine, newly fledged as a doctor, and the girl he was to marry, who had an elephant and a factory ...

Ben said, 'I remember you too,' as more memories came flooding in, the scent of rain on dirt, Mum's laughter in the kitchen, the smooth lapping of the flooded river's tangled daughters that gave their place its name. Overflow. Next year ... no, before that ... he would be there, with Moira and with Gavin. He'd have to get Gavin up on a horse, if Dad hadn't already done it. Or Nancy — she'd have been the one. Gavin probably had his own pony already. They'd ride together, and Moira too, riding in the cool of night as the Cross turned over.

'Watch out!' said Dr McAlpine sharply, as the log leapt out at him.

He fell.

Chapter 52

Underneath the water six feet deep
Old man Hitler fell asleep
All the mermaids tickled his feet
Underneath the water six feet deep

SYDNEY, 6 FEBRUARY 1945

MICHAEL

They marched four deep from the army trucks over to the station platform, their heavy boots thudding on the concrete. The entire company was dressed in jungle green, wearing slouch hats with chin straps and puggarees and carrying full battle kit.

He could feel the stares of the civilians. Someone called out the old battle cry: 'Ho-ho-ho! Ho-ho-ho!' Others in the crowd began to chant it.

Michael grinned. For the first time he actually felt like a soldier. A woman's voice began to sing.

'*Once a jolly swagman ...*' Her voice wavered with what might have been a sob. But other voices took up the song. It swelled above the stamping feet. '*... you'll never take me alive, said he!*

'*And his ghost may be heard as you pass by that billabong,*
You'll come a-waltzing Matilda with me.'

It was a song of defiance, sung like this, a song of determination too.

The men settled their kits on the station platform and waited. And waited.

Night came. The train did not. But this was war. Trains were late in wartime.

Women in print overalls brought around trays of tea, the mugs already milked and sweetened, and slightly stale buns. He drank the tea and ate, then wished he hadn't. He felt vaguely ill, his stomach tight. He had ever since he started training, and had blamed nerves.

Just now, though, he couldn't think exactly why he should be nervous. His mind felt thick.

And then the pain hit.

He had a moment to realise it, then the agony took over, dropped him to the platform, clutching his belly, retching. Someone yelled, 'It's Thompson. He's down!'

Concrete against his face. Thought and memory vanished.

He woke to whiteness. White walls. White light. A white sheet stretched across him. Pain lurked somewhere, but not the same pain as before. He tried to move his toes, then stopped because that hurt too. But at least they were there.

'Michael? Tommy! He's awake.'

'Mum?' That croak wasn't his voice. 'What happened?'

'Shh. Tommy, darling, tell the nurse he's woken up. Your appendix burst. They thought you were going to ...' Her voice cracked, and then she recovered. 'They sent a telegram. We've been sitting here for two days and nights. They've been very good to us,' she added, as a nurse in full starch bustled up, her heels tapping briskly on the wooden floor.

He knew enough of hospitals and had enough of his mind back to know that Dad must have been handing out ten-shilling notes, if his parents were staying past visiting hours. Or the nurses had expected him to die ...

The nurse felt his forehead. 'Temperature's eased,' she said, sounding slightly surprised. 'A good thing it happened at the station in Sydney, young man, with a doctor on hand too. If they hadn't got you into the operating theatre when they did, we'd have lost you.'

'How long?' he whispered.

'Have you been here? Four days and nights.'

He shook his head. 'How long till I can get back to my company?'

The nurse looked at him with both sympathy and understanding. 'A few months. Then light duties.'

Months! Light duties. Standing guard. Or paperwork. I'm sorry, he said silently to the men he'd trained with, who might even now be waiting in Brisbane or Townsville for embarkation, who would fight for him, perhaps die for him. I'm sorry, Nancy. Sorry, sorry, sorry, sorry ...

'No New Guinea for you,' said the nurse. As she turned to go, he heard her mutter to his mother, 'You're lucky.'

Chapter 53

Flinty Mack
Rock Farm
Rocky Valley
15 April 1945

Matilda Thompson
Drinkwater Station
via Gibber's Creek

Dear Matilda,
I am so glad to hear that Michael is recovering. It must have been a terrible shock for you. I am so glad he is safe and even gladder that he WILL be safe, and not sent overseas. Is that a terrible thing to say? But with so many of our young men gone, it is hard to see even one more leave.

You may have heard about our bushfires. We are quite all right here, but the Whites' main house was quite burnt out and all of their lower pasture. They've moved in with their son and daughter-in-law, and we've all been lending a hand gathering up what we can to help them, as they lost all their clothes of course.

I thought our place would go too, and I had the silver and my latest manuscript and photo albums under the tank stand, ready to let it drip, and dressed in wool which was as hot as a Sunday oven but at least doesn't burn. The flames had got up as far as the Rock when suddenly the wind changed, almost as fast as I can write about it, and blew the fire back over the already burnt country. The edges were smouldering, of course, but we had it entirely out in about two hours. We're all on roster to patrol it, in case there are some burning embers in hollow logs, but the cool change has come in. No rain — I think it has forgotten how to rain. But there is still water in the creek up here and the corn crop is safe and (I'll whisper it) if the fire hadn't got the Whites' old place, the white ants would have had it down next winter.

I heard on the radio some professor saying the war might actually end this year. Do you think it really might? What does Tommy think? He is so much closer to People in the Know than we are up here. Or maybe People in the Know just think they are in the Know. If they really did KNOW, we might not have had this ghastly war at all.

Now the latest book calls me and so does the washing up. We will see which one wins.

Do give Michael my love and very best wishes, and Jim, and love to you and Tommy,

Flinty

SOMEWHERE IN THE PACIFIC, 17 APRIL 1945

GILLIE O'GOLD

Gillie O'Gold checked her mirror as the plane circled the island below them. Another touch of lipstick. Women across the world were staining their lips with beetroot juice now, or kept their worn-down lipstick stubs for special occasions, but not Gillie O'Gold. There were always lipsticks for Gillie O'Gold, no matter how severe the rationing. A dab of powder ...

Was that a wrinkle? She peered, then relaxed. But when you had been twenty-eight years old for two years — and planned to be twenty-eight for at least six more, when she might reluctantly admit to being '... nearly thirty, darling. Isn't that terrible?' — you had to be careful. Even more careful than she'd ever been on the trapeze, back in her circus days, when she was Gertrude Olsen. If only Blue and Mah could see her now! And Fred. Fred had insisted that Blue was more beautiful than her, but you could never believe Fred, and anyway, he'd never seen her with peroxided hair, permed and perfect, the professional make-up that made a beautiful face one that men adored.

She glanced out the window as the plane headed down to the runway. Another fringe of white sand, more palm trees, more Nissen huts and young men doing calisthenics, the Red Cross flag flying over the hospital, and in the middle between the two green-clad mountains a strip of grassed runway, with aircraft in rows at both ends, some as small as the one she was in, others larger, big enough for army jeeps and ... Gillie shrugged mentally. And whatever other machinery was needed for the war.

War was everywhere, even in the life of Gillie O'Gold. Half the movies in Hollywood had war themes now. The other half had resolutely nothing to do with any fighting — romantic goofball comedies, like her last. *Jungle Girl*, starring her and Rock Hudson, who was a sweetie. She'd played the orphaned daughter of a rubber planter, living in the jungle after her parents' deaths, a sort of female Tarzan swinging through trees, her old trapeze skills still perfect, but with *much* better clothes than Tarzan ever wore, evening dresses artfully fitted and torn just enough to be revealing ...

But no more revealing than the costumes she'd worn as a child and young woman, back in Australia. Gillie frowned, then stopped. Frowning caused wrinkles.

Vaguely she was aware that the country of her birth had been threatened with invasion. But it hadn't happened, nor was it likely to. Mum sent food parcels to Australia from their home in California, big fruitcakes full of eggs and dried fruit, to everyone she'd known at the circus, telling everyone she knew in America that the USA needed to help Australia right up until the USA had finally joined the war after the Japanese attack on the US fleet at Pearl Harbor at the end of '41.

Gillie could sing 'The Yanks are Coming' and even 'The White Cliffs of Dover' with the best of them (where *was* Dover anyway?), but she had, in fact, little love for the land of her birth.

Stuck in a Queensland mission as a half-Aboriginal kid — and if anyone knew *that* she'd be done for, which was why she kept her hair peroxide blonde. Sold to a circus — and a cruel one — when she was four years old; snuck away by an older trainee who then pretended to be her mother till finally she was 'Mum' so firmly that neither they nor Ginger ever questioned it again. Thank goodness Ginger had a desk job now, at a place called Los Alamos, well away from the fighting. The war wouldn't touch him there.

The plane seemed to hover on the hot air above the runway, then dropped and rolled almost to the edge of the cliff. Gillie put away her compact. When you had spent the first eighteen years of your life swinging from ropes and the high trapeze, landing on coral atolls or jungle landing strips didn't faze you. And Mr Wirrenheim, her agent, said that doing a tour for the troops was just what her image needed. Plucky Gillie O'Gold, just like the characters she played.

Except, of course, that the shows never went where there was real danger. War happened to others. Not to Gillie O'Gold.

And the troops adored her. She peered out, and grinned. Men lined the runway now, a crowd with one voice, 'Gillie! Gillie!'

She stood, arranged her best smile and stepped out. The heat hit her like a slap. So did the noise.

'Gillie! Gillie! Gillie! Over here!'

And then her signature tune, played by a military band.

Tell me the sun can't shine,
Give me a star to climb,
Hand me the moon to throw,
Just don't tell me "no".'

She waved, blew kisses, let the shouts wash over her, cleaning away once again the small scared child up on the high rope, the urchin with her hair cut like a boy's, the teenager spooning stew from a tin plate as she sat on a bale of hay with Blue and Mah, grateful for a squished-fly biscuit and a hunk of damper.

She was Gillie O'Gold now. And they loved her.

An hour later she had admired the dozen aircraft painted with a picture of her smiling provocatively in a bathing suit; had held the hand of every man in the hospital, except the imprisoned Japanese ones in the guarded section at one end.

At last she was alone in a hot Nissen hut, a generator pounding away outside to power the fan and the tiny fridge, where at least there was some ice for her gin.

Gillie had work to do. First oiling her hair — peroxide made your hair brittle if you didn't take good care of it. A face mask of grated coconut — good advice from the studio make-up artist: 'They always have coconuts out in the Pacific.'

Nails retouched, cold compresses on her eyes. One hour to lie down, empty her mind, then the work again: washing her hair, rolling it in curlers — at least it dried quickly in the heat. Face mask off and then make-up: foundation, a new blank face to work on. Cheeks outlined with rouge; eyebrows and lashes coloured; eyeshadow smoothed on; false eyelashes applied; and then she teased out her hair and slid a little — a very little — coconut oil on it to make it shine, then a dust of glitter.

Now the cage, wire and old silk stockings, to keep her face from being smudged and her hair intact as she slipped into her clothes, cursing that the space available in the planes didn't allow her to bring her dresser. She still drew the line at pressing her own frocks. The colonel's batman was doing that …

First the girdle, then the silk stockings, the heels, finally the gold lamé dress, a final puff of powder. No full-length mirror — the things she had to put up with — but actually she could do this in her sleep.

A knock on the door. 'Miss O'Gold?'

'Come in!'

It was the colonel, far too young to be a colonel, so she gave him the ninety-five-watt Gillie smile — a one-hundred-watt one could stop a man in his tracks and this bloke had to get her to the stage.

'Flowers for the fair, Miss O'Gold.'

'Flowers? For me?' She took the slightly wilting orchids. Great. Now someone would have to hold them while she went on stage. Whatever stage they had knocked up in this place ...

The island smelt of heat, of sea, of men and sweat and tinned beef. It was cooler now, the sun sitting on the horizon. The breeze from the sea even had a hint of chill. The colonel led her between the Nissen huts, empty now, not a man to be seen. All of them, waiting for her.

And there was the stage, rigged up from planks, a curtain strung across it on ropes stretched between two palm trees. The colonel led her to a set of stairs. She couldn't see the audience but she could hear them, could taste their expectation thick as treacle, could hear their hearts beating. Tomorrow they might think of wives and sweethearts, but tonight, she thought, every one of you is mine.

The warm-up act was on first, in front of the closed curtain. She could hear men's voices singing falsetto; blokes in evening dress with coconuts for bosoms, she expected, hearing the laughter too. '*Dance with me, romance with me ...*'

The song finished. Applause, and a few whistles. Three men ducked behind the curtain in grass skirts and, yes, coconuts lolling in giant brassieres, blond wigs made from dried grass. One of them grinned at her. 'We got them warmed up nicely for you.'

She gave her ninety-seven-watt smile back, made her voice husky. 'Honey, I'm hot enough to get them sizzling.'

'Miss O'Gold.' The young man blushed under his stage make-up. He didn't even look twenty-one. Had lied about his age, she expected. 'Could I ... have your autograph, please?' He pulled a piece of paper out of his brassiere. Gillie smiled as his fingers trembled.

'I'll do better than that.' She took the paper, signed it and pressed a lipsticked kiss onto it, then leant over and kissed his cheek. 'Dream of that, soldier boy,' she whispered, then turned the wattage up to full.

The curtain opened. She counted to ten and strode onto the stage.

The cheers could have lifted her above the clouds. Did lift her. She lived for this. She ate cheers for breakfast and dinner too. Her veins flowed with love. She let the shouts wash up and over her, standing still in the spotlights of a dozen jeeps' headlights, unmoving, letting them drink her in.

Twenty seconds, standing in the glow of cheers. Fifty. She lifted her arms, and blew a kiss.

The yells grew shriller, wolf whistles, hoots.

She lifted her hand. And there was silence.

That was the best of all. One flutter of her fingers and two thousand men went quiet. She smiled, and nodded to the colonel offstage to start the music on the gramophone.

The bullets raked across the stage.

Blood dripped down her evening dress. She had been shot, but felt no pain. Then she realised the blood was from the young man who had asked for her autograph moments earlier, whom she had kissed. He lay, his body torn, only a few feet from her. Had he rushed to shelter her as the first bullets flew?

More firing. Instinctively she dropped and rolled across the stage, still a limber acrobat. She was behind a box backstage even as the shooting grew more intense.

'It's the Japs from the infirmary! They got the guard —' The shout was cut off.

She listened. Two machine guns, she thought, drawing from her extensive knowledge of firearms — she had seen every war movie ever made, and been in three of them. One at the back of the audience, the other at the far end of the stage. Screams. A moan that went on and on, and stopped. The colonel screaming, 'Get Miss O'Gold!' then his voice too was cut off. Men yelling, running for tents, huts, weapons.

At last the bang, bang, bang of a rifle. The machine gun at the rear of what had been an audience ceased its chatter. The one at the other end of the stage snorted again, at the retreating men. No more rifle shots. Perhaps they could not fire without hitting their own men. Or her.

She peered over the box, glimpsed a small figure, bent and intent behind the machine gun. Using the curtain as a cover, she thought. Using tonight as a decoy, the whole camp for a few hours focused on her, not war. For a few seconds she admired the prisoners' showmanship. For that was what it had to be. A few men, especially wounded, could never hope that this attack would win them their freedom. They would die here. But what a show!

Then anger took over. She looked at the colonel's body, at the young man in the grass skirt and coconut breasts. Then she looked up. And smiled.

Somewhere in the past, the man with the machine gun had a home above a bakery in a village with rice paddies and fields of buckwheat on either side. His father made the best ramen in the world.

But that was gone. His life was gone. All that mattered now was honour, wiping out the shame of capture. He would die as a soldier, not a prisoner, among the bodies of the enemies he'd killed.

Three more rounds of ammunition. The audience that had sat there like dummy targets was moving now, a wave of bodies so easy to shoot down. He fitted the next round and moved to fire again.

Something dropped on him from the top of the curtain — a woman in a torn lamé gown. Her hands still held the rope that had pulled the curtain across. Her thighs, strong as a vice, crushed his neck between them. He felt himself lifted as she swung them both up on the rope again, then dropped him onto the stage beyond. For a second he was free of her, too stunned to move, then she was on him again, holding his shoulders down onto the stage. How could any woman have strength like that?

Her brown mascaraed eyes peered into his. 'You lousy dingo,' said Gertrude Olsen. 'You spoilt my entrance.'

Chapter 54

Gibber's Creek Gazette, 22 May 1945

Sleep-Outs to Relieve Housing Shortage

The government has announced a program of 'sleep out' construction to help alleviate the housing shortage.

It was reported on the ABC today that a house owner advertising his house to rent in Sydney received more than one thousand applications.

Bungalows twelve feet by nine feet will be built by the government and can be hired for fifteen shillings a week. They will be available for householders who will give board to one or more persons engaged in the war industry, or for the accommodation of service personnel or their dependants. The AIF Women's Association has highlighted the plight of families of Diggers living in appalling circumstances, such as the wife and two children of an Australian prisoner of war living in two damp rooms behind a butcher's shop, with no cooking facilities other than a gas ring, a privy across the backyard and no bathroom.

SYDNEY, MAY 1945

MICHAEL

He had learnt the age-old soldier's skill of sleeping standing up on sentry duty. He had learnt to stamp *Received* on correspondence and to change the date on the stamp each day. He had learnt to feel that this work was still part of the war effort, was necessary, for if it hadn't been, he would have been released unfit for duty.

He was still of use. It meant a lot.

What he hadn't learnt was how to cope with loneliness.

He had never been lonely before, not at home, the main house at the centre of a small village of sheds and workers' cottages; not at school, where privacy had been hard to find, but not friendship; nor in basic training either, where a couple of World War I veterans who had lied convincingly about their age had forged their shared first-week blisters into some level of comradeship.

He knew no one at the barracks here, nor was likely to as his shift ended at four am — the least favourite shift given to the newcomer, the young man who couldn't even lift a box of envelopes, guarding the colonel's car.

Taylor had joined up the same day as him. He had no wish to visit Skimmer and, anyway, by the time he had a meal and slept through the civilised part of the day, the rest of the world was still working until his next shift began.

The first week he had simply wandered through the night after his shift was over. The city was shut, the reception areas at the big hotels where he had stayed in the life before his uniform; the cafés, even the pie van at the Quay had gone. After the first night he avoided Surry Hills, where the brothels' patrons wandered drunk and weary through the streets, and Kings Cross, with its forlorn tarts desperate enough to still hope for custom as the dawn broke over their heads.

On the seventh night he found himself in the Anzac Buffet. Even the buffet was quiet at five am, the dancers and the music gone. But women still buttered bread and cut sandwiches, stirred cocoa and brewed vast pots of tea. For two mornings he sat at a table, making his cup of tea, his toast and scrambled powdered eggs last.

On the third morning, he found a dark-haired woman standing by his table. She picked up his empty teacup. 'If you've got nothing better to do, you could give us a hand.'

She looked like his mother, though she was firm-hipped where his mother was wiry and her hair was untouched by grey ... She was nothing like his mother, in fact, except in her air of taking charge.

He followed her. She handed him a knife; placed him by a vast tub of butter and an even more enormous pile of bread slices. He began to butter. And kept buttering, letting the laughter and the gossip flow over him, so like the women at home at any of the 'bring a plate' affairs, women making food and sharing it, the heart of life.

He graduated to slicing bread by the second week; he tried assembling sandwiches the week after and was sent back to slicing. Whatever the knack was needed for carving two slices of bread filled with cheese and tomato into four pieces, he didn't have it. His sandwiches fell apart.

He was no longer lonely.

Those were his days now: sentry duty (he didn't even try to get his roster changed), signing off and signing on, slicing bread and talking of home and sheep and cows, of sunlight on the river and the smell of rocks in sunlight, and once, in the silent recesses of the pre-dawn morning, about a girl called Nancy of the Overflow.

They listened to him, these women, as he spoke of her — the strength of her, the curl of her hair, how she had run away to join the drovers pushing cattle up to Charters Towers and back, how they would be together, when the war was over, now it seemed that, truly, the war might one day end.

In return they spoke of husbands, sons, fiancés overseas, family lost, untraceable until peace was declared, in the bitter chaos that was Europe. And then they wiped their tears and went on buttering and slicing, making sandwiches and stirring cocoa, putting on toast and scrambled eggs as the first of the uniformed breakfast eaters appeared.

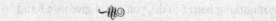

The war went on.

The referendum to give the Commonwealth government power over national health, family allowances, giving citizens the right to free speech and ex-servicemen the right to government-funded rehabilitation failed. Michael paid it little attention. At nineteen you could die — or stand guard duty — for your country, but you could not vote.

The flagship HMAS *Australia* was badly damaged by a Japanese kamikaze suicide bomber. Michael wondered if 'badly damaged' meant sunk — it was impossible to know the truth. The High Court had ruled that newspapers could only be published if they reported nothing that might damage the government's handling of the war, or that hadn't been passed by the censor.

Yet it seemed that victory was at last possible, at least, even if it might still take years to achieve. There was victory after victory in New Guinea, and across the rest of the Pacific, and in Europe too. The Japanese had underestimated the resilience of the USA after the bombing of their Pacific fleet at Pearl Harbor, and had overestimated their own ability to supply their troops as they conquered lands further and further south.

Michael wondered if the Japanese newspapers and wireless too were governed not just by the censor, but by propaganda news writers. Did the Japanese generals believe their own propaganda so deeply that they based their decisions on it? Did the Allies?

Impossible to know, when you were just a midnight guard at the barracks. He suspected his father, with his war contracts, might know more. Michael wore the uniform, but his father spoke to men who knew how the war was truly progressing. Or thought they did.

He stood guard. He sliced and buttered bread and sometimes even toasted it. He thought the latter was probably more use to the war than guarding.

He had been buttering for three hours, was thinking of becoming a customer and having breakfast when he heard voices at the counter. 'You wouldn't credit it, would you?' The voice was high, indignant.

'No,' said Mrs Krantz flatly. She handed the soldier his scrambled eggs, then came back to pick up four more plates.

Michael looked up from the crock of butter. 'What is it?'

'A piece in the paper about Japanese prisoner-of-war camps.'

'Anything new?' he asked urgently.

'Another lot of our boys were picked up when a Japanese transport ship was sunk. The article's what it was like in the prison camps.' Her voice was still carefully uninflected as she said, 'Same story as all the other ones. Pretty bad.'

He untied the apron over his uniform. 'I'm going to get a paper. Would you like me to bring it back for you?'

'No.' She realised she was being curt and added, 'Thank you.'

Her husband was missing in action, one of her sons too. She said quietly, 'There is only so much you can bear if you are to keep on going.'

He wondered if this was wisdom, cowardice or pragmatism. Whichever it was, it was her choice. Instinctively he kissed her cheek, then headed out.

The sunlight hit him like a wave. Mum's letters spoke of the drought getting worse. Here in Sydney it meant too much light reflected from the pavements, even the harbour. He needed trees and mountains.

Instead he followed the cries of 'Papah! Papo! Read all about it!' to the paperboy, and handed him threepence. Usually he first turned to the lists of missing, wounded and dead, but today the story was on the front page. It was as Mrs Krantz had said. Australian prisoners of war rescued from a torpedoed Japanese transport ship. No other details except what the rescued men had said.

Torture. Men burnt on the soles of their feet; their heads held back while water was forced down their throats; bamboo huts with earth floors or ankle deep in mud when the wet season came; hacking a way through thick jungle, laying railway sleepers, digging through mountains to bring supplies to an increasingly desperate enemy; working barefoot and in loincloths; living on a handful of rice and water stew; and finally thirteen hundred POWs crammed into a transport built for one hundred and eighty-seven passengers, to be sent from Singapore to labour in Japan instead.

The photo said more than the words. Faces like skeletons. Eyes, too big, too blank, looking out of faces like skulls. What had those men seen? What had been done to them?

Singapore. Malaya. Nancy.

Above him fighter planes roared and dived, a War Bonds stunt. His body shivered with the shock of noise.

Surely they would not mistreat women like that. Perhaps Nancy was not even a prisoner. Maybe she was living with her sister-in-law and nephew, made to work at a factory job perhaps. No, not in a factory. He could not bear to think of Nancy between the grim walls of a factory. She'd be working in a native village, conditions no rougher than when she'd slept in her swag up north, planting rice, picking bananas, maybe managing a rubber plantation if he knew Nancy ...

His mind offered the solutions. His body and his soul would not accept them. As deeply as he knew that she was alive, he knew that whatever she was doing, wherever it might be, it was bad.

Chapter 55

Matilda Thompson
Drinkwater Station
via Gibber's Creek
16 August 1945

Flinty Mack
Rock Farm
Rocky Valley

Dear Flinty,
The war is over. Oh, Flinty, my sons will be coming home. I felt
so guilty yesterday when that was the first thing I thought of — my
sons have made it through the war alive. I know I shouldn't write
this to you, not till Joseph is found, and that I should have been
thinking profound thoughts about world peace forever, and sorrow
for so many with so much lost, but instead in that moment I was
entirely, totally selfish. They are safe. They are safe. They are safe.

I can't even tell Tommy this. He is thinking logistics, how the
economy needs to change from war to peace, how will the men be
demobbed and when. But I know that you will understand. When
I heard about the thousands dead at Hiroshima and Nagasaki, I
even thought 'I wish more of them were dead' and then was so
ashamed of myself I was nearly sick. How do you weigh so many
horrible deaths against so many just as horrible that would have
happened if those terrible bombs had not been dropped? Not just
the deaths of our people but those tens of thousands of Japanese
women and children committing suicide as the Americans took

Okinawa, all the other Japanese civilians who might have done the same. How do we judge this, Flinty? What should we even feel?

I think I am writing to you because I have to talk to someone who will understand and I can't to Blue, not till we have word of Joseph. I am worried about her, to tell the truth, but I do not think there is anything any of us can do until she gets word one way or another. You must feel the same.

How did you celebrate up in the valley? I didn't even know about it till I heard the Land Girls screaming. I was down in the river paddock and thought one of them had been bitten by a snake. I raced up and they were throwing their hats around and dancing and Annabelle, she's the one who was on the music hall before the war, was at the piano singing, 'They're coming home, they're coming home!' to the tune of 'Jingle Bells'. She yelled at me, 'The war is over!' I managed to smile and hugged each one of them and said, 'Generator's on tonight, hot showers for everyone. I'll tell Mrs Mutton to make a cake,' then vanished to my study and just cried. But happy crying this time.

There. I feel better now. Thank you for listening, dear friend. Thank you for being there all through this war, someone I could talk to, even if just by mail. And now God has given me back my boys and we must pray He gives us Joseph too.

Love always,
Matilda

Chapter 56

Gibber's Creek Gazette, 16 August 1945

Party for the End of the War
By Elaine Sampson, aged thirteen

Today the students of Gibber's Creek Central School decorated the school to celebrate our victory. We put up red and blue streamers in all the classrooms. Later we marched to the CWA rooms, where the CWA ladies put on a splendid afternoon tea with scones and jam and cream and pikelets. We sang 'The White Cliffs of Dover' and 'Along the Road to Gundagai' and 'Waltzing Matilda'. Later the town band played. Mr Henderson the headmaster said that we will sing the songs again when our brave servicemen come home.

PULAU AYU PRISON CAMP, 20 AUGUST 1945

NANCY

The war had changed.

She didn't know how it had changed. The guards did not bring out their radio again. None of the villagers left messages in the precious parcels in the bushes outside. Perhaps they too did not know.

But for five days the young guards had kept their helmets on their heads, formal with their chin straps fastened, and stood ringing the camp with machine guns in their hands.

The guards did not talk. She wondered if they even ate, for most were almost as gaunt as their charges. But they must have drunk, she thought vaguely, or they could not have stood there.

She could not stand. Her dysentery was worse again; every sip of water she took seemed to leave her within minutes. An ulcer on her leg was as big as an orange.

'Nancy, darling, you must eat.' Moira sat by her bunk, holding out the bowl of vegetable gruel. She had taken over picking hibiscus buds and greens.

'Give it to Gavin.' Nancy tried to smile. 'It'll just end up in the latrine if I eat it. Won't even stop on the way through.'

She peered out the door as Gavin chased butterflies across the dusty yard. He was thin, desperately thin, his tiny legs slightly bowed; his skin so tanned that he might be a native child, native of here, native of there ...

'There' was home. She had to keep thinking of home. While she could think of home, she would still be alive; she could still watch for Gavin, even if the other women gave him his meals; she could still hold him warm against her each night.

An engine rumbled. She blinked until she recognised the sound. A car. She hadn't heard a car since the commandant left. She propped herself up on her elbows to look.

A shining car, very black under the sun. A Japanese man got out, small and tall and upright. He opened the back door for another man, this one in a uniform that shone almost as much as the car, covered in medals and braid.

The ring of guards bowed as one man. They kept their heads down while the newcomer stepped sedately into the officers' house.

Nurse Rogers grabbed Gavin, and joined the others by Nancy's bed.

'What's happening?' asked Mrs Hughendorn quietly. 'Do you think this means they have lost the war? Or won it?'

Nancy shrugged. Even that was too much work. I have to keep what's left of my strength for when it's needed, she thought. Not

429

waste it on shrugs. The war was the world, would be the world forever. How could it be lost or won ...?

The youngest guard came out of the soldiers' quarters, machine gun in his arms. He barked an order at the prisoners. The meaning was clear. The women lined up, Gavin holding Nurse Rogers's hand. Only Nancy didn't stand, but stayed lying on her bunk inside. Once that would have prompted yells, a beating.

Now the guard ignored her.

Another yell.

The women bowed. Nancy bowed her head too, on her bunk.

The officers' house door opened. Nancy watched as a line of three officers came out, each in a clean uniform with medals on his chest, every officer carrying something in each hand. The translator followed them.

The three officers and Mr Shigura marched to the centre of the compound. They bowed to each other, solemn bows and deep. They lifted their left hands. Nancy saw they held small cups filled with liquid. The four men raised these to the sun, and drank.

'Auntie, what are they doing?' Gavin broke from the line.

'Shh. Gavin, come back here!'

Nurse Rogers was too late.

'I want to see!'

The boy ran towards the men.

The world slowed. Nancy saw small footprints left in the dust by his bare feet, saw Mr Shigura's look of shock. She hauled herself out of bed with every last shred of energy, hurled herself towards him, pushing her rags of body across the hut, out into the daylight, reached out her arms, yelled out, 'Gavin! No!' as she waited for the machine guns ringing the camp to clatter out his death.

They didn't. Everything stayed quiet, except for the sound of her feet, and Gavin's.

The world exploded.

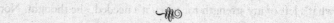

The world returned, in waves of agony and too much light. She was alive. She was alive because she hurt, hurt so much she didn't have the strength to feel the pain.

The camp had lost its sound.

No, she thought. I am deaf. The world was going on, because she could see it did. Could see her skin, coated with scattered dapples of dark brown. Could see the shadows of the hut.

She was inside. Moira lay on the bunk next to her, curled up small, not moving, her face buried in her hands.

Nancy said, 'Gavin.' Her lips made no noise.

A hand took hers. A face bent down. Mrs Hughendorn's. Her face too was stippled brown, though tears had washed some of the muck away. Mrs Hughendorn's lips moved.

Nancy said, 'I can't hear.'

Mrs Hughendorn's face came closer. She shouted, which was soft as well as loud: 'They blew themselves up. The officers and Mr Shigura. They had hand grenades. Nancy, I'm sorry. I'm so sorry.'

Nancy asked again, 'Gavin?'

Though she knew.

'He was right next to them.' Mrs Hughendorn's too-liquid, too-soft voice. 'It wasn't your fault. None of us realised what was happening. Oh, Nancy, I'm sorry. I am so sorry ...'

She couldn't bear it. Had no strength to bear it. Nor was there any reason to bear it now. Gavin was gone. She should comfort Moira, but what comfort could she give? He was gone, the bright child who had laughed and chased butterflies, who had not registered the horror in which they lived because he had been loved. He had accepted death as part of life, and now it had come for him as well.

Her reason for survival had gone.

Why should she stay living now?

Chapter 57

Gibber's Creek Gazette, 3 September 1945

Japanese Leaders Sign Surrender

Seventeen days after the announcement by Japanese
Emperor Hirohito, Japanese leaders yesterday signed the
agreement aboard the USS *Missouri*.

PULAU AYU PRISON CAMP, 3 SEPTEMBER 1945

NANCY

Each morning she opened her eyes and thought, I am alive.

Each morning Mrs Hughendorn brought her ration of watery
stew; held it up until she drank it. It took more strength to refuse
than to drink, and so she did drink, then lay back and tried to
make the world go dark again.

In those brief glimpses she did not recognise her body. Thin
ankles now swollen, as though she had been fed cream cake the
entire war. Even her fingers had swelled and darkened.

Vaguely she was aware of days passing; of morning roll calls
she could no longer attend. The enlisted men had not followed
their officers' example and so continued to guard the four
starving women. Perhaps they knew no other life to live.

An aircraft's roar beat over the hut's roof. She heard it, but
took no notice. Heard screams and could not care. Then thuds
around the camp.

It did not matter. Nothing mattered. Not even when someone cried, 'Food! Oh, you darlings, food!'

Later, minutes, years later, another cup was lifted to her lips. She sipped automatically, then spat out the unfamiliar fluid. 'What ...?' It was the first word she had spoken since ... Her mind closed, on both thought and words. She could not bear to finish them.

'Milk, my dear,' said Mrs Hughendorn's voice. 'Powdered milk dropped from the sky. And corned beef and flour and canned cheese. The guards have gone from the gate too. Nurse Rogers has gone to see if she can find the village, exchange some of the canned meat for medicines.'

Cheese. How could the world have cheese?

'We have won, my dear. I don't think I truly believed it till now.' The hand holding the mug began to shake. 'Oh, my dear Nancy, you have to live now. We have won.'

It was dark so it was night. She felt someone sit on the bunk next to her, felt a hand soft on her hair.

'Nancy? Can you hear me?' It was Moira.

She said nothing. What was there to say?

'Nancy, if I can live, then so can you. There is life beyond this.' The voice broke, then went on. 'Nothing ... nothing can ever bring Gavin back. Perhaps Ben is alive. Perhaps he is dead too. I don't know. But there can be more, if we can just live a little longer. Truly, my dear, there can be more.'

She looked at Moira in the dimness, the moon a flaming coconut in the black outside, this woman who a hundred barbaric years ago she had disliked. How stupid she had been.

'We can't think of what we have lost,' said Moira softly. 'If we do that, we are like the officers who killed themselves. We are more than that, my dear. We are going to live. We will leave the war behind, but keep the good.'

'The good?' Her voice was rusty, as though she had swallowed nails.

433

'Friendship,' said Moira quietly. 'And generosity and compassion. What we have given each other here. The kindness of the villagers. We must remember that. We must take the good with us and leave the bad.'

Her voice trembled only a little as she said, 'I want someone to paint Gavin's portrait when I get home. I will have to tell them what he looked like. I want Ben to see him. I want his family to see him. If we die here, Gavin will be forgotten. They will have killed him forever, and I can't stand that. I want a painting of my child laughing at butterflies. Gavin must remind us that even in the worst of times, there can be good.'

The room filled with silence, except the creak of insects, the scuttle of a rat up on the roof. Moira said at last, 'Did you hear me?'

'Yes.'

'Can you live, do you think?'

Nancy reached out and found Moira's hand. She said, 'I will try.'

The stew changed. It was, if anything, worse tasting than before, a mix of flour, corned beef and powdered milk, with whatever vegetables and coconuts the villagers could supply. Vaguely she supposed it was more nourishing. Equally vaguely, she did not care.

Voices. New voices. A woman, the accent Australian, bewildered: 'But where are the rest of you?'

'There,' said the voice of Mrs Hughendorn, and Nancy felt tears slide through her clenched eyelids at the memory of the graveyard, with that one grave at the side, smaller than the others.

Hands, men's hands. For a moment she fought them, remembering years ago the Japanese officers, what she had feared. And then she remembered that was gone. Everything was gone.

Her body was lifted onto something hard, flat. A stretcher. She was borne out into the glare of light. She forced her eyes open, suddenly desperate. 'Over there,' she whispered.

Two men, Australian uniforms. They didn't hear her. But Mrs Hughendorn did.

'She needs to say goodbye,' said Mrs Hughendorn.

They carried her, the kind uncomprehending men, trying not to show revulsion at the four wretched, skeletal beings they had rescued, who no longer looked like women, dressed in shreds of cloth, mostly bald, bodies grotesquely both thin and swollen. They carried her to the little graveyard. For the last time, Mrs Hughendorn lifted her: known arms, not strange ones. Nancy looked down on the graves.

Eight graves. They had names now, carved with scraps of bone on wood, tied with string made from grass onto crosses made from branches. That last small grave had a name too. *Gavin Clancy.*

She heard a dingo howl. But it was her. She hadn't known she had the strength to weep. The others stumbled from their own stretchers to kneel beside her. Moira and Mrs Hughendorn held her hands. Nurse Rogers put her own hands on Nancy's shoulders.

The watchers stood, only dimly comprehending, as Mrs Hughendorn muttered what might have been a prayer or final eulogy. 'Dear Lord, they are our hearts, forever more. Keep them and cherish them.'

The watchers helped the women back onto their stretchers. Women who until today had cooked, lit fires and carried water, supported each other and survived were deemed not able to walk even a few steps now.

Nancy turned her head as her stretcher was carried away, gazing at the silent graves. They will not be lost, thought Nancy. Others will come, and give them proper headstones. Ben might visit here. If she had lived, then Ben might be alive too.

But I am going to die, she thought. As the stretcher turned the corner to the road, leaving the graves behind, she lay back to do it.

A shadow crossed her stretcher, so close she felt the breath of wings.

435

She opened her eyes again. A heron, pale-topped, grey-backed. Wings rode the thermal up past the trees, towards the sea.

She had never thought what animal Gavin might belong to. Those things were for the world of Overflow, not Malaya. But now she felt Gavin's small soul tucked into the embrace of a thousand ancestors, part of the trees, the rocks, the river of his father's home.

The heron had gone. But now she saw another bird in her mind's eye. A pelican, strong-winged, spearing down to land feet first along the river, its wings beating against the spray. A river where swans still nested.

She only had to live and she would be there.

She only had to live.

Chapter 58

Gibber's Creek Gazette, 28 September 1945

Cheer the Boys as They Come Home!

Special, pre-war stock of hair curlers at Lee's Emporium.
Buy now before stocks run out!

MOURA, 28 SEPTEMBER 1945

BLUE

Blue strode down to the letterbox, Shadow nosing at wombat droppings or wallaby tracks in front of her, the young dog a gift from Matilda last Christmas. These days Blue could admit that it was impossible to focus on work — on anything — until Mrs Flanagan had passed with the mail.

There had been no word. Nothing. Or rather there had been many words — men and women starved to death and tortured in prison camps; the extermination camps of Germany; and Japanese slave labour camps of prisoners of war being slowly gathered into hospitals to recover enough to travel. But there were also stories of families told their loved ones were dead, yet they'd come home, unrecorded in a prison camp, hidden by kind people, or those who were not kind but hated those in power.

Yet not a word of Joseph. He had vanished in the jungle of Malaya. One day, would a headstone be erected over his grave, inscribed with the words *Unknown Soldier*?

No! Joseph was known. Was loved.

She stopped so suddenly that Shadow bounded up, sniffing her to see if anything was wrong. She rubbed his ears, then moved purposefully up the gully again.

There was a rock, half as tall as she was, with a flat top, as if aeons ago it had split in half, though if there had been a matching piece an ancient flood had shifted it. She had always meant to climb that rock, to sit on it just because it was so flat.

Why? She didn't know. But when she had found a foothold, clambered up and sat as Shadow settled himself at the base of the rock to guard her, she knew why.

It was warm. Warm like Joseph had been the last time she had held him. Warm and solid and *here*.

She lifted her face, and let the sunlight stroke it. She put her hands upon the rock. The words that came were not a prayer. Or perhaps they were.

Please, let me know. If he is dead, my heart will break but I will go on, and live my life even if he is not with me to share it. But please, please, do not leave us wondering, Flinty and Kirsty never knowing if their brother is alive, me not able to be wife or widow. Please, please, let us know.

A tear fell onto the rock, glinted for a moment, then evaporated. Please, my darling Joseph, be alive. Please.

She sat till Shadow grew restless; he barked once, then looked up at her. He must have heard Mrs Flanagan's horse. The mail had come.

She slid down the rock, patted Shadow, then walked back to the track. For some reason she felt calmer now. Perhaps, she thought, because I have allowed myself to cry.

Crying was good. Knowing would be better.

There was a letter. Only one. She knew the writing.

Joseph's.

She did not let herself feel joy. This might be a letter he had written long ago, when he knew that he might die. The postmark was Sydney. If he was in Sydney, he would have called her, not written. This must have been posted by a friend, who had kept the letter till it could at last be sent.

Once she opened the letter she would know.

My hands should tremble, she thought. If this was a book, my face would blanch.

She never had been able to do what was expected of a nice young woman.

Yet when she opened the envelope, she had to lean against the letterbox, her legs suddenly — appropriately — weak.

Singapore

September sometime or other. No time to find out the date! 1945

My darling Blue,

I am coming home. I am scribbling this to give to a good bloke who is being shipped off this morning to hospital in Australia to post to you. If I know the sodding army, they may not have even managed to tell you I am alive, or even tell themselves. My hospital bed had 'Dr McKenzie' on it till I noticed this morning and made them change it.

I am all right. Well, no, to be precise I have dysentery, malnutrition and two interesting tropical ulcers. But I am recovering fast. Most importantly, I am still myself, in one piece, if tattered, and if I know my Blue, you are still you too. I am needed here for a little while longer — while I am officially a patient, some of the men need the assurance of a doctor who knows what they have been through, and privately, some of the medical staff need my insight too. But soon I will find myself on a plane or ship bound for Australia. We will sit in the valley and listen to the cicadas call and, no matter what, my darling, I will not leave you or our valley again.

I am coming home to you.

All my love,
Joseph

She slid down onto the dust of the road, the plans rushing in like water shimmering down the gully after rain. She would make fruitcake, sponge cake, banana custard ... Joseph loved banana custard. Paint the bedroom — there was still a can of pre-war paint in the shed. If she did it now, the smell would be gone by the time he arrived home. She would garland Sheba in paper flowers, like they had done back in the circus for Madame's birthday.

I must get a new dress. Thank goodness she still had the coupons. Get her hair done. Another holiday at the factory? No, the profit margins were still too slim.

Today the factory would be without her. She must send a telegram to Flinty, tell Mah and Andy and Matilda and Tommy, send a telegram to Kirsty, still up north. Go to the stores to choose material for her new dress, paint the bedroom. Get a quarter of hogget from Drinkwater. If Joseph turned up unexpectedly, she needed to make sure she had a roast in hand. Did Matilda have any pumpkins from last autumn still sound in the shearing shed? Roast pumpkin ...

Shadow trotted behind her as she strode back up the path. His mistress was smiling again. And a dog like Shadow was good at guessing that a smile meant a lot of bones soon in his future.

Chapter 59

Gibber's Creek Gazette, 29 September 1945

Carlton beats South Melbourne in VFL Grand Final!

OVERFLOW, 29 SEPTEMBER 1945

SYLVIA CLANCY

The letter came to Overflow in the usual cloud of dust. She couldn't face the kind eyes of the postie, so she waited till the cloud had vanished around the corner before she walked down the track and took it from the old milk can that had been their letterbox even before her father-in-law's time.

The address was simple: *Mrs Sylvia Clancy, the Overflow, via Gibber's Creek, Australia.* A stranger's hand. Not good news then. The only good news would be from a hand she knew. She walked back to the house before she opened it, glad that it was empty, the others at the cattle sale.

Dear Mrs Clancy,

Forgive a stranger writing to you. By now you will have the news of poor little Gavin, and heard about Moira and darling Nancy. I hope you don't mind my referring to your daughter in that familiar way, but she was very dear to me, as dear as any daughter. Her courage and her determination helped the rest of us survive. We owe her our lives.

I am posting this before the ship sails for Bombay, where my

husband waits for me. If you wish, the address of the club on this
envelope will always find me. Please accept my sincere condolences
for the news that you must have found so hard to bear.

> *Yours sincerely,*
> *Mrs Horatio Hughendorn*

Her first thought was, she thinks we already know. There were
so many prisoners of war, so much confusion, so few ships or
medical staff, so many records destroyed. They'd had no word of
Ben, nor Nancy, Moira or Gavin. No word but this.

Poor little Gavin. The words were wrenched from her as
though they were too heavy to stay in her body. Dead then. She
had to think the word, accept it. *And Moira and darling Nancy.*
Which implied that Nancy too had died, and Moira also, the
woman she had never met, part of her family but gone now too.
All of them gone.

The second thought was, how will I tell them? For she must
tell her husband this, and her mother-in-law. The old woman
had been so sure that Nancy would return.

Now she would have to give her this.

Chapter 60

Gibber's Creek Gazette, 4 December 1945

Australian Wins Nobel Prize for Work on Penicillin

Australian pathologist Professor Howard Florey has been awarded the Nobel Prize for medicine for his development of the antibiotic penicillin.

Gibber's Creek's only current doctor, Dr Archibald, said, 'These new drugs mean that for the first time we can truly treat many diseases, instead of simply applying hope and careful nursing.'

Dr Archibald also stated that he hoped that Gibber's Creek's Dr Joseph McAlpine will soon be with us again. Dr McAlpine has been a POW since the fall of Singapore and has been recovering there since his liberation. His wife, Mrs McAlpine, says she believes that Dr McAlpine will be with us by New Year.

Gibber's Creek will give him a hero's welcome when he returns.

MOURA, DECEMBER 1945

BLUE

She couldn't wait for him. The telegram said his ship would dock in Brisbane, so that was where she was going.

443

She packed her white linen with blue spots, bought for his return, half her clothing coupons for the year. Hesitated over sensible shoes, then packed her new high-heeled 'Yank snatchers', keeping out a pair of pre-war low-heeled sandals for the journey. She packed the silk nightdress, unworn for four and a half years. His flannel trousers and two shirts, some socks and underpants. She didn't know if they would let him wear civilian clothes before his demob but he could at least wear them at the hotel.

His dressing gown — she had almost forgotten. His pyjamas too, soft cotton with the smell of home. Oh, and the photo of Kirsty's wedding in Darwin, though Kirsty still hadn't thought to mention her husband's surname, just the telegram *MARRIED JOHNNO TODAY STOP HAPPY HAPPY STOP LOVE KIRSTY* and the copy of the photo in the mail a week later for everyone in the family, inscribed *Johnno and me and Brownie* on the back, the thin young 'Brownie' presumably being the best man.

What else? Flinty's latest novel, though Joseph never read them, but might like to see it, and she could read it on the way. *Our Mutual Friend* for him, his favourite and a strange one, a tale of a world he'd never seen nor wanted to. Perhaps that was why he'd liked it.

Would he still like it now? She looked at herself in the mirror, and thought, will he still like me?

She took the train to Sydney, two nights at a hotel and seven baths. The last tank at home was half empty and she was saving that water for Joseph — had made do with a soapy flannel and a billy for the last three months, and a dip in the river after work to feel clean. She called the chambermaid three times for fresh towels. She ordered oysters for three people, to get around the austerity rules. Australia might have 'peace' but 'plenty' was still years away, as factories like hers changed from war production into making goods for home, as the labour force of women and the elderly gave way to returned servicemen.

A train to Brisbane leaving from Central Station, a blur of uniforms and women in impossibly high heels. She remembered the first time she had seen Central Station, with Mah and Gertrude and poor Fred.

Would Mah ever know what had happened to her brother? There had still been no word of Ben Clancy either. Even though the war was over, the newspapers still listed more dead each day, as camp after camp was opened, records slowly put together, camps across the Pacific, across Europe, not just prisoners of war but millions more — Jewish, Romany, anyone who had opposed the Nazi regime.

What did George Green think now of the fine Aryan race? Now the need for secrecy was over, Flinty and Matilda had told her his story. How many families had been lost, not just in war, but through hatred?

But I know where Joseph is, she thought. He is coming home to me.

The carriage was crammed, but she got a window seat. No sleepers available now, not with so many who must travel. She managed to doze, while stations slipped by, South Grafton, Casino, Kyogle, woke to see Jersey cows and green grass, the first she had seen for more than a year, a river, ten times the size of the one at home. Did they never have droughts up here? A straggle of houses that she thought was Brisbane. It wasn't, but when the train stopped she managed to buy a cup of strong stewed tea from the station buffet, the same women manning the urns as had fed the troops through the war, still doing sterling service now.

Brisbane was small. There were no taxis at the smoke-stained station. The stationmaster gave her directions. She picked up her case and walked across a bridge over yet another river, broad and winding, up two streets and then along to Lennons Hotel, where Tommy's agent had performed his usual miracles, and booked her a room.

A small room. Hot, even with the window open, but at least that stirred the breeze. The bathroom was down the hall. She had a bath, then room service — roast chicken and roast potatoes, charred pumpkin, no salad offered even in this heat. She spent most of the next day in the bath, and wondered how to get to the docks tomorrow, when Joseph's ship came in.

She needn't have worried. As she stepped out of the reception area, she was carried forwards.

Every person in Brisbane was heading to the docks today. 'Don't know any of the lads myself,' said the woman next to her, as round as a pumpkin and with a tan much the same colour. 'What them poor lads have been through! Never thought this day would come. Did you?'

'Yes,' said Blue.

The woman looked at her more closely. 'You got someone on the ship?'

'My husband.'

'Oh my, dearie.' The woman stepped into Queen Street and held up her hand like a policeman. She stuck her head in the window of the first car that stopped. 'This lady has a husband on the ship.'

'Oh my.' The man in front reached back and opened the door for her. The woman, obviously his wife, turned to Blue too. 'We'll give you both a lift home again.'

Blue tried to laugh. 'Home is more than a thousand miles away.'

They stared. She added, 'I'm staying at Lennons.'

'We'll drop you back there,' said the woman. 'How long since you've seen him?' She didn't ask, 'Does he have both legs? Can he see and talk and walk?'

'1941,' said Blue softly.

The woman began to cry silently.

'Our boy was reported killed in '41,' said the man, his face to the traffic. Every car in Brisbane was here, it seemed. And every dog. 'But you never know. Made mistakes, didn't they? Might have been a prisoner all that time. Might be on that ship.'

'Yes,' said Blue. What else was there to say? But Joseph will be there, she thought. Joseph.

The crowd and noise increased as they neared the docks. The ship was in sight, as Blue thanked her benefactors and got out of the car to struggle forwards through the crowd, pushing and apologising, 'My husband. I'm meeting my husband.' A hundred small craft accompanied the ship down the river, car horns tooting, two separate and competing brass bands playing, the heat breathless around her.

She strained to make out faces on the deck. Men crowding over to the rail.

He wasn't one of them. But of course, she thought, he doesn't know I'm here.

And then she saw him. Thin, looking at the other bank, not at the crowd.

She waved, she yelled his name, knowing it was futile.

'Joseph!' she cried again.

The people on either side of her took up the call. They made it into a chant, like at a football game. 'Jo ... seph! Jo ... seph!' Two tall men and an even taller woman hoisted her above their heads. She held down her skirt for modesty, and waved.

He saw her. She saw him stare. And then, slowly, she saw him grin.

The fear that she hadn't known was there unfroze — that after all that he had seen he might return, but without his smile.

She waved again.

They put her down.

She waited, as she had waited for four and a half years.

They had four minutes, one long embrace, before he was marched off for medical tests. She couldn't find the couple who had brought her, but another gave her a lift to a barracks behind barbed wire. Ironic, she thought, to put prisoners of war back behind barbed wire.

She finally found a public telephone box to call for a taxi back to Lennons. She tried to call the barracks once she was back there, but the operator said that the lines were always engaged. So for two days she waited on the footpath outside, on a camp stool lent to her by the hotel, in a broad hat with a Thermos of cold water against the heat.

On the second day they let him out, for an afternoon, miraculously with an army driver to take him and three others — and her too — into the city. Half an hour to get there, half an hour to get back. Which left them two hours together, spent with the other men, almost strangers, one from Perth, two from Adelaide, all of whom knew no one else in Brisbane.

Impossible to leave three men in a strange city, especially as the army had, it seemed, forgotten to give them money. They found a Bank of New South Wales with difficulty; with even more difficulty managed to convince the manager the men were who they said they were, and could withdraw a few pounds from their accounts without their savings books. Blue suspected if she hadn't had her own bankbook and gone guarantor, the men would have been left penniless till they reached home.

In the remaining hour she took them and the driver to the Ladies' Lounge at Lennons, where even more miraculously three cold beers were produced, and a shandy for her, before the car carried the men back behind barbed wire. Later, alone in bed, she counted: three kisses in four and a half years, and two whispered 'I love yous'.

But she was smiling as she slept.

A week later they gave him leave.

They'd still had no time alone together. They were not alone now. Once again, crammed in the train carriage, touching each other at least. Joseph was dozing on her shoulder by the time they reached Kyogle. She stayed awake, watching the miracle of him, alive, gaunt and pale under his tan, but alive.

The train rumbled below them on its tracks. *Alive. Alive. Alive.*

Somewhere in the long tunnel of the night he woke. They spoke, private at last while the other passengers slept. Later, she thought, I'll cry. I'll say I've missed you. I'll sob and tell you never to leave me again.

For now she whispered news, hour upon hour, year after year of it: '... then a year later Brenda married an American lieutenant she met at the Anzac Buffet. She's waiting for a war bride ship. Mick Henderson is back — he managed to get out of Crete. And the Clancys are hoping to hear from Ben any day now. They may have got a letter already —'

Joseph said in a queer voice, 'Ben Clancy?'

'Yes. They were notified he was a prisoner of war not long after I received the telegram about you. He even got a message to them using Tokyo Rose. Mr Clancy's been shining Ben's saddle ...'

He looked at her, his eyes full of pain. He said gently, 'Ben is dead, darling.'

'How do you know? Are you sure?'

'Quite sure. I was there when he died. Tried to save him —'

'Of course you tried to save him. Joseph, it's not your fault.'

'I know that,' he said quietly. 'You learnt to accept that or you couldn't go on.'

'How did he die? I'm sorry. Don't talk about it if you'd rather not —'

'I want to talk. The brass told us not to, back at barracks. Did I tell you that? They said the Japanese are American allies now, against the communists. They can't keep it all quiet — too much happened to too many people. But they demanded that we give them any papers or diaries we'd kept — against the rules, but some blokes kept them anyway. I kept medical records at one camp, but had to leave them behind. Anyway ...' He stared out at a glimpse of light in a fibro shack by the railway line. 'The papers were supposed to be fumigated. But no one got them back. We were told they had been burnt.'

'So it's all gone? Everyone's records?'

His smile was grim. 'Some of the lads still haven't learnt to do what they are told. They didn't hand over their diaries. And we'll remember, Blue. It won't be like the last war, when everyone worked hard to forget. The things that have been done in this war, to our lot, the Jews in Europe — if we don't remember them, they'll be done again and again.'

The woman next to her stirred, gave a snore, then a snort, then nodded back to sleep. Blue squeezed Joseph's hand.

'Ben Clancy?'

'He was in another camp. I only met him near the end. He nearly made it through. The camps were burnt, I don't know why. Everyone had to walk, even those too sick to stand. If they didn't ... Well, Ben walked. Managed to make it to just outside my camp, then he fell, that first afternoon, soon after we recognised each other. He was just struggling to his feet ...'

His voice stopped.

'Joseph?'

'They cut his head off. Two guards swooped down. They left him there by the track. We all had to leave his body there.' His voice cracked. When he had recovered he said, 'I think he'd have made it to the next camp if they had let him keep going. They murdered him, Blue. It wasn't war. Just murder. And there will be no war crimes trial for his murderers.' He met her eyes again. 'I'll have to tell his parents, won't I?'

'I can tell them for you if it's too hard.'

'They'd still need to hear it from me. Should I ...?'

'Lie? Say he died quietly in his sleep?'

He nodded.

'No. If it had been you, I'd want the truth. Want to know you'd fought to live until the end. Want to know every detail anyone could tell me. The Clancys will need that too.'

He accepted it without speaking, leaning back against the seat.

'Try to sleep,' she said.

'I'll sleep later. You don't know how good it is to talk to you. I used to have conversations with you in my head.'

'I did with you too.'

They smiled at each other, the moment lengthening. He bent and kissed her, then tucked her under his arm. They rode in silence for a while, the train rattling around them. At last Blue said, 'The poor Clancys. They have no one now. Ben's wife and son died, and Nancy. Did I tell you? They didn't even know they'd been taken prisoner. Just kept hoping. Then they got a letter from someone who'd been in the camp with them, saying how sorry she was.'

'Nancy Clancy? She's not dead.'

'What do you mean?'

'Her little nephew died. But Nancy is alive. Her sister-in-law too. Nancy was in the ward next to mine.'

'But ... but why hasn't anyone told her family?'

'Maybe the hospital doesn't know her name,' he said slowly. 'Things were pretty confused up there. Half the beds had no names on them. Half the others were wrong. I used to walk through the wards, a doctor's habit I think and, anyway, it did me good to move around. I recognised her. We even talked a couple of times, that's how I know about Moira — that's her sister-in-law — and little Gavin. Nancy was pretty sick. Nearly died. Maybe whoever wrote to her family thought she had died.'

'I ... I don't know.' She tried to remember what Matilda had told her about the letter. Had it really said straight out that Nancy was dead?

'She'll be coming home, Blue. Just like me,' said Joseph.

The stationmaster at South Grafton promised to send the telegrams himself, when she gave him the words and the money to send them. 'Reckon people need to know news like that,' he said, reading her scribble on the page torn from the back of her bankbook.

NANCY ALIVE STOP ILL IN SINGAPORE WILL RECOVER STOP JOSEPH SAW HER STOP MOIRA ALSO ALIVE STOP WILL TELL MORE ARRIVE TUESDAY BLUE

More cups of stewed tea, stale buns, and cheese and pickle sandwiches, some warm oranges, shared with the others in the carriage.

'Roast lamb,' Blue said. 'Roast pumpkin, roast parsnips, roast potatoes, gravy, apple crumble, baked custard ...'

Joseph looked at her enquiringly.

'Mah promised to have them all waiting for you. Sherry trifle — pre-war sherry, opened but still quite good. Apple teacake.'

'Shh,' he said. 'You'll put me off my crust of bread.' And laughed and kissed her, while the others in the carriage pretended not to watch, except for a six-year-old girl, who did.

Blue wanted him to rest in Sydney before they took the train to Gibber's Creek. He wouldn't. They sat at the station buffet, drinking more stewed tea, eating a salad of limp lettuce, sliced tomato, a radish rose and half an egg. She apologised for the lettuce, and for the brown paddocks that he'd see at home. He caught her hand again. 'I've seen drought before, darling. More than you have. You see the bones of the land in the drought, that's all. Beautiful, like a skeleton.'

Only a doctor, she thought, could think a skeleton beautiful. But she was glad he wasn't expecting lushness and flowers.

The train was an hour late leaving the station, waiting for a troop train. They clattered through Sydney and Joseph slept at last, over the Blue Mountains, where mist hung on fire-burnt trees, down onto the plains. *A chug a chug a chug ...*

He slept till Yass, woke up, then slept again.

They had nearly reached the Gibber's Creek station when it began to rain.

Chapter 61

Moira Clancy
Raffles Hospital
Singapore
16 January 1946

My dearest Nancy,
I have asked the nurse to give you this when my ship sails: to
England, not Australia.

    I hope you can forgive me, both for my desertion and for not
having the courage to tell you myself. But I didn't want our last words
together to be tears and goodbyes, but of looking towards the future.

    Yours is at Overflow. I don't know where mine is yet. But
I do know that before I find it I need to see my home, my real
home, green fields and brown streams and leaves turning yellow in
autumn. I need to hear English voices. One day, I promise, we will
meet again. Perhaps I will even come to stay at Overflow, if you
will have me.

    Overflow is your home. It is not mine. Please believe me that
this is not because of anything in your heritage. I admire whatever
ancestors made Nancy of the Overflow, and the man who I will
always love, and my son, whose face I will see every day, for as
long as I may live. If either of them had lived, I would have gone
with them to their home and made it mine. But they're gone
and somehow I must live with that. I do not think I can do so at
Overflow, or not yet.

    Goodbye, my dear, until we meet again. You have been closer
to me than a sister, another mother to my son. Please do not ever

blame yourself for his loss, as I try not to blame myself either. One day, perhaps, we might succeed.

Give my love to your river and to your family, who are still mine, even if I can't bear to meet them yet.

With all my love, always,
Moira

MOURA, 26 JANUARY 1946

MICHAEL

Michael sat in the Moura kitchen, looked at the woman opposite him, knowing she was trying to help. Knowing too that she could never understand.

Blue held up the teapot. 'Tea? It's stewed, not fresh, I'm afraid.'

'Don't think I'd recognise fresh tea if it bit me.' He accepted a cup and a biscuit.

'A new one of Mah's. No sugar, and beef tallow instead of butter. The tallow makes them better keepers too. We're hoping to get the factory back to domestic production by the end of the month.'

He bit into the soft pillow of the biscuit, trying to guess its flavour.

Blue grinned. 'Prunes. But don't tell anyone. We're calling them "Luxury Fruit Rolls: a pudding in a biscuit".'

'You wanted to talk to me about Nancy?'

Everyone wanted to talk to him about Nancy. His mother, her mother, her father, all trying to say without actually using the words that five years was a long time for two young people whose lives had diverged so much. That while of course everyone would be delighted if the girl who was now the sole heir to Overflow married the man who would inherit Drinkwater, he should not expect Nancy to feel the same, should not pressure her, should give her time to adjust, to know what she might want. Time to recover.

Only Nancy's grandmother had not tried to take him aside for a quick word, though she'd given him a hug and a kiss at the Christmas party. And now Blue had invited him over and he suspected it was not for a trial taste of Luxury Fruit Rolls.

'Yes.' Blue seemed to hunt for words already rehearsed. 'You know she's been very sick. Much, much sicker than Joseph. And the child ...'

He nodded to stop her talking more about the little boy. He didn't have any way of even thinking about that.

Nancy had been sent from Singapore to recuperate further in Darwin, where Kirsty had visited her. Kirsty had written to the assorted families. Nancy's hands were still unable to hold a pen, she'd said. But she'd sent her love to everyone, naming them one by one, including Michael. But then she had sent love to a couple of school friends too, and the dogs, and her horse. She had also asked that no one meet her in Brisbane, or even Sydney.

Michael knew that her mother, at least, wondered whether this meant she wanted to be home before she told them things they might not want to hear: that she had met a doctor, perhaps, in the hospital in Darwin, and was going to marry him and live far from Overflow. Perhaps even that she felt she could never marry now, after what she had seen or perhaps had had done to her in the prison camp.

'Joseph has nightmares,' Blue said flatly. 'They're easing a bit now. He's going to be fine. But ... it might be worse for a woman. Joseph says many of the men will never recover. Others will bury it so deep they won't know what frightens them.'

'You want me to go gently with Nancy?'

'I ... we ... want you to understand that she may never get over what has happened to her. Even once her body has recovered, her mind ...'

'She won't be Nancy of the Overflow?'

Blue said nothing.

'How is Joseph? Really?'

'He is home. Really home now. Not just in his own house. I ... I'm not very good with words.'

'And the bush has friends to meet him, and their kindly voices greet him,

In the murmur of the river and the whisper of the stars.'

'Banjo had the words, didn't he? Though I think some of those are yours, not his. I suspect,' Blue's smile was a true one now, 'every second, sleeping or waking, every step he takes, Joseph knows he's home.'

'It will be like that for Nancy too.'

'Maybe. She ... she did choose to leave, you know, for Charters Towers, then Malaya. Maybe for her ...' Again she floundered.

'The roots of home don't hold her close, like Joseph? They do. I've seen it. Felt it. Nancy will be all right, Blue. Thank you. But once she's home again, she will be fine.'

And she would be. She would belong to Overflow. The swans still nested down on the river, more and more of them each year. But would the girl who returned from war still want him? The swans and pelicans couldn't tell him that.

Blue nodded, her face still uncertain, and poured him another cup of tea. Michael took it.

The beginning of the old poem came back to him. *I had written him a letter ...*

It was time he wrote a letter too.

He looked at the paper on the desk in front of him, bare of words, then out the window. Cicadas yelled. Sheepdogs panted in the shade. Sheep clustered under the gum trees.

Somewhere out there his parents were by the river with a picnic basket and an elephant, in what he suspected was their first day off since the war began, except when they'd gone down with food poisoning, and he'd seen the swan, and known Nancy was alive.

Jim was at the factory, interviewing new employees, his uniform mothballed in a chest up in the attic with Michael's.

Their parents had accepted with what might even have been relief that neither of their sons planned to go to university or college. As Jim had said, it was time for real life now, old men and weary women, paddocks tired from war, welcoming back the young.

Michael gazed at the paper again, as if words might have grown there by themselves. He knew no etiquette for what he had to write. Just put down the bedrock, he thought, like the stones of the land under its fuzz of green. Just tell the truth.

Dear Nancy,
It is strange to have an address at which to write to you after so long. I have been sitting here wondering how to say things, some words to hide behind in case you don't feel as I do. But there should be no hiding now.

There has never been anyone for me except you. I know that you will not be the girl who left here five years ago. I am not the same boy either. I feel guilty that my war has been an easy one and yours unimaginable. You have endured so much more than me. I don't think the last five years have changed me, just made me more of who I was back then.

The morning you left Overflow you told me: 'We are birds, both of us, but we are rock too. I want to soar with you, and know the land below is us as well.' I did not know how to reply to those words then. Now, if I ever get the chance, I do. I think, I hope, that you still are the person who said them, and who will want my answer.

But if you are not — or if you are, but do not want to be that person with me — then please do not feel bound to me either by memory, or by my helping to manage Overflow as well as Drinkwater now.

Both of us will survive and thrive if you decide your life is not with me as a husband or as a farm manager. It made sense to combine the shearing this year, especially now Jim is back. He is putting the factories into post-war production. Between the two of us we're able to take much of the load from our parents and yours. He is well and happy, and engaged to a WAAF he met on the ship coming back.

Joseph McAlpine is back too, and hoping to begin practising again soon.

I have no words enough to tell you how sorry I am about the loss of Ben and Gavin, and what you have been through, but glad that you are coming home to us, no matter what you choose after that.

If I send you all my love, please don't think I expect you to do the same. But still:

All my love,
Michael

Chapter 62

And he sees the vision splendid of the sunlit plains extended,
And at night the wond'rous glory of the everlasting stars.

From 'Clancy of the Overflow'
by Banjo Paterson, 1889

SYDNEY, FEBRUARY 1946

NANCY

She dressed carefully, that last day: the cream linen dress with green edging Kirsty had bought her in Darwin, the one that the nurse with kind hands had taken in for her so it fit. Tan peep-toe shoes — she had to catch her breath after putting those on. Bending down still made her dizzy.

She looked at the mirror in the hospital bathroom. Thin, but no longer gaunt. Short hair, growing back at last. She lifted the lipstick, a present from the American doctor who had done such magic for the ulcer on her leg, and who had produced from that miracle the Americans called a PX store a lipstick and powder for every woman in his care.

She applied the lipstick carefully. This is for Moira, she thought.

Moira's letter was in her bag. Moira's loss was like a cord cut from her heart. She had read the letter, reread it, cried over it a hundred times. Knew that what Moira had chosen was right, just as what she was going to do today was right for her too.

The bag also contained a crumpled photograph of a Japanese girl that she had hidden from the 'fumigators' back in Singapore, a note from Nurse Rogers, back home in Albany, the whole town it seemed conspiring to fatten her up, and a slip of paper that had reached her in Darwin that said simply: *Dear Miss Clancy, I saw your name in the shipping lists. Welcome home. Yours sincerely, Cyril Harding (Colonel)*

A Red Cross volunteer took her to Central Station, walking slowly, carrying the bag, ready to help her up onto the train. It was good to have help. The noise, the size of everything, the mass of people were bewildering. But her legs could have walked for miles.

My last day, she thought. No more after this. Ever.

The train chugged and muttered. She closed her eyes, not to sleep, but to remember her last train ride, fleeing through the jungles of Malaya, Gavin laughing as the girls held him. Her arms ached as well as her heart when she thought of Gavin. Her arms felt empty now.

If she opened her eyes, perhaps they would be there: Gavin gurgling, Moira with her face concerned with appearances and her heart closed to everything but her husband and baby. It was almost as if there were two women, that one and the other she loved. But Moira had not really changed, there on the island. Hardship had simply stripped her down to the woman she had always been.

Moira was right. She must remember the good of the past four years today, the love, the friendship. Gavin, laughing as she told him about the bunyip. No, not that. She almost sobbed aloud. That memory was like a bayonet, pain that stabbed, too much to bear. Just get through today, she told herself. That was what she had decided, way back in Darwin.

Just get through the journey. Then get through today.

She opened her eyes, but there were only strangers in the carriage. It was still hard to smile at strangers, after the years with just themselves, so close at the end that they were almost one person. Only me, she thought. How can I live with only me?

The train stopped in a vast protest of brakes. Yass, and another woman in a Red Cross uniform who had obviously been told to look out for her, who bought her tea, which she drank gladly — was Mrs Hughendorn drinking tea now, with scones and her father's plum jam perhaps? — and a rock cake, which she didn't want but ate, because eating was what people expected her to do. She needed Mrs Hughendorn to help her eat it. Needed Nurse Rogers. Only today to get through ...

Chug a chugga chugga chug I want Moira I want Moira cannot bear it cannot bear it *chugga chug* ...

She grasped the window ledge and looked out. She knew the shape of the country now. There'd be water in that gully, where the hills creased. That was where the wind would meet itself, fragment and tear, roaring one way then another, shoving the clouds back and forth across the sky. Wallabies would gather after dusk.

She tried to smell the air, to taste for rain or drought, but all she smelt was train smoke.

She had waited five years for this. Suddenly it was too hard to wait this next half-hour. She sat back, trying to still her heart, telling herself that nothing could stop the train now, no invading enemy would pull her off. Her mind sang to the music of the train: *I will be there, I will be there, I will be there, one more day to get through, Moira, Mrs Hughendorn, I need you now.*

Ten miles, three ... The train should be slowing now. What if it didn't stop at Gibber's Creek at all, but went flowing on forever? In a world where small boys could be ripped away from life, anything could happen.

This is the last day, she reminded herself. After this all the panics would be gone.

The brakes screamed again. The land outside stopped bouncing past.

'Gibber's Creek! All out for Gibber's Creek!'

She couldn't move. She had asked her family not to meet her in Sydney because she didn't want a taste of home. She wanted

461

the real thing. The song of cicadas, the taste of hot rock in the air, the faces of those she loved in the land she loved. All of it, together, not in bits and pieces. Everything, on this one last day. But now she needed someone to take her hand, and lead her back to it. Moira, she whispered. Mrs Hughendorn.

A man's voice said her name. 'Nancy.' He held out his hand.

She took it, and there was Michael. Taller, broader shouldered, thinner faced. Not the same. Never the same, but still himself. The river changes every day but it is still the river, and he was Michael, and she was Nancy of the Overflow.

Five years ago her life had changed its course, as if in flood, uncontrolled, impossible to stop. Now, suddenly, it was in its banks again. She knew where she was headed, just like the river.

She would step from this train and the last day would be over. And the first one would begin.

My children will be your children, she thought. My land yours, and your land mine. One day we will talk of these things, but there is no need today. Today I'm me, and you are you, the war is past and we have tomorrow and tomorrow, stretching before us like the plains.

He said nothing, this new man who was still the one she knew, would always know, this man who was the land as she was too. He looked into her face, and nodded. He didn't kiss her then, just took her bag from the luggage rack and put his other arm around her. He did not let go.

They stepped from the train. Beyond the platform was what looked like the whole of Gibber's Creek; a banner saying *Welcome Home, Nancy* and two small girls with bunches of bright flowers and a band. A band! The Gibber's Creek Brass Band playing what was probably 'Waltzing Matilda'.

She shook in Michael's arm. Too much. Her first breath was train smoke and soot; the second mothballs and dust.

The third was home. The smell of dirt, of sheep, of kangaroos, the tang of river. She steadied.

She wanted to cry. She wanted to stamp a dance of rage and joy, for what was lost, and what was still to come.

Couldn't. But something seemed to wriggle through the soles of her feet, up through her legs, twining about her heart, gathering her arms, the core of her being. Roots, she thought. They can grow again now.

She glanced up, knowing what she would see. The heron, the traveller, the bird of here and far-off Malaya too, winging below puff-white clouds across the town towards the river. Gavin, she thought. For the first time she could think his name without agony so great it turned to blackness.

She would never leave this land again. Her life would be bounded by Overflow and Gibber's Creek, and the country in between: Drinkwater and the billabongs, the brown hills and the ridges. Only by staying here — knowing she was staying, would never leave, *could* never leave — would she be healed. Knowing that every breath she took would be warmed by this soil, the breath of a hundred thousand trees to give her life too.

The land would feed her body, feed her life. And she would give it love, and children, who might wander the world, free, because their mother was anchored here.

She looked along the platform. There was Gran — so small, too small, how she had shrunk the last few years — with Michael's parents, and Mum and Dad a little way in front of them, strangely hesitant, as if this meant so much that they too knew not quite what to do.

She had no words yet, not for Michael, nor for her family. Her father's lips twisted like he had a toothache, and she knew he could not speak. She saw her mother's face, small, so small, and knew her mother had no words either.

So Nancy had to find some. She broke from Michael's arm, keeping only her hand in his. She said, 'I'm sorry, Mum.'

What else was there to say? For she had failed: lost Ben, Gavin. Lost them both.

Her mother's face looked like it might shatter. '*No*. I'm sorry. We should never — but you're home,' she whispered. 'That … that is everything.'

Her father choked something unintelligible and reached for her, and suddenly they were all hugging, Dad and Mum and Michael, every person crying and somewhere children singing and the band still playing even as tears dripped into the tuba player's beard and she knew that the band played for all that had been lost and won these last years. The flowers, the banner and the music were for more than her.

Only Gran stood back. Smaller, darker than she remembered, but the same hat, the white straw with the cherries, the perfectly ironed white dress that she wore defiantly as though to emphasise her black skin.

As the hug slowly broke into separate people, Gran stepped forwards, looked at her, then looked at Michael, his arm around her shoulders, hers about his waist. (How had he grown so tall? So solid? My rock, she thought. My eagle.)

'Well,' said Gran. 'About time you were back. There's things you have to learn, girl.' She laughed, but Nancy knew she was not joking when she said, 'I had to keep myself alive long enough to teach them to you. You ready to learn your own place now?'

Michael's arm was warm around her.

'Yes,' said Nancy of the Overflow.

Author's Notes

None of the POW camps in this book are based on any one real camp. Instead, they are composites of many. Every major incident in the book, both atrocities and kindnesses, happened, but not at the same camps, or even in the same occupied Japanese territory. The radio of the Aerodrome Labour Camp is based on that of the one in Sandakan, formerly the number one prisoner-of-war camp in North Borneo. The camp was built by the British for the internment of three hundred Japanese and other enemies of war. In July 1942 it was taken over by the Japanese and held fifteen hundred men.

Nor is any character in this book based on any single person, apart from major historical figures such as General MacArthur, Sir Robert Menzies, John Curtin and General Heath, who are mentioned but do not actually appear in the story. The one exception is 'Miss Reid' (see below), who appears in the chapters set in Kuala Lumpur and is a homage to an extraordinary woman, Carline Reid, and her superb memoir of Malaya and Singapore from 1940 to 1942.

BRITISH AND JAPANESE TACTICS IN MALAYA 1941–1942

The supposedly impregnable fortress of Singapore fell when Lieutenant-General Arthur Percival, the Commanding General of British forces, surrendered over one hundred and thirty thousand British, Indian, Australian and local volunteer troops to fewer than half that number of Japanese military. The Japanese were almost out of ammunition, were physically exhausted, and with no proper supply lines had little chance of reinforcements or more firepower.

If the British forces had continued to fight, they might have won. They surrendered to a force half their size through sheer lack of nerve. The British intelligence services had advised that Japanese supplies were desperately low and without reinforcements. In New Guinea, the Australian and US troops kept fighting, and won — or rather, the lack of efficient Japanese supply lines helped them win. The British surrendered.

If the British had organised the defences of Malaya and Singapore efficiently — or even less extraordinarily incompetently — before the invasion, providing spare parts for planes that they had been advised were becoming inoperable and needing repairs, the campaign might have been won.

Japanese military strategy during the Malay invasion was good, even brilliant, though similarly to many British military decisions, and as with so many of the Japanese campaigns, the generals back in Japan overruled those on the ground, who stated that their supply lines were overstretched, food and ammunitions scarce and defeat a real possibility. The Japanese strategy in Malaya melded their navy, air force and army forces in the campaign, each supporting the others — something that the British forces failed to do. Rather than march down narrow roads and tracks, running the obvious risks of running into a larger force marching the other way (the tactics of the Battle of Waterloo and World War I — one large force battering another), they parachuted men in behind British lines, put them ashore by boat, or waded through the swampy jungle, climbing trees and hiding from British patrols. This was seen as 'unsporting'. It also worked.

The British had assumed that the dense jungle to the north was enough to protect Singapore; that no army could surge down the

Malay peninsula. The island's defences were focused on the sea to the south. But the Japanese did not invade Singapore by sea. They came by air and land.

The battle-hardened Japanese soldiers, who had already fought in China, were led by Lieutenant-General Tomoyuki Yamashita, and trained by Colonel Masanobu Tsuji in jungle warfare, including a simulated attack on the island of Hainan. Each division was equipped with about five hundred motor vehicles, but also six thousand bicycles. With no traffic congestion, they could move fast. They did — on roads. Even in the jungle they advanced about two kilometres a day, cutting their way through thorny vines, covered in leeches, trying desperately to avoid venomous snakes, hot during the day, cold and wet at night.

As the war progressed, the Japanese command became more and more victims of their own propaganda. Intelligence officers and journalists were not permitted to report on failures or starvation. To do so was not just unpatriotic but might lead to death and disgrace for themselves and their families. Japanese commanders in New Guinea knew their supply lines were non-existent, their troops starving, even while those in Japan were announcing the imminent invasion of Australia.

Why didn't the British adapt to the Malay conditions too? Partly from conservatism — time and again requests to use commando tactics were refused; and partly possibly from racial prejudice, a genuine belief that Japanese soldiers were innately inferior warriors. Racist clichés were frequently quoted as proof of this theory: they rode bicycles, not tanks (often true — and, as mentioned above, a much more effective mode of transport in that terrain); they all wore glasses (untrue); and that the Japanese air patrols could only operate because they were led by German pilots (also untrue). British high command was a victim of its own mythology. But there is also evidence that the British commanders on the ground were often inept, ignoring their own intelligence, and unable to either understand or implement effective strategy. After the war there would be extreme bitterness from many of the men who had survived the Malay campaign and who felt they had been betrayed by poor leadership.

The Malay campaign is possibly one of the few times when history could have been profoundly changed by a small action: if the British had withdrawn and left the defence to the Indian, Malay and Australian troops as well as the local defence forces made up of those who had lived in the country, I suspect the Japanese would not have even captured Kota Bharu — the Japanese ships would have been blown out of the water three days before they attacked.

If the Australians had been allowed to order their spare parts for their aircraft directly, and not go through British channels, the Japanese would have been outflanked, though admittedly that is based on the report of the single Australian airman who survived their last effort — ordered to fly in daylight in what they knew was a suicide mission with no chance of success, thus leaving northern Malaya with no air defences at all.

And if Malaya had not fallen? There might have been no New Guinea campaign; no Thai–Burma railway prison-camp horrors; no Changi prisoner-of-war camp; and possibly even no atomic bombs dropped on Hiroshima and Nagasaki. If forced to fight on a Malay–Thai battlefront, Japan would have been severely hampered in other areas of the war. Hundreds of thousands would not have died.

Perhaps.

But the Malay campaign is a lesson to any who would be conqueror or defender: adapt or die. Change your tactics to suit the circumstances. If necessary, forget all that you have been taught by those who have never fought under the conditions you now face and create new tactics, with the only rule being: Will this work? Believe your own intelligence sources (or replace them if you think they are incompetent). Do not believe your own propaganda. And if the war matters so much that you have chosen to fight it, do not give up, at least not while you are still capable of a vigorous defence.

And a small personal note here: nearly six decades of reading military history has led me to suspect that all armies are, and have been, incompetent, despite small parts of them that show strategic brilliance. Some are just more incompetent than others. I'm not talking about bravery here: extraordinary bravery is often shown by those who have incompetent leaders, and who may even know they are being led badly, but do their best — an extraordinary best — regardless.

Humans aren't particularly good at killing each other. Even if we do so much of it — and at times sadistically enthusiastically — with some exceptions, admittedly horrific, we have not yet managed to do it reliably well. The very fact that I use the word 'horrific' for genocides, and you, the reader, accept that genocide is horrific, underlines this point.

Most societies manage with a very small portion of their numbers acting as police, except where more are needed to enforce the government's ideology, rather than just to stop citizens from clouting each other on the head and robbing corner shops. Peace and cooperation really are written into our default code. And an ability to remain deliberately ignorant. Being able to pretend that genocide is not happening elsewhere does make life easier, and is perhaps a survival characteristic too. But not always, especially with our growing ability to affect the entire planet.

AUSTRALIAN PREPAREDNESS FOR WAR WITH JAPAN

Publicly in 1941 Prime Minister Menzies downplayed the threat Japan might pose to Australia. Privately he was well aware of the danger. Prime Ministers Fadden and Curtin (1941 was the year of the three PMs) both spoke within government ranks about their fears of Japanese southern aggression, Britain's inability to do more than try to hold off Germany's planned invasion of their homeland, and the likelihood that the USA would not enter the war if Japan attacked British and Dutch possessions.

But when Japanese attacked British-held Malaya without warning, negotiations that many hoped would lead to a lasting peace were still proceeding. A treaty between Australia and Japan had been signed, guaranteeing that neither would attack without a formal declaration of war. While Australia was mobilising onto a war footing that acknowledged the likelihood of attack on the Australian mainland, the public was still being reassured. To some extent, this understatement of the true danger and degree of shipping losses and bomb casualties in Darwin, Broome, Townsville and other northern areas continued throughout the war, to minimise panic and despondency. There continued to be a major difference between what the government knew and expected, and what the population was told.

Australia's major problem in preparing for war with Japan was the British refusal to send back Australian men and planes and other equipment from the Middle East. For Britain, defence of the motherland by defeating German and Italian armies was more important than defending Australia against Japan. The colonies — with the exception of India, the 'jewel in the crown' needed for its resources — were to be abandoned. By 1942 Australia lacked not just most of its fighting force, but desperately needed planes and spare parts for those it did have. Only by directly defying British Prime Minister Churchill, and accepting the command instead of American General Douglas MacArthur, could Prime Minister Curtin ensure that Australian troops were redirected to the war in the Pacific.

One of MacArthur's many famous quotes was: 'Wars are never won in the past.' He advocated hard-hitting manoeuvres against important strategic positions, rather than taking every island the Japanese held.

THE AUSTRALIAN PRISONERS OF WAR

Twenty-two thousand Australians were taken as Japanese prisoners of war (POWs) in World War II. Almost fifteen thousand of these were taken prisoner after the surrender of Singapore. The largest prison camp was Changi, and from there men were taken for forced labour for the Japanese, primarily to camps in Burma and Thailand to work on the infamous Thai–Burma railway, and Japan. About eight thousand men died in the labour camps. Many more men died from the conditions of their imprisonment than from fighting. Men and women from the conquered nations were also taken as slave labour.

About one hundred and thirty thousand civilians from the Allied nations were interned by the Japanese in the areas they conquered but, as in many cases no records were kept, nor, as in Nancy's case, were relatives at home informed, it is impossible to know the exact number. Although the civilians were usually not made to labour as the POWs were, the death rate from disease and starvation appears to have been much the same. Conditions varied from camp to camp, and also depended on the commandant of the camp at the time. The largest camp was Tjihapit in Java, which held fourteen thousand prisoners, but there were many much smaller camps. Pangkalpinang in Sumatra, for example, held only four internees.

My early childhood was haunted by men who had survived the POW camps. My best friend's father walked hunched over. I screamed when I first saw him, thinking he was a spider, with his gaunt face and haunted eyes. I still feel horror to think what my childish reaction must have done to him. He avoided me — and everyone — after that. I do not know what had been done to him, or if he recovered, for we moved soon after that. All I knew were the whispers, 'He was tortured by the Japanese.' A distant relative killed himself the day after the funeral of another. He left a note saying he could not live with the memory of the camp, with knowing what men could do to each other.

How did such appalling conditions happen? Part — a large part — was necessity. Even soon after the Japanese advance, when conditions were relatively good, their supply lines were badly overstretched. The only food was what was available locally, and that often wasn't enough for the locals, the soldiers, the internees and prisoners. Nor did many of the Japanese and Korean guards understand that prisoners with the usually larger build of Australian, British and Dutch men needed more food than they did, especially with long hours of labour.

As the war continued, the Japanese too starved. It must have seemed logical that the small reserves of food be kept for themselves, so they could continue to do their duty while their strength lasted. The use of slave labour on the Thai–Burma railway, the Sandakan airstrip and other projects, the lack of medical supplies and food, the yells of 'Lakas, lakas!' — faster, faster — can be seen as the growing desperation of men far from the centre of Japanese high command. Generals and war leaders believed their own propaganda — that their forces were invincible and were forging across the world, not desperate, starving and disastrously undersupplied. There was a general refusal to accept the word of their own intelligence services and they regarded anyone who countenanced the possibility of defeat as a traitor.

It is this concept of 'duty' that explains so much of the treatment in the camps. The Japanese soldier caste lived by the code of 'Bushido'. They owed unquestioning reverence and allegiance to the emperor, who was a living god. To show this allegiance, to prove themselves, they were required in training and in service to show unquestioning/absolute obedience, even to the extent of cutting off the heads of prisoners or bayoneting civilians. To question an order was to risk death and dishonour, not just for yourself but your entire family, who might kill themselves from the shame of your disloyalty.

Japan had not signed the Geneva Convention on the treatment of prisoners of war. To them suicide was preferable to being taken prisoner. Prisoners of war were, by definition, cowards to be held in utter contempt.

For this generation, the torture of prisoners is reprehensible. At the time, corporal punishment was a routine part of Japanese military order. Soldiers were expected to perform what we regard as atrocities to show their unquestioning obedience. If they had refused, they too would have been killed. Their training would also have included situations where they had to kill or brutalise others when the order was given. Humans of all nations are not naturally sadistic, apart from a small percentage of sociopaths and psychopaths, for whom war can be a delicious opportunity. But humans of all nations can be trained to be sadistic, nor do I know of any culture with no atrocities in its past.

GOOD AND EVIL

Humans prefer things neatly categorised into good and evil. War is bad; peace is good. But if your country — and those who live in it — are threatened, the only choice may be to fight or die. My grandmother, who had seen the suffering of family and friends who survived the prisoner-of-war camps and mourned others who did not, would never buy anything made in Japan. The only time she ever showed anger in my presence was when I, unthinkingly, told her about an exhibition of Japanese art I had attended and loved. 'How could you go there?' she asked. 'How could you?'

The Japan of 1942–1945 is not the modern-day Japan. It was a land and culture ruled by a military dictatorship, where protest was silenced with death, and even those who felt horror, shame or terror were unable to express it for fear of repercussions to themselves and their families. It was also a land that had been at war for more than a decade, partly to ensure the supply of minerals and other natural resources Japan needed to modernise but lacked in its own islands.

In a culture like this, psychopaths, sadists and sociopaths can, and did, flourish. But there are also many accounts of Japanese soldiers and guards who acted as expected when other Japanese people could see them and report back about their behaviour, but were as kind and compassionate as possible when alone with their prisoners.

The swift beheadings, the beatings that the prisoners were subjected to were the same punishments given to Japanese military and civilians who transgressed the rules. Prisoners starved, but so did their guards — as mentioned elsewhere the Japanese supply lines were almost non-existent, and both the Japanese Army and the remnants of the armies they had conquered had to subsist on what war-devastated lands could supply, or quickly tame the jungle for essential rail-lines to create desperately needed supply lines.

The stories of Japanese cannibalism in what is now Papua New Guinea indicate desperation and starvation, as well as a culture where much effort had gone into training citizens to see other races as less than human, where boys as young as twelve were thrust into war in the jungle, untrained, terrified, with discipline breaking down around them.

Most of the best-known prison-camp stories are also horror stories: horror is more vivid than boredom. But for a good part of the war, and until conditions deteriorated, some of the camps at least were left to the inmates to run — gardens were encouraged and work was paid for. Boredom and homesickness — and guilt at being a prisoner — were the most pressing problems. This is not to underestimate how hard those were even then, but they were not the result of Japanese cruelty, but the conditions of war and lack of resources at the time.

As the old imperial and samurai culture was swept away after the Japanese defeat, Japan changed swiftly to become a liberal democracy, with freedom of expression. Many Japanese did and still do express horror at what happened in the prison camps, the torture, medical experimentation and the genocide committed by the Japanese Imperial Army. But, unlike in Germany, the Japanese government has never officially apologised to any of the victims of imperial expansion and aggression, and there is also a strong movement that defends Japanese foreign policy between 1935 and 1945.

When we are quick to condemn Japan's lack of an apology, it is worth remembering that it took until 2007 for an Australian prime minister to apologise for the forced removal of children of Indigenous Australians during the twentieth century. Official apologies are rare and endangered beasts in world politics, partly, at least, because they can lead to demands for financial reparation.

In a culture as regimented and totalitarian as Japan was in World War II, and the war years preceding it, would any of us have had the courage to face death not just for ourselves but for our families by speaking out, or failing to obey orders? As I first wrote about Hitler's daughter, when the world around you is insane, how do you know what is good, and what is evil?

When I was a child we played cowboys and Indians, good guys versus bad guys. As an adult, I discovered that I am descended from both the cowboys — or at least the jackaroos — and the Indians, and the world cannot be neatly divided into goodies and baddies. A good person is capable of a bad action, a bad one of a good. It is enough, perhaps, to say, 'I will try to do my best,' and to absorb as many of others' widely diverging views as possible, to try to work out what that best may be.

This book is about those who do what they believe is good.

JAPANESE WORDS IN THE TEXT

Arigato — thank you
Sayonara — goodbye
Shindai — bunk
Tasukete — help
Watashi no musume — my daughter

RADIO TOKYO

The quotes from Radio Tokyo are based on real broadcasts, but as with the prison camps and characters, they are compilations, not direct transcripts. The broadcasts were widely listened to in the camps, not just for the entertainment value, with music and comedy routines, but because they also often gave messages from POWs or lists of those held. While their intended aim was propaganda, to give those in Australia and in the Allied armed services a sense that Japanese victory was inevitable, the news items seemed to have been treated with derision by those who heard them. The victories claimed were too exaggerated to be believed.

Tokyo Rose was the most famous broadcaster (most prominently voiced by Iva Toguri, a Japanese-American woman who was stranded in Japan at the outbreak of war, although other women also broadcast under that name), but there were many, including Australian POW Charles Cousens, pressured both physically and psychologically to give broadcasts. He was charged with high treason after the war, and stripped of his commission, although the treason charge was eventually dropped. Cousens also helped sabotage Japanese broadcasts, and gave as much information about prisoners as he was able to get away with. It has been argued that his 'contribution' to the Japanese war effort should have been treated with the same latitude as was given to those who worked on other military projects, like the Thai–Burma railway or Japanese airstrips.

THE NEW GUINEA MARTYRS

As the Japanese Army advanced through what was then known as Papua in 1942, most European civilians evacuated. On 31 January 1942, the Anglican Bishop of New Guinea, the Rt Reverend Philip Strong, broadcast a message — the sub-dean had already been broadcasting twice a day to mission stations. The bishop stated that he was thankful that all Anglican missionaries were still at their posts.

'I have, from the first, felt that we must endeavour to carry on our work in all circumstances, no matter what the cost may ultimately be to any of us individually. God expects this of us. The Church at home, which sent us out, expects this of us. The Universal Church expects it. The tradition and history of missions requires it of us. Missionaries who have been faithful to the uttermost and are now at rest are surely expecting it of us. The people whom we serve expect it of us. Our own consciences expect it of us. We could never hold up our faces again if, for our own safety, we all forsook Him and fled when the shadows of the Passion began to gather round Him in His Spiritual and Mystical Body, the Church in Papua. Our life in the future would be burdened with shame and we could not come back here and face our people again; and we would be conscious always of rejected opportunities.'

That speech is from *Faithful Unto Death: the Story of the New Guinea Martyrs* by the Reverend E C Rowland, published by the Australian Board of Missions, 109 Cambridge Street, Stanmore NSW in 1964.

While other missionaries evacuated, the Anglicans stayed. Forced to abandon their mission stations, they took to the jungle, supported by members of their flocks. The Reverend Henry Matthews, priest at Port Moresby; the Reverend Henry Holland, priest at Isivita Mission; the Reverend Vivian Frederick Barnes Redlich, priest at Sangara Mission; the Reverend John Frederick Barge, priest at Apugi Mission, New Britain; Sister Margery Brenchley, mission sister at Sangara; Sister May Hayman, mission sister at Gona; Miss Lilla Lashmar, mission teacher at Sangara; Miss Mavis Parkinson, mission teacher at Gona; Mr John Duffill, mission builder at Isivita; Lucian Tapiedi, Papuan teacher-evangelist at Sangara; and Leslie Gariadi, Papuan evangelist (from Boianai), assisting the Reverend Henry Matthews at Port Moresby — these people all died rather than abandon their congregations.

MR HARDING

Like the others in this book, Mr Harding is not based on any real person, alive or dead. He is, however, a composite of several.

FRED SMITH

Fred's extraordinary feat, and possible survival, is based on the true story of Private Thornton/George Maidment, who may, or may not, have survived wounds suffered at Eora Creek on 27 August 1942. For more details read *Lost Hero* by Nick Fletcher, senior curator in the Military Heraldry and Technology Section at the Australian War Memorial. This was published in *Wartime*, the official magazine of the Australian War Memorial, Issue 48. Fred may appear in the next volume of the Matilda Saga. Or, being Fred, may not.

MISS CARLINE REID

This book owes much to the invaluable *Malay Climax*, written and self-published as a limited edition by Carline Reid, giving a detailed and superb account of her experiences in Malaya from 1940 to her escape in 1942. I have been unable to find out more about Carline Reid, or her book, but it provides a vivid and first-hand account of the period from December 1941 to February 1942 that I have relied on heavily, as it adds so many personal and visual details to the other accounts available.

MY FATHER AND THE ANZAC BUFFET

Michael's war experience closely matches that of my father, who joined the air force as soon as he was old enough — I think in 1944. En route to embarkation overseas, he was taken off the train platform in Albury, with a ruptured appendix. He was expected to die. He didn't, but spent many months recovering and then was put on 'light duties'. For a young man with no experience and dodgy health, this mostly meant guard duty, on the late-night watch no one with more seniority wanted. He'd come off duty in the early hours of each morning.

He was desperately lonely. His friends were in New Guinea, facing the enemy. He was living away from home for the first time. There was no one around in the early hours of a Sydney morning — or at least no one that a nice young Presbyterian boy would associate with.

Except at the Anzac Buffet at Hyde Park. He found it his first morning off duty. He said he sat there alone for the first two mornings, with a cup of tea and tomato sandwiches, trying to make them last as long as he could before he went back to the barracks to sleep. On the third morning a woman making sandwiches called to him: 'You there, don't sit there doing nothing. Come and be useful.'

He said it was the kindest, most understanding gift a stranger had ever given him.

His first job was wiping up. Then he was put onto slicing bread.

He spent all his time there after that, as soon as he came off duty, having a quick bite and then back to slicing bread and the friendship of the kitchen. He'd been missing his mother and now he had at least a dozen of them, letting him talk about this and that and the meaning of life, the way young men do to their mums.

He didn't tell me this story until a few years before he died. We were coming back from the launch of my book *A Rose for the Anzac Boys*. I mentioned how I had been to the Hyde Park Memorial, had seen the plaque dedicated to the women of the Jewish community who had run the Anzac Buffet. His face lit up.

'I never knew they were Jewish,' he said wonderingly. 'They never mentioned religion at all.' That meant a lot to Dad. When Dad's Presbyterian mother had married his Catholic father, both families disowned them, and there would be more religious battles when Dad married my mother. Dad had seen much good work done in the name of religion, but mostly while making sure all knew exactly which religion it was.

The Anzac Buffet wasn't like that.

Dad said that the women of the buffet might have saved his life, or at least his sanity, their small corner of normal life offered to a young soldier. He wanted to go back to thank them, but was too frail to make it to Sydney again. 'When you go there again, will you thank them from me?' he asked.

Dad died in June 2011.

BUSH MEAT

Nancy's grandmother's 'rats' were antechinus — not rats at all, but small carnivorous marsupials — and bettongs, which aren't rats either. Do not eat any of the 'bush meat' or wild foods mentioned in this book, firstly because it is illegal to kill native animals unless it is part of your Indigenous tradition, and secondly because if you don't know what you are doing you may end up seriously dead — or extremely ill. Lizards, snakes and goannas are especially dangerous, as they may have poison glands (even ones considered non-venomous) and you need to be an expert to know where they are, how to remove them and how to cook the meat to make it safe. Some lizards, especially, can be toxic unless prepared by someone who knows their characteristics extremely well and their medicinal applications.

HIBISCUS BUDS

The buds that Nancy picked for their vitamin C content were probably *Hibiscus sabdariffa*, a hibiscus that is not native to Malaya but was widely grown at the time, the buds eaten, cooked or raw, both as a vegetable and flavouring.

TRADITIONAL MALAY HERBAL PLANTS

The villagers of the island where the prison camp was located would have been familiar with many dozen traditional native medicines. Nancy's gunshot wound may have been treated with a poultice of *Allium cepa* (bawang merah), *Ampelocissus gracilis* (kertas api), *Ipomea aquatica* (kang kong), *Talinum triangulare* (pokok duit) and many more, as well as the cultivated gambir leaves from the plantation or from wild gambir trees. As with all herbal remedies, do not try to use these yourself, as identification may be incorrect, and plants may also vary in the amount of active ingredients they contain.

MRS COUNCILLOR BULLOCK'S AND OTHER RECIPES IN THIS BOOK

These are based on those in the handwritten cookbook kept by my grandmother, Mrs Thelma Edwards, from about 1915 to 1988. Several of the recipes collected or given to her in World War II were for dishes that didn't need rationed sugar, butter or eggs.

HOME-GROWN FRUITCAKE

This was sent to men serving overseas, to kids at boarding school, or to friends and relatives in England, where rationing was far more severe than in Australia. While eggs, sugar and butter were rationed and dried fruit hard to find, many households, certainly in farming areas, grew their own. This is essentially a boiled pudding, but it makes a light and extremely moist cake.

250g butter (or cleaned mutton dripping)
1 cup brown sugar, if available (or honey or golden
    syrup, but all can be and often were omitted in World
    War II)
5 eggs, from the chooks (if left out, the pudding is still
    good but can be crumbly)
5 cups *fresh* breadcrumbs (i.e. not the very dry and dusty
    ones from a packet, though you can use stale bread;
    Grandma grated hers, but I use wholemeal bread, crusts
    removed, and whizz it in the blender till light and fluffy)

1 cup plain flour

2 cups dried plums (prunes), stones removed, and 2 cups
dried grapes (sultanas) soaked in 2 cups fresh orange
juice (not from navel oranges as these can turn bitter
after squeezing)

1 cup grated carrot

juice of 1 lemon

1 cup dried red currants if you have them growing, also
soaked in orange juice overnight until soft (currants are
tiny fruit and easy and quick to dry at home)

Beat butter/dripping with sugar, if using, till light. Beat in the
eggs one by one, then add other ingredients. Grandma then put
hers into a pudding basin and fastened down the lid. If you don't
have a pudding basin, put the mix in a plastic storage container,
tape down the lid with duct tape, then tie the whole thing in an
oven bag. Bring a large pot of water to the boil — it must be
boiling or the cake will be heavy. Plonk in the pudding and boil
for three hours. This keeps in the freezer for several months, and
for several weeks or even longer with refrigeration. The better
the fruit is dried, the longer it will keep. Grandma sometimes
used grated apple instead of dried grapes or prunes. The result
was delicious, but it needed to be eaten within three or four days,
or it grew whiskers. If it does, or becomes mouldy, throw it out
at once.

Note: even if you don't like fruitcake, you might love this.

SWIMMING

Modern readers might not realise how few country kids could
swim before the post-World War II swimming pools began
to spread across towns and suburbs. Even where there were
swimming holes, they were usually too small to take more
than a few strokes. Rivers were either shallow or dangerous in
flood. Billabongs in the days before widespread herbicides and/

or overstocking with cattle in a drought were usually filled with waterlilies, which could trap an unwary swimmer.

PREJUDICE

These days much racial prejudice is cultural, based on clichés of behaviour, not colour of the skin. But in the colonial world of which Australia was part, colour mattered desperately. Asian royalty would be entertained; anyone below that rank was classed as 'native'. English was unarguably the best of all 'races' to be descended from, followed by Welsh and Scottish and, a very poor fourth indeed, Irish. European nations were also acceptable, more acceptable in well-to-do circles than (Catholic) Irish.

'Native' was always an insult, with its implicit assumption of inferiority. Anyone with an Asian background faced extraordinary prejudice — but at least by World War II, if they were determined enough, they could break through it. This was not the case if you were Indigenous, no matter how brilliant. Great Australian poet Oodgeroo Noonuccal, whom I knew as Auntie Kath Walker, was employed as a housekeeper when she first had access to the books that would mean so much to her. Eddie Mabo, who fought for and won legal recognition of the rights of Indigenous people to the land they and their ancestors occupied, was employed as a university groundsman, though he was giving lectures at the same university.

Even in my school years a girl who sat next to me in class claimed she was Indian rather than admitting to an Aboriginal heritage. An Indigenous Australian couldn't get any but the most manual job, and then only if no white person wanted it, was denied access to hotels, public swimming pools, many cafés, restaurants, movie theatres and most schools, and was often only allowed to live on a settlement, able to leave only with the white superintendent's permission. Those who had left often found they were not given permission to come back and visit their families, in case they spread 'troublemaking' ideas of equality. My Indigenous friends at university were routinely picked up by police for no reason. It is almost impossible these days to comprehend the depth — and pettiness — of racism back then.

It is also difficult for the present generation to understand the depth of prejudice against women. A woman with a job was seen as 'taking the bread from a man's family'. Many professions like engineering, piloting and mechanics were closed to women entirely; the few women doctors, lawyers, police officers and journalists were expected to stay working in 'female' areas. Female teachers and nurses had to resign when they married. Women received less than a quarter of the average male pay for the same job — if they could get it.

WHO WAS CLANCY OF THE OVERFLOW?

Banjo Paterson wrote the poem 'Clancy of the Overflow' in 1889. Paterson was working in Sydney as a lawyer when he was asked to write a letter to Thomas Gerald Clancy at a property called Overflow, asking him to pay a debt. The answer came, as quoted in the poem, looking as if it had been 'written with a thumbnail dipped in tar': *Clancy's gone to Queensland droving and we don't know where he are.*

But the Clancy of that poem and the later 'The Man from Snowy River' isn't Thomas Gerald Clancy, the man who owed the unpaid debt, who would later write a rebuttal of the poem: he hated droving and was going to dig for gold instead.

The Clancy of the poems is a man of honour and vision, the sort of man who would be a friend of Paterson. He is undoubtedly a composite of the many bushmen and property owners Paterson knew personally, as he never knew Thomas Gerald Clancy.

What would induce a man like Clancy of the Overflow to leave his property to 'go to Queensland droving'? This book, and *The Girl from Snowy River*, attempt to answer that question.

I fell in love with Clancy of the Overflow when I was twelve years old. But why do we have him, and all the other male heroes of the bush, and not women heroes? Paterson's and Lawson's works do contain women, but usually as victims, suffering hardship, waiting for their men, or as sweet damsels.

So here is 'Nancy of the Overflow', tough as her grandfather, horsewoman, drover and heroine. I hope you like her.

Acknowledgements

At the finish of each book it is usually easy to decipher the web of gratitude to those who helped create it. This book was the most gruelling to create emotionally of any book I have written, and the acknowledgements equally difficult to untangle.

Firstly, to dear friend and colleague Emeritus Professor Virginia Hooker, more thanks than I can express for giving me so much of the skeleton of this book, from the name of the island where Nancy was imprisoned to the precious copy of Miss Carline Reid's extraordinary book and eyewitness account of those last months before the British surrender in Malaya. All errors are mine, not hers, especially as a form of cowardice I am too wary to analyse prevents me from giving her the unpublished manuscript to read through.

To Lisa Berryman, who wept as she read the first draft, and whose response helped me to be able to face creating draft two, not for the time or intellectual effort, but because it was too soon to face the world I had recreated again: thank you, always, for making me the writer who writes this.

To Kate O'Donnell, who began her editor's letter to me with 'I may never forgive you for killing Gavin. There. It's said. Narrative genius? Yes. Perfect climax? Sure, fine. BUT MY HEART IS BROKEN AND MAY NOT MEND. Just so you know.': thank you for guiding me again through the novel, for your comments, your insight and your understanding.

So many thanks to Kate Burnitt for guiding the book so perfectly through the editorial process; to Angela Marshall, as always, for deciphering what was possibly the most garbled of all manuscripts I have given her, as well as — being Angela — also being familiar with all the places and histories in this book, and accompanying me and correcting me on the journey through them. And to Bryan too, who probably won't read this, or the book itself, but who muttered sympathetically with only one eye on his *New Scientist* article when I cried as I explained plot devices, and how I wrote that final scene with Gavin only by writing it before I had even begun the book, or created the character who must die, the innocent who war kills, the child who shows that there can be joy even among suffering and squalor.

There are too many other thanks to fit here. To the family friends of my childhood, who had the courage to live well after all they had been through in World War II, to my parents Barrie Ffrench and Val French, whose stories are in this book, as are those of my grandparents Thelma Edwards and Dr T.A. Edwards, as well as the parents of friends, or those who kept their diaries and letters from that time, or wrote memoirs or collected oral histories afterwards, so we can hear the voices again. The Japanese voices show extraordinary courage and integrity in recording those years. There are many ways to love a country, and to serve it.

We owe much to every person on both sides of the conflict who had the strength to pass on their stories, despite their anguish, so that we can learn and understand.

The Secret Histories Series
Birrung the Secret Friend • Barney and the Secret of the Whales

Outlands Trilogy
In the Blood • Blood Moon • Flesh and Blood

School for Heroes Series
Lessons for a Werewolf Warrior • Dance of the Deadly Dinosaurs

Wacky Families Series
1. My Dog the Dinosaur • 2. My Mum the Pirate
3. My Dad the Dragon • 4. My Uncle Gus the Garden Gnome
5. My Uncle Wal the Werewolf • 6. My Gran the Gorilla
7. My Auntie Chook the Vampire Chicken • 8. My Pa the Polar Bear

Phredde Series
1. A Phaery Named Phredde
2. Phredde and a Frog Named Bruce
3. Phredde and the Zombie Librarian
4. Phredde and the Temple of Gloom
5. Phredde and the Leopard-Skin Librarian
6. Phredde and the Purple Pyramid
7. Phredde and the Vampire Footy Team
8. Phredde and the Ghostly Underpants

Picture Books
Diary of a Wombat (with Bruce Whatley)
Pete the Sheep (with Bruce Whatley)
Josephine Wants to Dance (with Bruce Whatley)
The Shaggy Gully Times (with Bruce Whatley)
Emily and the Big Bad Bunyip (with Bruce Whatley)
Baby Wombat's Week (with Bruce Whatley)
The Tomorrow Book (with Sue deGennaro)
Queen Victoria's Underpants (with Bruce Whatley)
Christmas Wombat (with Bruce Whatley)
A Day to Remember (with Mark Wilson)
Queen Victoria's Christmas (with Bruce Whatley)
Dinosaurs Love Cheese (with Nina Rycroft)
Wombat Goes to School (with Bruce Whatley)
The Hairy-Nosed Wombats Find a New Home (with Sue deGennaro)
Good Dog Hank (with Nina Rycroft)
The Beach They Called Gallipoli (with Bruce Whatley)
Wombat Wins (with Bruce Whatley)

Jackie French is an award-winning writer, wombat negotiator and was the Australian Children's Laureate for 2014-2015 and the 2015 Senior Australian of the Year. In 2016 Jackie became a Member of the Order of Australia for her contribution to children's literature and her advocacy for youth literacy. She is regarded as one of Australia's most popular children's authors, and writes across all genres - from picture books, history, fantasy, ecology and sci-fi to her much loved historical fiction. 'Share a Story' was the primary philosophy behind Jackie's two-year term as Laureate.

You can visit Jackie's website at:

www.jackiefrench.com